"Did you see D1449032 she asked,

making an effort at mimicking a worldly tone as she stood at the window. The top of her blouse had slipped to just above her breasts, leaving her shoulders uncovered.

Brandon issued a short laugh in response to her question. "My dear young lady, only a blind man could have missed that performance."

"Since you weren't blind, did you like it?"

"Like it? Perhaps 'stunned' would most aptly describe my reaction."

"Some seemed to enjoy it," she said haughtily. "*Some* seemed to like it *fine.*" Nervously, Melissa traced a pattern on the windowpane. She suddenly had no wish to prolong her charade of worldliness and drew up one side of her blouse to cover her nakedness.

But at once, with a shock, she felt the material being lowered again.

Brandon had come up behind her. He stood so close that she could feel his sword's scabbard against her hip.

"Tell me, madame, is this why you danced?" he whispered, his fingers running along her shoulderblade and straying to her neck. "Were you curious, perhaps?"

Dear Reader,

Welcome to the world of Harlequin Historicals. This month, we bring you another tale from the faraway islands of Hawaii with Donna Anders's *Ketti,* the story of the daughter of Mari and Adam from the author's April release, *Mari.*

For those of you who have long enjoyed her contemporaries, we are pleased to have *Odessa Gold,* Linda Shaw's first Harlequin Historical. Don't miss this delightful tale of honor and betrayal set against the backdrop of turn-of-the-century high society in Saratoga Springs and New York City.

Private Paradise by popular author Lucy Elliot and Jennifer West's first historical romance, *Passion's Legacy,* complete the roster. To start your summer reading off right, look for all four Harlequin Historicals at your local bookstore.

From all of us at Harlequin Historicals, our best wishes for a relaxing and enjoyable summer.

Yours,

Tracy Farrell
Senior Editor

Passion's Legacy

Jennifer West

Harlequin Books

TORONTO • NEW YORK • LONDON
AMSTERDAM • PARIS • SYDNEY • HAMBURG
STOCKHOLM • ATHENS • TOKYO • MILAN

Harlequin Historicals first edition June 1991

ISBN 0-373-28682-1

PASSION'S LEGACY

JENNIFER WEST's

first career was in musical comedy, as a professional singer and dancer. She turned her love for drama to the printed page, where she now gets to play all the parts—and direct the action. She lives in Southern California but travels frequently in search of adventures—and sometimes misadventures!—to share with her readers.

To my wise and kind friend and mentor,
Teppy Boraks

Chapter One

Cornwall, 1735

"Mother Mary, save us!" gasped Moll Farber, giving Melissa a shove. "Odsfish! What a sight it is! Comin' over the hill, a devil on horseback, not riding, but flying.... Look at his hair, black as night, and the eyes, I'll wager, are burning like hot coals...."

The jolt came unexpectedly and was almost enough to make Melissa drop her basket, filled neatly to its brim with goods purchased at Saturday's market.

"Oh, take *care*, Moll!" cautioned Melissa peevishly, finding herself irritated as usual by the silly girl, who with increased drama now staggered backward, looking in the direction from which they had come.

Melissa marched on, ever mindful of ruts and stones that might scar her good black shoes and not paying a whit of attention to her companion's story. Moll always had some wild tale, the only merit of which was to direct attention to herself.

"It's one of the Four Horsemen of the 'pocalypse, it is!" Moll squealed, and this time she grabbed Melissa's shawl, tugging hard on it to make her turn around. "Do look, Melissa, a'fore it'll be too late and he'll be upon us."

Melissa shrugged herself free. "If you don't stop your pulling and pushing and playacting and bellow-weathering, Moll Farber, you'll have everything on the road. It's all balanced perfectly, and it took me forever to fit it all in, just so.'' With an accompanying ''tsk'' of annoyance, Melissa shifted the large, heavy basket to her other arm, where it would be safer.

It had been a lovely May afternoon, and the early evening was still warm enough for nothing more than the green wool shawl Melissa had drawn about her shoulders. The shawl had once belonged to her guardian, who had worn it in London when she worked there, and Melissa thought it went well with her gray linsey-woolsey skirt, tucked up over the deep green petticoat. It was her best outfit—in fact, her only good one. Her white blouse was the only ordinary item from daily wear, and it had been freshly laundered for the occasion of going to market—a social treat coming rarely into Melissa's sheltered existence. Her black stomacher had been laced tightly, with premeditated purpose, so that it drew her breasts voluptuously high and forward in addition to emphasizing the smallness of her already slender waist.

Her efforts had not gone unappreciated; many an admiring glance from the opposite sex had been thrown her way that day as she paraded self-consciously through the stalls with her basket, collecting items on Goodie's list. As for the envying looks of the girls, and the disapproving clucks from the older women, she had ignored them for being what they were—signs of petty jealousy and further proof that she was exceedingly pretty.

In truth, she was far less vain than she was curious about her status as a woman. Sequestered on the farm, with no company but her two old guardians, she had rarely had opportunity to see herself mirrored in the eyes of others, and now she found herself almost ravenous to discover herself as a female.

She was eighteen, of marrying age, and soon she would have to choose a husband. It was imperative that she have an idea of her market worth.

Melissa would have preferred to make the four-mile walk back home alone, during which time she could have embroidered romantic daydreams around a few of the young men who had flirted with her that day. But as bad luck would have it, she had been accosted by the silly Moll, who, going in the same direction, insisted on trotting along, filling every quiet space with her incessant babbling.

Melissa did not like Moll on several counts, one being that she truly was a lamebrain prone to melodramatic exaggerations, another being that she had said mean and gossipy things about Melissa from behind her back—although not beyond her hearing.

Now Moll had stopped in her tracks entirely, and with a hand clasped over her heart and eyes wide, she went on to exclaim, "It's one of the Four Horsemen, truly it is! Look, look, now, Melissa…it's coming our way. What'll we do, what'll we do?" Moll prattled breathlessly, half in dread and half in delight, and this time she grabbed hold of Melissa's arm so forcefully that the basket tipped completely over, spilling its contents on the dry road.

In the mishap, a turnip fell hard on one of Melissa's neat black shoes. The shoes had lovely small red heels and plain silver buckles, and they were her most prized possessions in the entire world. The vegetable rolled away, leaving dirty scuff marks.

"Oh, now look!" Melissa cried out. She had so little that was nice, what she did possess she valued far beyond its actual worth.

She whirled about, fury igniting her blood. Curls which that morning she had painstakingly arranged atop her head tumbled loose from their pins and collapsed in thick, golden disarray over her shoulders. Melissa stared down at the mess surrounding her. "You silly, silly cow! Now do you see what you've done!"

First her time for daydreaming stolen, and now the added trouble of having to rearrange her basket. It was a tiresome task, and patience had never been her strong suit.

"You and your dramatics!" Melissa raged, her temper thoroughly aroused. "You're a bother and a bore. I never wanted you along in the first place, and I never want to walk with you again, do you hear?" She raised her hand

and might have sent Moll sprawling in return for the assault on her basket, but then she, too, became suddenly stricken by the sight looming on the horizon.

Good Lord... she had done Moll a disservice.

Coming over the crest of the graveyard positioned atop the highest hill for miles about—a place chosen in order that departed souls would be closer to heaven—rose the specter of a man on horseback.

His speed was so great that indeed he did look to be flying rather than galloping over solid earth. The evening sky behind him had recently turned crimson, adding to his eerie appearance.

Moll had begun to snuffle and whimper.

"Oh, do stop that," Melissa said absently, her eyes never leaving the rider, "it's only a human man and not something religious."

"You're so wicked, Melissa Danfort," wailed Moll, no longer fearing for her life, but instead concerned over her injured pride. "I was only having a bit of fun, trying to liven things up, and you said I was boring and a bother and stupid."

"I didn't say you were stupid," Melissa amended, her eyes riveted on the figure, as her imagination began to turn.

The man was still a good distance off but was making rapid progress, cutting directly across the treeless fields rather than following the cow path. He seemed in a terrible rush to Melissa, as if chased by the devil himself.

A glint of metal caught the sun's dying rays, and Melissa took in the sword buckled to his side. A sharp thrill, such as she had felt that day at market when she had noticed several of the young men looking hotly after her, rushed up her spine.

Never before had she seen a man with cause to wear a deadly weapon. Men like that were of a breed apart from those she knew. A staff to push the sheep along was all that was required in Cornwall, or a hoe to pick at the stony earth. But a sword—that bespoke serious matters, belonging to a world far beyond the scope of Melissa's experience, although not entirely beyond her knowledge.

Goodie, her guardian, had once resided in London, and had entertained Melissa with tales of its dangerous environs and roguish citizenry. In truth, Melissa's wildest hopes—which unfortunately also equaled her slimmest chances—were to one day rub shoulders with a tiny bit of danger and to glimpse at least a spot of such glittering debauchery as Goodie had described taking place in King George's Court.

So although innocent, she was not entirely naive, and thinking hard, her green eyes narrowed to slits, Melissa assessed the possibilities attached to the figure on horseback. There was little doubt, from what she had heard that day at market, that the situation required hasty action.

"Hurry, Moll," urged Melissa, stooping to gather up the fallen articles and place them, any way she could, back into the basket. Her green shawl dragged in the dirt and for the time being even her shiny black shoes were forgotten. It was, however, impossible to overlook Moll, who was making a racket sniffing and sniveling. "Oh, do stop all that, Moll. You haven't got an audience now, and I could use your help. Can't you see, it's one of those villainous highwaymen...."

"A highwayman!" Moll echoed, her voice all at once genuinely tremulous. She took up her apron and began to wring and twist it. "What ever'll we do?"

"It's what he'll do that ought concern you," Melissa returned.

Earlier that day, the marketplace had abounded with lurid and much embellished tales of highwaymen who looted travelers and ravaged beautiful women. To hear it told, the scoundrels were as common as flies, turning up on every road and even frequenting inns. Although they were criminals, a few of the more well-known robbers had actually been elevated to the status of folk hero, their exploits against the aristocracy becoming the subject of ribald songs and romantic tabloid adventures hawked for a few pence at London bookstalls and in the streets.

Moll, now truly alarmed, stood frozen, her mouth agape, her eyes widened to the size of saucers. "He'll have my maidenhead!"

"Oh, forget your maidenhead. Help me with my beets and flour. I'm sure he'd much prefer those."

"Oh?" Moll planted her hands on both hips. "Oh, really? And just how do you know *that?*" huffed Moll, the fear forgotten as her face filled with indignation.

Melissa shot her a withering glance. Although they were the same age, Moll was a good foot shorter and as square as Melissa was willowy, with a large flat nose, a small mouth and eyes the color of mud. Adding insult to injury, nature had crowned her with a full head of startling flame-colored hair that only served to emphasize the rest of her plainness.

"I can guess," Melissa said, and let the insult go at that. She continued to collect her goods, and at the same time looked up frequently to gauge the distance remaining between them and the man. If she hurried, they could cross a field and disappear behind one of the stone walls, crouching low until the brigand had gone, thereby saving her purchases.

By Melissa's reckoning, money was in far scarcer supply than a woman's virtue, and she seriously doubted that either she or Moll were in danger of being ravished. To her mind, the true crime would be to return to Darben and Goodie empty-handed.

Her trip to market represented two months of their savings, earned from Darben's efforts at farming their hard earth and from selling five of their remaining fifteen sheep—thirty of the others having fallen sick and died during the past season. Her guardians had been middle-aged when they took on her care sixteen years ago, and now, well past their prime, they were beset with a series of ailments that made earning a living even more of a trial, although Melissa did everything she could to lighten their load of responsibilities.

Working feverishly, Melissa stuffed her goods into the basket, pounding down items to make room for more.

"I suppose," said Moll, glaring, "you think the brigand'd prefer you."

Melissa looked up with disgust. Strands of the outrageous hair shot from beneath Moll's white cap like flaming needles. "Oh, please, if you can't help, then at least do keep still." Melissa threw a bag of sugar into the basket.

"If you even *are* a virgin," said Moll imperiously, continuing on her own track. "The way you're always tossing yourself around, like you're better than anyone here." Her voice rose and the words tumbled out as if her grievances had been held for a long time. "Putting on airs because you can read and write and speak in your hoity-toity way. Well, y'don't even have real parents. So there! God only knows where you do come from. And if you want to know, Miss High-and-Mighty, they say you're a bastard, that's what people say. And no decent man'll have you without a proper name, so maybe it would be just as well you get ravaged on the dirt by some black-hearted devil. Then at least you'll be knowing your proper place, and keeping to it!"

Jerking her head up, Melissa gripped a turnip, itching to hurl it at Moll. "Are you finished?"

"I've got more, if I've a mind—" But seeing Melissa, she stopped.

Melissa's back was rigid, her eyes were green fire and she looked about to spring. Instead, she said with deadly calm, "Hold your silly, poisonous tongue, Moll Farber, or I'll rip it out and stick it in your ear—or someplace a good deal more fitting."

Moll backed slightly away, as if uncertain whether Melissa's threat might be more than a figure of speech.

The truth was, this wasn't the first time Melissa had heard the malicious gossip that she was illegitimate, and in spite of the fact that Goodie and Darben denied the vile rumor, Melissa had always had her doubts.

Turning her face from Moll, Melissa fought back the tears that were gradually replacing her initial anger.

All she really knew was that when she was two, she had been sent from London to live in Cornwall with the Dorchesters. She had been told that the couple had been under retainer to her parents before their untimely death in an ocean crossing. She was also to believe that the ill-fated voyage had cost her parents their entire fortune, the trade ship having sunk off the Cape with the whole of their investment aboard. It had been a covenant of their will that Melissa, along with a small inheritance left from the estate, be placed in the Dorchesters' care.

So the story went. And it was a story Melissa had clung to, for want of any other personal history. Anyway, it was far more preferable than believing she was a bastard, as Moll Farber and others claimed.

But whatever other venom Moll might have unleashed was forestalled by the sound of hooves fast approaching, and both young women turned at the same time to discover much to their horror that escape from their fate—whatever it would be—was no longer possible.

Rather than take the long way around, the horseman had managed to jump a high stone wall. Sailing over the mound of gray stones, he came hurtling forward now, the sound of his great brown beast's exertion as loud in Melissa's mind as the racket of her heart.

He was almost upon them.

Melissa stepped quickly to the side of the road, followed by Moll, who sent out a shriek and flung herself behind the taller woman. As she peered from behind, she clutched Melissa's shoulders, screaming feverishly, "Please . . . mercy, I beg of you! Have mercy on us!"

He showed them more than mercy.

He all but ignored them.

Sweeping past, the highwayman barely glanced their way, looking down only briefly with black shining eyes when Moll shrieked out her plea for clemency.

Both girls stared after him as his form fast became no more than a cloud of dust, with the thunder of hooves retreating quickly into memory. Silence, not lusty male arms, enveloped them. For all their grandiose fears, they might have been two pesty, flea-ridden mutts, judging by the amount of attention they had warranted.

"Gemini!" Melissa breathed out. Her legs felt like water beneath her. The man's image, from the leather bucket-top boots to the dark head of shoulder-length hair bound with a strap, still burned in Melissa's mind as she shook off Moll's death grip.

"I saved us," sighed Moll, and more smugly added, "I might've been ruined just now, but for my quick wit. Did ye see the way his eyes burned down at us? Black eyes, filled with lust . . . hot lust, that's what. . . . But I found the barest corner of pity in his black soul, and instead of having his way, he rode on to do his evil elsewhere. You have me to thank for that."

Melissa gave her a look, rolling her eyes. "I have you to thank for nothing. The man hardly saw us, we were that important to him. And if you had lain on the road with your skirts raised, he wouldn't have been interested."

"Well, a lot you know about life. Without my intervention, there'd have been a tragic crime this day."

"The only tragic crime is your company," moaned Melissa, looking about to assess the damage committed by the man's passage. A beet had been smashed, but that seemed to be the only casualty.

Her eyes trailed off in the direction the man had flown. Of course, he was gone, vanished around the bend and out of her life. Not even a trail of dust remained.

She had never seen anyone like him before. There had been power in his body and determination in a face that was as ruthless as it was spectacularly handsome.

He was her first highwayman, her only highwayman, the most handsome highwayman who could ever exist on any road. . . . And Melissa wished with all her heart that she had been his victim. That he had carried her off into his world, away from Moll and the mean town gossip and the bumpkin lads—one whom she would be destined by circumstance and not passion to wed, and who could not begin to compare with him, her highwayman.

If she had lain with him all night, she could not have been more his than she was then. She stooped and picked up the injured beet, holding it tightly against her breast as if it were something precious.

Chapter Two

Goodie and Darben Dorchester said not a word as the stranger, identified as Brandon de Forrest in a letter written in the hand and bearing the familiar seal of the Duke of Danfort, explained that he would need lodging for the night, but would be leaving at the first light of day for London—with the Duke's granddaughter in his company.

It was early evening, with the last bright rays of the day falling below the horizon. The small main room of the cottage had turned to gloom, and at the conclusion of de Forrest's speech, Goodie rose from her chair at the table next to her husband and brought a candle stuck in a bottle to light their discussion.

"You know, of course, Melissa has no knowledge about any of this," Darben said worriedly, looking across to where the Duke's emissary stood, his form partially in shadow. "Melissa believes she's an orphan, with no living relatives. Monsieur de Forrest, it's what we had been instructed to tell her." Darben's eyes flickered, his face burdened with guilty conscience.

"Yes, I was made aware of that, and of course the deception's not yours." Brandon had no stomach for domestic issues. But still, the old couple were plain and honest folk, and he felt a tinge of regret for their pain. "But explanations to the girl will be in order before we leave... and *your* responsibility," he emphasized leaning against the wall.

He was a tall man, over six feet, and the ceiling was low. He found himself wanting to slouch, felt himself hemmed in on all sides by the small confines, and then realized that part of his discomfort was in his mind. He had been trapped into the visit.

"Deceived all these years...what will she think?" Goodie murmured, shaking her head. Her eyes were taking on a moist look. "And how will she manage without us? She doesn't know the world beyond this village. She wasn't meant to know it." Goodie's voice rose slightly in panic, as the future appeared in her mind. "Nothing was done to prepare her for more than what she had here. We were in service in London, Darben and I—we know the life at Court. But, of course, you know what I speak of, Monsieur de Forrest. You know that a girl like Melissa, an innocent...she could be easily used, easily wounded."

Brandon could offer her no solace, nor did he feel it was his position to intervene with insipid assurances that the girl would find a pleasant life in her new environment. He knew very well the lures and traps awaiting any young woman who ventured from her village into the City of London. In Melissa Danfort's case, the situation would be further aggravated by her being thrust into the social and political limelight. A sheep being led to slaughter was not too farfetched an analogy.

"She's a strong-willed girl," comforted Darben, although his voice sounded every bit as despairing as his wife's. "And clever, too. It'll be all right. And in London there'll be others to watch over her, to teach her what she needs to know." He also looked to Brandon, seeking confirmation of Melissa's bright future.

"I hope you understand," Brandon cautioned, "I've no personal connection nor allegiance to this matter. My involvement is solely in the capacity of escort. A temporary escort," he qualified, more for his peace of mind than for their edification.

He longed for sleep, but before taking his leave for the night, felt obligated—perhaps even a bit curious—to meet the female who had caused him so much inconvenience.

The girl was to return soon from marketing. Dimly he recalled passing two girls not long before reaching the cottage. He'd taken no particular notice of either, except that one had screamed something as he rode by. If one were the Danfort girl, he hoped she wasn't the screamer. Hysterical females did not sit well with him.

While the couple commiserated between themselves, he reflected upon the sour fortune that had led him on a hard two-day journey from London to their doorstep.

It was a journey he deeply—no, violently—resented making and one he would have avoided had there been any possible way. But Danfort had dropped his web, and as usual there was no escape, merely survival—if one was that lucky.

Brandon's eyes fell upon the leather pouch in the middle of the table, seeing it as a symbol of all that was wrong with this meeting, and with his life, for that matter. Several coins lay glittering, spilled loose on the wood.

He had placed the bag there himself some minutes before, and in his mind he could still hear the heavy thud of its weight echoing through the room. The pouch contained a thousand pounds in gold pieces, ostensibly to be taken as severance pay from the grateful Duke for the Dorchesters' services in raising his only grandchild.

But Brandon saw the gold in different, far more realistic terms.

For a scant thousand pounds—a fortune to the Dorchesters, but a pittance to Danfort—the Duke was in essence purchasing the life of the girl, a life he had buried in a remote Cornish village for sixteen years. And well did Brandon know that the Duke would have let Melissa Danfort mold there, had not the political climate in India suddenly altered to the Duke's financial advantage.

No, there was no germ of kindness in this resurrection, for Danfort had no such emotion within his being. He simply had in mind to trade the girl's life for a fortune so vast it dwarfed all but the Crown's coffers and would one day quite possibly even rival that. With the girl as his pawn the Duke stood to become the richest man in the kingdom. Not since Lorenzo de' Medici had risen to supremacy over kings had there been such a man in the world.

And, ironically, Brandon mused, still with his eyes on the glittering gold, he also would profit mightily from this one hapless female.

In transporting her to India, as the Duke had ordered of him, he would finally be released from Danfort's web. The shipping empire he had established seven years before, with money borrowed at usurious terms from Danfort, would be solely his, free and clear of debt and any other entanglements.

Conversely, should he fail at his duty, Brandon knew all would be lost. The Duke would see to his downfall; it would be swift and certain, there was no doubting that.

Using his influence with the Crown, Danfort had the power to pull Brandon's charters of trade. And lacking those agreements with the government, Brandon could not legally berth his ships in English ports, nor would he have protection on the seas. His trade vessels would be easy prey to pirates and the ships of hostile countries. There was no way his fleet could survive the ongoing attacks.

It was this imminent threat of losing his charters that had spurred him to make his breakneck ride from London. The Duke would have him leave for India as soon as possible, with the girl in his care.

Brandon's black eyes glittered as brightly as the golden coins lying loose on the table, and his lips curled into a smile that was far from pleasant as he realized the full irony of his situation.

Paradoxically Melissa Danfort would be both the most valuable and the most loathsome cargo he had ever carried across the seas. As the Duke's flesh and blood, she was automatically vile to Brandon, but she would also serve as his deliverance from his archenemy.

But as the Duke's thin, pallid face arose in Brandon's mind, the cottage door burst open, and before him appeared the flesh and blood pawn whom, in actuality, fate had contrived to make more powerful than even the Duke. The girl's eyes were wide saucers of shimmering green light, eyes filled with unconcealed excitement as she sought him out. But, of course; she would have suspected a guest awaited within. His horse, tethered outside, was a fine animal, clearly valuable, and strange to these parts. She would have sensed an extraordinary element to its presence at her cottage.

Yet even Brandon was taken by the moment at hand.

How remarkable, he thought, his eyes slowly moving over the slender form of Melissa Danfort. The bedraggled-looking creature who had just entered with her basket of vegetables had the power to possess two kingdoms and wreak havoc upon the fortunes of men who had withstood every manner of assault from every manner of enemy.

She was staring at him in wonder, much as if he were an apparition.

Well, life was interesting, if not always pleasant, Brandon mused, and he pushed himself from the wall to greet the woman who held—along with her basket of vegetables—his fortune in her hands.

"This is Melissa," said Goodie, standing to make the introduction. Her voice quaked slightly. "Melissa, this is Monsieur de Forrest. There is much to explain, but he has come to take you to London."

There was a long moment of silence, during which time Brandon saw the girls' mind move, assimilating news that had to be catastrophic. But no cry came, no fit of the vapors, not even a maidenly gasp. God's mercy, he thought, at least she wasn't the roadside screamer.

Instead, she eschewed all melodrama and inquired quite reasonably, in a soft, breathless voice, "To London? I'm really to go to London?" Her large eyes, as clear and bright as green cut glass, roamed from Goodie to Brandon and then to Darben, seeking further assurance.

Goodie cleared her throat. "There are certain things, Melissa, about your life...things you have not been told...."

And so, thought Brandon, the travail began in earnest. Next would come the requisite female display of weeping and questions and answers and recriminations. God help him, he would rather face pirates or fifty-foot waves than weather this situation.

"... and Monsieur de Forrest has been enlisted as your escort for the journey to your grandfather's," Goodie finished.

Resignedly Brandon stepped forward to officially assume his part in the Duke's domestic drama. "Your servant, madame." Smiling slightly, he made a proper sweeping bow, the formal gesture ironic amid the rustic surroundings.

But when he straightened again, he was not met with the anticipated hysteria.

Instead he found two slanted, emerald eyes regarding him intelligently and cautiously from within a delicate, oval face, the cheekbones high, the nose straight, the lips full. It was a countenance of mixed associations—that of the noble aristocrat, that of an exotic pagan—and it brought instantly to Brandon's mind the impression of a jungle cat, a creature proud and sinuous and dangerous.

Having known his share of women, he found little left in any of them to provoke his interest much beyond the casual social encounter or passing physical liaison. But for a lengthy moment, he found his attention bound fast to this last remaining member of a great dynasty. There was a quality about the Danfort girl, a certain elusive presence. Did he face a wise child, he wondered, or a woman who had not yet quite grown into herself? Certainly he had not expected such composure as she displayed.

But as he held her gaze, a slow flush crept to her face, and she smiled shyly—a child's smile, he noted. Lowering dark lashes to cover her thoughts, she returned his elaborate and well-practiced bow with a small, uncertain curtsy.

"Monsieur de Forrest..." Melissa Danfort's voice was a soft and low caress, as innocent as spring—while to the contrary, he could not overlook that her waist was cinched tightly and that above her simple peasant blouse the rising swell of milky white breasts was entirely evident. When she looked up, she said, "Do you think that there might be highwaymen along our way?"

"If there are, you needn't worry."

"Oh, but I'm not afraid," she said quickly. "I'd rather like to meet one. I've heard stories of them."

"I can assure you that stories make life far more glamorous than what life actually is."

"I wouldn't know that," she said. "But perhaps I'll learn in London."

"Perhaps you will," he said, knowing that in no time at all, the girl standing before him would learn a great deal, perhaps more than she would like. Dressed so unpretentiously now in her country garb, she would soon enough be fitted in a low-cut gown of satin, and men would find her to be more trouble than a hundred of her gender.

As for him, his only desire—a fervent one—was to rid himself of both her and her grandfather as fast as humanly possible.

As she followed behind Brandon de Forrest, who followed behind the host, leading their way to the upper story of the Boarshead Inn, Melissa was less caring of her aching, saddle-sore bones than she was excited to be on this unforeseen adventure, an adventure that was turning out to be her life.

For one thing, she was not a bastard, but the granddaughter of a rich and powerful duke, to whose home she was being taken—and not by a highwayman, but by a gentleman.

But to Melissa, it made little difference if Brandon de Forrest was criminal or saint; in her eyes he was the most intriguing creature on the face of the earth, and regardless of his formal, almost disinterested manner towards her, she was determined that they would never part company. From the moment she had seen him pass on the road, she had felt her soul bound to his, and in her mind a feeling that potent had to be reciprocated by the other party.

The inn was already filled with travelers when they arrived, and they found only a single suite remaining, available because of its higher cost. The lodgings consisted therefore of two adjoining rooms and a door between. At home she had slept on a straw mat in a loft above the cottage's main room, and to Melissa her current surroundings, with sturdy oak furnishings and a large bed, appeared no less than luxurious.

But when Brandon scowled, suggesting to the innkeeper that he was displeased with their quarters, Melissa realized that if she didn't want to humiliate herself in his eyes, she had best keep her tongue idle until she was more worldly-wise.

She was therefore disappointed when she was required to have her supper alone in her room, while Brandon ate below in the gay atmosphere of the inn.

"I'd much prefer to eat with you," Melissa said hopefully, and engaged him with what she hoped was a beguiling smile. She had practiced the same smile at market, to good effect on the village boys.

But Brandon was no such easy mark. He shook his head, appearing unmoved by her charm—if he even noticed her at all.

"It's best you eat here in your own quarters. There's often bad company at inns such as this, and there's no reason to go out of your way to court trouble." He strode toward the door without another glance her way.

"But I'll be in your company," countered Melissa, not knowing what he meant by trouble. She couldn't help secretly thinking that bad company sounded very exciting and that, in the interest of broadening her education, she wouldn't at all mind experiencing some.

"This isn't an environment for a young woman, no matter whose company she keeps," said Brandon dismissively, reaching for the door handle.

Melissa called out plaintively, snatching at her last hope. "I've never been away from home... I've seen nothing at all. Oh, please... let me come along with you."

Turning, Brandon took in her pathetic appearance—that of a waif with a tumble of thick golden hair. She stood in the center of the room staring at him with her large sorrowful green eyes, the small bag of shabby belongings by her side—hardly worth the effort it took to carry them to London, where he knew she would be outfitted in an entirely new wardrobe in keeping with her station. No one would suspect that she was one of the wealthiest women in England. In fact, even she had no knowledge of her true worth.

For an instant, Brandon was tempted to alter his decision to avoid all but the most necessary personal contact with her, and allow her to dine with him below.

But, he reminded himself, she was the Duke's pawn and therefore as dangerous a woman as any could be. In the months to come, in service to the Duke, Melissa Danfort would be moved against a good many people, and he could easily be one of them. He and the Duke's granddaughter could never be more than enemies, and it would be no kindness to allow her to think otherwise.

Relying upon reason, he said, "You'll see a great deal of the world very soon . . . more than you can possibly imagine—or may want to," he added cryptically. "Anyway, you'll be safe here alone, and I'll check later to see that you're all right."

And there the matter ended.

At least for him.

For Melissa, it was otherwise.

Gloomily she sat at her table alone. She chewed her stew, tore pieces off the loaf of bread and drank the flagon of ale brought by the maid, all the time listening to the sound of laughter and voices raised in what she knew had to be vibrant discourse.

It was maddening to be left out of the fun—not to mention being separated from Brandon de Forrest's company—and finally, unable to bear the torture any longer, she took to her bed. She placed the pillow over her head to drown out the revelry from which she had been excluded, and invented a long and happy future with Brandon.

She slept for some time, until roused by music from below.

* * *

The exotic, atonal music spun a heavy spell over the crowd assembled in the inn's public room. A traveling band of gypsy performers had recently arrived and, like everyone else, Brandon's attention had been diverted to the raven-haired beauty who danced atop a table, taunting the male audience with her black flashing eyes and teasing smiles.

Two gypsy musicians accompanied her performance, which she herself abetted with the use of a tambourine. Now and again a coin would be thrown at her feet, or a nearby hand would slip into her bodice to deposit a reward for her performance.

No one, including Brandon, noticed Melissa as she slipped discreetly into a vacant place at one of the long tables. Beside her, a man well into his cups was pawing a woman with a brightly painted face, and on her other side, a man was snoring with his head on the table.

When Melissa looked around, the first man caught her eye and winked lasciviously, snaking fingers around the woman's back to grab Melissa's leg. Indignant, Melissa blushed, gave the hand a hard swat and moved closer to the snorer, who at least could do her no harm.

Still, it was all extremely exciting.

Searching the room with her eyes, she found Brandon at last, seated with two men garbed in dress coats and wigs and hats, men obviously of a higher class than most others there.

She also noted that there were four empty wine bottles before them. As she looked, a full bottle was brought by a pretty but slatternly girl who, in Melissa's estimation, stayed far too long in Brandon's company, making big eyes at him and twisting her body so that for a moment he took his attention off the gypsy and gave the girl a long, discerning look.

Melissa closed her eyes. Her stomach turned, twisting into tight knots. In her visions of Brandon, there had been no other woman but herself.

When she forced herself to look again, Brandon and the other men were laughing heartily among themselves at something the girl had said.

But then, to Melissa's increased dismay, the gypsy woman hopped down from her table-top perch and began to wind through the room, spinning directly into Brandon's presence. With a challenging thrust of her hip, she pushed the sloe-eyed hussy away.

Everyone laughed, including Brandon, who threw back his head, his black eyes shining as the woman leaned close, shimmying her breasts in his face and thrusting her hips suggestively.

Only Melissa did not laugh.

Now she knew exactly the meaning of bad company.

This gypsy woman was very bad company indeed, and to help herself bear it, Melissa reached for an empty cup and helped herself to the contents of a bottle left on the table.

The liquid went down like hot fire, but that discomfort was only slight compared to the vision before her, and she took another swallow, then another and another, all the time watching Brandon and hating the gypsy for her worldliness and exotic beauty.

A new entertainment had begun in yet another part of the room. The gypsy musicians traveled among the tables, encouraging a pretty female here, and another there, to display her own talent at dancing. It was great fun for everyone, and Melissa laughed when even a very fat woman stood upon a table and began to parody the gypsy woman's sensual performance.

It was several minutes and three cups of brandy later when the two dark-eyed gypsies spied her.

"Come! Come, pretty one!" they goaded. "Show the others how badly they dance."

Melissa was aghast. She tried to shrink into herself, as if to become invisible. But now even the people near her were encouraging her to rise and dance.

"No—please..." she said, demurring with a shame-faced smile and wave of her hands.

But it was no use. With a hearty laugh, one of the musicians swept her up against her will and placed her atop the table. Tipsy from the drink, she wobbled for a moment, got her bearings, and then immediately tried to climb down. Her way was blocked by fervent admirers.

"It's only in fun," came the encouragement from the sidelines.

"The devil won't have your soul for naught more 'an a jig," sounded another voice.

And a glance at the other tables showed her that three other girls were having no more than innocent fun prancing about, each in her own manner trying to imitate the more expert moves of the gypsy.

"All right," she said softly. "All right, I will." Her voice hardly sounded like her own, which she supposed had something to do with the amount of liquor she had imbibed and the noise that seemed to absorb everything but music and laughter. Suddenly she too was laughing. She was feeling far more gay and not nearly so shy.

"Yes, I'll dance," she repeated to herself, and fixing her somewhat blurred vision on Brandon, whose back was to her as he watched the gypsy dancer, Melissa began to move in time to the music.

Across the room, the gypsy woman gave a sudden yelp. Dizzily, Melissa looked up, startled to find the woman laughing and gesturing, as if in good-natured challenge, for Melissa and the others to match her performance.

Melissa laughed, too, and caught up in the revelry, trained her green eyes on the woman's movements, doing what she could to approximate the expert's dance. She began uncertainly, shyly, and found it more difficult than she had imagined it would be to move all her separate bodily parts as the woman did, in time to the music, which had taken on an urgent, driving beat.

But she watched carefully.

When the woman ruffled her skirts, so did Melissa.

When the woman swayed, leaning backwards, Melissa followed suit, although out of fear she didn't venture quite as far back.

This was all to the delight of Melissa's table companions, who were more than pleased to watch the dark and passionate expert performing on one table, while her opposite in coloring and purity—judging by the country garb the girl wore—executed a variation of the dance on another. And in the minds of many, it was the naiveté and freshness of the younger girl that most heatedly stirred the blood.

"Good Lord! Now there's a tasty morsel to wet one's appetite," said one of the men in Brandon's company. Both gentlemen were from London and sophisticated when it came to such bawdy entertainment, yet a wide smile had sprung to the man's face, whereas a moment before he had been watching the gypsy with no more than a mild interest.

"I say...indeed...a veritable feast," murmured the second man, both travelers now switching their attention to an area of the room behind Brandon's back.

Brandon's own gaze had not veered from the gypsy, although she might not have been there. He hardly heard the music. His eyes were cloudy and unfocused, his thoughts in London and on ships that were due to sail within the week.

"She looks wet behind the ears, but judging from the raw talent being displayed, she'll learn the trade fast enough. With a face and body like that, London's the place for her," the first man drawled. "Perhaps she could stand a sponsor...."

Both men laughed heartily.

"Maybe I'll have a hand in her education myself," the second added, his eyes growing slightly hazy as his mind flowed into the future he envisioned. "Later. Tonight. Umm...yes...shall I stop her before she's too tired to enjoy her lessons?"

"What say you, Monsieur de Forrest?" prompted the first gentleman. "Do you agree there's rich potential here?"

It was only then, roused from his reverie, that Brandon turned toward his dinner companions, who urged him to look behind him.

"Bloody hell," he muttered, hardly believing what he was seeing as his eyes fell on Melissa. He followed the first curse with a long string of oaths, issued through clenched teeth. "She was warned . . . told to stay in her room."

"You know her?" one of the men asked.

"I know her. I know she's trouble," replied Brandon, more to himself than to the others.

His first impulse was to stalk across the room, yank her off her makeshift stage, drag her up the stairs and into her room; but this intention was stayed momentarily as Brandon, like many others in the room, found himself captivated by the vision she presented.

Melissa was finding it difficult to remain on her feet. Her head was beginning to swim from the combination of liquor and her twirling. She knew she had gone much too far in her antics and that she should get down at once and make her way back up the stairs to her room—although she was beginning to wonder if that would even be possible. Her legs did not seem to be quite hers anymore . . . nor did any other part of her body seem related to her former self. The brandy had dissolved *that* Melissa, creating this new one in her place.

And *this* Melissa wanted Brandon to look at her the way he had the gypsy. That, at least, remained clear enough in her head.

A few times she had tried to find him in the sea of faces, but it was nearly impossible to focus on anything amid the jostling crowd.

Even now the gypsy's stringed instrument spun a driving, hypnotic melody to the accompaniment of small drums, and Melissa felt her newly acquired nature flowing out with every pulse of the music. Closing her eyes, she lost yet another shred of her old self to the notes.

But across the room, Brandon did not close his eyes. Nor, unfortunately, could he look away. Nor could he act to stop what he knew should be ended immediately, before the situation got any further out of hand.

Judging by the crowd's reaction, there was bound to be trouble as drunken men, of questionable ethics at best, lost their restraint.

It was understandable, if not conscionable. A metamorphosis had taken place before their eyes, as with every new phrase, the music peeled away another layer of the girl's innocence. Unveiled in her place was an enticing woman, whose raw sensuality had temporarily broken through even Brandon's jaded exterior.

Stirred to desire, he let the heat last, experiencing the sensation in his groin as a pleasurable pain as old memories mixed with physical excitement.

He had taken many women over the years but had loved only one, and only with her...with Pavan...had he felt the wildness and longing to unite with a woman body and soul. But there was something of that feeling now as he let the girl's artless charms draw him out of his old anger and pain and into the experience of raw, ardent desire.

Damn the girl! He stood at last, killing the elusive pleasure that had briefly held him captive.

Melissa moved with authority now, eyes closed, arms entwining above her head. Her green petticoat flowed about her legs as if it were no more than a gossamer veil, and although her white blouse had slipped lower off her shoulders, there was no feeling of shame. Instead there was a certainty in each step, in every thrust of hip to the beat of the instruments.

Someone called to her...called her name, she thought.

Opening her eyes, she saw the room as a blur, and then the faces of the men, and even those of the women, telling her what she already knew—that she was beautiful, that she was desirable. That she had within her an extraordinary power.

"Melissa!" Her name came again, and suddenly, amid the jumble of noise and bodies, she saw Brandon—also watching her. He had risen from his seat and was slowly making his way toward her, his eyes black and hard and dangerous as he pushed through the room.

This was not the look he had given the gypsy woman. This was not the look she had wanted from him.

She was dimly aware of the music, and that her body continued its sway. She heard rough male voices calling for her to come closer. The shouts merged into an unintelligible cacophony as she held Brandon's eyes, searching for some sign of his admiration.

A hard object struck her foot, and she looked down to find a coin there. Almost immediately there came others, a shower of money amid yelps and applause. Someone was grabbing for her skirt, pulling her down so that they might deposit money in her bodice. A hand gripped her wrist. She tried to regain her balance. She was no longer dancing, but was struggling to free herself, and she was losing the battle.

Vaguely she noticed that the other girls who had been dancing had now stopped and were watching her along with everyone else.

A man's hot, wet fingers brushed against her flesh, pulling at her bodice, moving downward toward her breasts.

Cringing, she screamed for him to let her go.

And at once her plea was answered.

She was released, torn from the man by an even stronger force, which sent her reeling and almost toppling from the table.

But she was not alone in being displaced. In the time it took her to catch her next breath, her attacker flew backward from his bench, landing in a thud on the floor with a dazed expression on his face.

Half in shock herself, Melissa looked down, examining the man for injury. A thin trickle of blood trailed from his cut lip, otherwise—but for his pride—he seemed intact.

Brandon de Forrest stood over the man, who remained sprawled against the floor. In contrast, Brandon was utterly still and composed. One would have thought he had risen from the dinner table after an evening of pleasant conversation.

Melissa further noted, with a sudden catch to her heart, how utterly splendid he appeared. Although he still wore his sword, he had changed from his traveling clothes into a fresh white linen shirt, its sleeves gathered at the wrist and the straight white collar fastened neatly. Against the fabric, his dark hair, pulled back with a leather strap at his nape, shone with a rich brightness, with only a few loose strands attesting to his part in the recent fray.

For an instant Melissa thought—and fervently hoped—that amid this apparent calm, she could simply disappear up the stairs as quietly as she had descended.

But this was not to be. Inching her way to the edge of the table, she was making ready to slip to the bench in preparation for her escape, when, without turning her way, Brandon said in a flat voice, "Stay where you are, madame."

And she obeyed.

Slowly, calmly, the black eyes of Brandon de Forrest surveyed the room for additional trouble. But the crowd had quieted, becoming suddenly mannerly, and even the musicians had wisely switched to a less frenetic rhythm.

"*Now*, madame," he said coldly. Saying no more, he swept her off the table and, dragging her behind him, led the way up the stairs and into her room, where he shut the door.

He locked it, and for a long moment remained where he was, making no move to turn toward her.

Meekly Melissa moved to the nearest chair by the table and, taking her seat, waited in nervous dread for the storm that was certain to erupt.

Brandon turned slowly, measuring his anger, which was, at the moment, great. Although part of it was directed at the girl, he was equally furious at his own momentary weakness. Old passions and tired sentimentality had gripped him while he watched Melissa Danfort dance. He had thought himself finished with that part of his nature, with that whole humiliating and debilitating era of his life, when his obsessive affection for a woman had all but caused his ruin. It was troubling to find himself wrong.

He spoke deliberately and harshly, Pavan's image crisscrossing in his mind with Melissa's. "You behaved stupidly tonight. You could have caused yourself, me, and others a great deal of trouble and possibly harm. What you did was not in keeping with the conduct of a lady—and it was dangerous."

Melissa felt each word of the rebuke as a whiplash to her pride. The heat rose to her face and her eyes began to flood with tears.

"I seem to be in one piece yet, thank you," she said stiffly, trying to retain some semblance of dignity and finding it hard to meet his eyes, which bore nothing but disdain. The brandy still mixed with her blood and made her susceptible to a thousand fleeting and diverse emotions. She wanted to cry, wanted to scream, wanted to die from shame and disappointment.

"Perhaps you misunderstood," Brandon said, his tone lower and more even, but the words no less hurtful as he continued. "My presence here is not to educate you in the ways of the world, as perhaps you thought. Fortunately that duty will fall to others...and—" he sighed "—God help them in their work. I, on the other hand, am pledged to be your escort—not your private militia. I've very little desire to lose my life for you, fighting over your honor—or dishonor, as the case may be. From here on, I would strongly advise you to do exactly as I say. If not, then you're free to suffer your own consequences. So," he concluded, "have I made our positions absolutely clear?"

With nothing to say in her defense, she cast her tear-filled eyes downward. "Yes...yes, completely," she murmured.

"Excellent. Then we may happily presume that the rest of our journey will be without incident." He made a movement, as if to leave, and Melissa looked up. His eyes were still on her, examining her coolly, with dull disinterest.

She remembered how his eyes had glittered when he looked at the gypsy. It was that look of desire that she had wanted to claim for herself. Only for this reason had she danced. And drunk on brandy, she had also experienced the heady intoxication of her newly discovered power over the opposite sex. Surely, she thought, Brandon hadn't been completely immune to what others had so obviously found favorable. And as there was nothing left to lose, she decided to launch one last attempt at capturing his admiration.

Rising from her seat with her head held high, she moved toward the window, with every step trying to recall the authority she had possessed when all eyes had been turned her way.

"Did you see my dance, then?" she asked, making an effort at mimicking a worldly, offhanded tone. She was very unsure of herself, as if feeling her way through a dark and unfamiliar room. At any moment she might stumble, and her heart sank as it suddenly occurred to her that she had been wrong; perhaps even now she could make things worse than they were already.

She had reached the window, and the cool air from the leaded panes hit her bare skin. The top of her blouse had slipped to just above her breasts, leaving her shoulders uncovered. In the tumult that had taken place below, she had forgotten her state of disarray, but as she saw herself reflected in the window, she was stricken with a sense of confusion.

The image was hers . . . and yet not hers.

Her hair, which was thick and generally unruly, ranged loose and wild about her small face, and her exposed flesh gave her a wanton look that did not match her actual level of confidence.

Behind her, Brandon issued a short laugh in response to her question. "My dear young lady, only a blind man could have missed that performance."

"Since you weren't blind, did you like it?"

"Like it? Well, let me consider that. Perhaps 'stunned' would most aptly describe my reaction."

"*Some* seemed to enjoy it," she said haughtily, with a swish of her hair. "*Some* seemed to like it *fine*."

Nervously Melissa traced a pattern on the windowpane. The reflection wished to prolong her charade of worldliness, but the inner-girl of Cornwall wanted to retire from the drama. Hoping the action was too subtle to notice, she drew up one side of her blouse to cover her nakedness.

But at once, with a shock, she felt the material being lowered again.

Brandon had come up behind her. He stood so close that she could feel his sword's scabbard against her hip.

His hand was hot against her skin. "Tell me, madame, is this why you danced?" he whispered, his fingers running along her shoulder blade and straying to her neck. "Were you curious, perhaps?" His voice had become a dark, velveteen purr.

"I—I...?" Melissa had lost her train of thought. It was partly the remnants of the brandy that made her head spin, and partly fear, but it was primarily the sensation caused by Brandon's touch that was unraveling her mind and dissolving her will.

"Is this what you wanted?" he persisted. "To make love? I think it was for this that you danced tonight. What say you, madame? I'm sure I'm right...."

Stunned by her success at finally having gained his attentions, Melissa now didn't know how to respond. Nothing in her soft and romantic fantasies had prepared her for this raw sexual encounter. This was not at all the way she had envisioned his pursuit of her.

In the mirrored glass, his face looked back at her. He had a strong, sharp jawline and lips that seemed rarely to smile, unless he was amused by some unpleasantness of life.

To her dismay, she saw that he was now smiling.

"No," she said, becoming truly afraid. "No, that's not what I wanted."

"There's no need to be coy," Brandon whispered in her ear, his breath like a sweet warm mist against her skin. Wrapping his arm about her waist, he pulled her against him. His eyes shone in the window's reflection. "I know I'm not mistaken. What you wanted was very obvious to me—and to so many others tonight."

His fingers played against her neck. Softly, she felt them twining in her hair, brushing against her cheek, luring her into a world she knew nothing about.

Melissa shivered, but not from desire.

"Do you really want to know what I was thinking when I watched you dance tonight? Do you know what *I* wanted?"

Melissa shut her eyes, wishing the moment would disappear in the blackness behind her lids. "To have me in London and off your hands."

Brandon laughed.

She tried to pull away. But he held her back, his hands strong, gripping her shoulders, and she felt his breath against the side of her face as he moved closer. His body heat burned through the thin fabric of her blouse.

"I wanted this...." He spun her effortlessly around and in to him, bringing his lips hard against hers, pressing her mouth open.

"I don't think that I should—"

"Ah, but you don't need to think," Brandon said, and lifting her into his arms, he carried her to the bed. "Thinking is hardly necessary now." And he dropped her onto the mattress.

She bounced slightly, without dignity.

"Well?" he asked, his dark eyes boring into her, half with amusement, half with anger. "So? Here we are. Shall we get on with it?"

Melissa stared up at him, studying his face, reading the humor behind the facade of seriousness. *He was only playing with her!* Ha! He was attempting to teach her a lesson, that was it. He meant to humble her—not to have her. And she had been doubly rejected by him.

Burning with humiliation, she suddenly hated him as much as she had formerly adored him.

"Come now," Brandon said, his half smile in place, "undress... We're both anxious, aren't we? Your curiosity about lovemaking is shortly to be satisfied—and my appetite, as well. Your education begins, madame.''

''No,'' Melissa said lightly. ''No. I don't think so. I'm not so very hungry as you.''

Brandon arched one brow, and she watched the amused, smug light come to his black eyes ... along with the relief.

''Well, then. I've been misled by you,'' Brandon said grimly. ''Because by your behavior tonight, I—and any other man—would have imagined your desire as being other than cool.''

Propped on her elbow, Melissa smiled. She looked up at him and said, ''What I meant was ... I'd rather *you* undress me—slowly. You see, I'm not that anxious.''

She was fully aware that her bodice had slipped lower again, and that half her breasts were exposed to view. She fought the impulse to cover herself; she was too angry to care about modesty now—plus, what was one more disgrace after a full evening of them? Besides, she knew now that she was safe, that this was all a game. Her grandfather was a powerful duke; no man in his service, who was in his right mind, would be so stupid or so bold as to harm her.

And she was sure that Brandon de Forrest's mind worked very well. But not well enough.

She would play Brandon's game, and they would see who won.

''Perhaps, because you have the experience, you should begin to undress first ... teaching me. Slowly, but surely,'' she said softly.

''As you wish, slowly but surely....'' Smiling coldly, Brandon looked into the girl's sparkling green eyes, slanted up at him from where she sat on the bed as his hands went to his belt and he released the Scottish dirk, the sword that had saved him from many a dangerous situation but which was no good here.

He had recognized the sound of triumph in her voice, the glint of advantage in her eyes. So ... she had caught on.

He had meant to frighten her into submission by demonstrating the dangers that could be brought on by her behavior; it would make their future together far easier. But he had misjudged her. The girl was not just head-strong, she was also astute. Her grandfather's blood ran in her veins, all right....

Brandon knew full well the tricks and turns of battle. He knew that if he backed down now, all would be lost. She would run him ragged, getting into all manner of mischief and quite probably into some serious trouble on his ship, if she retained her penchant for flaunting her body.

The conflict would have to be settled here and now. And he had damn well better be the victor.

He blew out all but one of the room's five tapers and then returned to the foot of the bed, where the girl re-clined, watching him.

He began to undress, slowly. Boots, stockings, belt, shirt....

As he removed each piece of clothing, he allowed time for her to plead for the end of the game. When she did not, when there was nothing remaining but his breeches—and his hope that things would not progress any further—he snuffed out the last candle. Even so, moonlight flooded through the window, casting the room in a silver glow.

God help him, but the girl did look lovely, he thought, looking down at Melissa Danfort, whose golden mane of hair was spread over the pillow and across her shoulders, her breasts high and full beneath the shirt she wore. Any man would want a woman like her—no matter how much trouble she was out of bed. And having thought that, it was with a shock that Brandon discovered himself hard-ening. Then the reality of being the lover of the Duke of Danfort's granddaughter returned him to his senses.

"Come, you still haven't removed a stitch of your own clothing—must I do everything?" He slipped beside her on the bed, hoping like hell, as he drew her hard against him, that she would capitulate before the next breath.

But the next breath was his to take, quick and stabbing, as the warmth of her body melted into his bare chest, and she turned to him, yielding to his embrace.

"Melissa," he murmured, "Melissa..." He fought against two equal foes, panic and desire, as he drew his hands from her body and raised them to her face. Arching away from her, he searched to find some sign of artifice in her expression. But the lips were parted and moist, the green eyes wide and peering into his. *Good God,* he thought, *this was real.*

He had made a mistake.

With a long sigh, the girl twined her arms about his neck, and her mouth, warm and wet, searched hungrily against his chest. He tried to pull away, but the pleasure was too intense. He shuddered, cursing his stupidity, cursing his weakness. But in the next instant, he had forgotten both flaws, and with a savage groan he pushed himself atop her, the game entirely lost, as he kissed her once, hard, with an angry violence that came from the depths of him. Her body was like liquid fire beneath him, and he reached beneath her skirts, touching her legs, sliding his hand up the silken flesh to reach—

"No! No..." Melissa cried out, and pushed from him with enough force to separate their bodies, blessedly breaking the moment's temptation.

For an instant, they stared at the other, their bodies softly, magically silvered in the light from the window. Brandon's breath came as quick, short gasps, as he fought against his still violently intense state of arousal. Even his hands trembled. *Madness! He had come so close to....*

"All right!" Melissa cried, tears glistening in the large eyes filled with pain. "You've won your game! My lesson's learned! I *am* a stupid young girl who's played with fire. Scorched already, I'm not so dim-witted that I want to get crisped completely. There, now are you happy?" She drew in a long uneven breath and closed her eyes. Tears squeezed from beneath the veil of thick dark lashes and began a sad trail down her cheeks. "In London, I'll learn everything. In London, it will be different."

She did not add *You shall see!* but this was in her heart as she buried her face in her pillow. If it took her whole life, she would make Brandon de Forrest respect her and want her. Someday she would have him on his knees to her.

Brandon let her be. He felt no satisfaction in his triumph. At any rate, it was a Pyrrhic victory. Using the door separating their quarters, he escaped to the safety of his room, seeking refuge in solitude.

But tired as he was, sleep eluded him. Restless, he lay upon his bed in morose contemplation. What had happened this night had been totally unexpected. He had considered Melissa Danfort a child, or at most, a half woman, and he still held to that opinion. But when he felt her body against his, passion had swept like wildfire through him. Rocked by the emotion, he had, for an instant at least, become a slave to his senses—once again....

A bitter tide of feeling washed over him as he recalled how he had loved Pavan de Noialles with his entire soul, not to mention his body, and how she had misused that devotion, until there had been nothing left of him to lose to any other woman.

After Pavan, he had not thought himself capable of experiencing the kind of raging, burning desire that had swept over him this night. He had hoped to be free of the emotions that only brought torment to a man's life.

In the half light of his room, Brandon studied the door to Melissa's room. He felt the pulse of his body quicken. Good Lord, he had wanted her, and he still did.

He closed his eyes and let the sensation eat away at his soul until, churning and twisting within him, the desire burned itself out and left him hollow and clear-minded again.

Chapter Three

Melissa knew that any gain she was to make in her campaign to humble Brandon lay in the future.

And to this end, her mind wove a voluptuous tapestry of her coming days in London—although, annoyingly, the pictures she created did lack a certain definition. The fact was, she had very little insight as to what exactly she might expect of her new life.

To begin with, she had only the vaguest notion of what it meant to be the granddaughter to a duke. Still, she assumed from Goodie's reverence when speaking of her newly acquired relative, that beyond merely owning a title, he was a man of considerable wealth and social substance. Not only that, but she was said to be his only living relative.

Then, again, this fact led to a perplexing question. Why had he kept his only relative in exile for sixteen years? Thinking on the subject during the day's ride, Melissa had at last succumbed to her natural optimism and concluded that his decision must have been based entirely on her welfare. Now that the mysterious obstacle to their reunion had been removed, she was certain they would greet each other with open and loving arms and their lives would be forever splendid.

Further, she considered—with the subject of captivating Brandon de Forrest still paramount in her mind—it would naturally stand to reason that her grandfather would want to see her shine in the eyes of London society.

Wouldn't he want her to be outfitted in the finest dresses and jewels? Of course. Wouldn't he insist that tutoring in all manner of social refinement would commence as soon as she arrived? Indeed. He would feel exactly this way and would issue these commands immediately.

Her crusade for self-improvement would proceed methodically, with vigor and with her full determination to realize her goal. One day soon she would bring Brandon de Forrest worshipfully to his knees.

Melissa's intricate plan of revenge and triumph had been formulated early that morning, even before Brandon knocked at her door with instructions to make ready for the journey.

Now she sat haughtily astride her horse, doing her best not to appear at all interested in him—while actually observing him with a hawk's intensity from the corner of her eye.

He was engaged in last-minute arrangements and was fastening a sack of provisions for their journey to his saddle when a coach drawn by four horses came trundling noisily into the inn's cobbled courtyard.

There was an immediate hue and cry as the driver bellowed news that highwaymen abounded on the road from London.

"Not just set upon once, mind you," he blustered, his face flushed with outrage as he climbed down from his high seat, "but stopped three separate times, we were."

A small crowd of workers and guests began to assemble, eager for the gruesome news. Melissa's own attention was likewise riveted. Highwaymen still held a heady fascination for her.

The man played to his audience, narrowing his eyes and dropping his voice. "Lucky to have our pants left on us, the bleedin' thieves."

"Although, in truth, one was most charming," piped a young woman of Melissa's age, who alighted from the coach. She held out a dainty gloved hand to a stable boy, who guided her safely to the ground. "And most attractive," the girl added, casting her eyes demurely downward as soon as the statement issued from her pink rouged lips.

She was the prettiest thing Melissa had ever seen, and a sting of envy mixed with awe assailed her as she studied each detail of the girl's appearance.

The female passenger had burnished copper hair assembled in a graceful display of small curls atop her head, and on her cheeks were two decorative black patches—a half moon and a star.

As the girl moved **forw**ard on her satin shoes, she came within inches of Brandon—whom, Melissa noted, she could have easily avoided by choosing a slightly different route. But passing close by him, she suddenly looked up, widened her blue eyes as if surprised at his presence, then smiled coquettishly. When his eyes met hers, she instantly procured from within the winged cuff of her gown a small gold and blue silk fan, and snapping it open, she peered over its top with shining eyes.

The minx! thought Melissa.

And, also, what an utterly charming gesture, this fan business. . . .

She made a mental note to immediately seek out a fan, once in London. Perhaps she would get several of them.

Hungered for clues by which to better herself, Melissa continued to study the girl's costume, taking in the cut of her light blue damask gown, with its sleeves ending in stiff, flared cuffs, lined in gold material.

Unfortunately, it was also impossible for Melissa to ignore that Brandon's eyes followed the woman for a few seconds as she made her way to the inn's entrance. Pricked by hot needles of jealousy, Melissa was all the more determined to one day own his eyes, his body, his mind, his very soul—exclusively.

That, and nothing less, would do.

Yes, she thought with dark resolve, *she would make him pay dearly before she finally accepted him back into her bed.*

"Are you well armed, sirrah?" asked the coachman, taking in Brandon's preparations to depart. "And accompanied by staunch friends?"

"Indeed." Brandon touched his fingers to the hilt of his Scottish dirk. "With my trusty, sharp-edged friend here."

The man's eyes settled respectfully on the blade. "Aye, and well it is you're traveling with such a one at your side." He looked back up at Brandon. "Though if you don't mind me saying so, sirrah, better you should have some fire power along as another companion." The coachman grunted, shaking his head. "One scurvy knave brandished his musket about, but I didn't want to test him." He gave Brandon a keen look. "Meaning no disrespect... if you take my advice, better to wait and travel with a group of others headed in your direction. Safety in numbers," he said, and while dispensing this last bit of advice, he slid his attention to Melissa. An instant glow of male appreciation lighted his eyes as he ran his gaze from her face to her toes and back up again.

Melissa couldn't have been more pleased. In fact, she desperately wished she had a fan to snap, although perhaps it wasn't done to waste fans on coachmen.

"You wouldn't want to lose the pretty miss there, would you?" the man said with good-natured gallantry. He slid another telling glance Melissa's way.

"I thank you for your concern," Brandon returned with polite dismissiveness, choosing equally to ignore the compliment paid to Melissa. "Unfortunately we've no time to spare on precautions." As if to demonstrate, he mounted his horse.

"Then God and luck go with you and against the blackguards," murmured the coachman, tipping his three-cornered hat in a respectful good-bye.

The town was soon behind them, and they traveled in silence, keeping to the highway rather than ranging over the meadows and taking shortcuts as Brandon had done on his trip to Cornwall.

He went at a good pace, but not so fast that Melissa could not follow close behind. Now and then they would stop to rest the horses.

During these brief interludes their manner toward each other was one of polite indifference, strained on Melissa's part, for she felt a tumult of emotions ranging from fury and thoughts of vengeance, to the sad longing that he would want her and find her as fascinating as she did him.

Like this, then, their journey continued into the afternoon, with Melissa finally growing weary even of her daydreams.

The sun was gradually lowering over a thickly treed hill that had long been a distant landmark.

Close now, the hill seemed far steeper and the shade more dense. It was a place Melissa did not find appealing and which brought to mind some of Goodie's old tales of goblins and witches.

They had just passed from sunlight into the dark hollow of the hill's shadow when Brandon veered his horse around and galloped back to where she straggled at her slower pace.

His face was grim, and for once, at least, she knew that the cause of his concern was not her doing.

He trotted next to her, his eyes scanning ahead as he spoke in a low, tense voice. "If anything should happen, should there be trouble... you're to let me handle it without any interference." He turned and his dark eyes gripped hers. This time she did not dare to question him; she did not think to defy him. "You're to ride ahead and ride hard. Continue down this road, and once near London, ask directions. Here," he said, and handed her a pouch that he drew from a larger leather bag strung to his saddle. The bag bore the heavy feel of coins. "Ask for King Street. Then inquire for Danfort House, where you'll find your grandfather. Is that clear, Melissa?"

She nodded once, an icy fear chilling her far more than the shadows wrapping darkness around them.

"Good. Then you're to follow my instructions to the letter. And a warning... other than asking for directions, you aren't to trust anyone—not even someone who claims they'll assist you. London is not Cornwall. People wear masks of many types—kindness, poverty, even gentility— anything it takes to separate the naive from his purse. And sometimes even a life is snatched. So for this once, at least, I urge you to curb your curious nature and stifle your appetite for adventure. There's to be no deviation from my instructions.''

"But, why could I—"

"Melissa…" he reprimanded, one eye on her, the other on the dark hillside, whose silhouette loomed above them.

"Yes … yes. All right," she sighed. "Ride hard in case of trouble, London, King Street, not to trust anyone. Obey your commands to the letter. There, are you happy?"

"To the letter," he echoed, and he didn't sound at all happy. "It isn't to be like last night." He gave her a sharp glance.

Melissa looked away.

Of course it wasn't to be like last night. Last night she had been a young, infatuated girl without a dollop of sense. This day, she was a young, cowed girl bearing the burden of humiliation, wishing only to rid herself of the onus of shame she had brought upon herself.

"I understand perfectly," she said, with a prim dignity. "If we are to be attacked by highwaymen, I'm to flee for my cowardly life, leaving you to heroically fend off our attackers."

He was not amused. "And?" he prodded.

"And I'm to make my way to my grandfather. There, now, are you pleased at last?"

"Very good—exactly." For once, a smile lurked just behind the dark eyes. For an instant his stern face softened. Melissa thought he might have smiled, that he had wanted to smile, but that his thoughts seemed split between her and the hill with its tangled gloom of trees.

But her own mind was still alive and burning with questions. "But, Monsieur de Forrest, I must ask…what if you *can't* fend off the attackers? And what if the attackers come after me?"

"Then God help them in their black fortune. It would be a blunder of monumental order," he said dryly. He spurred his horse forward, leaving her to straggle behind.

The sun had at last fallen completely behind the hill. All that remained were radiant shafts of light, which seemed to grow out of the tree-lined mound to burst against the sky.

Brandon rode before her, at a fast gallop. Although she could tell from his bearing that he was alert, watching for trouble, the only sounds were those of their horses and the occasional bird, and in the absence of any visible peril, her thoughts turned easily to more mundane matters.

She wondered where they would spend the night. She would be a model of decorum wherever it was.

What would she eat? She was thinking of roast beef and dumplings and damson pie, she was thinking of trifle and stewed pippins and quince jelly on toast, she was thinking of her stomach...when the sound of horses drew her eyes to the crest of the hill.

At first she could see nothing. The combination of the sun's brightness behind the hill and the shadows in front obscured her vision.

But a moment later the shapes of four horsemen formed out of the fuzzy light, and the distant rattle of hooves became a growing thunder in her mind, which had completely forgotten about pheasant and vegetables.

Ahead, Brandon stiffened in his saddle. He reined in his mount, quickly changing direction to come hurtling back to her.

"*Now,* Melissa. Go now—ride!" he ordered, the better part of his attention fixed on the men coming their way.

"But, Brandon—"

"Damn you, girl! Do what I say!" He looked into her eyes, and she saw a new man there, a man she had not met before. *Oh,* she thought. She would not defy this man—not ever. "Go!" he said, and gave a hard swat to her horse's flanks.

The beast dove forward, straining at a breakneck pace down the road as if under the control of Brandon's will.

Melissa looked behind to see that Brandon had already crossed onto the hill's lower slope to meet the four men.

Her heart turned over. All her glamorous visions of courtly highwaymen faded as her ears filled with the sound of metal cutting against metal, and the next time she looked back, her eyes drew in the horrifying scene of Brandon bearing down on one man, only to be attacked by another from a different side.

She couldn't leave him!

But Brandon's words to her rang in her mind . . . *Do as I say, Melissa.* He had made her promise.

But while she remained undecided, slowing her horse one minute, pushing ahead in a gallop the next, two of the attackers left the fray. They rode fast toward Melissa.

The decision was made for her.

Digging her heels into her horse, she bent her head low against its mane, urging an increase in speed, now and then looking behind to gauge the distance separating her from her pursuers. Her skirts rose high over her knees, climbing to her thighs, and the lightweight woolen cloak whipped behind her.

The men were gaining, riding at a remarkable speed she did not have the skill to match. They were close enough now that she saw the flare of their nostrils amid unshaven faces and could all but smell the stench of their grime-spotted clothes.

These were not the highwaymen of her friends' girlish gossip. These were not "charming" as the girl in the inn had claimed. They were foul, disgusting oafs!

Laughing gutturally, one reached her side and lunged for her reins. But with a violent kick, Melissa sent him reeling, only to find herself in combat with the second man. Releasing her cloak, she sent it flying directly into his face, at which point she did a complete about-face and sent her horse careering back in the opposite direction.

Ahead of her she could see Brandon beating off the remaining two men. Her heart leaped with hope of victory, then fell.

Blood. A deep red stain seeped through the white sleeve of Brandon's right arm, causing him to fight with his unfavored left.

And all the while, behind her, her pursuers were gaining.

From one came an oath, cutting through the din, and Brandon turned just long enough to take the brunt of a crippling blow to his back. The flat impact of his foe's sword sent him sprawling.

"Brandon!" Melissa screamed in warning.

But to no effect.

The second man plunged his sword into Brandon's side even as he made to rise.

Helpless, horrified, Melissa watched him totter, reach for his fallen sword, then doubling in pain, collapse slowly to the earth.

Her two pursuers continued to snatch at her, but she evaded them, dodging back and forth with her horse, all the while racing to the arena of battle where Brandon lay fallen.

"Oh...Mother of Mary!" Melissa cried, looking down at Brandon's still form on the earth. She brought her horse around and leaped to the ground, throwing herself to her knees and bending over him. "Oh, Brandon...Brandon...oh, no, no..." she said over and over again, looking into his face and then back at the wound, which was gushing forth red blood against his white shirt.

The enchanting dark, velveteen eyes had fallen closed, but at her voice, his lids fluttered and he looked into her face.

"Melissa..." he gasped. "Damn it...I told you—"

"Don't die, Brandon. Oh, please, please don't die!" she cried. Frantic, she touched his face, touched his hand, squeezing his fingers with her palm as if the force of her love might sustain him. "Brandon, I can't bear to live in this world if you aren't in it! Please, please don't leave me.... Please—I'll do anything you say. Anything. Everything...forever and ever, Brandon. I'll mind whatever you tell me. Oh, God!" she cried, looking to the heavens in anguish. "Save him!" And again, pleading, she said, "I don't want to live without you in this world, Brandon, Brandon...don't leave me. Please..." she sobbed.

His hand moved in hers, and she bent closer to listen as he whispered her name softly. The dark eyes were open, taking in her face as if in wonder, as if memorizing it. "Melissa..." But the light was fading from his eyes even as he strained to speak. "Be careful in London.... Melissa, last night—" He struggled to find the breath. "I did...I wanted...you."

And then he spoke no more.

His eyes were closed. His breath was still. He was gone.

Sobbing, Melissa threw herself over him, covering his still form as if to protect him from the harm that had already befallen. But no sooner had she embraced him, than she was rudely yanked up by her arm and spun around to face one of the attackers.

"Now then, that were a touching good scene," the man said. He had a missing tooth, and his grin was as evil as a devil's. "But s'finished now. Come on, your ladyship. We handled that one...now we've got you to finish with."

Helpless, Melissa backed away, her eyes still on Brandon's slain form. Sobbing, she looked up into the four pitiless faces, "You can't just leave him here. He's got to be buried properly."

The men laughed in unison.

"We can do whatever we have a mind, Miss Pretty." And that one stepped forward, pulling her roughly against his body, so that her heart stopped, fearing the worst. But instead, he hoisted her into his arms and threw her atop his horse, climbing up after and wrapping one arm around her middle in a tight vise.

"What are you going to do with me?" Melissa gasped, hardly able to find the breath to speak.

"Why take you to London, yer ladyship. This be'n the road to London town...now isn't that the place where'n you were headed? Yer new escorts, we be. Keepin y'safe's our pledge."

The horses were reeled around, and Melissa was able to steal one last fleeting look at Brandon lying white and still and dead in the shadow of the hill.

"Brandon!" she screamed. "I shall never, never love anyone but you!" she cried out, as the horses set forth in the direction of London.

And all the men laughed.

It was the dead of night when the four horsemen and Melissa entered the city. She was blurry-eyed with fatigue, and cold and aching. Brandon's face still burned like a fever in her brain.

The streets of London were empty but for an occasional rider and a few carriages. Now and again a few dark and ragged wraiths darted from the shadows, caught for an instant in the moonlight before being swallowed by night or an alleyway. The streets were narrow, with some of the high buildings five stories tall. Signs swung, creaking and whining on hinges over doorways. They seemed a macabre display, their painted and carved wooden faces depicting all manner of pleasure, from food and libations to dry goods. Indeed, there was no joy in any of these new sights for Melissa, who all but gagged at the faint foul odor of sewage, even worse than the smell of the man holding her locked against his body.

Finally a new scent arose. The pungent odor of seawater came to mingle with a dense fog as the motley band reached the wharves.

Melissa heard the lap of water against stone and the creak of ships straining against their moorings. *Brandon had known this city. Every sight, every sound she now experienced had once belonged to him. Oh, God... would that he had lived, that she had shared that life with him!*

An occasional light would filter through the heavy gray mist, but otherwise, they were unseen travelers in a dank gray world.

The last sound Melissa heard as she was ushered from the mist, through a door into a dimly lit corridor, was the sounding of a ship's bell.

The next sound she heard was that of a woman's voice. At this, Melissa took heart—but too soon, and foolishly.

For when the woman appeared, the face peering at Melissa in the candle's glow was twisted into a permanent state of cruelty. The woman surveyed her unsympathetically, running her eyes down the length of her, then coming again to rest upon her face. Too weary even for fear, Melissa could only stand and stare back.

"A fine one," the woman said, her voice harsh and gravelly as a man's.

"She'll fetch us a pretty price," said Melissa's captor. He held her arms pinned behind her back.

"Aye, that she will. Take her below. Throw her in with that other brat. It'll save trouble with the keys at feeding time," said the woman. Giving Melissa one more appraising glance, she tossed a ring of heavy keys to the man.

Melissa's struggles were useless. She was pushed down a narrow flight of stone steps, then through a damp underground corridor. The candle's glow danced against the walls of the long, narrow passageway, lined on both sides with short, stout arched doors. Most were open, a few were closed. Melissa thought she heard whimpering from behind one door.

"Here be yer quarters, m'lady." The man jiggled the ring of keys in her face and laughed.

"What is this place?" Melissa asked. Her voice was so weak she hardly recognized it as her own.

"Yer lodgin's . . . yer fine quarters, like I said." He kept one hand on Melissa's wrist as he worked a key in a lock.

"Please . . . what will happen to me?" she asked him, deliberately pulling back as he made to shove her through a hollow opening leading to absolute blackness beyond.

"The back of me hand'll happen t'ya, if'n you don't shut yer mouth and get in there."

With a shove, he sent Melissa flying forward into the black hole. She fell face first, landing against cold stone. The door slammed shut.

There was no light left. There was only silence, absolute silence, and then the scrape of the key in the thick
lock, sealing her in.

"Oh, God..." Melissa sobbed. "Gracious, good,
merciful Lord, what is this place?"

And from the dark came a voice, so soft that Melissa
thought it was her own maddened mind answering.

"It is hell."

Her Ladyship, the Countess Glenmillan Danfort's violet eyes were ablaze with an evil light that frightened the
chambermaid far more than the vase her mistress had just
hurled at her, and which, through experience and being
fleet of foot, she had only barely avoided.

"Shall I clean up the pieces, ma'am?" the girl asked
timorously, her eyes widening as Glenmillan's hand
reached for a second missile, a valuable porcelain figurine
of a Venetian boatman, with a little clock imbedded in his
chest.

Glenmillan stayed her hand as she gave thought to the
girl's question. "No," she snapped, "leave it." And to the
maid's relief, she moved away from the figurine. "Go to
my son's rooms and see if he's returned yet. Tell him to get
his rump here immediately. Tell him if he doesn't come at
once, I shall have his arse disinherited and thrown into
debtor's prison!"

"Yes, m'lady," said the girl, and with a bobbed curtsy
she rushed as quickly as possible through the double white
and gilt carved doors to attend to her task and save her
own skin.

"Yes, m'lady, yes m'lady," Glenmillan mimicked, and
whirling about in her enormous cane-stiffened panniers,
she toppled the boatman figurine from its perch on a
carved Grecian pedestal. "Oh, Lord!" Glenmillan cried,
sobering suddenly as she examined the debris.

Now what had she done? The clock statue was a gift
from King George, who had personally presented it to her
at Court after she had read a little poem she had penned
for the occasion of his birthday. The gesture had been a

tremendous social coup, and now, witnessing the statue's sorry end, Glenmillan became gravely alarmed that the accident might portend disaster for her.

Nothing, simply nothing, had been going right for her, from the very moment Danfort decided to bring that girl back into their lives.

Glenmillan's gaze followed the trail of physical destruction she had wreaked that morning. As she took inventory, her sorrow grew proportionate to the cost of the items she had savaged beyond repair.

Among the casualties was the smashed hand mirror, its gold back encrusted with blue sapphires and lavender amethysts—to compliment her eye color. It was a gift from the Earl of Brynwald upon enjoying her favors one night. The next time she slept with him, he had presented her with a music box with a lid of sterling silver and diamonds to signify the eternal nature of his devotion. The tune hadn't been anything much, but the diamonds were charming, and she was looking forward to their next assignation.

A sharp knock against her door interrupted her musings. Glenmillan tensed. *Let it be Quentin. Please, God, let it be Quentin with news that all is well.* "Yes? Who's there?"

"Me, it's me, ma'am...." The maid's voice sounded from the other side of the door. "His lordship's not returned yet. Would you like me to start with your hair now?"

"Go," said Glenmillan dully. "I don't care for my hair, you ninny. What use is hair when the world is collapsing? Go from me...go hang yourself, useless wench. Fling yourself from London Bridge...you'll not be missed...."

"Yes, ma'am. Thank you, ma'am."

"Oh, misery," Glenmillan sighed. "I am surrounded by half-wits."

Fifteen minutes later, Glenmillan was still staring blankly out a window looking upon the Duke's intricately sculptured gardens when another knock sounded, abrupt and emphatic. Glenmillan had only just turned when, without invitation, Quentin burst through the doors.

"Well! At last! There you are!"

"So I am," said Quentin pleasantly. "And, I dare say...so are you."

"My God, but you do reek. I can smell your breath from here."

Quentin merely smiled and made a show of closing the door quietly and securely. He carried a cane with a mother-of-pearl handle. Still in elaborate evening dress, he wore a waistcoat of blue velvet, overlaid with intricate silver-gilt embroidery and tiny seed pearls and sequins.

Glenmillan stared at him, as if transfixed by the vision he presented. "Have you any idea of what time it is? What if the Duke saw you? Have you any notion of the sight you'd make?"

Quentin arched one brow and said, "And you, Mother, are a picture in your chemise, your stays, your petticoat and panniers, with strings of coal black hair streaming like snakes across your shoulders and dangling down your back. A fine Medusa you'd make." He cast an entertained glance around the room, taking in the destruction. "Have a care, Mother, or the Duke might catch *you,* and off you'd go, a fit candidate for Bedlam, judging by your looks—not to mention your, uh, antics...."

"Oh, very well," Glenmillan said with a sigh, following him as he strolled toward a chair and sank wearily into it. "We shall forget fashion for the time being. Have you any news?"

"News? News...let me see," said Quentin reflectively.

"I will kill you, Quentin—"

"Ah, you mean *news*. Yes, mother," he drawled, and hit the cane against his shoes, "I *am* the bearer of news...which is precisely why I happen to be late. You mustn't be so quick to condemn. In fact, I've been attending to business. *Our* business," he finished pointedly.

Glenmillan stood stock-still. She believed her heart might give out. "And, Quentin? And...?"

"And..." said Quentin, studying his satin-encased toes, which he flexed and wiggled, "the girl is ours." He looked up, measuring his mother's reaction.

"Oh, oh...." Glenmillan moaned with ecstasy and brought her fingers together. "Thank God!"

"Better to thank me, mother," said Quentin, whose eyes bore the same round shape as Glenmillan's, but which were a less dramatic shade—pale blue rather than Glenmillan's startling violet color. But, whereas Glenmillan's intense violet was counterbalanced by equally dramatic raven-colored hair, Quentin was less fortunate. The light eyes, combined with the same black hair, presented him with a somewhat disquieting, otherworldly quality that had the effect of shifting attention from his words to his appearance. It was a trick of nature, which Quentin often used to his advantage, luring women into his web with his patter while they concentrated on his opalescent irises, or disarming an opponent with his crystalline gaze while in a card game at White's.

"I'll thank you," Glenmillan said, her head awhirl with thoughts for the future. "I'll thank you fully, with an enormous inheritance, once you've wed the girl and we're safely out of the woods." Her eyes sharpened as she caught the tail end of another unpleasant thought. "Brandon de Forrest?"

"Finished."

"Ah." Glenmillan was uncommonly silent for a moment. "Finished."

"Alas, it *was* the only way," Quentin said, studying Glenmillan with an ironic smile.

"Yes...yes, of course."

"But...it seems you regret it?"

"Perhaps, a shade...."

"Careful, madame, one might think you had a heart."

"He is—was—an unusual man."

"Unusual because he didn't capitulate to your charms?"

Glenmillan smiled weakly, but her smile was without malice and bore a deeper degree of sadness than she generally displayed. "I wasn't seriously interested in him—he's a foreigner, and without a title."

"Of course. And only silly little girls from Cornwall might be tempted to fall in love and marry such a man as that."

"Exactly," said Glenmillan, turning and moving toward the window again. She peered out at the garden, seeing a summer's eve two years before, when the tall, handsome and unpredictable French expatriate had kissed her, then refused her invitation to accompany her up the stairs to her bedchamber. At forty, she had been thirteen years Brandon's senior, but she was beautiful and she was convinced that age had not been a factor in his refusal. He simply didn't want her. And she had never wanted any man more.

"Anyway, I'll effect the grand rescue in two days," said Quentin, rising wearily from his seat.

"Why so long?" Glenmillan asked, her mind still clouded with the past. "Can we risk the time?"

"The slaver sets sail in five days time, so there's no hurry. But if the girl's sprung too soon, it will diminish the impact of my rescue. Let her suffer. A bit of hardship will make her all the more grateful when I arrive to save her."

"You are heartless, aren't you?" Glenmillan commented dully, watching through the panes as a gardener slashed at a tree branch.

"Indeed. I am my mother's son," said Quentin cheerily. "And now, with your leave, madame, I shall take to my bed. I must reserve my strength for my forthcoming heroics."

Behind her, Glenmillan heard the door click shut.

Only then did she turn. Her eyes were red, and tears hung in them, but did not fall. She had not allowed herself to cry for many years.

"Oh, Brandon..." she whispered, and a lone tear slipped free, trailing randomly down her cheek. "A damned shame...."

Chapter Four

They began their friendship in the merciless darkness. In the beginning, they were only two voices, halting, soft, frightened.

She said her name was Celia Allen. She was twenty-two, four years older than Melissa. Like Melissa, she had come to London from the country—a village in Yorkshire—to seek a better life. Having no skills, but possessing a passably good education and a few nice manners learned from some of the landed gentry of the area, she had found service in the London town home of the Duke and Duchess of Beltonwick.

"A very fine lady, whose daily works are dedicated to helping the poor and unfortunate," Celia had said, her voice holding the pride of association.

"Then I certainly hope she'll do something for you, because under the subject of misfortune, you qualify to the very letter," Melissa returned with lack of heart. Her natural optimism had at last dwindled to harsh acceptance that neither of them would see freedom again.

"She will. I'm sure of it. Once she realizes..." But Celia's voice, which had begun with authority, drifted into a sigh of despair.

It had been almost two days since she had been thrown into the dungeon, and Melissa felt as if her very soul were being bled into the stone walls. Soon nothing of her would remain. And perhaps she did not care. At least the torture of loving a man she could never touch would be finished.

It was an awful place, a nightmare that would not end.

During the night it was entirely black within their small cell, and only during the daylight hours did a small patch of illumination seep down from above, where an air vent allowed sunlight to enter.

In the faint light, Melissa had made out her companion's features, taking in a hint of what must have been auburn hair and eyes that Celia described to her as gray.

It was hard to tell some things. She could, however, tell that enormous rats were nocturnal visitors to their quarters, dropping in from the air vent and scurrying across her feet as they made for whatever remained in their food bowls.

Celia had been right: this was hell.

Melissa also learned from Celia that they were not alone in their misfortune. There were others kept behind the locked doors she had passed when being led to her cell.

"Mostly they take prostitutes from the street, and others down on their luck," Celia explained. Celia knew a great deal, her mistress having explained the horrors that it was her life's work to rectify.

They were in a temporary holding place—probably a warehouse, once used for the storage of goods—for women who would be transported aboard ship to various English colonies and India. There they would be sold into houses of ill repute catering to the pleasures of sailors and other Anglo transplants, or else absorbed into harems.

In some cases a transported victim had only a life of hard labor to endure, working in the fields or as a household menial. If more unlucky, she would be sentenced to work a mine.

"It's a scandal," Celia said, in understatement, and Melissa thought she must have heard the Duchess of Beltonwick's tone in the phrase. "And all of London knows about it. My mistress petitioned the King to have it stopped."

"Apparently with no success."

Celia sighed. "My lady was much discouraged. Some say it's because some of His Grace's friends have a coin or two of their own invested in slavery, and it's because of them he looks the other way . . . needing their support for his own matters, you see.''

''I see that we're doomed—that's what I see.''

''No. Someone will come,'' Celia said emphatically. ''Someone will come. They *must*.'' She was silent for a while, and then said in an ashamed voice, ''I've a child . . . a little girl, Melissa. It was her I was going to see, when I got nabbed. I was sneaking out at night, so as not to be seen by anyone. No one in the household knows about my baby,'' she said. ''I haven't a husband, you see. And I was afraid that the Duchess might have me sacked for being immoral. She's a very good woman, and what I did was a sin.''

She broke off, and Melissa knew that she was waiting for a reaction to her confession.

''It isn't ever a sin to lie with someone, not if you truly love him,'' Melissa offered at last, thinking of how she had wanted and loved Brandon. And her heart felt as though it had been wrenched apart as Brandon's face drove more deeply through her dark thoughts, filling her with a rush of love-tinged sadness and terrible regret.

''Oh, I did love him,'' Celia said forlornly. ''It was he who didn't love me . . . he only wanted me.''

And again Melissa's mind flew backward in time, hearing Brandon's last words to her as he lay dying. He had wanted her . . . he *had*.

''Have you ever—have you ever lain with a man you loved with your whole heart and body and soul, Melissa?''

''No. I've never been with any man. But once . . .'' she hesitated, finding it difficult to speak ''. . . once, well, I wanted to. And almost did.'' *It would have been so perfect between us.*

''And you loved him very much then, I'll wager.''

''I will never, never love another,'' Melissa said softly and fervently. She wiped away the tears. They would not help anything.

''And the man you loved, did he feel the same for you?''

"No...I don't think so. Not the same. But he felt something perhaps. If we had had more time... He died, you see."

She remembered Brandon as he had looked, lying still as the earth itself yet handsome as ever, when she had ridden off, screaming into the dying shadows that she loved him and would never love again. She had told him that she did not want to live anymore if he were taken from this world.

She had meant it.

And now, it seemed, her prayer was coming to pass....

But their captors did not want them to die—at least not yet.

Once a day the heavy arched door of their cell would be dragged open, and someone would bring in enough food to keep them alive. It was tasteless and foul fare, but Melissa was forced by hunger pangs to have at least some of it; the rats helped themselves to the remainder.

It was on the second evening that the door opened and a man's face appeared quite suddenly, illuminated by a candle. Melissa had not seen him before. He wore a heavy stubble of beard and a leer, as he stooped to peer in at them.

He thrust the candle forward to get a better look, and the glow shattered the dark of the tiny room. Melissa blinked and brought her arm against her eyes to shield her vision from the bright flare. When she looked again, the man was boldly appraising her.

"Where's our meal?" demanded Melissa, hunger driving past her depression and fear. She was hungry, so hungry that she could feel a burning sensation eating away at her stomach, and her eyes left the man's hideous face to seek the two bowls of food that were to replace their empty ones. "We won't be any good to you if we're dead, or scraggly like skinny chickens!"

He laughed and, hunching down to clear the doorway, slipped into the cell with them. He was not tall, but square and muscular. "Hungry are you? Wouldn't you like it, then—your nice hot delicious meal? What would you give me for your dinner?''

From the corner of her eye, Melissa saw Celia creep back against the cell wall, but Melissa did not yet understand. Her thoughts were elsewhere, her nerves on fire as she looked past the man to the hall, in search of the bowls that might lay beyond. There she saw them, just the barest outline in the half light.

''There they are! You've left our bowls outside,'' Melissa said, panic edging each word.

''Have I now?'' He continued to eye Melissa. ''If you're good to me, I might get them.''

Melissa recoiled, shrinking back as she finally understood the intention of his visit.

''Who'll be first to get her dinner?'' he asked, flicking his eyes to Celia, then back to Melissa. ''You're the hungry one, I think it'll be you.''

He reached forward to grab her arm, but Melissa dodged his first attempt at capture. Narrowing his eyes, he nodded, and set down the bottle holding his candle. ''Then you'll have it rough.''

This time he was more agile. With a snarl, he lunged, caught her arm and, hurling his weight against her, toppled her to the stone floor.

Melissa screamed and kicked at him, but he smacked her hard across the face. The blow made her dizzy, until black enveloped her from within. She felt his fingers rip at her skirt and lift the material over her waist.

''No!'' Melissa begged. ''Please, no...'' She was silenced as his mouth covered her words and he forced his tongue between her lips. She could feel his hard organ, thrusting to enter, and closed her eyes, from which hot tears of shame and rage erupted. *Brandon!* her mind cried. *Brandon!*

And suddenly, as if her plea had been answered, the man was no longer on her.

''Leave her be! Get away from her!''

It was Celia's voice.

And then it was the man's, his panicked curses filling the cell as he rolled off Melissa and leaped to his feet, swatting at the flames that engulfed him and rose higher with every frantic gesture he made to extinguish himself. The walls were alive with wild, shimmering, flying shadows as he flapped hysterically about.

Beyond the flaming torch he presented, Melissa saw Celia's face, contorted in a different kind of pain and horror. It was Celia who had smashed the bottle over his head, it was Celia who had inadvertently caused his clothes to catch fire from the fallen candle as he rolled off his would-be victim.

"Oh, Lord!" Celia cried, throwing herself forward. "I didn't mean to—" With her hands, she began to beat down the flames.

Even Melissa, horrified at the sight, fell to his aid, trying to stifle the fire. With savage strength, she tore off his burning shirt, but he was crazed and screaming as if still afire. His curses of rage and panic echoed down the long hallway as he ran from the room.

"Quick," Melissa said in a rush, "he's left the door open."

The cell had only the barest amount of light from the shaft, but it was enough for them. Cautiously, they felt their way to the short, arched space that was their gateway to freedom. Melissa's heart beat like a hammer.

In the distance they could hear the rantings of the man as he clambered up the stairs. Melissa's mouth had gone cottony as the notion of liberty became ever more real; but whatever hope she held was cancelled by the knowledge that the man, or his friends, could suddenly return and seek vengeance against them.

And then suddenly, just as they reached the door, the distant cries stopped. An eerie silence seeped through the damp cellar, wrapping tentacles of new fear around Melissa's heart.

"What's happened?" she whispered to Celia.

"Has he reached the top of the stairs, perhaps gone out?"

"Do you think he's dead of the fire?"

"I don't know, I don't think so. The sounds stopped so suddenly." Celia clutched at Melissa's arm. "What should we do?"

"We've got no choice, do we? We've got to escape."

"But if they catch us—"

"What more could they do? Kill us? We're bound to die anyway. Better now than later, when all we'll do is suffer more at the hands of some other rogues." And so saying, Melissa stepped boldly into the hallway, only to gasp and fall back at once. "Mother Mary . . . save us. There's another of them. He's coming fast down the hallway now with a torch and a drawn sword."

With a small cry, Celia fell to her knees and began to pray.

Time seemed to rush. The hall grew lighter as the steps sounding against the stone grew louder—and closer. In prayer, Celia's voice was small, ardent, plaintive.

Melissa heard her ask forgiveness for all her sins and for Melissa's soul to be spared, as well. She begged that their end be painless and fast, and that her little girl would be taken care of by good people and taught the Lord's way, and that somehow her child would come to know that she hadn't been abandoned for lack of love.

As for Melissa, she spent her time grappling around in the dark, searching for the bottle that had held the candle the man had carried into their cell.

By the time their new persecutor entered their keep, Celia was ready for heaven and Melissa was ready for him.

No sooner had the man shown his head through the door than down her weapon came with a crash.

She heard a deep groan, then a thud and the clash of metal, as body and sword connected with stone.

"Now!" Melissa cried to Celia, who was already scrambling to get possession of the torch, as Melissa grabbed for the sword.

"God's saved us!" Celia exclaimed triumphantly. "He's saved us!" And with that, she fainted.

"No...no..." came a weak male voice from the floor. The man's fingers began to scrabble at the stones as he attempted to raise himself, but he sank down immediately as Melissa pressed the point of his weapon into his ribs. "Not God," he said, "me. Me. It's I who've come to liberate you...." He turned his face, his features etched in pain and confusion as he stared up at Melissa. "Which of you is my stepsister? Which of you would be Melissa?"

Chapter Five

"Now, my dear, you've undergone a horrendous ordeal, but thanks to Quentin, it's all in the past."

Melissa, who was propped in bed against satin cushions, looked directly into her stepmother's beautiful violet eyes and said, "It isn't in the past at all. Not until Celia is safe."

"Yes, well...you do understand that Quentin is doing what he can—we all are—to see that the situation is rectified."

"All it takes is going there!" Melissa said adamantly. "We know where she is, and all that needs to be done is to carry her out, the same as I was. She should have left when I did. There's no reason for her still to be there."

"But, my dear, you saw what happened. Our dear Quentin had to fight his way out with you in his arms."

"I was perfectly capable of walking myself."

"Quentin didn't think so."

"I told him so."

"Well, he was wild with worry over your safety."

"And I'm worried about Celia. I swear to you, if I don't have proof that she's been set free within the next day, I'll get her myself."

Glenmillan fixed her violet eyes on Melissa and silently cursed the girl. Rather than exhibiting gratefulness, for two days the wretched wench had done nothing but yammer and complain about that servant girl she had been holed up with. Of course Quentin hadn't bothered with her. He hadn't bothered because he simply didn't care a whit what became of the chit. Nor did she care, thought Glenmillan. Nor did anyone else on the face of the earth—except for Melissa—care what became of such baggage.

London was teeming with the likes of this Celia. They came in droves from the country to make their way in a city that was already full to overflowing with too many bodies.

In Quentin's mock battle with the men he had hired to stage his heroic rescue, he had simply made it seem impossible to free the servant girl.

Of course, now it seemed that it would have been far easier if he'd liberated her. At least they wouldn't have had to listen to Melissa's lamentations. On the other hand, it was fortuitous that Melissa had been shown a genuine sample of Quentin's efforts on her behalf.

It had been a happy bit of business that he had met with the complaining fire victim, who had presented a nasty but short-lived challenge to Quentin's rescue operation. Quentin had easily silenced his curses with a blade, and there the body remained, conveniently sprawled at the top of the stairs for Quentin to step over as he spirited Melissa away from her miserable fate.

One would have thought the girl would have been more impressed...certainly more grateful. Instead, she was filled with complaint. Even now.

"Don't you see," said Melissa, "if we don't act at once—this very day—then there's the chance that the slave ship might sail. There's no time to spare."

"Whatever makes you care so deeply for this servant?" Glenmillan asked, bored beyond endurance.

"For one thing, she's a human being, just the same as you and I. For another, she risked her life to save me from being ravaged—or maybe even killed. And for another, although this is in strictest confidence, she has a child...a little girl, dependent upon her support."

"Yes, well—" Glenmillan sighed "—in that light, everything is far more understandable. Now you had better rest, my dear, and I shall go to speak about this matter to—"

"My grandfather?" Melissa inquired. "I'm sure if you were to ask for his assistance, knowing what it would mean to me, he'd use his influence with the King on Celia's behalf."

"Yes, of course he would," soothed Glenmillan. "But you must remember, it wouldn't do to trouble him with such matters now. When he heard the details of your dismaying journey, he suffered a terrible shock. It's important that he not have any more excitement, any additional reminder of your ordeal, lest he...well, I'm sure you understand." With that, Glenmillan rose gracefully from the small bedside chair and, with a kindly parting smile, drifted toward the double doors opening onto the great gallery lying beyond Melissa's quarters.

Absently, half thinking of Celia, Melissa studied her stepmother as she moved away. Glenmillan was undeniably the most beautiful woman Melissa had ever seen in her life. The violet eyes, of course, were her most outstanding feature, but everything else about her seemed equally perfect, from her flawless white skin to the shiny black hair, and the exquisite manner in which she dressed, talked and moved.

With more consideration, Melissa studied the deep purple gown Glenmillan wore that morning, and thought that such a color would be equally becoming on herself, and that with her hair done similarly, Brandon would not fail to find her irresistible.

But with a sudden jolt, as if the blade of a guillotine had come flashing down on the thought, the past lay bleeding before her. *Brandon de Forrest was dead.*

Melissa closed her eyes, her chest heaving as she fought against the misery that now and again rose up, stifling in its intensity, cutting off her will to live. How strange it was that not knowing of him, she had spent her life freely and easily; then, in that fateful discovery of his existence, she had realized that not one day of her life had been truly felt, truly lived, until the moment he had passed her on the road. From that instant the world had become a different place, exploding into a wonderland of delights, of excitement, of moment-to-moment anticipation!

And then, just as suddenly as the world had opened for her, the blazing light had died away, and all of life had grown cold, withering into a meaningless existence. *Brandon was dead.*

Though it was true, it was a fact impossible to fathom while her passion for him remained alive.

In an attempt to save herself from sliding into a deeper crevasse of pain, she put her mind to what she must do to rescue Celia Allen. Since her life held little value to her without Brandon in it, she determined that she would spare nothing of herself in her efforts to extricate Celia from the jowls of misfortune. If she could not count upon anyone else to help her, then she would help herself.

"And how is my granddaughter this morning?" inquired the Duke of Danfort from his desk, without looking up at his daughter-in-law, a woman he detested almost as much as he despised her wastrel of a son. That it was he who had arranged the marriage of the woman to his son Philip, some sixteen years previous, was testimony to the fact that he, dare he say it, was capable of human error. *And human conceit.*

During his robust years, he had never likened himself to other men, holding himself above the masses of humanity in all ways, and yet, for all his shrewdness, he had—like even the most humble yeoman farmer—fallen prey to the universal delusion that time would never run out for him.

And then, suddenly, a scant month ago, infirmity had pounced, broadsiding him with the certainty of his mortality—his very imminent mortality. He could no longer evade the annoying evidence that he was, after all, merely human and would not continue, as the sun did, to rise and set unendingly.

However bitter a pill *that* was to swallow, it was not the oblivion of death that disturbed his soul's serenity. No, when the time was upon him, he would concede to the grim reaper with gentlemanly tolerance. It was the probability that the proceeds of his life's work, and that of his ancestors', would fall into the hands of his estate's only remaining—and undeserving—heirs that made the bile churn in his gut.

Insufferable! He gripped the slender stalk of his quill pen as a dangerous heat arose from his depths. It was always so. Just the thought of the rapacious and cloying duo squandering all that he had amassed drove him into a black, irreconcilable mood.

At any rate, the exiled grandchild was now a necessity to him on two counts, the most pressing one being that he needed a blood heir to thwart the expectations of the two vultures awaiting his demise. That he could use her to expand his empire to India came simply as a stroke of good fortune.

He fought down his temper and continued to work at his papers, piled in several neat stacks on his desk, a large French *bureau plat* only recently imported from across the channel. He was aware of Glenmillan observing him, gauging his mood from across the room. He was aware that she was taking a suspiciously long time to answer his question.

The library was an enormous rectangular room, the two longer walls devoted to high bookshelves lined with leather-bound volumes in English, Greek and Latin. Family paintings hung above the volumes, generations of the illustrious Danforts looking down upon the world in death, just as they had in life. A third wall consisted entirely of a bank of three windows, which the Duke had thrown wide. From without could be heard the noisy play of sparrows.

As the Duke worked, a patch of May sunlight spilled over his shoulder, brightening the mole gray velveteen fabric of his jacket and occasionally sending off a ray of iridescent light from the heavy gold embroidery.

"I'm afraid your granddaughter is ailing, your lordship," said Glenmillan at last.

The Duke gave her a brief glance. Rustling forward in her satin, she wore a distressed expression, and the violet eyes held a hint of empathy.

"The experience she suffered was extremely debilitating," Glenmillan said. Her tone matched her facial appearance. "You can imagine…" And with that, she all but collapsed onto a sofa.

Located next to the hearth, the couch was the nearest seat to the Duke, and at right angles to his desk. She repositioned herself in order to watch him more easily. It was always necessary to catch every nuance of the man—the better to protect her interests. "If it hadn't been for Quentin," she went on, "well, God help us all. We'd never have seen her in any condition."

From the corner of her eye, she examined the Duke for response. They had explained Quentin's rescue of Melissa by an intricate but plausible story. Out of goodwill, he had ridden ahead to meet her and, not finding her, had suspected foul play. Totally distraught, he had hounded every possible source of information until he had tracked her to the warehouse.

It was a charming, touching little fable. No one would have believed it was Quentin himself who had arranged for the entire abduction in the first place.

Danfort raised his white, periwigged head, the small rolled curls at the sides looking like two extra little ears. *Or, better yet, thought Glenmillan, like horns.* But there was nothing laughable about the Duke. His very presence inspired respect, and along with that, fear. His eyes were hazel, with flecks like gold dust scattered amid the greenish brown cast, and for a man well into his seventies, the glance hitting his daughter-in-law was sharp and cynical and still bore the vital gleam of life.

His voice, likewise, had a cutting edge to it, devoid of warmth when he spoke. "I've heard enough of your secondhand tales, madame. I am interested in meeting her for myself and won't be put off any longer."

"But of course," said Glenmillan, whose fervent wish it was to delay that meeting as long as possible. They needed time to ingratiate themselves with Melissa before the Duke pulled her into his web. Glenmillan shifted her skirts, smoothing the folds into neat creases in order to have something to do with her hands. Only the Duke could cause her to shake like that.

"Then I want her here, without any more excuses. I expect her to be here this afternoon to make our acquaintance."

"But—"

"Madame, let us have no more of this delay. I want a look at her." He paused then and asked consideringly, "Tell me . . . how does she appear?"

"Oh, quite wan, and she has these fits of trembling, I'm afraid. Probably due to the shock . . . although it might be something of a permanent nature. Who's to know yet? Naturally, I'm doing what I can to—"

"Madame, I do not inquire about her condition. I wish to know about her appearance." The Duke's mouth had curled with displeasure. His once fleshy face had degenerated in age, and the pale skin now covered sunken, angular cheekbones that had not been apparent in earlier years. "Pray, what does she look like, madame? Is she fair or a toad?"

"She's middling, your lordship," Glenmillan responded, lying through her teeth. "A typical country girl, rather plain and undistinguished, as you might expect."

The girl was bloody exquisite, Glenmillan thought begrudgingly, and anyone with even half his vision intact would be blinded by the sight of her once she was fixed up with the proper clothes and had that wild yellow mane of hair managed into something fashionable.

But it pained Glenmillan to provide the Duke with any more pleasure than was necessary—especially since she knew precisely why he had asked about the girl's appearance. He had in mind to marry her off to some clever rogue with a title and properties of his own, one who'd watch over the Duke's estate—as he claimed Quentin was incapable of doing—impregnate the brat and thus prolong the Danfort dynasty, which was dangling by its thin, blue aristocratic veins. Except, looking more closely, Glenmillan also had to admit that the Duke did not seem particularly fragile lately. This new project of his, the reclaiming of his granddaughter, seemed to have enlivened him beyond what was decent for a man who had been steadily diminishing for the past year.

"Well, it doesn't signify about her looks," said the Duke, waving his hand. "It's the money and the title that counts in the end when you try to marry them off. Isn't it?" And he smiled at Glenmillan, whose stomach turned twice before she responded.

"I suppose I'm a romantic, your lordship. I would think otherwise." Her insides had soured. If the Danfort fortune—or *her* fortune, as she had come to think of it—were to pass out of her grasp, she would die. Not only would it be a terrible, no, a crippling humiliation, but the loss of the inheritance would also provide a financial hardship that was too gruesome even to contemplate. Anticipating the Duke's estate, she had all but gone through Philip's huge legacy, spending lavishly over the years since his death. Anyway, could she have done otherwise? She had certain standards that needed to be maintained. The cost had simply been, well... exceedingly high, that was all.

Her mind spun crazily, like the wheels of a coach drawn by horses gone out of control. Quentin would have to make his move fast. He would have to be all things at all times to the girl, and have a ring on her finger, and a baby in her belly—or vice versa—before the Duke would have time to hatch his miserable scheme to marry her off to someone else. Otherwise...

"Madame, on second thought, why wait any longer? I would have the girl brought to me immediately. This day. This moment. Yes... bring her here."

"But..."

"Yes, madame? What is it this time?"

"Well... she's abed, you see, and—"

"Then get her out of it. I shouldn't want our first visit to be under such awkwardly intimate conditions as a bedchamber. Such things as family reunions are best managed in more formal and somber settings, wouldn't you agree?'' He did not wait for a reply, but went on rapidly as was his habit. ''I will, of course, have to tell her about her father and mother—''

Glenmillan gasped. ''Your lordship! I beg of you, do reconsider. It would be such a shock. And so soon after everything else that's happened.''

''She seems sturdy enough to have survived her ordeal.''

''But what good would it serve to let her know she's a, a...you know?''

The Duke arched his thin white brows. Again, his lips curled, and his eyes lit more brightly, as if he was remembering something. ''An Anglo-Indian? A half-caste?''

''Yes, why, if she should let it slip...being young and naive to the ways of the world...well, it wouldn't go well for her in Court...nor for you—'' Glenmillan rushed on, a pink stain tinging her flawless alabaster cheeks. She was thinking of the scandal Quentin and she would have to bear when Quentin married the girl.

''And for you, madame? I trust it would not go at all well for your reputation?''

''Well...perhaps. It might be just a shade unpleasant—always having to defend her in Court.'' The violet eyes beseeched him to reconsider. ''Please, your lordship...she'll be ostracized at Court. For her sake—''

''I would think your understanding of human nature would be more keen, Glenmillan. You surprise me. The fact is, she's too rich to be snubbed. Now, go...go...I'm busy.'' He waved his hand, and bending his head back to his task, said, ''Just get her.''

Heavily, Glenmillan drew herself up from the seat and for an instant stared down at the Duke with hatred. He had always gotten the best of her. Well, at least she had had the distinct satisfaction of seeing the Duke's implacable demeanor disturbed two days prior when she had announced that Brandon de Forrest had been slain.

How deeply she had enjoyed seeing the expression of shock, and even—she hardly could believe her eyes—the

glimmer of regret. For an instant something almost sentimental had inhabited the cold hazel eyes. It was a small,
rare moment of triumph amid years of defeat…which bore
repeating.

"It's a pity," she said casually, just as she turned,
"about de Forrest. I can't help but to remember the tragedy. He was a brave and unusual man."

"He was a privateer bastard," the Duke shot back with
vehemence. "The man respected neither King nor country, nor any other man but himself."

"Yes…but to die in the prime of his life—"

"He had to die sometime. He just did it sooner. Leave
me, madame, and tend to the business I've given you."

But as she flowed across the room in a billowing haze of
purple satin, feeling sorely deprived of her little revenge,
the Duke of Danfort let his quill settle to the page on which
he wrote. His thin lips trembled slightly, and he brought a
liver-spotted hand up to cover the telltale sign of an emotion he dimly recognized from years ago.

de Forrest. He could still see him standing before him,
defiant and brilliant, a worthy foe if ever he had had one,
and more to the point, a perfect match for his granddaughter. He had not grieved for any man since his son
Philip had died.

Claimed by angels or devils, wherever he was, de Forrest would undoubtedly make his new domain as interesting a place as he had made this world.

Remembering, the Duke closed his eyes.

"She's gone?" Glenmillan's eyes flew open. She stared
at Quentin, whom she had met coming around the corner
as she made her way to fetch Melissa. "Ye gods, Quentin!
What do you mean, she's gone?"

"Melissa…has gone. Poof." He made a spiraling motion toward the ceiling with his hand. "She's left. Vanished. Disappeared from sight. I thought you'd like to
know, and was just now on my way to alert you of our little dilemma."

"Impossible. I left her no more than minutes ago. She was propped against her pillows with nothing more than a nightdress on. How could she be gone? Impossible." Nevertheless, she raised her skirts and started at a run for the girl's room.

Quentin followed behind at an easy stroll. Two of the footmen and three upper chambermaids stared at Glenmillan in wonder as she rushed down the corridor, almost crashing into a candle man going about his chores, and swung into the large gallery opening on to Melissa's room.

"You needn't hurry," Quentin called from behind her, but Glenmillan, clattering ahead, paid him no heed.

Reaching the double doors, she flung them wide and rushed forward in a frenzy, only to stop stock-still as she stared into the pale blue, white and gilt rococo room that she herself had decorated two years ago at great expense—it was the Duke's money paying for it.

Quentin ambled up beside her and brushed a sweetly scented lace handkerchief beneath his nose. "You can't change anything through hysterics, Mother," he said in a reasonable, modulated tone.

"She's gone," Glenmillan said, looking about in a daze.

"Precisely," Quentin agreed with the exaggerated languor of an adult dealing with a slow-witted child.

She turned and faced her son, widening her eyes. "Well, Quentin, we must find her then."

"Yes, I suppose we should."

"You *suppose?*" Glenmillan blinked her violet eyes in disbelief. "You seem to be taking a rather curiously cavalier attitude about this disaster, Quentin. Especially," she went on, breathless with nerves and the physical exertion of her dash through the halls, "since if anything happens to that girl before you marry her, Danfort will in all probability leave everything to the Crown and nothing to us."

"I'm merely being reasonable, Mother. I presume," said Quentin, tucking in his chin to better investigate the state of his lace cravat, "that she's gone after that girl. That Celia." He adjusted the neck-piece with his fingers, fluffing its folds. "She'll be back. After all, she has nowhere else to go."

"How could she do it? She has no means," objected Glenmillan, chewing on her lower lip as her mind darted to and fro. "Why, she has nothing to wear!"

"She has her wits. The girl, if you haven't noticed, isn't stupid. In fact, I'd judge her to be a crafty little minx, or I haven't known my share of women. She'd almost escaped out of that hellhole herself, and it was just luck that I arrived precisely when I did. Otherwise—"

"Don't!" Glenmillan said, holding up her hand. "I don't want to hear about past potential disasters when we have an actual one in our very midst."

"We must never lose sight of the fact that our little Melissa has got the old scoundrel's blood in her veins. That has to count for something. In matters such as these, to underestimate is to dig one's own grave." Quentin sauntered to a full-length oval mirror and tipped its base toward him. With a critical eye, he examined his form from different angles. "Do you think this jacket's a might too long?"

His casual response to what was clearly a disaster of the first order annoyed Glenmillan. "If she does make it to the warehouse, she might find that your heroics were nothing more than a ruse."

"Not entirely," Quentin returned. Their eyes met in the mirror's surface. "Giving credit where it's due, I did kill a man on her behalf."

Glenmillan waved his contention away. "Oh, think what you'd like about it...but *later,* I beg of you. For now, screw your brain to the subject at hand and come up with something to undo this mess we're in." She fell into a chair with a cloud of purple skirts billowing up around her.

Quentin revolved on his heels and fixed his cool blue eyes on his mother. "I suggest that you let me handle the matter."

"Really?" Her eyebrows shot up. "Can you? Will you? I'm beginning to wonder if you understand the significance of our situation. Rome is burning, and you fiddle, sir!"

"Trust me, madame. We are safe. And, now, if you will excuse me, I have matters to tend. Or would you rather have me stand here quibbling—or is it fiddling?"

He bowed and took his leave, in turn leaving his mother to bite her lips, even as his own curved into a secret smile as he made his way through the corridors of Danfort House, which would one day very soon belong to him.

It was a magnificent palace, one of the finest in the entire kingdom, and he would stop short of nothing to own it.

Yes, he thought, as he now skipped quickly down the wide marble stairs leading to the vast formal reception hall below, he would stop at nothing to possess Danfort House and all that it contained.

His mother had been entirely wrong when she thought that he was oblivious to their situation. Even as they had spoken, his coach was being readied for his journey to the wharves. He might have laid her mind to rest, but, really, that was not possible. There were some secrets that even she could not know.

The two footmen stationed at the front entrance bowed and swung wide the front doors, as Quentin passed through into the pleasant afternoon air.

A hundred servants were employed in the palace in London, another two hundred scattered among three country estates. And if Glenmillan had her way, they would have a few extra.

But those who worked at Danfort House were sufficient for his purposes. A good number of them, from under to upper servants, were clandestinely in his own employ, reporting to him gossip heard from any and all quarters, from the buttery to the steward's room. Quentin was scrupulous in rewarding a careful ear with a good tip.

"To the wharves," he commanded of the driver, whom he had made a point of rewarding well for keeping his lips sealed about these little escapades to the docks. It would not do to have his name connected to the slaving scandals. The postilion beside him would also need to be taken care of, which was a nuisance of an expense, but Quentin had thought a four-horse carriage would be more impressive than a more modest conveyance.

"The usual place, sir?" the man queried discreetly.

"The usual place."

Quentin got in and settled himself against the comfortable burgundy upholstery. The coach lurched forward, and shortly Quentin found himself swaying toward glory as they passed Charing Cross headed toward Whitehall and the Thames.

In reflective moments like the present, Quentin could not but fail to liken himself to Walpole, the King's prime Minister—a financial genius and master of political intrigue.

Quentin had found it to be extraordinary, the things one could learn through his household network of shabby, uneducated spies. Why, that very day, he had been informed of Melissa's clever tactics in securing herself a ride from a groom. Quentin had discovered to the minute when she had left, and where she had gone; of course, he knew to what purpose.

He also knew that it would not do her a bit of good to make the journey. Celia Allen was a lost cause.

The ship, one of those in which he had invested, had left yesterday for India with the girl and others of her ilk aboard, and her keepers had already moved on to a new location due to some recent bothersome pressure from the annoying Societies for Reformation of Manners. The coalition of do-gooders were of late exerting pressure upon King George to eradicate the slaving operations, which had proven to be extremely lucrative. Quentin and many of his friends could always use a few extra coins to fling upon the gaming tables at White's.

Already, as an appeasement, a few indiscreet commoners, unprotected by rank and privilege, had been publicly hanged or executed.

Therefore, Melissa could count on finding nothing more than an empty warehouse, devoid of captive and captors, after which she would turn, distraught, into a disorienting world—from which he, bold cavalier that he was, would suddenly appear to rescue her a second time.

No doubt she would be extremely grateful; enough so that in short order she would consent to his hand and—most importantly—to his partnership in marriage. Quentin fluffed his cravat and looked past the window to the passing view of St. James Park. He had every confidence in himself.

Ah, but it was a shame about Glenmillan. He felt a tinge of disloyalty. He had been forced to leave her biting her lips, chewing her nails, all for naught. It could have been enjoyable for them both to share in this recent turn of events, which would only work to their advantage.

But his mother had no inkling of his slaving investments, and he thought it best to keep her uninformed. Not so much because he thought she might disapprove—Glenmillan would never snub a way to increase wealth, by any means—but because the money he had amassed afforded him a feeling of autonomy. Both the Duke and Glenmillan had cast long shadows over his life. In his small way, he enjoyed his brief outings in sunlight that shone upon him, and him alone.

Melissa had no idea a house could be as enormous and enormously confusing as Danfort House, which it took her a good half hour to escape.

Having to beware of the footman who had seen her arrive, and who would undoubtedly try to hinder her from leaving without consent of someone in authority, she had followed her nose and made her way to the kitchens, where, looking a sight in her ragged, sooty clothes, reclaimed from the floor of a cabinet, she passed herself off as some menial attending the hearths.

It was yet another matter to flirt with one of the stable boys, as she *had* looked a sight more appealing in her day. But in the end, she managed to get him to ride with her through the city to the wharves and to stay with her until she found the area resembling her prison. It proved still *another* matter to get the lad to wait for her when she refused him the promised familiarities, and, angry, he left her there with a rudely delivered "Pox on you!" trailing over his shoulder.

The wharves were a smelly, bustling affair teeming with all manner of humanity, from mincing, well-dressed merchants to sun-darkened sailors walking with broad rolling gaits as they heaved crates and barrels up ramps to tall-masted ships. Rudely constructed carts trundled along beside fine carriages bearing gilt crests. What space remained was taken up by urchins and fishwives, prostitutes and beggars.

The clamor was horrendous...and exciting. It appeared to Melissa that all the world's diversities were represented in this narrow patch of earth bordered by the Thames, and had she not been so intent on freeing Celia, she would have enjoyed the spectacle.

Although she had been ushered into captivity in the dead of night, and out again through particularly confusing circumstances, her directional instincts were innately accurate and she had an unfailing eye for detail. Calling upon both these resources, she was able to locate in only a matter of minutes the hated building that had housed her and still held Celia.

But entering it was quite another matter, requiring an amount of courage she suddenly doubted she owned. In a flash of sickening insight it became apparent to her just how foolish she had been to go off on her own to liberate Celia. Still, she had no other choice. Time was of the essence, and her prodding of Glenmillan and Quentin to assist in Celia's release had come to nothing but a succession of stalls and vague excuses.

She had thought of approaching her grandfather, but reconsidered; according to Glenmillan his health was fragile and he was only just recuperating from the emotional trauma caused by her abduction. It was best, she had decided, to be respectful of such a delicate constitution. She didn't want to be the death of him, now that they had found each other.

The door before her was gray and weathered from the sea air. On the lintel over it, a partly battered stone gargoyle warned away intruders with its evil leer.

Forcing herself onward, she covered the remaining steps to the door and, without daring to hesitate for fear that she would abandon her mission, tried the handle. Unlocked, the heavy door swung slowly open.

Warily, Melissa stepped into the fetid interior. There was enough light from the open door to locate a candle in the first room off the hall. Lighting it, she moved slowly through the corridor with a poker she had claimed from the room's cold hearth, with every step listening for sounds.

Even before she had made her way to the cell in which she and Celia had been kept, it was clear that her efforts were in vain. Celia was gone. There was not a sign of human life on the entire premises, as if, Melissa thought, her memories of those two days had been nothing more than a terrible dream.

In less than five days she had lost the only man she could ever love and a girl who, in risking her life to save Melissa's, had become dearer than any friend Melissa had ever known.

The weight of the two tragic losses bore heavily on her as she moved again through the crowded wharves, her mission come to nothing.

Through her tears, she did not notice anyone or anything: the usually alert green eyes were locked inward in grief. She did not see that a drunken band of six sailors, recently arrived from a turn at sea, had discovered her lonely progress and had begun to trail her. Nor did she recognize the lewd propositions being made for her services. Others more sober and of higher quality, who did notice the situation, took the matter for what it appeared: a beautiful girl in rude, tattered garments plying her trade as a prostitute on the waterfront. It was an ordinary sight, not worth a second glance, certainly not worth the trouble of intervention.

But reality suddenly exploded through Melissa's wall of sorrow.

Stumbling and lurching, the largest and most drunken of the group of six seamen caught her by the hair and spun her around and in to him.

"Let me go!" Melissa shouted, pummeling him with both fists as he attempted to kiss her.

Around her, the others laughed and gawked, urging their compatriot on.

"C'mon, pretty, I'll pay for it," the man said, slurring and belching between words.

Melissa spat in his face.

"Little bitch!" And with a shove, he sent her sprawling to the pavement, his lips curling into a snarl as his hands went to his breeches.

In horror mixed with disbelief, Melissa stared up at the six faces. All Goodie's stories of the misfortunes of country girls in London played themselves back in her mind in a rapid blur of words and moral repugnance. And then there were Brandon's admonitions to her on the danger of placing oneself in compromising situations.

Even as she thought of Brandon, seeing him in her mind as he had looked that night when they had lain together on her bed—she loving him, wanting him to want her back, but sweetly as well as passionately—a loathsome beast, stinking of liquor and smelling rank enough to raise the dead, was lowering himself atop her. Scratching and flailing at him did no good. Two of his companions swept upon her, grasping both arms and pinning them to the cobbles.

She was going to be raped.

Oh, God! Oh, God...Brandon...Brandon....

Melissa screamed.

She screamed so loudly that her lungs felt as if they were being ripped wide.

Chapter Six

Just as the cold lethal thrust of a blade had come close to ending his life days before, the scream sliced through Brandon's mind, cutting his thoughts.

It was his first hour back in the city, and, distractedly, he had been listening to his company's manager, Ross McKay, as they walked slowly along the waterfront to the de Forrest Company's offices. But now the scream had turned Brandon's attention to a group of drunken sailors off to the side.

From what he could see, they were sporting with a girl who lay beneath the bulk of one of the laughing, jeering men. She was undoubtedly one of the many prostitutes who made their living along the waterfront. Her skirts were raised, obscuring her features, and her arms were pinioned above her head by two of the rabble; even so, Brandon could make out her feeble attempts to thrash free. Her efforts were pathetic and hopeless, and they brought to Brandon's mind his own recent situation, in which he had fought against unmatched numbers.

Ross also broke off from his accounting of the past week's events. Narrowing gray eyes at the scene, he shook a head of burnished, coppery hair and said darkly, "Lightning blast the scurvy lot. Doxie or not, I've a mind to even the odds on that contest." At the same time he gripped the hilt of his sword.

But before he could move forward, Brandon had already outdistanced him by some paces. He advanced with a rapid but uneasy gait, the faltering steps evidence of his still painful wounds bound tightly in gauze.

Had it not been for the band of gypsies—the same who had presented the entertainment at the Boarshead Inn—he would have been no more than a stone-cold corpse lying at the side of the road, helpful to no one. That he was able to even limp along as well as he did was a miracle Brandon himself was hard pressed to accept.

But in spite of the physical disability, his sword was already drawn, and by the time Ross had joined him, the five abettors of the would-be rape had scattered like dazed, frightened chickens, with the larger man flung off his hapless victim by Brandon.

Brandon advanced with his sword, a cold, amused glint in his dark eyes as the bully turned cowardly, edging backward toward a high stack of pallets. When he could go no farther, Brandon moved in, only half-playfully whipping his blade to and fro. He thought of the men on the hillside, men as rank and brutal as the man before him. Animals were better. The world would not miss any of them.

"Come on, Cap'n, no quarrel 'tween us—ugh! That pricks!" the man howled as the point of Brandon's blade pressed against his Adam's apple. "I'm not armed . . . you wouldn't take down a man with no way to defend himself, would ye?"

Brandon laughed. "Would you take down a girl with no means to defend herself? Would you?" he mimicked.

"Aw, now . . . it was only a little itch on m'Johnny jump-up needn' scratchin'. You know how it is, Cap'n. Ain't right a man's got to die for livin' his nature, is it?" he pleaded wildly.

"I've a mind to lop your Johnny off, you bloody bastard," said Brandon, a tick of angry emotion pulsing at his forehead. The memory of Melissa Danfort being carried off by the band of ruffians was still fresh in his mind. For the past three days he had been haunted by his last view of her, the green eyes terrified, the plaintive cry of her voice echoing in his mind, even as death threw its icy blanket over his body and his eyes closed to the living world.

For the rest of his days, he would not sleep without seeing that small, terrified face in his mind. It was not hard to imagine her fate. If she wasn't dead already from misuse by the men who had made off with her, she would most likely be sold into some manner of slavery—either abroad or forced into service as a thief or a whore in the bowels of London.

Even that morning he could take no step without anticipating a glimpse of her face in a crowd; and in the years to come, wherever in the world he would sail, he knew he would search for her. There would be no peace for either of them on this earth until she had been found, or until he knew that she was never to be found.

He had tried to convince himself that his concern over the girl was professional, moral, obligatory; but that was not the whole truth. Failing in his duty was only the smallest part of his regret.

Not since Pavan had any woman stirred his desire so hotly, nor touched his emotions so deeply as the girl had done during their brief and peculiar relationship. He had wanted nothing to do with her; she was but a parcel, a thing to be delivered. Worldly, hardened, superior, he had played with her, protecting himself from the folly of human passions, and he had been ensnared by his own conceit. How richly humorous life was! And how darkly hideous its other side. The girl had offered him the gift of her innocence; he had trampled it with his cynicism.

What if he had lain with her that night at the inn? The question haunted him, obsessed him with vivid pictures. What if they had accepted each other's longings and luxuriated in the moment given them? Where would the remorse have been in that honesty? The night would have ended and a new day begun, but what of it? They could have lived that day as it unfolded, weeping if weeping was due, escaping if flight was necessary, fighting if war arose between them. But at least, God curse him, they would have lived—fully, dearly and not regretfully, as he tasted the minutes now left to him without her.

Tomorrow he would meet the Duke. He would stand before him and give him his report, extend heartfelt regrets that the Duke would dismiss as meaningless, and, undoubtedly, in the aftermath of that meeting, he would pay for the loss of the girl with the loss of his charters.

A savage fury arose in him for all the many losses he had been forced to suffer in his life—from his parents, his family and native country; to Pavan, who would not wed a poor man; to this latest of life's capricious misfortunes, the dissolution of a company he had sweat blood to build. And he thought again of the girl, of Melissa, and how her own life had been affected so tragically by happenstance, by merely being on a road at the wrong time....

The man before him suddenly screwed his ugly face into a companionable expression, his gravelly voice edging into clownish humor, harmless, placating. "So, Cap'n, me Johnny just crept out to have 'im a bit of air, innocent like, and look at the trouble 'e's let me into. What can a poor fool do with such a fellow?"

"Let him dangle around your neck," replied Brandon caustically.

The man's eyes widened into huge pools of fearful comprehension. "But she were only a whore! No harm done to a whore....a doxie, she were, and we was havin' no more 'an a bit o' fun," he rattled on, ever mindful of Brandon's hand holding the blade. "Look at 'er...a sorry sight, she's not worth dying over," he rushed, a note of indignation creeping into his plea for clemency.

It was only then that Brandon took any notice of the girl, who was being aided to her feet by Ross.

Their eyes met at the same moment—Melissa's dazed and disoriented, Brandon's disbelieving and horrified.

"Holy Mother..." Brandon breathed, hardly trusting his senses.

From a face swollen from blows sustained during the attack, and eyes puffed from crying, Melissa peered at the apparition of Brandon de Forrest.

"No!" she gasped, the single word emerging more as a strangled note. With a violent thrust of her body, she wrenched herself free from Ross's hold and backed off as if having sighted the devil. "It's not—it can't be. . . ." She put her fingers to her forehead and took a halting step in one direction, then, at a loss, stumbled the other way, as if to make her escape from her own madness.

"Melissa!" called Brandon, hard pressed himself to accept her presence. At the sound of her name, she stopped, dared to look over her shoulder.

Sparkling with tears, the green eyes bore a new, strange depth. For a moment, Brandon could think of nothing to say, so struck was he by her beauty. It seemed that the girl had matured ten years since last he had seen her—if anything she had become more stunning, more desirable than before.

"Oh, oh . . . it *can't* be you," she sobbed, and the voice he heard had lost its fight.

Gone was the familiar mocking humor, the self-confident vexatiousness she had displayed in the inn. His insides gave a sudden leap of raw male fury. What had changed her? What had she been forced to endure? Whatever it was, it had killed the innocence and smothered the fiery nature. As she stood there, trembling, it was hard to imagine her as she had appeared dancing atop a table, joyous in her youth and beauty. *The devil curse him! He had failed to protect her.*

"You're dead, dead!" she cried fearfully, and staggered backward away from the terrible vision her mind had created.

He told her once again that he was alive and there, that she was safe, but nothing he said seemed to reach her. Instead, her complexion beneath the dirt and red scratches began to take on a waxy pallor; her body swayed uncertainly.

Brandon had long since lowered his lance—forfeiting his revenge on the sailor—and he rushed to take hold of her before she dropped in a faint to the cobbles again.

"It can't be true!" Melissa wept, as Brandon pressed his arms around her, holding her tightly for both physical and emotional support, his face buried in the wild mass of golden hair. Joy mixed with sorrow, swamping him with emotion he could barely contain.

"There now, you're safe, I'm alive, there's nothing to fear anymore," he said, raising his head from the tumble of hair. "I won't let anyone harm you. Never again," he said, looking into the future. "Never again." His eyes met Ross McKay's. By Ross's expression, the man appeared every bit as startled by the scene he was witnessing as Brandon was to be experiencing it.

"But I saw you die!" she insisted hysterically, as Brandon continued to stroke her back, her hair, brushing his fingers lightly, tenderly against the side of her face as he moved away golden strands to see her more clearly. He tensed at the sight of the bruises, already turning color. "They ran a blade through you," she said. "I saw the blood... they cut you."

"That they did, but not deeply enough to do the job. Look at me, Melissa. I'm here and I'm very much alive. Look at me," he said repeatedly, trying to jar her from her inner world, and when she slowly, with fearful caution, tipped her face to peer up at him, her eyes held unveiled joy. But the happiness was only fleeting. In the next instant she flew against him again, huddling and crying in his arms like a small child.

Over his head, Ross and Brandon exchanged looks that needed no words to be mutually understood.

The girl in Brandon's arms was the Duke of Danfort's granddaughter, and by logical association, any attachment he developed to the girl could—and probably would—be used as a manipulative device against Brandon in ways that would benefit the Duke and be of detriment to the de Forrest Company's interests. Therefore, what the hell in God's name was Brandon doing! Offering comfort was one thing, but this was altogether a different matter.

In truth, Brandon could not come to his own defense. Feelings of protectiveness and tenderness surged through him as he surrounded Melissa Danfort with his arms. To think clearly was all but impossible.

Her outfit—which she had once told him was her very best, and which she'd worn for their journey to make a dignified entrance into the great city of London—was now torn and filthy, tattered beyond repair. It was impossible not to feel some sympathy for the harsh disillusionment the girl must have already suffered since leaving her small village. But, regardless of how it might look to Ross, Brandon knew his judgment was still intact; he knew who she truly was beneath the grime and rags and tear-stained face. She was the Duke of Danfort's heir, and nothing he felt would change that very disturbing fact.

Still, despite her unfortunate blood lines, at the moment she felt in his arms like a broken bird in need of care, and although he made the valiant attempt to install firmness in his words, his voice was too soft and unresolved when he said, "That's enough now. There'll be time for weeping later. I don't know who—or what—in hell brought you to this wretched place and circumstance, but you're to be sent to your grandfather at once."

Dazed, she nodded, the liquid green eyes surrounding him, pulling him under. He struggled against the undertow of desire. *She was his enemy's granddaughter!*

Forgetful of his own wounds, he swept her up into his arms, then gave a sudden sharp cry as the flesh parted beneath his bandages. Ross stepped quickly forward to relieve him of Melissa, but Brandon waved him away, at the same time lowering Melissa gently to the ground. He was reduced to offering her the support of his arm, rather than risk having the both of them crumble to the pavement.

"She's still afraid…she knows me," Brandon said, and in the look they exchanged, they both knew that wasn't the reason he would not relinquish his burden to Ross. "Hire a carriage," Brandon ordered, and with Melissa's limp, trembling form against his body, they made their way through the throng.

Their progress was not unobserved.

Quentin Danfort sat slumped in the back of his own

coach, his eyes fogged with dismay as he peered at the shocking sight of Brandon de Forrest—*alive, blast him!*—carrying off the prize he himself had come to fetch.

"Home, damn you!" he shouted at the driver. "No! Not there... to White's!" He would not face Glenmillan unfortified. Brandy, a good deal of brandy, would instill the courage that the sight of de Forrest had drained out of him.

And, as if things were not bad enough already, he remembered that his accounts were far past due at the club. He was in sad arrears at White's, even at Almacks, and his allowance was drawn ahead by a good three months from the goldsmith who executed what inheritance of his was left of Philip's estate.

The situation was dire. There would be no way out of his predicament unless he were to snare Melissa Danfort and her hundreds and hundreds of thousands of Danfort pounds.

And, quickly....

Not one of the liveried footmen had the nerve to stop the notorious visitor who swept past them. They could only stare at the man's audacity—in a sense treading where angels feared to go, that is, into the very hub of the Duke of Danfort's lair.

He took the main staircase as if he were lord of the house and not an unannounced guest. Beside him, he supported a beautiful girl in rags, her face swollen and covered in dirt, her long gold tresses matted and tangled about her shoulders.

Of course they all knew who he was. How could they not?

Although Brandon de Forrest had been no more than an infrequent guest over the past several years, his visits had made deep impressions among those household servants fortunate enough to have observed him personally on other occasions. From their lips passed stories of what the famous privateer and tradesman looked like, wore, said, did;

and for once embellishments were unnecessary to build a hero.

Everyone knew his history; after all, scandals were always welcome in conversation. Of French descent, his family had been stripped of their titles and lands when his father fell into disfavor over a tax issue some years before with Louis XV. His mother had died several years earlier, during childbirth, and his father had taken his own life a year after having been dispossessed of both his personal dignity and material wealth.

It had fallen to Brandon, the eldest, to hold what he could of the family together, and with no opportunity in France to support his four younger brothers and one sister, he left France as a privateer.

Seven years before, he was a stranger in Danfort House, little more than a beggar who had come that day to petition the Duke of Danfort for a preposterous loan. He had come with nothing more to recommend him than a single ship, and a somewhat legendary reputation as a seadog, along with many exalted visions of his future. To his credit, he was known as a shrewd trader, an able captain and a fearsome warrior in combat with the Spanish and Moorish pirates, and also the Portuguese, all of whom had tried to run him from the seas to no avail.

To everyone's surprise, the Duke had granted him the loan he requested—charging what everyone knew had to be usurious rates, along with the added burden of being under the constant jeopardy of forfeiture if de Forrest were to default on even one payment.

Among the aristocracy and well-heeled merchants, even money had been laid that de Forrest would fail, that he would be unable to compete against the giant East India Company and the South Seas Company, not to mention being sabotaged by the Duke himself, who would have much to gain in terms of material collateral if Brandon de Forrest were to forfeit his enterprise.

But they had been wrong—so far.

Since that time, the French expatriate had managed to build a shipping and trade empire consisting of thirty ships. He was said to be a man who owed allegiance to no country, to no man, nor any woman. He stood alone, and because of it, he seemed to stand even higher in the eyes of everyone who gazed upon him, for few men could boast of such independence, and all women felt the challenge of taming such an unobtainable prize.

So, no sooner had the legendary de Forrest passed through the great downstairs hall with the limp form of the girl at his side, when the tongues began wagging anew. Speculations were rampant: was the forlorn-looking creature really the Duke's granddaughter, previously sequestered in private chambers? Wasn't it said that de Forrest had been slain some few days ago? What would become of the Countess Glenmillan and her son now that there was a blood heir to the old Duke's estates?

By coincidence, the Countess Glenmillan was also a part of the strange tableau assembled on the staircase.

Only moments before she had received another angry summons—the third in three hours—from the Duke to bring Melissa to him immediately; if not, there would be serious repercussions, which Glenmillan understood to mean that, as on other occasions, the Duke would restrict her personal allowance for a period long enough to cause her severe social distress. The money left from Philip's estate was a pathetic amount. It was further restricted from her clutches by the terms of her inheritance, which allowed her to withdraw sums only at monthly intervals.

She was clearly in a fix. In the miserable state of a prisoner condemned to the pillory, she was just making her way across the upper hall, and past the stairwell, thinking of what excuse she might make for the disappearance of the Duke's granddaughter, when her mouth all but fell open.

There before her, coming up the stairs, was none other than the deceased Brandon de Forrest, with the disappeared girl hobbling along, her slender body pressed against his for support.

Pangs of guilty horror and fear collided with feelings of joyous relief that the Frenchman had survived the grave and was even at that very moment delivering the contemptible girl, the cause of everyone's grief.

So astounded was Glenmillan by this latest perplexing turn of events that she could only stand like a statue, frozen in place and gaping, until de Forrest noticed her.

Looking up, he caught her stare. He spoke at once, brusquely, "Where may I find his lordship?"

"His..." Overcome, Glenmillan choked and had to begin again. "His personal closet..." Both her eyes and voice trailed after him, until suddenly roused to action by the instinct to save her skin, she rustled after him in her satins, and had only just made it to the Duke's private chambers when Brandon pushed open the doors—and then slammed them in her face.

God's eyeballs! Glenmillan thought in shock, and stopped short of her intention to follow. She had better think this through. She might do better to avoid that scene altogether until she knew more the length and breadth and depth of the trouble that awaited. There were too many things happening at once for her liking. Things were getting out of hand. No matter how carefully she planned, everything seemed to be constantly slipping out of her control.

And in the spirit of self-preservation, she turned and rushed back to her own rooms to worry about her allowance and await Quentin's return.

At the sound of the door slamming, the Duke of Danfort snapped his head up from his reading. He sat at his desk in his personal closet. Located off his bedroom, the retreat was his favorite room, and the most private for him in the entire house, a vast labyrinth of specialized chambers.

For one thing, Glenmillan had not gotten her hands on this room, which he had overseen himself. Over the French parquet floors lay a brilliantly colored Turkish carpet, and the walls were covered with floral-patterned green, gold and maroon Chinese silk. There were mahogany shelves lined with books, a fireplace and a fine wall clock, its case designed by Chippendale, ticking off the moments of pleasure the Duke found in his comfortable hollow.

Only his valet and one specially selected maid were privy to this room's confines, and when the door opened without so much as a knock, the Duke was as surprised as he was outraged.

But in the next instant, his heart gave a start, and even his mind stopped. "Good God..." he uttered, staring at Brandon de Forrest, who stood before him supporting the slack form of a dishevelled young woman. The girl herself made an extraordinary picture.

She had eyes as bright and green as stained glass with the sun shining through, and thick golden hair that might have been an asset had it not been tangled and matted.

But one puzzle at a time. His attention jumped back to Brandon. "I was given to understand—under the strictest authority... the devil take you, de Forrest, you're supposed to be dead!" But in the next breath, Danfort collected himself, for surely de Forrest was very much alive. In a more customary tone of vexation, he said, "What in hell is the meaning of this intrusion! For that matter, what bundle is that beside you?"

Brandon smiled at the irony of the situation. "The bundle, your lordship, is your granddaughter."

The Duke scowled, his thin eyebrows knitting together at the filthy vision in rags who fixed him with equal curiosity, even as he spoke of her in the abstract.

"Impossible! How can this be my granddaughter?"

"An excellent question, one I've asked myself." With that, Brandon pressed Melissa slightly forward. "May I have the honor of presenting, Her Ladyship, Melissa Danfort."

The young woman and the old man stared across the room at each other, taking stock of their only relative on the earth's surface.

"Grandfather..." Melissa said, making a curtsy as best she could. She was humiliated to appear in such a shoddy state and to have made such a strange—but necessary— entrance into his life.

She had almost no strength in her limbs, and it was for this reason and not for gallant effect that Brandon had been forced to support her like an invalid through the streets and into the house. The entire afternoon still seemed like a dream, and never more so than now, as she stood beside the man she loved and thought she had lost, and her own flesh-and-blood grandfather, whom she had never known existed. It was a deeply stirring moment for her and one she hardly felt up to.

"So," Danfort said, raking her with his hazel eyes, "so... this is Melissa. The famous Melissa who it appears has a penchant for adventure. Or should I say disaster? Interesting... your father seemed to have the same streak of unfortunate recklessness."

"Your lordship," Melissa said, wanting desperately to please this only living relative, "I give you my word that I shall never cause you so much as another scrap of trouble. I have had enough adventure, and misadventure, to last me the whole of my life. And I'm deeply sorry, sir, for having sent you to bed in worry."

The Duke scowled. "How was that?"

"Her Ladyship, the Countess Glenmillan, told me when I wanted to see you that you were taken ill from excessive concern over my welfare."

The Duke grimaced. "Did she now? Well, her ladyship is always concerned about my welfare—as no doubt she'll be concerned for yours." And something in his eyes flickered, a thought that made his eyes grow hard and cold. But he waved his hand, dismissing the subject, and said, "Turn, turn... it's been sixteen years. Let us see what time has wrought. Let me see you."

Melissa turned slowly, uncertainly, feeling like a broken doll atop a music box. She knew very well how dreadful she must appear. With a sick heart, she recalled her plans to bewitch Brandon in her silks and fans and pretty black satin patches affixed to her face. How did he see her now? She shuddered to think of it.

Across from her, the Duke leaned back in his chair. His interest was speculative, not sentimental.

She was a mess, of course; that went without saying. Although the cause of her disarray was a mystery yet. But beneath the grimy exterior lay a stone of gem quality that would sparkle once shined and properly mounted. Aye, yes, *properly mounted.*

And giving weight to the crude meaning of the thought, the Duke looked again at Brandon de Forrest, who was his choice to see to that task. No doubt with all the ports the man had visited, he'd be up to the job of bedding the heir to England's greatest fortune.

"So," the Duke said to Brandon, "you've just barely managed to save your skin. And your company. I shall have to wait, I suppose, a while longer until I take over the de Forrest Company."

"It will have to be over one of our dead bodies then," said Brandon agreeably. They often traded threats.

The Duke smiled, reacting to the double irony in the remark. "Exactly what I had in mind."

There was no man in the kingdom, nor any man outside of England that Danfort had met, who could better manage the legacy he would leave behind at his death. And the Duke would suffer the pangs of hell before he would leave a single farthing of his fortune to that useless milksop Quentin or his conniving, spendthrift mother.

"You look frail," the Duke said, breaking his train of thought and turning his attention back to the girl whose job it would be to bring de Forrest to his knees and into the family fold. "I understand you've suffered various unpleasantries these past days, and you look none the better for whatever new misfortune has apparently befallen you. But we have other matters to discuss, and since you are here and alive—the both of you," he added, his glance taking in Brandon as well as Melissa, "we shall dispense with what no longer has any significance." He waved his hand toward two chairs set before his desk. "Sit, both of you."

No sooner had they taken their places, Melissa glad to oblige, Brandon suspicious and reluctant to remain, than the Duke of Danfort rose from his chair and took his position beside a large globe suspended from a circular stand.

He gave the globe a spin. Round and round it went, Melissa looking from it to her grandfather wonderingly. He smiled, catching her curiosity. "Do you like history?"

"I don't know," she said.

"You are about to learn then. More to the point, you are even to create it." His eyes moved to Brandon, who already knew where this tale was to lead, then returned to Melissa. "You are in a particularly curious position. It seems that through a quirk of fate, by what might be called a veritable accident of nature, if you will, your father has left you an unintended legacy. As legacies go, it's a rather strange inheritance. Your legacy is passion." The Duke smiled without warmth, letting the last word linger.

"His passion," the Duke continued, "to a woman he should never have loved, and certainly should never have married, and most assuredly should never have had a child with, has created for you an opportunity to hold half the world in your hands. Would you like that?"

Melissa merely stared. She didn't know what to say. She had imagined there would be a warm family scene...tears, kisses, a kindly old gentleman doddering about. "To— well, I don't really know...."

The Duke gave the globe another spin. He stopped it abruptly, his finger pressing down on a patch of green. "India." He jabbed his finger at the spot. "Have you heard of the land?"

Melissa's mind reached out, gathering vague, odd facts she'd heard of the country. "Only that it is far away.... That it's strange, a heathen place where the people worship many gods. That it's very mysterious, but with great riches..."

"Exactly—great riches!" A light flared in the Duke's hazel eyes. "And you will bring them all back to me."

This time Melissa ventured a weak smile. "Ah, this is a game." She glanced at Brandon for confirmation. His face was remote, stern and noncommittal.

"Yes," said the Duke, seeming pleased with her analogy, "a game, if you will. But for very high stakes. And you, my dear, are the pawn that will take the King. I will explain."

"And I will take my leave," said Brandon, rising abruptly.

"You will remain," the Duke snapped. "As this game very much concerns your involvement."

Melissa saw a deadly look pass between the two men. It frightened her. There was so much—too much—that she did not understand. She was surprised, also, that Brandon obeyed her grandfather; she especially did not understand that. It was hard to believe that Brandon de Forrest would bow to any man.

For an hour Melissa listened to a story that was as fabulous as any Goodie had ever invented, complete with evil rulers and beautiful women and handsome men, with riches beyond imagination, with murder and intrigue.

But it was a story without an ending; the final word would be hers to write.

And, as she discovered, she had no choice but to write it.

Chapter Seven

Melissa stared at herself in the dressing table mirror. There was much to examine in this mirror...*much*. She had sat immobile before it for the past hour, ever since being dismissed from her grandfather's presence.

"That will be all for now," the Duke had said to her, his voice filled with all the warmth he might shower on a new household menial. He turned his eyes to Brandon. "Monsieur de Forrest will remain, however. We have additional matters to discuss between us."

Rage had overcome fatigue, and she had flown down the hallways, twice having to ask directions to her room from servants she passed. Once there, she had locked her doors and had not allowed anyone to enter, not even Glenmillan, who had beat upon the door two or three times already, wanting to be let in.

Quentin had also come. She did not really know about Quentin—whether or not she liked him. True, he had rescued her when she had been jailed, and he *was* very good looking, in his own sort of foppish, elegant way, although he could not come close to the standard for masculine perfection set by Brandon de Forrest.

But who could? In Melissa's mind, even the sun would be eclipsed by Brandon's light.

Perhaps she was being unfair about Quentin. Her reservations about him rested mostly upon his failure to rescue Celia as he had promised.

Later two maids had appeared on separate occasions—their voices quite different—each tapping politely on the locked door.

"May I draw water for your bath, madame?"

"Perhaps I may see to madame's toilette?"

Melissa had answered none of her callers. For one thing, she did not know if *Melissa* even existed anymore.

Who was Melissa?

That was the question holding her spellbound to the reflection. There she found a stranger, a girl with her face, but not her at all.

Her grandfather had told her what she was. *She was a half-breed. An outcast. An Anglo-Indian.*

And as such she was a humiliation to everyone, including herself. She fit nowhere on the earth—at least not in decent society, and from what she was able to surmise, even the Indians would not accept her, for they had no love of the English, either.

Brandon had known of her mottled history from the very beginning, of course; he had been told everything before he had been sent to collect her in Cornwall.

No wonder he had not made love to her. He had said he had wanted her, but still he had not taken her. Perhaps he had thought lying with her would taint him physically as well as socially.

Melissa's fingers curled tightly into her palms, her nails cutting against her flesh. But no amount of physical discomfort could equal her inner misery. The shame of her situation was almost unbearable. All her pride, her many plans to captivate London society in order that she might win Brandon's admiration, his heart...ha! What a mockery it all seemed now as she stared at her face in the mirror.

Under the circumstances.

Her grandfather had used the phrase often—*under the circumstances*—in order to emphasize that she had no other choice but to do his bidding.

When she had left her grandfather's quarters, Brandon had of course remained. Already she could tell her grandfather was someone whose word was heeded as law. Even Brandon was beholden to him. Brandon, whom she could not imagine bending to any man.

She had felt Brandon's black eyes on her as she made for the door. With each step she shrank deeper inside of herself, wanting to slide from his vision unobserved. She knew what his eyes held, and his mind, too: pity, and the curiosity one reserves for peculiarities of nature.

Melissa studied her reflection, looking for her parents in her face: her English father, dead now; her Indian mother... still alive.

Strange. For all her life she had wished for parents, and now to discover that even one of them remained should have gladdened her heart beyond belief. But instead she felt nothing but mystification that she could be the living product of a heathen, the child of an exotic. Her mind could form no connection to this kind of mother. And yet, it was only this unknown woman in all the world who apparently cared for her.

She *could* see Philip, her father, in her mind... could feel his presence in the very walls surrounding her, for he was English and fair of coloring.

"You got your coloring from your father," said the Duke, "the fair hair, the green eyes. This is all to the good, a saving grace. As for your mother... she was said to be very beautiful—not by our typical English standards, perhaps, but enough to cause serious damage to at least two men who could have had their pick of any woman they fancied, with far less trouble connected. And far less tragedy, alas." The Duke had broken off, fixing her with a penetrating look. "It's the Indian in you that accounts for the... the strangeness. Or perhaps I should more accurately call it your unique appearance."

The *strangeness* to which the Duke referred was suddenly clearly evident to Melissa, who stared at her face with its high cheekbones and large, slanted, almond-shaped eyes, its full-lipped mouth. But there was also delicacy—a small, pointed chin, the straight, narrow nose.

Saluina. That was her mother's name.

The Duke's son, Philip, had fallen in love and married Saluina in a secret ceremony while in India nineteen years before, as he attempted to expand the Danfort interests. Philip's plan was to remove her to England, but the love alliance between two of such diverse cultures was predictably ill-fated.

The Nawab, or local ruler, was also obsessed with Saluina's beauty. Discovering the marriage, he denounced it on religious grounds and sent men to kill Philip and their newly born child, in order to claim Saluina for himself. Barely did Philip manage to escape with Melissa—Saluina having been providentially forewarned by one of the Nawab's sympathetic concubines.

When he returned to England, Philip went into a deep emotional decline over the loss of Saluina. She had been forced to marry the Nawab. There was no chance to rescue her; the forces surrounding the Nawab were formidable and impossible to penetrate.

It was during this bleak period of Philip's life that Melissa was removed to Cornwall under the care of the Dorchesters.

"We felt it best . . . under the circumstances," the Duke had explained to Melissa.

Again, *the circumstances.*

"You mean you wanted to protect my father's reputation. You mean it would not have done to have a strange, dark child grow up with the Danfort name," she had returned sharply, with mocking bitterness. Anyway, she had considered, why should she make an effort to please? Let the devil take their miserable souls. There would be no love from anyone here. Hopelessness had engulfed her. And, always aware of Brandon by her side, she would not humiliate herself further by a pathetic apology for being such a lowly specimen of humanity, nor would she offer a show of gratefulness for being tolerated in their polite company.

"Your father never thought of that—unfortunately social dictates meant very little to him. No, the fact was, he would weep uncontrollably whenever he saw you. You were a reminder of Saluina.''

So she'd been taken away to be raised in Cornwall—for her own emotional well-being as much as for Philip's—to be cared for by simple people who could give her love.

"And what did you tell people?" she had inquired, with wry amusement at how easily callousness was handled. "Philip's daughter suddenly sent away... didn't anyone want to know?"

"A plausible story was contrived. Your mother was French. She died in childbirth.''

"How convenient," Melissa had said beneath her breath.

"We simply told people you were sent to France to be raised by your mother's people. Goodwyn spoke the language—one of the reasons she was selected for your care. You were to be instructed in French, in case there became a need—"

"To trot me out in the future?"

"You have as much to gain as anyone in this enterprise. What talents you have at your disposal are as much to your advantage as to mine. It's my understanding your education is complete in the area of linguistics, as it is in certain other areas. For instance, I'm pleased with your elocution. It will hold you in good stead when you are presented at Court.''

"But my father remarried. Why wasn't I brought back then?" Melissa had pressed, already knowing the reason, but needing in some perverse way to hear it said aloud.

Even then, some voiceless ally buried deep within her was beginning to rise up, to fortify her against dissolving completely into the wretched little contrivance others would have her be for their benefit. They did not want her in their midst because of her tainted bloodline. No one wanted to risk her turning out to look Asian, for that would tarnish the family name.

"Yes...under my urging, Philip took another wife," the Duke had said, avoiding the issue of her continued exile. "I felt a new involvement would help him. He had to go on, to forget the past. He was wasting away, you see. And, also, I had hoped for a grandson, an heir to carry on the family name after Philip was gone.''

''So *you* found Glenmillan.''

''To the contrary. *She* found Philip,'' said the Duke, wincing slightly at some distant memory of that event. ''The marriage was, of course, a failure…dismal from the start. Philip was already by then reduced to a shell of what he had once been as a man, and the widow Glenmillan Darnley was a self-centered opportunist who had already gotten what she wanted—the Danfort name for herself and her son. I need not even mention that she also managed to secure a life-style far beyond her former means. After three years, Philip caught a cold during the winter and allowed it to turn into pneumonia. He had no will to live—that was the real cause. In three days he was gone.'' The Duke had paused, as if by remembering the event he too had suddenly lost his own will.

''But still you didn't bring me back,'' said Melissa, returning to her previous question.

''That's right.'' There was no apology in his voice, nor in his direct gaze. ''Frankly, Glenmillan was not a fit mother. She had parties and wigs and new coaches on her mind. It's a very small mind, and there was no room in it for a growing girl.''

''But *you* were my grandfather.''

He raised his thin eyebrows, took a moment to look her over, as if surprised that she could actually formulate ideas of her own. At last he said, ''I was no longer interested in familial bonds. Philip had been my life up until then. My own wife was gone, and then my son. After his death I wanted nothing more to do with the human comedy.''

''The human tragedy,'' Melissa murmured, beginning to feel that perhaps she was invisible and that whatever she did or said wouldn't count for much anyway; why not speak her thoughts aloud? Who would care? Who would hear?

Brandon, beside her, sat still as a stone. Now and then she felt that his attention was on her, but she did not want to look at him for fear she would react to the scorn, or pity, in his eyes. She was a rich pariah, an oddity on two continents. But she was a pariah with pride.

To her surprise, the Duke had caught her mumbled comment and a slight smile curled his thin lips upward. "Indeed, taken from a certain perspective they *are* one and the same. Rather than wallow in a sentimental bog, I preferred instead to build an empire that was invulnerable to the passage of time. And I have done so—or, should I say, I have almost done so. You shall finish my dream for me."

Melissa's heart hammered against her chest, shattering all her expectations that life in London was to be gay and happy, that she would find a permanent home with a loving relative. "So," she said calmly, "I am brought back here because you need me and not because of any affection on your part?"

"Would you have me lie?"

"No. There have been lies enough."

"Exactly. You're a sensible girl, realistic. That's very good. The fact stands, we are strangers. Would you pretend to love me? A man you know nothing of but that our names are the same?"

"I was prepared to be loved . . . prepared to love," Melissa had said. "That was *my* dream, perhaps. Obviously, a foolish one. I can only hope that yours has more substance."

It did.

Her mother's husband was now the powerful Muslim ruler, Alviradi Khan. Saluina had written frequently during the past few years, begging for word of her daughter. It seemed that the Nawab had softened over time, finding sympathy for Saluina, who could bear no additional children after Melissa. Up until recently, the Duke had found it prudent, for political reasons, not to reply to Saluina's pleas.

However, the political winds had shifted, and it was now the Duke's intention to form a safe and lasting trade agreement with India. Since 1746 France and England had been engaged in a war of supremacy in India. Each nation had been supporting rival Indian factions. The Moghul strength was collapsing against the Hindu rebellion, and the resulting civil unrest was further exacerbated by various Moghul provincial governors vying for their own territorial dominion. The Duke was convinced that Britain would eventually dominate India. He would have his own personal interests established and secured. Saluina plus Melissa plus the Nawab were the equation that equaled success. It was the Duke's hope that to make amends to Saluina for depriving her of her child, the Nawab would grant the mother any favor the girl wanted. Melissa would ask for an exclusive trade agreement, banning Holland and France from the territory.

"And without me, you can do nothing," Melissa had commented coldly after listening to the details of the Duke's plan.

"And without me, *you* can do nothing," her grandfather had replied, every bit as icily.

For a long moment they stared, each taking measure of the other. What Melissa saw she did not like, and although weakened from her ordeal, she had been prepared to rise then, to leave from her grandfather's presence and never look back.

She would return to Cornwall, marry a stupid boy, have a child that she would hold and love. When her time came, she would die in peace and be buried on the hill with its many crosses—that hill where she had first glimpsed her magnificent highwayman, who was merely an apparition, after all. She would run from this rats' nest of cold-hearted intrigue.

Yes, Melissa thought, staring into the mirror over her vanity table, all of this she would have done, but that the Duke suddenly said, "Monsieur de Forrest has agreed to escort you on the journey to India."

Up until this point, Brandon had remained mute. The matters being discussed were as much personal as business, and seemed not to concern him. Melissa now understood that whatever feelings had passed between them earlier were predicated on his own stake in the profitable future she could provide both men.

Naturally he had been glad to find her alive! Of course he had comforted her! She was to be expensive cargo on his ship.

"Agreed, you say? I'd hardly consider it an agreement by choice," Brandon broke in sharply, as if he had heard her thoughts and meant to dispute her accusation. But in his next sentence, she saw that he was only defending his own autonomy. "You could get anyone to make this voyage instead of me, and it's a damned inconvenience, as you very well know."

"And as you very well know, I need more than a captain. I need someone who can protect my granddaughter. The girl's soon to become the heiress to one of the greatest fortunes this realm has ever known and ever will know. I don't plan on having her perish before she is wed and gives birth to a male heir to carry on the Danfort name. You will see to it that she survives, if for no other reason than because you care about your company."

And that was when, suddenly, out of her burning fury at being treated as an object, Melissa understood the full extent of her power. She was not the lowly pawn that either of them considered her to be.

The way they had contrived the future, her grandfather would play the part of King, with Brandon as his rook, the knight who would ride into battle bearing the King's standard. But she was not a pliable, dispensable pawn as they thought.

In actuality, she now saw her position as that of Queen, and in the game of chess taught to her by Goodie and Darben when she was but a child, she had learned it was this player that held the true power. It was the Queen who had the actual mobility to sweep across the board in any direction, to pounce upon her prey or to protect when she was needed.

The King could not last without her, and the knight could not catch her. She was a Queen in a pawn's disguise.

And in time, they would see that.

So she had left the men, returning to her room, where she now stared at the stranger in the mirror...a stranger who would evolve into a woman none of them had ever bargained for.

When the girl had gone from the room, the Duke continued to stare at the door for a moment. "She's quite remarkable, isn't she?" he said with a bemused expression. "What think you, de Forrest?"

"She appears clever." She was many other things as well, such as beautiful, desirable, headstrong, arrogant, naive—although learning quickly, it appeared—and brave; but Brandon let his opinions remain his own. The less he had to do with either of the Danforts, the better it would be for him. That the girl had the ability to make him forget these caveats was unfortunate, and he would have to guard vigilantly against her allure.

"Yes, a shrewd one," the Duke concurred, adding, "And beautiful, too, in that unusual Oriental sort of way. But no one need know about that," he said dismissively, and then continued in a distracted, half-musing manner. "The girl will suit my purposes well. In a week I'm giving a ball for her, to make a formal presentation to the eligible gallants. That jade Glenmillan is seeing to all the plans. I've a mind to find the girl a husband, someone who'll take over my estate, all my enterprises. And I want to see her with child before I draw my last breath." He looked directly at Brandon, the hazel eyes smiling with a secret. "This dynasty will endure, de Forrest."

Something tightened in Brandon's gut. "Has it ever occurred to you that your brood mare may not be amenable to your vision of her future?"

"No," the Duke said. "It has not."

The remainder of Brandon's stay consisted of business matters, and for the first time in years—since his relationship with Pavan had upturned his world—he found it difficult to concentrate.

While the Duke laid out his plans for the India voyage, detailing what gifts he hoped to send aboard ship, reflecting on what manner and amount of bribery would be in order for servants of the Nawab and military members attached to his service, Brandon's mind wandered its own course, continuously returning to the Duke's scheme of marrying Melissa off to protect his investment in the earthly realm once he had departed.

It disturbed Brandon more than he cared to admit, the notion of Melissa's domestication into a life of dry matrimony to some fawning, avaricious prig of a nobleman. In no time at all her vitality would be drained. Fattened by childbirth, she would spend her days in gossip with the other women of the court, while her husband roved about increasing the Danfort fortune and taking his pleasure with an occasional mistress.

There was no doubt that this would occur; Brandon had seen the familiar pattern repeat endlessly during the seven years he had frequented the English Court and the drawing rooms of the wealthy. Melissa was doomed.

He tried to clear his mind, reminding himself that beyond India, her future was not to be his concern. He further cautioned himself that on their voyage he would do well to zealously guard against that part of his nature that would enjoy a few hours of purely hedonistic pleasure in her bed.

Like his nemesis, the Duke, he would be far better off to remember the toll wrought by sentimental involvements.

He, too, had suffered over his family's misfortunes, and then again, in possibly a more severe fashion, over the loss of Pavan.

In his youth and idealism, he had loved Pavan totally, with his entire being. It had been a young love perhaps, but a deep one. And when Pavan, beautiful Pavan, had married a man of high noble birth and extraordinary wealth, preferring title and money to him and his dreams, the wound had run deep.

The love affair had ended seven years ago. It was Pavan's rejection, as much as economic necessity, that had prompted him to make his fortune on the seas, but the scar had never truly healed.

Since then, since Pavan, women had been enjoyed solely for the momentary pleasure they afforded the flesh; they were not to be let close to his heart. Ships and the coin they brought were his great passions now and would always remain so.

So the Duke and he had at least this one thing in common—affairs of the heart were an anathema.

"You will attend the ball, of course," the Duke had said, as an aside, just as Brandon was about to depart.

Brandon glanced over his shoulder. The quick movement pained. He felt the stitches in his wound straining beneath his bandages, and suddenly he was tired, not just physically, but of all that he had to do merely to survive one more day in a world populated by jackals like Danfort. "Am I being invited or commanded?"

"Let us say, it would be to your advantage to make an appearance."

"I find such evenings a bore."

"Better to be bored than to find your company in jeopardy," the Duke said. Then he added. "Must you always cast me as the arch villain?"

"The role suits you so well. It would be a shame to give the part to anyone less worthy. I will *consider* the invitation."

He closed the door behind him and stared down the long corridor, wondering if he could stomach the sight of Melissa Danfort at the ball, being sold off like a piece of meat, and then told himself that he would have to. Her fate was sealed by her grandfather's intentions.

For all the woman's fawning acts of kindness, Melissa had determined that Glenmillan Danfort was not a woman to trust.

For one thing, Glenmillan's tongue, when speaking of others, had the slick, darting, venomous sting of a viper, the result being that Melissa learned as much about her stepmother's character as she did about those whom

Glenmillan verbally assassinated—which was almost everyone.

Still, for all her faults, Glenmillan did possess certain social talents, and Melissa was not in a position to refuse the lessons in fashion and etiquette daily being pressed upon her. What she did, she did entirely for Brandon.

Her every thought was of him and of how he must view her with pity. All along he had known she was nothing but a half-caste. Even while she had so clumsily tried to captivate him with her feminine charms he must have found her pathetic. How she hated pity! Hated it as much as she still loved him.

Pride driving her on, she allowed herself to be subjected to one after another of Glenmillan's efforts to make her socially presentable. But being merely acceptable was not enough for Melissa. Perfection was her goal, and nothing less. She was, therefore, to Glenmillan's delight, an avid student of feminine artifice.

For instance, the lesson concerning face patches: Melissa had thought them only whimsical motifs, worn out of vanity. She was, therefore, surprised to learn that the circular or crescent-shaped pieces of scarlet or black satin and silk were originally contrived to bear testimony to one's politics. They also served to hide the disfigurements of smallpox.

Melissa's first days in London were filled to overflowing with appointments from a variety of tradesmen, ranging from mercers and jewelers to perfumers and drapers. All of them were more than delighted to wait patiently in anterooms until they might present their wares to the shrewd but extravagant eye of Glenmillan Danfort, who had undertaken the outfitting of her young charge.

"You aren't to say a thing," Glenmillan instructed Melissa. "After all, you were supposed to have been in France all these years. You should know something of style. Which you don't. Of course, you will have been in the country. That's how we'll explain your—uh—gaps in sophistication."

The colorful bruises and scratches on her face were similarly explained away as the result of a carriage accident.

"These little men who come bearing their wares have busy tongues on them," said Glenmillan, "and they have legs that carry them from here to all the other houses in London. Anyway, by the time you are formally presented, you'll make an impression that will silence any conjecture about your past. Leave it to me and everything will turn out excellently for all concerned."

If in one week's time Melissa had gained a stunning new wardrobe, she had also lost her basic naiveté.

She no longer trusted anyone or anything on first sight. She was also well aware that Glenmillan's dedication to her social acceptance was at least partially based upon reducing the woman's own embarrassment. Her stepmother no more wanted a smudge on the Danfort name than did the Duke, and money was no object when it came to outfitting the future standard-bearer of the family name.

Melissa's education continued relentlessly.

The English, Melissa discovered from Glenmillan, were considered barbarians when it came to anything stylish, and with this in mind, an expert from Paris was commissioned to see to her unruly locks.

"*C'est magnifique!*" Monsieur Fountaine exclaimed, after he had arranged Melissa's golden locks in an upsweep of curls entwined with delicate white satin rosettes. He was, according to Glenmillan, as much in demand among his many wealthy patrons for his fawning compliments as he was for his handiwork. No woman minded a lie, she claimed, as long as it was delivered with sincerity.

And, indeed, Melissa had to agree with Monsieur Fountaine, she did look splendid—if one ignored the purple and red swelling on her forehead.

But in spite of Glenmillan's insistence, Melissa would not allow the white powder to be applied as a makeup base to her face—not even to lessen the sight of the bruises—especially after she discovered from one of the maids that it was made of white lead and that some of the workmen who made it were afflicted with serious illnesses.

Nor would she succumb to trimming her eyebrows and concealing them behind artificial mouseskin brows.

She did allow her cheeks to be roughed with a crimson leather, said to be imported from South America, and her lip coloring took on the heightened effects of a potion of ground and tinted plaster of paris.

When it came to other artifices, such as plumpers—small cork balls placed inside the cheeks to give them a rounder, more youthful appearance, plus assisting the wearer to speak with a fashionable lisp—Melissa laughed until her sides nearly split.

But in most instances she took her education very seriously. After all, she was a pawn only in disguise. There was much to learn for that day when she would step out into the world as Queen; in other words, as her true self, for Brandon to recognize and acknowledge.

Whenever she and Glenmillan ventured beyond the confines of Danfort House, they were always accompanied by a page or footman. They were never without their fans, or without a small gold case, carried by the servant, in which were placed bottles of scent and aromatic vinegar, precautions against the odors of the city and its unwashed populace, as well as a snuff box.

But if her outings with Glenmillan were instructive, her engagements with Quentin took on a decidedly different flavor.

It was clear that Quentin was smitten with her; she would have had to have been deaf, dumb and blind not to have noticed.

Her interest in him, however, was negligible. Brandon was her obsession.

He continued to occupy her every thought and owned all her feelings; she lived for the moment when she would next meet him, and every second of every day seemed given over to imagining how she would look, what she would say and do and how her presence would affect him. So, at least to this end, she allowed and even encouraged Quentin's adoration, as it afforded her the opportunity to experiment with her femininity.

"You are the most beautiful woman in London," he declared passionately one afternoon, as they trotted through St. James park in a carriage.

"And the most mysterious," she returned from behind the folds of her cloak. It had been a week since her ordeal at the wharves, and her face was almost healed, although she still took the precaution of covering the signs of her battering when leaving Danfort House.

But the unveiling would occur soon. There were plans to attend an afternoon garden party with Glenmillan within the week.

"You cannot imagine what the sight of your face does to me," Quentin continued in the same heated vein. He clasped her hands in his. "I dare say, for the first and only time in my life, I'm inflamed beyond the point of reason."

"I do believe you exaggerate, sir," said Melissa, in a tone she mimicked from others she had observed flirting. Retrieving her hand, she brought up her fan as she had seen Glenmillan do, to peer at him with mock alarm at his impassioned declarations.

He closed his pale, luminous eyes and sighed. "I do not exaggerate in the slightest," he returned, as if injured by her remark. The compelling blue gaze was again fixed on her. "If anything, I understate the truth. You are more beautiful than any woman I have seen, even on my grand tour. In all of Italy, France or Holland, there's not a woman who can compare. I swear to you, madame, on my honor, what I speak is the entire truth."

Melissa was extremely pleased. She searched his face for evidence of his exaggeration. For if she were even a half as beautiful as Quentin claimed, then Brandon would find it all that more difficult to resist her. Poor Quentin. It wasn't fair, but everything that he said or did merely reflected back upon what Brandon might say or do.

She did not feel *too* sorry, however, for she had never forgiven Quentin for not rescuing Celia. Celia...her poor friend Celia, whom she would never forget as long as there remained a breath in her. No, she would never forgive Quentin for the loss of Celia.

So with Quentin she flirted and teased and coaxed, shamelessly playing with him as she had heard Court sophisticates did with their suitors.

But perhaps she had overdone things.

All too late she realized that she had kindled too hot a fire in her stepbrother.

That unhappy realization came when she was alone in the upstairs library. She'd been leafing through books with descriptions of France, attempting to discover some notations on Brandon's family—as it was said by Glenmillan to have once been a great house—when Quentin discovered her whereabouts.

"Ah!" he said, his blue eyes alight with the same combination of longing and hope he always displayed when in her company. "At long last! I've been looking everywhere for you."

Under ordinary circumstances she would have used their meeting to hone her feminine wiles. But something had happened earlier that had upset her, that had wounded her to the quick, and she was in no mood for her flirtatious charade.

Brandon had visited the Duke that morning. She had only by chance happened upon him, just as he had been descending the stairs, about to take his leave.

Caught off guard, she had excitedly called out his name from the top landing. But no sooner had he turned than she realized what a blunder she had made. By his face, he appeared deeply involved with business matters, and her lilting voice sounded as childishly removed from his world as a beggar's concerns from a king's.

"Yes?" he inquired, turning only partially.

Melissa's breath had caught. Her mind stood still. He looked as handsome as ever. His breeches were a dark green velvet and his stockings a pure, clean white, showing the muscles of his powerful legs to good effect—legs that had once pressed against her flesh. He wore a waistcoat of brown and green, subdued and rich, not foppish as were the outfits worn by Quentin, but masculine. As always, the sword was fixed to his side.

He was waiting for a response, but with his dark eyes on her it was impossible to locate a cogent thought. Her heart pounded in her chest. Her throat had become a tight, constricted tube. *She loved him; she would always, always love him.* And he did not even see her except as an unwanted responsibility thrust upon him by her grandfather.

"Hello..." she said, at a loss. Yesterday at the same time she had been fully dressed in one of the new gowns Glenmillan had made up for her at great speed and cost. Her hair had been arranged by Monsieur Fountaine, who was experimenting on styles to discover one appropriate for her presentation at the ball.

But that was yesterday. Now all she wore was a morning dress of pale yellow and white silk, which made her appear young and innocent, not alluring and sophisticated. And her hair tumbled loose over her shoulders.

"Yes, hello." He bowed slightly and waited, his shoulders tense with impatience.

"I did not know you were coming," she said in a weak voice.

"Your grandfather had a matter to discuss."

She could feel him straining to be gone. Her heart pounded violently. She thought she might faint from fear.

"Is there something...?" he asked.

In a moment he would leave her! "I heard," she stammered, hardly able to think of what her next word would be, "that if we do not sail soon, we will be caught by the winds and not make it around the Cape."

Well. What she had said had clearly caught his interest. His eyes narrowed attentively. She went on, feeling more certain of herself and trying hard to remember what Quentin had told her about voyages to India. "And there's the tail of the monsoon...there's that, too. If we were to wait, we could catch the tail of the monsoon and ride it quickly...until the winds shifted. But if the winds shift before that, then we would never be able to go against them. So timing is of utmost—"

"Madame," Brandon said sharply, clearly annoyed, "if you were to require advice on what ribbons to wind through your hair, or what skirts to wear with what shoes, I presume you would seek someone with experience in those matters. Correspondingly, if I have need for advice on the sea—which I do not—I shall ask it from someone familiar with ships. Now, is that all?"

"Yes, yes... all..."

"Then I bid you good day." He bowed and left her—left her devastated, trembling from humiliation.

That was some time earlier, and now Quentin was also bowing to her, even as her mind was filled with Brandon.

"My mother tells me you're to be presented at an afternoon's gathering tomorrow."

"Tomorrow, yes... tomorrow," Melissa replied, sighing.

"And soon you're to be presented at Court. It will be the start of a whole new life, a whole new world...." His voice took on an excitement she did not share. "You will meet the King!"

She wondered if Brandon would be there when she was presented to King George.

"And soon, I vow, every man in England will be vying for your heart," Quentin continued on with more urgency.

Melissa sighed, the image of Brandon fading. "Then let them vie away. It means nothing to me," she answered listlessly. She was standing near one of the casement windows. A soft afternoon light filtered through the panes, falling over her pale yellow dress and tinting the air golden as she turned to place the book she had been perusing back on the shelf.

"But *I* care!" objected Quentin passionately. "Don't you see, I'm going mad thinking I'll lose you to someone else!" He grabbed her shoulders, spinning her around, his face contorted in anguish. "Surely you have to see what you mean to me—how much you have gained my admiration? Why, there...do you see?'' He broke away, almost flung himself away.

Melissa could only gape.

"Look what I've been reduced to, behaving like a brute, like an overwrought school boy!" he lamented, reacting to Melissa's surprise. "I *must* have you!"

The book dropped from her hands.

"Ah, now see, I've frightened you." He stooped and brought up the volume, his eyes straying to its title: *A History of French Aristocracy*.

Melissa caught the sudden change in expression. Even his body stiffened. The metamorphosis was remarkable. From wounded, impassioned suitor, the look he wore changed to one of cold calculation. When he handed the book back to her, his tone was again cool. "I see, madame, that you've developed a recent fancy for French history?"

"A passing interest," she replied, coloring.

"And why, may I ask? Why *French* history? Why this particular fascination with the French?"

Truthfulness was in her nature, but in this instance she knew that the truth would never do. For one thing, Quentin would only be offended in learning she had no interest in him, and for another, her feelings for Brandon were sacred. She would cheapen them by bandying them about. Still, an explanation was due, and Quentin was awaiting it.

"To be sure that if someone asks me about France, I can respond credibly. I find that prudent, don't you, as I was supposed to be living there for sixteen years?"

Quentin considered her explanation. He relaxed somewhat, but, she saw, not entirely, as he still eyed her suspiciously. He wore a deep blue velveteen suit, which accentuated the color of his eyes, and a tight white collar with a fluffy lace cravat. As he watched her his fingers fiddled with the lace, moved to the neck and pulled the fabric, as if it were too tight.

"Yes, now that you mention it," he responded, but she did not believe he was totally convinced. At any rate, he moved closer to her and said with slightly less feeling than had been in his voice previously, "You look very soft, very lovely in the light. You look...golden. Your hair, your skin...even your eyes, those wonderful green eyes, are tinged with gold...." He spoke softly, hypnotically, and his fingers stroked her face lightly. Quentin's eyes were blue and mesmerizing. "You are the most desirable woman I have ever known," he said, and before Melissa could suspect his action, he brought his lips against hers, his arms pressing her against him.

"No!" she protested. "No..." and she struggled successfully to free herself. "Quentin! Have you lost your wits? You're my brother!"

"We're not related...it isn't forbidden," he countered, just as she heaved herself out of his embrace.

"This is—it's going too far, Quentin!" It was hard to catch her breath. "Please...leave me. Leave me, Quentin!" And borrowing one of Glenmillan's imperious gestures, she pointed her finger toward the door.

But instead, he took her hand and drew her to him again. "Why don't you understand...I love you. I won't hurt you. I'll take care of you. We'll marry, have children. It will be...oh, so wonderful." He closed his eyes briefly. When he opened them, they were wide and blue and demanding. "I want you."

Melissa struggled against him. "Let me go."

"No...let me love you...let me love you now." He clasped her hands behind her back and bowed her body backward. "You don't know how wonderful it will be for both of us," Quentin said. "I love you—"

"I don't love you!" She turned her face from his seeking mouth. "I don't want you."

For a moment, he seemed to hesitate, considering her words. "Then you've only toyed with me. You've led me to believe—"

"There's someone else," she said, panicked that she had let things go too far with Quentin. She was not experienced in these things. "Someone else I care about." With all her strength, Melissa shoved him away.

Quentin staggered backward into a table, sending the items on top of it crashing to the floor.

He stared at her, the blue eyes wild. "I'm sorry," he said. Then, as if another man had suddenly taken his place, he became calm, more his usual self. "I ask your forgiveness. Of course, you're right. I've overstepped myself. But I had thought...I had felt..." He shook his head, then dropped his eyes. "Madame, over the past few days you *have* pretended an interest in me. You cannot say otherwise."

"I'm sorry. I shouldn't have...I'm not so wise yet in these worldly matters. We will both forget this incident."

"Yes, we must." He turned as if to leave, then glanced back, saying sharply, "You say there is someone else?"

"Only in my mind," she said quickly to cover her mistake. "Only a fantasy, no more."

"Then I can still hope. But, you must tell me, do you find me unappealing? If you do, I would like to know. I would change what I can, but if there's nothing, then—" He shrugged.

"No," she said, her green eyes softening, and her voice reverting to a kindness that was genuine. She had no deep feelings for Quentin Danfort, but she knew what it was to be rejected. "You're very attractive." That much was true. His type just didn't appeal to her. "It's just that—"

And he waited.

"You know that I am leaving for India." She sounded so sincere in her excuse that even she would have believed it.

His face went pale. "India?"

"I thought you knew."

"No," he said. He looked astounded. "Nothing. I knew nothing."

"Then I'm sorry. But I'm to sail within two or three weeks' time. The journey is long...perhaps it will take seven months, and whatever feelings you have for me now will certainly have cooled by the time I return." She went on to tell him that she was to be reunited with her mother.

But he wasn't listening to her. She could see that. His eyes had clouded over, and he sank down into the nearest chair.

Finally, he looked at her and said, "We will be wed then. Before you leave. And I will accompany you on your voyage."

"Oh, Quentin. I cannot marry you." Melissa turned from his ghostly paleness and burning blue eyes, seeking relief in the serene gardens beyond the window. "I cannot ever marry you, Quentin."

"Don't say never, Melissa. There are always twists and turns and new forks in the road ahead."

Behind her, she heard Quentin rise slowly from his chair and quietly make his way from the room.

He did not knock on his mother's door when he arrived at her quarters, but merely entered, pushing apart the double doors. When she saw him, her violet eyes lit up in anticipation.

"Well?" she asked. "How did it go?"

Quentin shut the doors, remaining slumped against them, staring into space. "She's in love," said Quentin, his voice as colorless as his skin.

Glenmillan clapped her hands. "Ah! There, I knew it! She wouldn't be able to resist your charm. Oh, Quentin, Quentin, we have won!" She twirled around in a circle, the green of her gown rushing like sea foam about her.

"Stop it! We've lost," he said flatly. "She's in love with—"

Glenmillan froze. Her upraised hands dropped leadenly to her sides and hung there. "No. Not . . . ?"

"Yes."

Mother and son stared at each other.

Glenmillan chewed on her painted lip. "Are you certain?"

"As certain as I am that I owe more money than I have."

"Yes, well, that *is* fairly certain, then." Glenmillan began to pace. She chewed on a nail. "But what of it? What if she does have an infatuation for de Forrest? He'll never be had by her—no one can have that man. At least not longer than a night.''

"And some not that long," Quentin said pointedly, with intended meanness. He saw no reason why Glenmillan should avoid the sting of being a discard if he had been forced to suffer rejection on her account. "But this girl is young and beautiful and soon to be the richest woman in the kingdom. Even de Forrest must have his price. Anyway, we are finished, Mother." He moved to stare critically at himself in the full-length mirror. "I'm not bad, am I? I'm rather handsome, actually. But I'm also no match for de Forrest and we both know it."

That evening Glenmillan attended the theater at Drury Lane with the Earl of Brynwald. She was pleased with the pearls he gave her, but even more elated when he gave her the latest gossip. It was all she could do to stay in her seat.

"Oh, dear me," she exclaimed, when the Earl suggested he retire with her after the performance. "But I'm having a terrible spell . . . my head.''

"You seemed in high enough spirits only a moment ago."

"Yes, well, these attacks . . . they come on very suddenly.''

In her hurry to return home to give Quentin the news, she actually forgot the case containing the pearls, and she was chased by Brynwald's coach half the way home until they could be returned to her. Anyway, what were pearls when she was now able to claim the world?

She burst in on Quentin, who lay in his bed with one of the maids. The room reeked of brandy. The girl gave a frightened little gasp and disappeared under the sheets. Quentin covered himself and, sitting up, said with a slurred voice, "Madame?"

"My dear, dear son!" She smiled her lovely smile.

Quentin stifled a brandied belch. "Madame?"

"Pavan de Noialles is in London.''

"Thank God," said Quentin, and he gave the girl's rump a hearty slap.

Chapter Eight

While others stared at her, speculating quietly among themselves upon her worth, the remarkable green eyes, the extraordinary mass of golden hair, the magnificent gown and diamond-studded fan—and particularly upon the power she might eventually wield in Court—Melissa could scarcely keep her eyes off someone else.

She was all but hypnotized by the beautiful silver-tressed Frenchwoman who wound through the gathering of women in the music room at Vauxhall that May afternoon. To Melissa, she bore the shining grace of a moonbeam fallen upon an earth unworthy of her visit.

The woman's eyes were the color of cornflowers, her skin like alabaster, and when she laughed, which was often, Melissa would have sworn it was the peel of delicate bells and not a human voice. If she could be anyone else, Melissa decided, she would be this woman.

Even Brandon, who seemed beyond idle infatuation, could not help but fall to his knees before such a radiant creature.

"Who is she?" Melissa whispered to Glenmillan, when they had a moment together.

For the third time since they had arrived, Glenmillan had pulled her into a private alcove, away from the main concentration of activity, in order to fiddle with Melissa's appearance.

"Who is who?" Glenmillan asked distractedly, as if she had not heard the question above the chamber orchestra playing a selection by Handel. Her long slender fingers continued to fuss with the delicate garland of miniature yellow tea roses Monsieur Fountaine had woven through Melissa's upswept hair.

The flowers went with Melissa's dress. A gown of the latest French fashion, it was a sack of white and yellow ribbed silk, complete with a train, and trimmed with pink-edged flounces. Braids and silk tassels had been added for additional effect. A necklace and earrings of diamonds, and an ivory fan studded with diamonds completed the ensemble, which was as spectacularly tasteful as it was opulent.

"*That* woman," said Melissa, peering out beyond the alcove. She tipped her dainty ivory fan slightly, just as Glenmillan had instructed during her lessons on proper etiquette. "The one in the blue gown with the silver threads. The one with the blue eyes and the silver hair. The one—"

"There now, we're perfect again," cooed Glenmillan, hardly seeming to listen. She stepped back to admire her work.

"She's perfect," Melissa said, annoyed that Glenmillan had such a stubbornly focused mind.

"*You're* perfect. Well, I've done it," she concluded with smug satisfaction, patting the closed edge of her fan against her palm. "It's entirely obvious, you're a tremendous success here, a credit to the Danfort name. They're all wildly curious and madly jealous, also afraid that the King will favor you above anyone else when you're introduced. You've quite upset their little world. Yes, I must say, I've quite outdone myself."

Melissa could not imagine her own presence counting for anything at all, not in the company of the woman in blue and silver. But if Glenmillan had a one-track mind, so did she. "But the woman . . . who might *she* be?"

Glenmillan smiled, hardly needing to glance in the direction Melissa had pointed. "Ah," she said, "you speak of Pavan de Noialles. French, as you might suspect. She's a scandal in Paris at the moment, and has come to visit a cousin here. Or so they say." Glenmillan lowered her voice somewhat. "Of course, the truth is somewhat different." And then she shut her mouth.

"What truth?" asked Melissa, almost ready to strangle Glenmillan for the information.

"Well, it's suspected that she's come here to reclaim her lover—a Frenchman who left the country years ago when she jilted him for another man with a great deal of money. It's said that neither has loved anyone else all these years. Her husband was felled last year in a duel with a man who preferred to lose his life rather than lose Pavan's occasional favors." At the last word, she raised her eyebrow meaningfully.

"Yes, yes. I understand," said Melissa, who daily was becoming more worldly-wise. "And then?" she prodded.

"And then she tired of the poor fool, who had risked everything." Glenmillan smiled brightly. "Tragic, isn't it?"

Melissa stepped to the alcove's opening and stared at the woman men were ready to die for. "Yes . . . tragic." Melissa did not smile. She sighed. "But romantic, too." The story of star-crossed lovers, pawns of fate and most likely of their own human appetites, appealed to Melissa.

Anyway, a tale with a happy ending gave her hope that she would one day be united with Brandon—no matter how bleak the present appeared. Using Pavan de Noialles as a model for what might be possible, there was always, apparently, a tomorrow.

"Of course, one can understand a man being willing to die for a woman like de Noialles," Glenmillan added, coming to stand near Melissa. Two sets of eyes, one violet, the other green, peered at the Frenchwoman.

Fascinated, Melissa took in Pavan de Noialles's every gesture, memorizing what she saw so that she, too, might display a similar grace when in the company of Brandon. "Do you know who the lover is? The one she's come to England to be reunited with?" Melissa asked, wondering what man could be such a woman's equal.

"As a matter of fact, yes." Glenmillan paused. She slanted her violet eyes to Melissa. "And you also know him."

Melissa turned her head in surprise, forgetful of her fan. It fell from her fingers and clattered to the floor. Even before Glenmillan said the words, she knew the awful truth in her heart.

"Why, it's Brandon de Forrest." Glenmillan smiled radiantly. "Ah, now . . . see, you've dropped your fan."

"It's hopeless," breathed Melissa, as her maid removed the pins from her hair in preparation for her retiring. To let in a breath of air, the thick swag drapes had not been closed, and Melissa could look beyond the open panes to see a tiny sliver of moon glittering like a hooked blade against the backdrop of indigo sky.

The girl tugged at a stubborn pin that had become twisted in one of Monsieur Fountaine's curls. Melissa was never to touch her own hair again, Glenmillan had told her. It wasn't seemly for a lady to tend to her own toilette.

Was it, Melissa wondered, seemly for a lady to waste away of a broken heart, or to fling herself from the window and end her misery in a single swift gesture? What, Melissa wondered, would Glenmillan find to be the socially correct expression of utter and complete despair?

Glenmillan would not grieve, not she; instead, she would most likely order a new dress. She would paste more patches of little moons on her face.

Oh, Melissa thought, would that I could have a heart like that—so cold, like a coin found on a patch of snow. "Oh, what wouldn't I give to be free of this torment," Melissa lamented in a whisper.

"My lady?" Anne cocked her head to the side.

Melissa had forgotten the maid, who looked at her questioningly.

"It's nothing, nothing, Anne." She had forgotten that she was rarely alone anymore.

There was always someone about, either her maid, worrying over her welfare, or else Glenmillan, bustling around with details about her dress for the ball or with news of whom she had invited and who had accepted. It seemed that everyone in the world had been invited, and none had declined.

During the day there was scarce time for Melissa to reflect upon her morbid circumstances, but at night there was ample space for brooding, and her mind would churn with pictures of the magnificent Pavan de Noialles locked in an embrace with Brandon, even as she herself lay alone in her bed, yearning for a mere glimpse of him.

"My hair is impossible," Melissa said, covering her feelings. She had learned from Glenmillan that gossip was virulent among servants. Any indiscreet word could have severe consequences later, in some distant drawing room. She would die before allowing Brandon to know she was pining for him night and day. "My hair is hopeless. There's far too much of it and it won't stay in place no matter how many pins Monsieur Fountaine applies." Anyway, that much was true.

"Oh, but my lady, your hair is wonderful. Everyone comments upon it . . . and on how splendid you look in all other ways, as well. Perish, there's not another woman who could hold a candle to you—lest it be the Frenchwoman come to see her ladyship today," Anne added with a note of reverence.

"What?" Melissa felt as if a bolt of lightning had passed up her spine.

"She was something amazing to look upon, that one was, like an angel in the palest pink. She hardly walked, but floated like a swan. Her hair so white, and the eyes as blue as the sky's most perfect day. But you're no less than she, madame," the girl said quickly, noting a look of disturbance on her mistress's face.

"This Frenchwoman? What name did she go by?"

"They say her name's Pavan de Noialles."

At the utterance of her name, Melissa's eyes fell shut. The enemy was even beneath her own roof. A terrible sign. A sign of defeat.

"And she brought a bolt of the finest cloth to her ladyship, violet and gold it was. Her ladyship's colors. She'll look splendid when it's all made up into a gown, don't you think?"

"Splendid," Melissa said softly. "Now leave me please, Anne."

"But your hair, madame, it's only half—"

"I can manage pins on my own." Demonstrating, Melissa pulled savagely at two pins and flung them into the little dish with the others. Her green eyes were moist with despair. But behind the veil of tears, a fire burned. "I can manage a great deal, actually! I just need . . . I need time." Anne was gaping at her. "Just—just go!"

And Anne scampered away, not understanding the outburst, but knowing full well the range of the Danfort temper.

The only thing, thought Melissa, with tears beginning to fall freely now that she had some privacy, that she couldn't seem to manage was to make Brandon fall in love with her. And now that Pavan de Noialles had returned to claim him, what possible good would all her elaborate primping and fine manners serve? Pavan was magnificent. She was not only beautiful, she was French. And thereby cultured. And worldly in matters of the flesh. Plus, she had also owned Brandon's heart once, and to hear it said, his emotions were yet bound to Pavan.

What could she do to save this situation from becoming more critical?

Melissa swiped at her tears, sniffed and forced herself to concentrate. Well, exactly what was the situation?

Within a month she would set sail for India, with Brandon as captain. But until then, Pavan would have ample time to seduce him. Why—Melissa projected with horror—they could marry in that period; why, he could get her with child! The thought of Brandon making love to Pavan, of loving her, of having a child by her, was too painful for her to think of for longer than an instant.

She had to do something.

Unless she could think of something unique, something that Pavan could not offer him, there was no chance at all for her to triumph over the Frenchwoman.

For fifteen minutes Melissa paced the length of the room in her linen shift, just as she had seen Glenmillan do when stuck on some thought. Pacing was very good, she decided, when at last the brilliant notion flew into her mind and with certainty she knew that Brandon would be hers.

That night she slept soundly for the first time in three days, since having learned of the Frenchwoman's hold over Brandon.

In the morning, her spirits revived, she was up and waiting for Anne to dress her even before the girl arrived. She forced herself to have the little cakes and fruit delivered on a tray for breakfast, and then she dashed to her grandfather's private rooms and waited to be announced by the footman who stood sentry outside the door. Her pulse was still rushing when she entered his closet.

The Duke looked up from his work. "Yes?" he said with a pinched note of annoyance. "You have some urgent matter?"

"My lord," Melissa said respectfully, making a proper curtsy. She had to behave impeccably; she very much needed her grandfather's cooperation. "I beg your indulgence."

This morning he looked severe, formidable. His waistcoat was of shot green and black silk, the reflected color making his hazel eyes appear darker, more penetrating. Small gilt buttons winked in the light from the candle placed near his reading material. They gleamed like additional eyes, all watching her with disapproval. As always when she came into his company, he initially wore a faintly startled expression, as if he had forgotten that he had let something dangerous out of its box, only to find it there before him.

"Then be brief about your begging, I have much to do," he said, but he sank back into his chair, ready to listen. She glanced down at the book he had been studying and found it to be a drama, the text in the original Greek.

He did not invite her to sit, and so she gave her speech where she stood on the bright Turkish carpet before his desk.

"Your lordship, if I am to be heir to your estate, then I would like to learn everything that you know. That is, I wish to learn about accounts, about shipping, trade, what businesses you possess, how to deal with goldsmiths. Everything. And I wish to begin immediately."

The Duke of Danfort appraised her. After a long spell, he finally sat forward and, pointing a finger at her, said, "These subjects belong to a man's world. Nothing you have mentioned is of a woman's domain. Your suggestion is preposterous."

Exactly, thought Melissa. *It was preposterous and daring and desperate.* But she had come prepared to counter all objections and said, "But I would not wish to entrust all that you have worked so hard for these many years to men who were less than your equal. And all men would be less than that." *Except for one man, whom I will catch with all the knowledge you shall arm me with.*

The Duke sank back in his chair. He nodded to himself and looked at her, his fingers fiddling idly with the pages of the Greek drama. The hazel eyes grew into tiny pinpricks of dark light that drilled through her skull, opening her to his inquiry.

Finally, he said, "Yes. Yes, actually, what you say is true."

Melissa was overjoyed. But she remained stoic, as she knew a display of icy reserve more than anything else would impress her grandfather. "I would hope to begin my instruction immediately."

To her delight and relief, they began that very morning, with Melissa listening raptly to her grandfather's explanation of his mining operation in Wales. She further learned that there were shipping warehouses and farms, not to mention a myriad number of investments in colonial enterprises. He dealt with three goldsmiths rather than relying upon one, preferring to diversify his funds and thereby create a competitive atmosphere among the merchant class. She was particularly interested in learning to read shipping charts and in the balancing of accounts for trading voyages.

Three days later, when Brandon arrived in the library for his appointment with the Duke, Melissa was prepared to shine.

She was dressed impeccably, in a blue damask gown trimmed in blond bobbin lace. Her hair was arranged neatly in an upsweep, but without the usual ribbons or flowers or feathers popularly in fashion. She wanted to appear subdued and elegant. If she could not compete directly with Pavan, then she would present herself as unique. Her mirror had verified that her intentions were a success, but the true test would be Brandon's reaction to her.

As for Brandon—ah, her eyes all but devoured him as he entered the library. It had been several days since she had last seen him on the stairs, and then he had been as cold as January frost. Still, no matter how elaborate her imaginings, the reality of his presence always seemed to exceed any fantasy she had drawn to sustain her while deprived of his company.

He was every inch a man, from appearance to manner: the self-assured stride; the dark eyes, taking in details of his surroundings that Melissa barely noted; a certain relaxed tension in his bearing, like a Tom on a hunt who knew his prey's habits and had only to pounce to take what he wanted. She prayed that he would want *her*.

The slightest movement of his hand stirred her heart, caused her pulse to rise and exploded heat through her body. That hand, those fingers . . . once they had caressed her body. *But also,* she thought, her heart clutching, *another woman, a Frenchwoman, might now be thrilling to that practiced touch.*

Brandon wore a leather vest and dark black pants. The shirt was similar to his others, white with full loose sleeves, bound at the wrists. There was no decorative finish at the neckline, merely an open slit, with linen ties. Instead of boots, he had chosen neat shoes with silver buckles and white cotton stockings that showed his tightly muscled legs to advantage. And, of course, as always, there was the sword buckled to his side.

Brandon bowed to the Duke, an automatic gesture, and then with a questioning look took in Melissa's presence as she moved from the shadows behind the Duke's desk into the light. The ground trembled beneath her as for a moment he simply stared, then presented a second, perfunctory bow.

"I was under the impression we would discuss business matters," Brandon said. He carried with him three long scrolls of parchment. Melissa took them to be navigational charts.

"And so we shall. We shall keep to our general schedule, as planned," said the Duke.

Brandon's eyes returned to Melissa, the meaning of his glance apparent. He disapproved of her presence.

"The girl will stay," the Duke announced. "My granddaughter's expressed an interest in matters pertaining to her inheritance. She has my blessing on this project of hers. With a bit of knowledge on affairs of business, she can keep an eye on her future husband's management of her estate."

Brandon looked directly at Melissa. "I see." She could not read what lay behind the black eyes—surprise, relief, or was it something else? But his voice was as flat and hard as his gaze when he turned back to the Duke. "Then I take it that a suitable match has already appeared."

"A suitable match has not appeared. But soon, in due time, a selection will be made to fill our purposes. I'm sure there will be no dearth of applicants. The ball will bring them all forth in droves. Now," said the Duke, "we have the matter of victualing to settle. We will begin with that and move on."

After that, both men all but ignored Melissa, who kept to the shadows as the men discussed their plans for the voyage.

As they conversed, she made notes for herself, but she found it hard to concentrate. Her eyes strayed constantly to Brandon, who spoke rapidly and to the point. For all the notice he gave her, she might not have been in the room.

Only once did she catch him stealing a glance her way. She smiled faintly, but he did not. At least for the present, he saw her as an intrusion. But that would change. It would have to.

It was impossible for her not to think of him with Pavan, and she listened for any piece of private information she could glean from his dialogue with the Duke.

It was on the third such meeting she attended that the Duke suggested they meet again one night in the future.

Brandon appeared momentarily surprised. "Surely you jest, my lord."

"I am not given to humor."

"That much I know," said Brandon dryly. "But since when have we begun evening appointments?"

"Since this moment." The Duke barely glanced up from his papers.

"Yes, well, that's unfortunate. Because as it happens, I've an engagement already," Brandon replied, the matter apparently settled in his mind, as he gathered his charts in readiness to depart.

"Perhaps you could change your appointment?" Melissa blurted desperately from the shadows. She rose out of her seat, propelled by panic, and stepped into the pool of light from the window.

Both the Duke and Brandon turned sharply and stared in amazement, as if a chair or table had suddenly spoken.

"There's scant time to prepare," she added, attempting to sound reasonable, even enthusiastic. "I would suggest we use every available moment to make this a successful voyage. There's much at stake."

Her grandfather wore a scowl; Brandon merely appeared annoyed. She might have been a yapping dog.

"Sit down," the Duke said firmly. "You overstep yourself. You are not Elizabeth Regina, ready to rule—*yet*," he added sourly. But to Brandon he said, "Nevertheless, she's right. The voyage is less than three weeks off. Break your engagement.''

"I'm sorry," Brandon said calmly. "But I must refuse."

"Really?" The Duke looked up, his face darkening. "And what could be more important than money to you, de Forrest? You intrigue me mightily."

"The matter is of a personal nature."

"I've never known social engagements to be that important to you."

"Some are," Brandon returned dismissively.

"Then tell the woman you'll see her another night," the Duke said dryly, and Melissa noted with pain that Brandon made no effort to contradict the Duke's implication.

Of course, it was Pavan he was going to see!

When he left, Melissa was beside herself. Moving from her place of exile, distraught and bewildered, she came before the Duke's desk. "I don't understand. You could have made him break his engagement. You never let anyone defy you."

The Duke looked up at her. His eyes were all the more dark in contrast to the white periwig. "Why should my seeming lack of authority trouble you so much?"

"It's in the interest of the voyage that I make my objections."

"Is that it? Well, don't let it trouble you. There's time enough to conduct our business." But he looked at her curiously, as if he were about to say something more but then thought better of it.

"No," she said solemnly beneath her breath, "there isn't. There isn't nearly enough time." And her head filled with a scene of Pavan and Brandon laughing, embracing, while she sat alone with a ledger of accounts. Maybe her plan wasn't quite what she had hoped it would be; maybe it was better to act the coquette, as that was all that could ever hold any man; maybe Brandon de Forrest was not really so different from others. Maybe she would die in her sleep and be out of her misery. . . .

* * *

If Melissa was unhappy with the meetings she attended, Glenmillan was far more so when she discovered the new hobby.

"It isn't fitting!" Glenmillan railed as they strolled in the garden, taking their afternoon's constitutional. "A lady of quality does not involve herself in financial affairs."

"That's strange. You seem extremely interested in all the Duke's financial affairs," Melissa returned pleasantly, and, lifting her skirts, she ran toward the high box hedges that formed the intricate maze designed by the Duke.

"Oh . . . oh, don't!" Glenmillan called. "I hate that wicked trap! It's for rodents, not humans."

But Melissa was already around the first bend. She laughed. "It's good training for the real world," she called out, her voice sailing through the hedges. "Catch me if you can! If you do, then I promise to heed any advice you wish to dispense. But if not . . . then count me free of all constraints. I'll do exactly as I please without another word from you. My wager, madame. Do you accept the challenge?"

Glenmillan did not answer. That would have given away her position. The hunt had suddenly become important. It was a symbol.

Instead of responding, she crept along the corridors of high green walls, listening for the sound of Melissa, just as Melissa pricked her ears for the nearby rustle of Glenmillan's skirts as she sought to discover her location.

At one point, they were obviously on opposite sides of the same hedge. "I want to know why you're doing all of this," Glenmillan said, as if the barrier of sheared privet was not there between them.

"It's fun."

"No, not this damn game of yours. I mean all this meddling in the Duke's accounts."

"That's also fun," Melissa said, moving along.

Glenmillan slid forward, pacing herself with Melissa's footsteps. She would catch her soon enough. An eighteen-year-old girl was certainly not going to best her. "Well, it isn't seemly. It's so...so blatant."

"I don't give a fig what other people do. And perhaps I'm not an indirect personality."

"But facts and figures are the province of men. People will talk."

"But, Glenmillan, they talk anyway. About nothing at all. So if they must talk, then let them at least have something real on which they may sharpen their tongues." And Melissa ran quickly around a hedge, doubled back and took another turn, which brought her directly behind the groping Glenmillan. "Aha!" Melissa cried.

"Good Lord!" Glenmillan's fan flew from her fingers. "What are you doing?"

"I've outfoxed you," said Melissa guilelessly, smiling as brilliantly as her stepmother had when she told her that Brandon was still smitten with Pavan de Noialles. "Ah, now see," she said, "it appears you have dropped your fan. And lost your cause."

Glenmillan glared at her, but with more respect; certainly with more caution. This girl was becoming dangerous.

It was not only Glenmillan who talked about Pavan. Everyone else seemed to have the woman's name on their tongues as well. They spoke about her at every gathering Melissa attended. They spoke about her as if she were a goddess and not a woman. She was already said to have captured the attention of the King, who had invited her for a private audience.

"Is there no one whom the lady herself admires?" Melissa had asked, fluttering her fan with a languid boredom that belied the furious racing of her pulse, as she sat in a box in Drury Lane Theater one night with Glenmillan and Quentin. Several of their friends were in attendance. Below, in the pit and galleries, the common people of London sat on long benches, happy to steal glances at the spectacularly plumed citizens above. At any given moment only half the audience watched *The Beggar's Opera,* so busy were they with what was happening around them.

"But, of course," said the Earl of Shropesmire, a friend of Quentin's, who made no secret of his infatuation with Melissa. The Earl spent his days in gaming salons and drawing rooms, and at cock fights. A macaroni of the first order, he dressed even more elaborately than Quentin, in extreme Italian and French styles, and knew every piece of gossip there was. "She's mad for that man...the sailor...what's his name?" He brought up a scented handkerchief and waved it before his nose, as if the perfume held the answer.

"Brandon de Forrest," said Quentin, watching Melissa's expression.

But she kept her face frozen, her eyes on the actors. Her brain was on fire.

"Ah, yes, that's the one. Clever bastard. Made a fortune in trade, I understand. So now the Countess wants him back, I'd expect." Shropesmire leaned toward Melissa. "She has an amazing fondness for money, I'm told. And de Forrest seems to have quite a lot of it."

"And with all the tricks that one has at her disposal, I'm sure de Forrest will find an amazing fondness for her," said Glenmillan, smiling at Melissa. Her eyes were very bright, her little chin pointed, the cheekbones accentuated in the shadows, and she looked like a crafty fox.

Melissa smiled back. She was not a chicken.

But the problem was, as Melissa saw it—while lying awake that night brooding as usual—precisely as her stepmother had outlined it: Pavan had tricks at her disposal; she, Melissa, had none.

She would develop some.

She listened with concern when her grandfather explained that he would be detained the following day; an appointment in Fleet Street required his attendance. When she was invited, she demurred, claiming a fitting for her ball dress. It did not disturb her when he mentioned that he had just penned a note to de Forrest, canceling their usual meeting. It did not disturb her because she quickly apprehended the page who was to make the delivery.

When Brandon arrived, she was seated at her grandfather's desk in the library.

Stopping short in his tracks, Brandon said, "I was under the impression that the Duke and I had an appointment."

"Yes," Melissa replied brightly. "You're quite right."

"Then the Duke will be here soon."

"Well, you see . . . he's not here."

"But you are."

"Yes . . ."

Brandon smiled, but it was not out of friendliness. "I see. You've decided to become Elizabeth after all, and I am to perhaps be your Drake?"

Melissa looked down at the papers she had prepared for their interview. He did not take her seriously. Well, she would change all of that soon. "I've become quite familiar with the Duke's plans."

"And of course he knows of this—" Brandon swept his arm in an arc "—this meeting between us? Somehow I doubt that."

Melissa said nothing; misrepresenting the truth was one thing, outright lying another. Instead, she rose from the desk and made her way to the large globe, giving the dyed leather ball a spin toward India. Dissembling, she said, "I suggest rather than the first two ports you have decided upon, you consider stopping here." She pointed with her finger.

Brandon shook his head. He turned to leave.

Melissa spoke out quickly. "I have it upon authority that the East India Company has not been particularly vigilant in maintaining its trade relationship in these areas."

Brandon stopped, turned, gave her a hostile look, and then spent a moment in consideration before coming forward. He strode across the room, closing the distance between them before she could continue with her masterfully designed plot.

She was suddenly frightened. He did not look at all impressed with her business acumen.

When he reached her, he snatched her hand from the globe, and, holding it for a long moment, looked thoughtfully into her eyes. Then, with a kindness that was more patronizing than anything else, said, "Melissa...this is foolish. I'm going to leave now. Tell your grandfather that we will—"

"I won't be talked down to. It's your pride that keeps you from listening. I'm not a stupid child," she said defiantly, claiming her hand from him and stepping back.

She wanted him to see her. She wanted to blind him with her beauty.

She had worn her best new gown, white and black satin, with black piping and a bodice that emphasized her tiny waist and full breasts. Never had she looked more lovely; she knew it. And it was important that he notice, as well. With satisfaction she saw the dark eyes course over her, saw his jaw tighten, and when he looked back into her eyes, she went on with more confidence. "All right...I may not be worldly—yet—and I may only be a half-caste, but I have abilities that no other woman in England has. Why can't you at least hear me out? I've learned, I'm learning, and each day I'll become more useful. To someone," she added softly, dropping her eyes. But when she looked back up, it was clear that she had shown her hand, and that he did not particularly care for her cards.

For an instant, she thought he was going to walk out, or worse, to merely laugh at her; but instead he went toward the cold hearth and stood by the mantel, where he remained lost in thought. "Don't you realize," he said, "that what you are doing is unnecessary and won't make any difference?

"Melissa," he said, turning slowly around to face her again, "I'm not ever going to belong to anyone—not king, country, man or woman. And I refuse to be manipulated by this game of yours."

She could feel her face catch fire from shame. But it was too late for pride now. She was fighting for her life...she was fighting for her love. She was willing to take whatever small crumb she could get, as long as she did not lose him entirely. "You don't have to belong to me. Just let me...let me merely help."

"No," he said, his manner again distant. "I don't want your help. Nor do I want your grandfather's help. After this voyage to India, my ties to the House of Danfort will be completely severed. It's what I want. This is my life, I've designed it the way I want it, and I want it free from anyone's interference. There's no room for this...there's no place for *you* in my life," he said finally, coming to the point.

For an instant Melissa was too stricken to respond. Then the sorrow erupted, spewing forth as self-protective spite. "At least I'd be more good than some pretty trinket to visit in the evenings!"

Brandon studied her coolly. "Perhaps," he said. "But maybe that's all I want—a pretty trinket."

His truthfulness was a slap to her face, but she could not let the matter rest there. She had to fight Pavan in the only way open to her, and that was through her wits, through the use of the economic power that would soon be hers. She swallowed her pride and went on, determined to present her case.

"And maybe that would be a mistake. If you love your ships so much, and you value the expansion of your company so dearly, then my position is relevant to your cause. Soon I'll have the funds and the power to extend my grandfather's estate, to make investments." With a shock of disgust, she realized her voice had taken on a pleading quality.

"I will not be owned, Melissa. I will not be commanded." He started away.

"Have you considered that you may not have any choice!" There—she was not pleading now.

Brandon turned and met her eyes with a direct gaze, nodding. He smiled coldly. "So, you *are* your grandfather's child, aren't you?"

"If you walk out without even hearing what I have to say, then you may do yourself a serious disservice." She could no longer look at him. Biting her lip, she moved back to the globe. She continued, not knowing if he would leave or not, not knowing if she had lost him entirely.

She heard him move behind her, but continued talking as if he were interested. "With the American Colonies, not to mention our own country, in competition with France for raw supplies, it would be to our advantage to establish a foothold in these forgotten ports. Anyway, they're along the way. There's nothing to lose. Sometimes," she said, "forgotten ports can suddenly become valuable. I have been somewhat of a forgotten port, myself, have I not?" When she finished, she dared not move. She had heard his footsteps as she spoke and did not know if he had already gone.

There was a moment of silence, and then she felt his hands on her shoulders, turning her to him. Melissa felt a chill travel the length of her back and down her arms. *He wants me,* she thought, feeling the power of his eyes as he looked down at her, feeling the heat of his hands, even through the dress's fabric. He swallowed and then dropped his hands.

"No, Melissa . . . no, this can't be. Not any of it. Especially not us."

Turning, he took a few steps, then looked back. This time his expression and voice were solemn, and the momentary flare of passion had been banished.

"I don't deny your plan has merit," he said evenly, and she caught her breath, hope spreading deep into her heart that at least she had pleased him with her brilliance. "But there's also a time element to consider, as we must sail within the month. There's the extra financial burden of increased fees to the crew, as the voyage will then become extended. Some of the men won't want to prolong their time at sea; it will mean replacing them. That could prove a troublesome task. I want this matter finished. Do you understand? I want my freedom, Melissa. That's my final say."

"But this is to be *my* future . . . so it's I who have the final say."

He stared at her. "You're a child."

"A child, am I? Then a child with power!"

"Not nearly enough," Brandon said, and with that he did leave.

The following day she was summoned to her grandfather. A letter was in his hand.

The Duke stood, then walked slowly around his desk to where she waited. He flung the letter at her. It dropped at her feet.

She did not need to pick it up to know who it was from.

"What have you done?" the Duke exploded.

Melissa had never seen anyone so angry before. "An alternate plan. I suggested an alternate plan."

"And you killed the entire voyage!"

Melissa felt the strength draining from her limbs. Staggering slightly, she sank to the nearest chair.

"Brandon de Forrest's broken his contract. He will not captain the ship."

Melissa tried to speak. Words would hardly come. "I—"

"You what?"

"But he must," she said, still disbelieving what she had been told. Now she would not even be in his company. "If he doesn't, then you can pull his charters. He'll lose everything."

"Don't you understand?" The Duke stared at her, incredulous, as if she had sprouted another head.

"No . . . no . . ." she said, meaning it. She had felt so sure of her ground. She had all the power. She had been the Queen, sweeping over the board.

"Then I will explain. And you will listen and heed what I tell you." The Duke walked away, choosing his words; returning, he spoke to the air, now and then glaring at her. "A man like de Forrest is willing to lose everything to retain his independence. We had a business deal. He upheld his end of the bargain . . . I upheld mine. There was dignity in that. But you have taken away that dignity by insisting that he adhere to your orders. Orders. And from a woman! From a girl. From a know-nothing upstart." His words and manner were merciless, but when he spoke his next sentence, he completely destroyed her.

"You will tame your tongue. You will apologize to the man and do as he bids. If you have to get on your knees, you will get de Forrest back!"

"No, oh, no..." she pleaded. "I can't." She saw herself as she would appear to Brandon, small and foolish, a laughingstock. And then she saw Pavan: cool and elegant, dignified. And desired.

"You will."

"We could get another captain."

"There's only one man for this voyage. You sent that man away. Now get him back."

The Duke of Danfort watched his granddaughter leave the room. If she had turned, she would have seen a faint smile touch his thin lips. Things were working out rather well, he thought...all things considered. He sat down, returning to the Greek drama he had been enjoying.

Chapter Nine

Glenmillan's spirits rose and fell each time a page delivered another response to her invitation to the ball.

"Is this all?" She glared at the young man who had just brought the latest acceptance.

"All that has come, m'lady."

"It can't be. There must be others." Her eyes searched the empty silver plate on which the note had been carried.

Blanching, the boy looked down at the same plate, as if hoping to find something there by which to redeem himself. "No, madame. I'm afraid, madame, only this."

"Oh, lord," Glenmillan sighed miserably, her eyes falling on the wax seal of a great London house, but not the one insignia she coveted—that of the de Forrest crest. "Well, then, leave me, leave me." She waved him away and sank into a narrow chair to brood, her voluminous skirts rising high around her.

The gala event was only three days off, and she had yet to hear from Brandon de Forrest. She was frantic. Pavan de Noialles had already sent her acceptance, and it was absolutely imperative that Brandon be at the ball as well.

Glenmillan wrung her hands, thinking hard. She had it upon good authority from her various spies that neither of them had yet been in the other's company. This did not bode well at all. A reconciliation between the two former lovers *had* to be effected. With Brandon claimed by Pavan and safely out of the picture, Quentin would have free rein to ply his charm and snare the golden goose.

Time was of the essence and, horribly, she could feel it seeping through her fingers.

She had to think. Frowning, she rose and began to pace.

From what she understood, the goose was soon set to sail from their shores in Brandon's company. The trip to India would take seven months. In seven months anything could happen; in fact, the very worst could happen: Brandon might fall in love with the girl, and she would certainly have him as her husband.

And then where would she be, the Countess Glenmillan Danfort, who had reigned over sixteen years of Court intrigue?

Out, that's where. Out with nothing . . . except for a lot of enemies who would rip her to pieces with their sharp tongues. *Oh, she had a terrible headache.*

"Is there any good word?" Quentin asked, arriving shortly after noon in his mother's apartments. He had only just finished dressing and was outfitted in a coat of gray silk and a pink satin waistcoat. Ruffles peeked from the sleeves, and in his hand he carried a lace handkerchief that he waved with every other word, an affectation, Glenmillan noted, he had recently adopted from being in the company of that fop, Shropesmire.

Glenmillan wasn't sure she liked all the flouncing—current trends had their limits. Still, she had to admit that with his dark hair and vivid blue eyes, Quentin was by any accounts a handsome man. If only, she thought, the little minx Melissa would see him that way. But Quentin had reported the girl was moody and non-communicative in his company, and of course they both knew why: their nemesis Brandon de Forrest was the cause.

Glenmillan had been reclining upon her silk-covered divan, a damp cloth on her forehead. At Quentin's question, she sighed listlessly and pressed a hand against the material, as if to blunt a stab of pain. The other hand she let trail to the floor. "No, no word, good or otherwise. Not a single word. Only silence." And she sighed again.

Quentin's blue eyes widened, then narrowed. His voice lost its theatrical lightness and took on a tight, officious quality. "And you lie there moping! This is crucial. You must *do* something. We can't allow this opportunity to slip away. It would be fatal to our purposes."

"Well, my genius son, what do you suggest?" Glenmillan snapped. She flung the cloth to the floor and glared at Quentin. "Do you suggest that I drag de Forrest here bodily?" She laughed bitterly. "Nothing and no one can move that man."

Quentin chewed on his lip, his mind working. "Pavan moved him once. She can do the same again. Does he know Pavan will be attending?"

"If he has any ear for gossip, he knows. How could he not? I've told half of London."

"And if he has no ear for gossip? What then?"

Glenmillan thought for a moment. "Then we must be more direct. You're right, of course. Nothing can be left to chance." Suddenly revived from her torpor, she lifted herself from the divan, and with an air of determination sat down at her desk. She picked up a quill and searched about to find a piece of paper without any markings of personal identification. In a few seconds she had penned her anonymous note.

"There." She handed the missive to Quentin. "I trust you will see that this will find its way before de Forrest's nose."

Quentin made a mock bow. "Your ever faithful servant, madame. The deed is as good as done." Kissing his mother lightly on her forehead, he started away. Then, almost to the door, he spun about on his heels and said, "Oh, by-the-by, I was wondering... that is, it so happens I find myself a trifle short in the pockets these days."

"No," Glenmillan said, before he had asked for the funds outright. "It's entirely your own doing. You have your passion for *trente-et-quarante* and *ombre* and lanterloo to thank for your empty pockets."

"Actually, in the present case it was faro."

"Keep away from the gaming tables. I will not finance another evening's foolish debauchery at White's. Especially when it's all I can do to scrape by myself." Glenmillan rose from the desk. "You may leave, sir. You've an errand of some urgency, if you recall?"

Quentin put up his hand. "Now, now...you assume too much too soon. Hear me out. Rather than what you think, your largess would be for a worthy cause. I thought perhaps I could get a little something glittery for Melissa's coming-out ball. Some meaningful token of my affection that might, in turn, draw her closer to me, her ardent suitor." He raised his eyebrows and smiled, pleased with himself. "In this case, don't you think you might find your way to parting with a few pounds to be well spent? One hundred should do nicely."

But Glenmillan paled before his eyes.

Quentin felt his knees turn to water. "Oh. My. Then things truly *have* become that serious? My..." he breathed, gloom descending over his former high spirits. He gave a feeble wave of his handkerchief. "I thought you were merely being contrary."

For a moment mother and son stared across the space at each other. Then Glenmillan said, "Wait. We are not completely indigent. Yet."

And she moved fleetly to her dressing table. Stacked on its top were small boxes of varying shapes and composition, from silver and wood and porcelain to embroidered fabrics. Hunting about, she removed a small white and gold box and pulled out a bracelet of sapphires and rubies.

She held it up to the light, taking one last regretful look before handing it over to Quentin, and with dismay said, "Sell it. It should bring a good penny. Enough to get the little jade something she might show off at the ball to ward off lesser, financially well-disposed admirers. May I suggest something sentimental...hearts entwined...something of that order. She's obviously of a romantic bent, what with her mooning about over de Forrest."

Quentin tossed the circle of stones in the air and together they watched the bracelet's descent, the stones appearing to Glenmillan like sparkling blue and red tears.

"Ah," Quentin said mournfully, closing his open palm around the jewels, "the sacrifices we make to secure our meager position in this hard world." He waved his handkerchief and with a disarming smile said, "Well, *adieu*. I am off to save our skins."

Brandon had read the note twice already when Ross McKay gave his perfunctory signature knock and entered. His boots made a hollow sound over the planks of the second-story office, and his resonant voice filled the quiet with its warmth and energy. "The *Horizon*'ll be taking on the five tons of lead originally meant for Surat. There's a crying need for it in Boston, and we'll do well to make the space, even if we've got to let go of some of the wool."

Brandon looked up. His eyes seemed to refocus, as if they had been trained on a distant point in space. "How did this come here?" He held up the note he had just read.

Ross scowled, looking down at the paper. "I know nothing of this." The paper fluttered slightly in the breeze coming off the Thames through the open window. Outside, the voices of sailors and porters could be heard, along with the creaking of ships against their moorings and the clatter and thump of cargo being loaded.

"I found it on my desk. You're the only one who has admittance to my office."

Ross colored under the rebuke. "What is it?"

"Gossip." And Brandon crushed the note in his palm, hurling the ball of paper across the room. A breeze caught it, carrying it halfway back. "Gossip that someone meant for me to know and was obviously willing to take a considerable risk to see that it came into my hands."

And suddenly Ross understood. He, too, had heard the talk, but had known there was no point in bringing up the subject of Pavan to Brandon. Passion for a woman sometimes died hard in a man, especially when he had been jilted. And especially for a man of Brandon's proud nature. He did nothing without intensity, whether it be to sail a ship or fight a battle, or even to make love—if one could trust the accounts of women who had lain with him.

Whatever Brandon now felt for the Frenchwoman was bound to be complicated, a tangle of love and hate, and Ross would have preferred to stay clear of the entire matter. But Brandon himself had brought it up.

He ventured a neutral comment. "I heard she was in London."

"I had heard the news myself." Brandon lapsed into silence. His expression registered feelings that were cold and hard and private. A moment passed and he said, "We have room for both the wool and the lead."

Glad to escape the topic of Pavan, Ross said quickly, "And the iron?"

"We can take the iron as well."

"Aye, Captain, the iron goes aboard!" He turned on his heels, but Brandon's sharp voice preempted his exit.

"Wait. I've something to be delivered."

Ross watched as Brandon bent to the task of writing a note. His strokes were quick, almost angry. He sealed the missive with the de Forrest Company's insignia, of a sailing ship with a lion-headed bowsprit.

"See that it's delivered at once."

With a sinking heart, Ross accepted the message, but he was surprised and gladdened to see that it was not addressed to Pavan, but instead to the Countess Glenmillan Danfort.

Melissa's mind churned night and day, working over alternatives and remedies to her dilemma. She had no choice. Her grandfather was constantly needling her to make peace with Brandon. The Duke was merciless, showing no fatigue in his campaign. At every opportunity he pushed, prodded, commanded, insisted and threatened her.

She was brooding over her miserable situation while having the final fitting for her ball gown in Glenmillan's suite when her stepmother was called away. The woman had been in a foul mood all morning, and Melissa was more than glad to be relieved of her company, if even for a while.

The seamstress finished her tucking and pinning and clucking over Melissa's need to constantly fidget, and for several minutes, while she worked at some preliminary stitching, Melissa meandered through the room, thoughts of Brandon heavy on her mind. It was during one leg of her idle wandering that she stopped at Glenmillan's cherrywood secretary to read the list of people who had accepted the invitation to the ball. There were at least two hundred names listed, perhaps fifty more on a separate sheet, and only ten people had declined.

It was then that she saw the note.

At first it was the strong, bold slant of the script that caught her interest, but it was the signature that made her heart stop and her legs grow weak. *Brandon de Forrest.*

She read the message hungrily; this was the only contact she had had with him since her terrible mishandling of their last meeting. Briefly, tersely, he had declined the invitation to the ball. There was no explanation, not even a "regretfully" included in his response.

Melissa's mind blurred, a heavy despair settling over her as she looked at the strong sweep of his signature. It was so like him in every way that she reached forward and touched the ink, following the flow of the script with her finger as if she might reach him through the paper. She closed her eyes, willing him to feel her mind, willing him back into her life.

And as she did, the answer came to her of how she could undo the damage she had caused.

"You've a caller," said Ross, coming into Brandon's office.

Brandon stood at the chest he had taken off a Spanish galleon some years before. He was pouring himself a flagon of ale, and when he turned Ross saw by the look in his eyes that he had sampled more than a few glasses already. Ross also suspected the cause.

"I'm not seeing visitors. Send him away," Brandon said sharply.

"Her," Ross corrected, observing Brandon with a knowledgeable wariness developed out of long and intimate association. He had rarely seen Brandon drink during working hours and had only on one or two occasions in the past seen him in a heavy state of inebriation. Both times the provocation for his loss of control had been Pavan de Noialles. Silently Ross cursed the woman. Most women were devils. His mind moved to the one below, and he all but shuddered; that one had to be the queen of all the she-devils! A pretty one, aye, but trouble from the first glance he'd taken of her.

"A woman?" Brandon's back stiffened and his eyes burned more brightly. For a moment expectancy softened the ironic, world-weary resolve that was his usual expression. But along with the excitement, a dim, cruel light glowed behind the penetrating dark look he gave Ross.

"No," Ross said quietly, understanding Brandon's mistaken hope, "it's not her."

And the light faded. Brandon turned, his jaw hardening as it always did when he fought against his deeper feelings, and he moved with his mug of ale to the window. With his back to Ross, he said dully, "I'm not interested in seeing anyone."

Ross would have been content to obey orders, but in this case, the situation was more complex. He knew he had best tread carefully. "If you'll pardon me for saying so, I think it's in the company's best interest to see... to see this one."

With annoyance, Brandon glanced over his shoulder. "You heard me, Ross." His tone was sharp, lethal.

"Aye, Captain. I'll tell her you're busy."

Brandon stared out at the busy scene below his office. Ordinarily, the sight of his ships would have brought a sense of satisfaction. The familiar smells attached to his trading enterprise—that of lamp oil and oak barrels, ink and paper and the sweat of men, would have been gratifying. Now they only reminded him that he had lost himself at sea for seven years in order to forget a woman. But he had not escaped the past, as he had hoped. He found himself stranded, awash in memories.

He did not know anymore what he felt; was it still love? Or was it the need for revenge that made him wish to see Pavan's face again? He brought the pewter to his lips and drank deeply, as if the liquid might lubricate his soul and end the dryness that had become his life.

Lost in thought, he did not hear the sound of the intruder until the clear feminine voice melded with his thoughts. There came a gentle clearing of a throat, and then, "Begging your pardon... sir."

Brandon turned. For a moment he stared without registering a response. But soon his brow furrowed, and when he spoke, his tone held no welcome. "I trust you were told to leave."

"Well, yes... that is, your man—"

"Then why didn't you?" He shook his head and shrugged. "Of course, that's an idle question, isn't it? After all, during our brief but tumultuous acquaintance I've never known you to follow social convention of any kind."

Melissa had not seen him since the terrible scene at Danfort House. Although he looked as handsome as ever in his white shirt and dark brown breeches, with his black hair shining like a piece of fallen midnight, there was a strained intensity to his speech, and the dark eyes seemed as much haunted as angry when he looked at her. "I understand how this may appear, but—"

"But what in damnation gives you the gall to barge your way in here? I would have thought our last meeting had settled all accounts between us."

"Matters of grave urgency urged me to risk this... this reaction from you," Melissa replied solemnly, steeling herself against his hostility. She had, of course, anticipated his reaction to her visit. She had even expected him to refuse to see her.

"Then take your serious matter elsewhere. Our business with each other has ended. There's nothing left for us to discuss. I should think that would be plain enough. You may leave now—the same way you entered, on your own."

She turned, but rather than go, she closed the heavy oak door. Then she leaned against it and unclasped the button of her cloak, knowing full well that no matter how angry he was, he could not help but find her attractive today.

She had spent the morning preparing for their meeting, and her dress was as beautiful as any Pavan or Glenmillan or a thousand other women might own. The silk champagne-colored fabric caught every nuance of light, and blended with her hair. Her velvet cloak was of the same shade, and was trimmed in brown mink tails. An emerald necklace given to her by the Duke, one having belonged to his wife, sparkled at her neck, and diamond and emerald earrings glittered against her fair skin.

Hiding her fear and desperation, she let the cloak fall slowly and gracefully from her shoulders. The cloth caught at her elbows, providing a graceful frame around her, and the dress was fully displayed to his view. More importantly, so was her body. But her heart raced; her fingers were numb from fright.

Brandon's eyes coursed over her figure, moving languidly along the high, full thrust of her breasts and down to the small waist and flaring skirt.

Warmth returned to her body; she had succeeded.

She knew the look well enough, and coming from Brandon, it thrilled her. Hot and admiring glances from men generally accompanied her progress these days. But it was never the attention of other men she craved. Everything she did to beautify herself was done as a dress rehearsal for the moments she would have with Brandon. A moment such as this one.

Brandon's lips curved in a slow, faintly suggestive smile. "Yes," he said, as if he had read her thoughts. "You're very beautiful today. So," he asked, a tinge of irony creeping into his voice, "is this your urgent business? To seduce me? If so, I can assure you, madame, it would be no particular triumph on your part. At the present moment—as you may or may not have noticed—I am slightly into my cups. Almost anyone would do, and I most likely wouldn't remember a bit of the ecstasy we would share."

He turned from her and went back to his chest to refill his cup.

"I've come on my grandfather's behalf," she said stiffly, hiding from him how much his words had hurt. As always, he made her feel transparent and stupid.

Brandon shot her a look of disbelief. "The Duke and I have ended our business together." He smiled slightly. "All that's left is his ax to fall on my head. We both know that, Melissa, so there's no purpose to this meeting."

"Some things don't end, at least not that easily," she said, and she thought of her love for Brandon. Then she thought of his love for another woman, and a part of her wanted to strike back at him, to wound him in some way, just as he had insulted her. But more than that, she wished to be in his company...forever if she could. She had come knowing she would have to pay a price, and this groveling was it.

Swallowing her pride, she made her way more deeply into the room. She placed the velvet cloak on a table and said, "You couldn't know...the Duke has taken seriously ill." A fabrication, of course, but it might have been true. "His heart has failed him and there's little time left. I've come here for this reason, even knowing...what you felt about me. It's for him I've come. It would be so generous of you if you could visit him."

"I lost my generous spirit some years ago. It was squeezed out of me by your grandfather."

"Perhaps you're not aware, but he's very fond of you."

At that, Brandon threw back his head and laughed. Turning to face her, he said wryly, "Come now, what kind of a fool do you take me for? Your grandfather is not fond of a single living creature."

"Oh, but you're so wrong," she objected vigorously. "He's a proud and complicated man. He hides his true feelings."

"Your grandfather is a clever, manipulative, unfeeling politician." He paused and drank down another swallow of ale. For a moment he was thoughtful, then he said, "If he wants me at all, it's because he knows that you've made a mess of things, and he hopes to prey upon my sympathies—of which I have none at all—to lure me back into his sphere of control. Frankly, I'm surprised. His mind must also be giving way, otherwise he'd have known I was immune to such obvious ploys." Brandon moved to the window again. "Tell him, if you must report anything, that India is a dead issue. I'm prepared to pay whatever price is due for my independence."

Melissa was beginning to panic. At any second she'd be tossed out. This was her one and only opportunity to draw him back to her.

"I can assure you," she lied further, but she hoped convincingly, "you've entirely the wrong impression of my grandfather. Perhaps he might have once seemed hardened to you, but his soul has changed greatly during these last remaining days of his life. I promise, you'd hardly know him as the same man." She had been moving steadily closer to Brandon, inching her way as if approaching a wild creature. "If you would just consider his invitation to the ball. It is, he feels, his last social engagement." She paused for effect. "To have his dearest friends with him . . . well, it would mean everything."

She was by this time within inches of where Brandon stood. When he turned, they were almost touching.

"There's no point to this discussion," he said coldly, looking down at her with scorn. "I've work to do. And I'm sure you have voyages to chart," he added sarcastically.

"But—" The objection died on her lips as he moved her aside. She could only watch helplessly as he grabbed up the cloak she had left on the table and, without pausing, returned to drape it over her shoulders.

For a moment they were connected. Neither of them moved.

But she could feel his thoughts, could sense the yearning of his body. If they stayed like this forever, she would have been glad. But the moment of enchantment would not last; even now she could feel the familiar feeling of loss as the tension between them shifted, as his stubborn resolve to have nothing to do with her began to displace the

existing magic. Like sand through an hourglass, the opportunity to recapture the relationship they had once
shared was slipping...slipping.... It was all but gone. And
at the same time that he withdrew his touch, she lost herself to grief and love, and turned to him, desperate to keep
their connection.

Her hand reached out. Her fingers were light against his
arm, but the touch was enough to stay him.

"Don't send me away," she whispered pleadingly. She
searched his eyes and with joy found what she needed. "It
isn't what you want. It isn't what I want...."

"What I want," he said, a dull flush creeping to his face,
"is one thing. But what you want, Melissa, past this, is
more than I am willing to give you." His words were a
warning.

"I know," Melissa said, willing to agree to his terms. In
her heart she believed that once she could demonstrate her
love, no power on earth would draw him from her. Not
even Pavan could take him. She did not look away like a
frightened girl this time but held his eyes so that he could
be sure she was a woman who knew her own mind and
body.

He closed his eyes and, drawing in a tortured breath,
pulled her roughly against him. "You're a beautiful fool,
Melissa. I ought to throw you out."

His breath was warm against her neck, and yet she
shivered, sighing with happiness. "I wouldn't go...."

"I know!" he laughed.

"Brandon, I love—"

"Don't...don't, Melissa," he said into her ear. "Don't
make beautiful speeches about this. Don't make declarations." He placed a finger lightly against her lips. "Don't
expect anything but this, Melissa." He made a vague,
helpless motion with one hand. "I'm not offering you
more."

He was looking at her, but in the reflection of his eyes,
Melissa saw Pavan's image, not her own. *She was only a
substitute for the one he truly wanted!* The pain that the
realization brought her was great, but she allowed it. She

had no alternative. To be separated from him would be a far greater hell to endure. Besides, she told herself, she would make him forget all about Pavan; she would make him love *her*. She only needed this chance.

"You're very beautiful, my dangerous, troublesome little green-eyed cat, and God help me for wanting you after all the misery you've caused. But I do...God knows I do." The dark eyes smoldered, and she knew that at least now it was *her* body he craved, hers and not Pavan's. She also knew that it was only this he wanted, the physical pleasure, the temporary release from his lonely pain of loving someone he couldn't have.

It didn't matter. She wanted *him*. And when he bent his mouth to hers, she returned his kiss with the pent-up passion of all the many days and nights she had lived with no more than the fantasy of this moment.

A sense of urgency enveloped them both as they came together, and for an instant they were two forces of equal desire, without names and histories, without right or wrong; only the need to touch and taste and lose themselves to their hunger.

And it was precisely this urgent, overpowering need that a moment later made Brandon break from their embrace. "No, Melissa...this can't be. It's wrong. I must be mad to think—" He ran a hand over his face. "I've had too much to drink, too much...."

"Ale's not responsible for this. Oh, Brandon...it's not the ale doing this to you," she said, breathing hard, her breasts rising and falling beneath the silk. "You can't tell me that. You can't believe that! You want me...*me*, Brandon." She was almost crying.

"No, Melissa. You have illusions about us that aren't real."

"Illusions? I have no illusions. Do you think that I can't feel what's real? Do you think I'm a child still, to be played with like a toy? To be taught a lesson about life? To be discarded so easily? Is that it? Too much has happened to me. Oh, Brandon...a lifetime has happened to me since we first met that evening in Cornwall." Her eyes were alight with rage and frustration and hurt. "Do you think that I haven't heard about Pavan? I know, Brandon. I know it's her you want in your arms, in your bed! But you want me, too! And you'll grow to love me. I know you will, and—"

"Shut up!" he said, having advanced on her as she spoke. His face was dark and angry.

"You're afraid," she said in wonder, in that split second reading the truth in his eyes. "You're afraid that you *might* love me! You're afraid that—"

He grasped her by the shoulders and she gave a cry of surprised anguish. "No," he said brutally, "I could never love you, Melissa. Not ever. You're not only beautiful, you also happen to be everything in life that I have grown to despise." For a split second both looked at the other, and then Melissa whirled about and flew toward the door.

Her fingers gripped the handle, but as she tugged, she was wrenched away, spun around and hurled with force against the hard oak door.

"Let me go!" she screamed at him, twisting her body to be free. "If you find me so—so repulsive, then let me go! I swear you'll never, *never* see me again!" Tears welled in her eyes and slid down her cheeks in rivulets.

But he didn't release her. His body strained against hers, fevered and cruel in its force. She heard him secure the bolt behind her. Then, his hands framing her face, he looked at her fiercely and brought his mouth against hers. His tongue searched, explored, the message urgent. She did not resist. His need was hers in equal measure.

He buried his face against her neck, and whatever remained of her resolve to flee from the disastrous meeting was scorched to ashes by the brush of his lips against her skin. Arching back, she made herself available, vulnerable, and she gave a small, faint cry of joy and sorrow. The love she had dreamed of was not to be hers, and she had no choice but to settle for the passion.

"Yes, yes…" he said in a rush, his face pressed into the mass of thick fair curls, "I want you. I have wanted you since I first looked at you in Cornwall. And I have wanted you at night when I lay awake. But I do not love you. I do not love you, Melissa,'' he said insistently, repeating it over and over, even as he ravaged her with his mouth.

''But I love you—'' she began, trying to salvage the sacred moment she had envisioned in her dreams.

He silenced her with a hurtful kiss. ''Don't,'' he said, lifting her chin so that she would read in his face how serious he was. The black eyes bore into her, angry again, commanding, and Melissa felt that even now he might draw away from her. ''It can't be the way you want. It can only be this way.'' And once again Brandon's face was a moving canvas of desire as he cupped the underside of her breasts, thrusting the pale mounds of flesh up above the silk bodice to meet his mouth.

Against her legs, even through the layers of underskirts she wore, she could feel his male organ, stiff and hard, and suddenly, though she wanted him, she was also afraid. From this point on she would never be the same.

But his hands were as certain as his mouth against her flesh, and she did not protest when he tore at the fastenings of her gown, pulling away her bodice and dropping her shift from her shoulders.

She had never allowed any man to look upon her before, and now, as Brandon brought her breasts between his hands, brushing his thumbs over her nipples until they hardened into taut peaks, she felt at once wild with desire and shameful to be naked. His eyes were glazed pools of desire when he looked from her bare skin to her eyes.

''Am I . . . ?'' And she felt foolish to have begun the question.

Understanding, he smiled slightly and answered in a voice that was tight and hoarse and unfamiliar to her ears. ''Beautiful? You are the most beautiful woman I've ever seen.''

For a wild, tempestuous instant, she wanted to ask if she were more beautiful than Pavan, but his mouth had found a breast and all thought ceased.

It was hardly an effort for him to remove her undergarments, and when he lifted her off her feet and brought her to a small narrow bed against a far wall, she made no protest. Her heart hammered wildly. It wasn't to be like this— not this way.... She had dreamed of it differently during her nights of longing.

But it was, of course, to be exactly this way.

There were various items on the bed. He threw off a coil of heavy rope and a cotton bag stuffed with what appeared to be clothes, and placed her upon the mattress. His own clothes were removed next, quickly, with his eyes raking over her body. Comfortable in his nakedness, he stood before her, the first man she had ever seen uncovered. He smiled knowingly as her eyes widened, and there was no shyness in him as he watched her eyes examine his form. He touched himself even as her eyes did, and slowly, with mesmerizing sensuality, walked to the bed and sank to his knees.

Pulling her forward to the edge of the bed, he twisted her around and buried his face against her stomach, his hands and tongue moving restlessly but gently over her flesh, so that Melissa shuddered as if racked by a sudden fever. Her hands twined in his dark hair, and she released it from its binding so that it fell loose to the sides of his face.

She did not know anymore what she was doing, nor did she care that he had complete control over her body. She felt her legs being parted, and her first thought was of modesty. But then a flood of warmth spilled from her as his fingers explored the wet triangle, and she stiffened against the delirious savagery of her feelings.

"Brandon," she gasped. Her eyes closed against the pleasure, then opened to look at him as her thoughts fragmented at the pleasure of his searching tongue.

The pressure of his mouth was more than she could bear, and she was afraid... afraid of the pleasure... afraid that she would be rendered senseless by the ecstasy.... And then suddenly all thoughts dissolved, splintering into a dark void at whose end a white hot star beckoned and at last claimed her.

She had never known...never known... And as the tide ebbed, Brandon moved atop her, his face taut with need, the black eyes absorbing her into him as he thrust slowly forward. There was a brief, sharp pain as he entered. She stifled a cry, but he knew...and he waited. "Is it bad?" he asked her, a caring tenderness mixing with the urgency in his voice.

Answering him with her body, she pulled him more tightly against her, and slowly they were matched in a rhythmic flow of liquid motion.

Their release was simultaneous and explosive. At the peak, he threw back his head, straining, and cried out her name. When he focused his eyes on her, he said, "Melissa...Melissa...Melissa." And she knew then that it was she and not Pavan he had made love to. No matter what he had said, no matter what he claimed later, she could at least be certain that he had wanted *her* now.

Afterward, he held her. The quiet aftermath was almost as good in its own way as the joining of their bodies had been. She could feel the beat of his heart. His body was slick with moisture and she moved her fingers softly over his skin, luxuriating in the feel of the man she loved. Slowly their breathing subsided to a soft even flow, and she felt herself at peace in his arms, completely happy, drifting into a dream in which this closeness would never end.

But it did. A moment later, Brandon roused her, saying, "Melissa...it's time you go."

His voice saying her name was far different than it had been a short time ago, now it was sharp and hard and distant.

He slipped from their embrace—escaped, it seemed to Melissa—and when he brought her discarded garments to her, his face had also altered, and he wore an expression of tense self-loathing.

Devastated by the change, Melissa looked up at him, searching for signs of the closeness they had shared. "It doesn't have to be this way," she said softly. "It doesn't have to..."

"End," he finished bluntly. He looked at her briefly, but went busily about his own dressing, collecting not only his clothes, but his emotional armor as well. "Yes, it does have to end. As you told me—as you assured me—you aren't a child. And I'd say you proved that." He glanced at her and, for a flicker of an instant, the man who had so passionately made love to her returned. But in the next breath he was góne, and a man with cold, hard eyes said, "You knew what the situation was before we—"

"Made love," Melissa finished dully.

He hesitated, staring at her for a moment before saying, "Don't delude yourself, Melissa. You'll only make it harder on yourself."

"I'm not," she said stubbornly but softly. "I know what I felt."

"But you don't know what I felt."

"You wanted me."

"Wanted you." He shook his head. "*Wanted* you. You're a beautiful woman. A man would be out of his mind not to want to lie with you. But that's no more than a physical act, and when you've had more experience in life, you'll understand."

"You're so cruel," she said, her eyes filling.

"You force me to be. You came here. You wanted this, you worked to make this happen. You understood how it was to be—and now it's that way. So do us both a service and get dressed, return to your ailing grandfather, inherit his wealth and find a man who will love you as you deserve to be loved. He'll give you children, and—"

"Don't!" Melissa said, her green eyes wild with despair. "I will not love another man. I will not have another man's child. And I will never forget that the man who made love to me today loved me. I will have no man but you."

Brandon stared down at her. His voice was as hollow as the look in his dark eyes. "Then you shall have no man at all. Because, Melissa, believe me when I tell you that you will never have me."

He left her, and she dressed as best she could. Unable to manage the intricacies of her costume, usually handled by Annie, she finally covered her failure with the cloak. She did not cry. She could feel nothing but a dull emptiness as she moved across Brandon's office, a room that had so briefly been paradise, and out the door.

She neither heard nor saw the world about her as the coach traversed the city, returning to Danfort House. The sights and sounds and smells of Covent Garden's confused markets, which in the past had thrilled Melissa, she passed as though they weren't there. Nothing in the world had any meaning for her. She felt like a maiden in a fairy story, a silly thing who had been given one wish and had squandered it. Had she not succumbed to temptation, had she been more dignified, more aloof—more of everything that Pavan de Noialles was—then she might have avoided this disaster. She might have persuaded him to attend the ball. There, they might have eased into some sort of personal relationship that could have flowered gradually.

But, instead, things had gone too far. Now all was lost. Forever.

From his window, Brandon watched Melissa Danfort climb into her coach. His face was grim and unforgiving. Behind him he heard Ross McKay's knock, and then footsteps.

"My apologies," Ross said, speaking to Brandon's back. "Believe me, I didn't even know she had sneaked past me until I saw her leave just now. Spunky wench, isn't she? And beautiful," he added somewhat wistfully.

Brandon turned, and the look on his face made Ross hold his tongue. "What do you think? That I'm a soft fool for a pretty woman?"

"Of course not," returned Ross. "The thought never entered my mind."

"To hell with you." And Brandon turned back to the window. He wanted to watch her drive away, wanted to feel the pain completely, wanted the ache to burn into him until there was nothing left of his insides and he would never, never be reduced to feeling anything again. *He did not want to love her.*

Chapter Ten

It was to have been the most important occasion of her life. Certainly by everyone else the ball was considered the crowning jewel of the London social season.

But instead of the thrill that a young woman of eighteen might experience at being presented to the most glittering folk in London—not to mention those guests who had traveled from as far off as Italy and Germany to attend the gala—Melissa found herself leaden with fatigue.

The fatigue was pervasive, and more than physical, it was emotional. There was no point to anything anymore. Life was dull, meaningless, even bitter now that she could no longer even dream of a future with Brandon.

It was an hour before her formal presentation. Already guests were gathering below, and Annie and Glenmillan were in a frenzy over making last-minute alterations and improvements in her appearance.

"Lud, m'lady, but you'll stop the heart of every gallant there t'night," exclaimed Annie in a breathless rush. "Your complexion's like ivory...and your eyes, madame...with the makeup...it's as if the entire sea were locked inside, clear and deep as can be. Any man'll drown in 'em for sure," she continued lavishly, and then giggled at her lyrical flight.

"You've been reading too many of those penny pamphlets," Glenmillan groaned, rolling her eyes to the ceiling. But even Glenmillan was wont to wax poetic, and she exclaimed a moment later that "There hasn't been a gown

like this in fifty years…maybe a hundred…perhaps never
in the entire history of the realm.'' Melissa smiled at that.
Glenmillan had designed the gown herself. ''You will shine
tonight with the brilliance of a thousand tapers, my dear.''

Melissa accepted all the praise with the detachment of
the dead.

The two women continued to exclaim about the size,
color and design of the diamond and amethyst jewels the
Duke had lavished upon her, to complement the gown.

But Melissa hardly paid any notice to her admiring audience. Her mind was lost to the constant stream of female chatter. For the past few days, she had survived the
futility of her life by obsessively going over and over the
only thing she would find worth remembering for the rest
of her life: the day she had made love with Brandon. For
that is how she thought of it—as love—no matter what he
had said.

She was ready when Quentin arrived. Glenmillan had
finally left to join the guests on the ground floor of the
palace, and not being able to stand Annie's hysterical
concern that she not muss her hair or gown or makeup,
Melissa had finally sent the girl away. But Annie's fears
were all for naught; left on her own, Melissa sat still as a
stone, removed from the world around her.

When Quentin knocked, she barely heard him, until finally the clamor roused her to say, ''Yes, come.…''

And she sighed upon seeing him; a glimpse of so much
robust enthusiasm drained her. As always when in her
company, he wore a perpetually alert expression, one that
made her ill at ease. It was as if he were constantly hoping
for something she was not prepared to offer.

In this case, she knew the purpose of his visit, and with
obedient resignation she rose from her chair. It had been
decided that Quentin would escort her down the wide
length of the main staircase. Her grandfather was engaged as host to the guests already arrived.

''Ah…'' Quentin gasped at the first sight of her and
took a step back, as if blown off balance by the powerful

force of her beauty. "But surely you're not mortal," he breathed. "Your hair... the jewels... your dress..."

"Which appears incredibly like your own outfit in color," said Melissa, looking him over in turn.

"Well," said Quentin, staring down at his violet-and-cream-colored suit, "so it does. We have Glenmillan to thank for that, I suppose."

Melissa's own gown was a work of art. Made from purple and white brocaded silk, on which hundreds of pale pink silk roses had been fashioned, each with its own dainty stem and green leaf, it showed her figure to full advantage. Her small waist had never appeared as narrow, and the tops of her smooth white breasts, thrust forward and up by the stays, tantalized from above the square neckline. And her hair... well, Monsieur Fountaine had considered her hair his supreme masterpiece. The weeks he had spent in rehearsal for the grand performance had paid off handsomely—even Melissa could not dispute that. Small semiprecious stones in pink and green glittered like stars amid the woven curls he had arranged to frame her face. The Frenchman had all but swooned at the sight of his final creation, which was followed by a venal hint from him that additional recompense might be in order.

And now Quentin appeared every bit as captured by her appearance. "May I—" he said, stammering "—might I—" He came to within a foot of her, and with a graceful bow and a flourish, presented a small silver box. "A small token to commemorate this very great occasion."

Opening it, Melissa found a bracelet of diamonds and pearls, the mixture both delicate and dazzling.

"You'll note," said Quentin, as he nimbly fastened it around her wrist, "that the diamonds are hard as eternity, signifying lasting love... and the pearls are the tears of one who loves without hope."

As he spoke, Melissa's eyes filled with tears of the very hopelessness he mentioned. "That's beautiful," she said, and seized by an overflow of emotion, suddenly needing human contact, she threw her arms around him.

Quentin, in his turn, stared into space over her shoulder. The display of affection had rendered him mute with surprise. He was hardly able to believe that his effort to romance her had been so successful, even though he had worked on the speech with Glenmillan for hours. *There was hope for him, after all.* However, if jewels and poetry were the way to her heart, it would be an expensive path to follow. Glenmillan would just have to cough up some other trinket.

"You're beautiful," he said, finally remembering to bring his arm up to hold her just as she slipped away.

As they walked down the stairs together, Melissa caught the light from her wrist—the diamonds of eternity flashing and the tears of one who loves without hope filling her with thoughts and feelings of Brandon. How strange that it was Quentin, of all people, who had found the perfect token to bind her to the memory of Brandon.

She was, of course, a dazzling success, just as Glenmillan had envisioned she would be. Before she had even reached the bottom step, a river of admiring sighs flowed through the crowd assembled in the enormous entry, with other curious spectators spilling out from the grand salon. Wouldn't they all die if they knew she was a half-caste? she wondered. With a sense of satisfaction she realized she was wise enough, at least, to recognize hypocrisy.

Melissa carried off her role with aplomb. It was curious, she thought, as she walked smiling through the masses of glittering, twittering bodies, how easy it was to go about life's business when nothing mattered.

Of course Quentin claimed the first dance with her, but after that a continuing stream of young and old men sought her partnership. Quentin was obligated by social dictates to let her be snatched quite literally from his clutches, but wherever she was, she felt his eyes fixed on her.

Likewise, her own attention became riveted on Pavan de Noialles.

If there was any other woman there that night who seemed to hold the attention of those gathered at the ball, it was the Frenchwoman. Her satin gown was white and encrusted with thousands of tiny seed pearls. With her striking white hair, she appeared to Melissa like a beautiful snowflake as she drifted by on the arms of her many partners. Once, in passing, their eyes touched, and Melissa felt a powerful wave of jealous resentment rise up from her lethargy.

It was Pavan who owned Brandon's heart. It was Pavan who had come to reclaim him. It was Pavan who would live out her days in Brandon's life. It was Pavan Melissa wished would be gone from the face of the earth.

She was drowning in her thick soup of envy when Quentin reappeared to lead her through the steps of a minuet, and for a moment, as they spun into the center of the dance floor, Melissa lost sight of Pavan. The jealousy ebbed, and a short time later, Melissa again found herself safely cloaked by leaden disinterest in the world about her.

In fact, so detached was she that she barely noticed the sudden murmur, twisting of bodies and craning of necks among the guests.

It was Quentin who ended her blissful ignorance.

"Ah, I see that a guest of particular distinction has thought fit to enliven our little gathering tonight. I daresay, if it isn't that attractive rogue Brandon de Forrest."

At the mention of Brandon's name, Melissa's heart soared. Every particle of her being sizzled, burning with life. Her heart was light, weightless, flying, as her eyes sought his presence in the crowded room.

"Where?" she asked eagerly, no longer caring what Quentin or Glenmillan or anyone else knew about her feelings. Only Brandon occupied her mind. She searched the room for the shining black hair, as dark and lustrous as a raven's.

Her mind was on fire: *so he had reconsidered; he did care about her!*

She would be more dignified this time...she would be perfect in every way, even kind. Yes, she would forgive him his coldness, his cruelty. Oh, to be in his arms again! "Oh, where is he?" she pleaded of Quentin, her frustration mounting.

And Quentin showed her. Slowly guiding her about, he nodded and said, "Why, he's there. You see him now, don't you? He's with her...with Pavan de Noialles. Don't they look marvelous together? A perfect match...look for yourself. He *is* a devilishly handsome man, isn't he? I can understand why everyone falls in love with him upon sight. He's as handsome as she's beautiful. One can almost feel the passion, can't one?"

Melissa could feel only a numbing, blinding misery. And when Quentin held her more closely to him, she hardly noticed.

He had come for Pavan—not her.

Brandon de Forrest surveyed the scene before him.

Colors of every hue swam before his eyes, the vision a patchwork held together by silver and gold thread, with silks and heavy brocades brought to these shores most likely by some of his own ships.

His own habit was of snowy white silk brocade, both jacket and knee breeches trimmed in gold. His shoes were of the finest delicate leather and encrusted with gilt fleurs-de-lis, with the typically French pattern also etched in golden thread upon his white stockings.

One by one he felt eyes discover him. He knew why, and had expected this. Smiling to himself, he began to stroll through the large salon, nodding to those he knew and cared to acknowledge, ignoring those in whom he had no interest. But tonight, he knew, friend and foe alike would have something to talk about.

Then he saw her... and their eyes touched for the first time in seven years.

He felt as if he were hurled back in time.

It was impossible to deny: her beauty still produced the same potent effect as when he had first set eyes on her. And she wore white, the same as he. They had worn white then, too.... So long ago, Brandon thought. So long ago.

He moved toward her as if borne on wings, their gazes still joined. She smiled faintly; he returned the smile.

Seven years.

He was no longer poor. He was no longer young. He was no longer the idealistic, infatuated fool Pavan had last seen. *And discarded.* But, he thought with a dosage of brutal honesty, he was still a fool. Were he not, he would not have come at all.

He reached her side and, bowing formally, said in French, "I have admired you from afar. Your beauty surpasses that of an angel." They were the same words he had spoken to her seven years before. How young he had been, how innocent. And although his choice of words was intentional, he did not allow the irony he felt to creep into his tone. Rather, he enjoyed the subtlety, and knew Pavan would notice.

"You are too kind, monsieur," she replied modestly.

The same words she had spoken to him.

"May I have the honor of this dance, madame?"

And Pavan dipped her head slightly, the blue eyes looking upward into his, questions flowing from their depths. "*Oui*, Monsieur." She offered her hand, and as he drew her to him, he heard her say softly, "And you may have far more than that."

Suddenly it seemed that seven years had melted away.

The sight of Brandon holding Pavan was too much for Melissa to bear. She wanted to run, to hide from the shame she experienced. She hated herself. Such a fool she was! She had exposed her deepest feelings and given her most sacred gift to a man who could not care for her ever…just as he had told her—that is, as he had *tried* to tell her. But she had been deaf and blind to the reality he had tried to make her see.

Well, now she saw. She saw him holding the woman he loved.

And Melissa hated him with as fierce a passion as she had loved him an instant before. She closed her eyes, searching within for the strength to last out this torturous evening.

The music ended and she was swallowed up again by a coterie of admiring guests. She supposed she smiled at them; perhaps she nodded; once or twice she may have spoken. She didn't know what she was doing. Her head swam. Her heart pounded. Her pulse was like a team of wild horses. And always in her mind was the knowledge that somewhere beyond the circle of faces surrounding her, the two most beautiful people on earth were in each other's arms.

The music began again. Quentin captured her, delivering her to the center of the dance floor. To be precise, he positioned her right beside Brandon and Pavan.

"I'd like to sit down," she whispered to Quentin.

"But this is a favorite piece of mine," he said quickly.

"I find it not to my liking," Melissa returned, and began to pull from him. When he gripped her hand more tightly, she continued, "I said I—"

"The guest of honor must at least appear to be having a good time," he interrupted, his eyes telling her more than his statement.

And she suddenly realized that he was doing this to her purposefully, to humiliate her for having turned him away so many times. At the very least he meant to teach her a lesson, to make it even more plain to her that she would never have the man she loved. Had there been the slightest doubt of his objective in her mind, his next words erased it.

"I do not mean to be cruel," Quentin whispered in a low, urgent voice, "which is what I fear you suspect are my motives."

"I have no idea of what you mean," she returned.

"I mean only to spare you pain, Melissa. You mean so much to me, and you have no idea of the wolves that lurk in this forest that is London."

"I have some notion by now, I'd say."

"Then you must realize that de Forrest will never be available to any woman—unless it's Pavan. That's always been common knowledge. A hundred women have tried to win the man and have failed. Don't make a fool of yourself over him. I pray, Melissa, that you have more pride and intelligence than to include yourself among his hapless admirers."

"You needn't lose any sleep on my account."

"Mustn't I?" Quentin returned coldly. "Your eyes, Melissa...your eyes betray the conviction of your words."

"Then perhaps it's your own sight that's defective, Quentin. You're seeing what's not there." She held her head high in defiance, determined now to see the dance through to the end. Her eyes looked straight ahead, into Quentin's, and the slow smile that spread across his face was bright with triumph. Why not? Melissa thought. After all, he had had his way.

As they danced, he now and then said something. She didn't listen. She merely continued to die, little by little, degree by degree, while on the outside looking splendidly happy should Brandon chance to notice her.

But clearly, that was another of her ridiculous notions!

How plain it was that for Brandon the world consisted entirely of the irresistible Pavan. Even as Melissa stole a secretive glance at the magnificent couple, the French beauty's light, fluting laughter brought enchantment to his expression. She saw him whisper into Pavan's ear.

Melissa recalled the warm caress of his breath over her own skin.

Pavan nodded, and when she broke away from his embrace, it was with a knowing smile that invited him to follow her through the crowd.

Melissa was not alone in her recent observations, and if her heart had shattered at the sight of Brandon and Pavan escaping from the ball, Quentin's spirits had risen to such heights that it was all he could do to contain himself from issuing a triumphant shout. *The deed was done!*

He had missed nothing. Not a single nuance of the affair being renewed between the two former lovers had escaped his attention. Without a second thought he would lay his life on the line, wagering that Brandon de Forrest and Pavan de Noialles would be lying in each other's arms in a sweaty heap before the hour was out.

And he would equally wager that before the month was out, he would be betrothed to Melissa Danfort, and he and Glenmillan would never have to worry again.

It was all he could do to finish the dance with Melissa, who was clearly as deflated as he was inflated with excitement. It was entirely safe to leave her now, and as soon as the music stopped, he excused himself to have an urgent word with Glenmillan.

Abandoned by Quentin, Melissa longed for peace and, although it was impossible, seclusion. But instead, she found herself the center of attention. Her stomach quaked as she murmured polite trivialities. Her eyes stung from the effort of holding back her tears. From inside out she felt as if she were coming apart at the seams. She fought away the crazy impulse to declare to those who crowded her with their eager and false smiles that she—the darling of the evening, of the season!—was a half-breed. They would scatter as if she had proclaimed herself a carrier of the black plague. Then, at least, she would have peace in which to quietly die.

But the music took up again, gay and lilting, and across the room she caught sight of Quentin rushing back to reclaim her for the next dance.

With every step he took toward her, she felt that much more deeply and irrevocably damned. She knew that Quentin wanted her for more than a dance and the idea of spending a night in his bed, or a lifetime as his wife, after knowing the ecstatic union she'd shared with Brandon, was so hideously wrong that she felt herself grow faint with revulsion.

But there was, at the moment, no way to escape his fevered and determined attentions. She sighed and closed her eyes, awaiting the inevitable. It came at once; her hand was swiftly claimed.

Opening her eyes, she was met by the amazing sight of Quentin's smile collapsing as she was twirled into the crowded mass of bodies.

It was Brandon who held her.

Her mind swam with joyous confusion as she felt him guide her through the steps of the dance. All eyes were on her... on them... and she could feel the speculation rampant among the guests as to what Brandon's return meant.

She wanted to touch his face, to throw herself against him and feel his heart beat against her own, just as when they had lain together.

But, of course, she could not show these feelings.

She had not forgotten the pain, nor her anger, nor her resolve to comport herself with dignity. Whatever his return meant, she would do well to recall his last words to her. He would never allow himself to be joined with a woman beyond the physical liaisons he occasionally made.

And she would also be wise to heed Quentin's words, for regardless of their bitter sting, they were true.

"It's good of you to come," she said stiffly, fighting against the thrill of his touch. "My grandfather will be much pleased by your presence."

"I'm sorry to disappoint you—your grandfather was not the reason I came."

And then he said no more.

Her heart raced to her throat, stifling her breath. *Why did you come?* her mind shouted. *Why? Was it for me you came? Or... was it for her?*

The music stopped, as if it, too, waited to hear the truth, glorious or horrible though it might be.

"Melissa..." he began, then hesitated. His smile of assurance faded and the deep, charcoal-colored eyes darkened, smoldering, as he looked into her face...

Just as Quentin claimed her hand and drew her away.

Chapter Eleven

He did not sleep the whole night for thinking of her. At last, at three in the morning, Brandon tossed aside his covers and rose from his bed to stare out his window into the foggy darkness of the sleeping city.

He had not gone to see the Danfort girl—or so he told himself.

He had gone for Pavan. He had gone to the ball in order to satisfy himself that Pavan no longer owned his soul, and at least in this matter he could claim some degree of satisfaction.

Strange how it had turned out, strange and unsettling, this visit to the past. The night had turned into the surprise of his life.

Below in the street, a carriage passed, its small lanterns glowing like eyes in the fuzzy gray night. The sound of horses' hooves filled the silence for a moment. Then the lonely, hollow quiet returned and he was once again plagued by his thoughts.

The truth was, he was almost sad to be free of Pavan's spell. In a way he would almost welcome it back. At least those feelings were by now predictable, understandable, a far cry from the unmanageable position in which he now found himself.

He had lived with his sentimental pathos for so many years that he actually felt its loss, much as if a difficult person he had known for a long time had died. There was relief—but also the undeniable tinge of regret.

Seeing her at the ball, dressed so spectacularly—and ironically—in her virginal white gown, he had found Pavan as beautiful as ever. At least there had been no disappointment there. And, likewise, initially she had shown herself to be as scintillating, as captivating, as mercurially entrancing as he remembered.

And yet, in spite of everything, after a few moments he began to find her...strangely dull, her conversation derivative of a thousand other conversations with a thousand other women he had known over the years. The realization came as a shock. She was not the goddess of his dreams, after all. Like others of her gender and social position, she was more or less predictable, not exceptional as his youthful idealism had allowed him to think. Her patter was practiced to a fine art, but it was talk without substance. The minutes in her company passed, and his bedazzlement began to wane...and yet, even as it did, he wanted to clutch back his dreams.

They had danced. Oh, yes, and he could not deny that for a moment it had been magic to feel her in his arms again—the seven years vanishing into time as if they had never happened.

She had murmured into his ear, inviting him to the garden, to a small gazebo where she assured him Glenmillan Danfort had promised them complete privacy.

For an instant he had been tempted to go with her. Yes, for an instant he had wanted her with as much intensity as he had seven years before, that day when they had first made love in a boathouse on her family's estate.

He had even gone so far as to follow her halfway to the gazebo. And suddenly he had stopped.

Pavan had turned to him, her blue eyes changed to dark glistening pools shining in the starlight, questioning, inviting him, luring him to come deeper into the shadows where she promised ecstasy.

And that was when he was certain he no longer wanted her.

For the first time, he saw Pavan as she truly was. He found himself facing a woman whose character was shallow, who was dedicated to romantic conquests having no more meaning to her than a new frock she desired to own. Once she had even cast him off. But he had risen from the ashes as a new man, and she wanted to test her charms again. That was the depth of her attraction to him. *What a fool he'd been.*

As she waited for him to follow, he saw her certainty waver—a slight flicker of light behind the eyes, a subtle twist of the head. She was a lioness gauging her quarry.

Her history, which he'd followed over the years through the channels of gossip replayed itself in his mind. He had listened, but had chosen not to hear. Now he recalled each telling remark. The woman he had suffered over was, in the final analysis, basically a silly woman, whose life was given over to superficial vanities. Her sole distinction was that she was more beautiful than the rest of her sex. That was her power—her extraordinary beauty.

It would have been laughable, this unveiling of the truth, were it not for the awareness that he had sacrificed seven years of his life for an illusion. For a delusion. He had pined for a woman who risked nothing of herself, yet demanded the very lifeblood of others. It was a shattering realization.

He had hesitated for only one more moment. Then, as if the night demanded it of him, and not to hurt her, not to triumph over her, he made his final accounting of their relationship. In a soft voice holding some sadness, but mostly resolve, he said, "I loved you once deeply, dearly...almost more than I could bear. I suffered more than any man should be asked to suffer for a woman. And I thought the love—and the misery—would never end. I'm sorry. It gives me no pleasure to say it, but it seems I was wrong."

Even as he spoke, she shimmered before him, close enough to reach in five steps, a lovely chimera in white. The luminescence of the thousands of seed pearls reflected the moonlight. His heart twisted in pain, remembering his years of need and knowing all he had to do now was reach out and take what he had wanted for so long.

"Pavan." He said her name as if for the first time truly hearing it, and its sound rang hollow in his heart.

She smiled, assured of herself again, and held out her hand for him to take. "You didn't mean it, you couldn't...you only meant to hurt me, my love. It is impossible for us to forget each other," she purred.

"No," he said. "It's ended."

She made a slight sound, either wounded or disbelieving, he couldn't be sure, and when he began to turn, she took a step toward him. But again he said, "No," this time more sharply, and she froze in place.

There was no more to say. She looked at him, stunned in the recognition of her defeat. It occurred to him, fleetingly, that it might have been the only loss she had ever known.

He left her, and behind him, as he made his way back to the brilliantly lighted palace of the Duke of Danfort, he heard Pavan cry out his name.

When he reached the terrace, music swelled over the chattering voices of the few hundred guests assembled for the coming-out party given in honor of Melissa Danfort. The main hall was ablaze with candlelight and jewels. Overhead, hundreds of tiny lights danced and winked from the enormous Austrian crystal chandeliers. Italian cut glass wall sconces threw illumination into every corner.

The night was a festival of happiness.

And he was unmoved. He was weary—seven years weary, a lifetime exhausted, or so it seemed then—and it had been his intention to merely pass through the house on his way to claim his carriage.

But it did not happen as he had planned.

He had been making his way along the periphery of the dance floor when there was a sudden opening in the crowd of observers, and the vision of Melissa Danfort dancing in the arms of her stepbrother caused him to pause.

He had meant to go on, but the glance turned into interest, and the interest to absorption.

The girl was easily the most beautiful woman there that night. Of course, he had known that once she was properly outfitted she would eclipse any other female at Court. Even Pavan, whose beauty was as close to perfection as nature could contrive, would find competition in the girl.

Like others around him, he was held spellbound by her, and although he knew he should leave, knew that there was no earthly point to him remaining, he found himself rooted to the spot.

Amazing. She had been raised in rude surroundings, hardly better than those fit for a goatherd, yet there was about her bearing an innate regality, a fluid grace that no amount of training could instill in a woman. Her slightest gesture was sensual, natural.

He saw her laugh at something Quentin Danfort said. The golden curls caught the light from one of the chandeliers; the green eyes glittered; the delicate, full mouth turned up and the even white teeth shone in sudden merriment.

Danfort whispered again in her ear, and, irrationally, Brandon found himself responding with irritation. He told himself he did not like Danfort. But when next he saw Quentin brush a finger intimately across her cheek, he burned a degree hotter.

Until that moment—call it a moment of truth—he had managed to convince himself that the intimate involvement the girl and he had shared some days before had been an aberration in both their lives. And he had been honest, frank from the start, absolutely forthright in telling her that their joining had been no more than sexual. From what he understood of women, he knew how she would react to his bluntness. In return for his raw honesty, she would find some way to scorn him, and there was no doubt that the romantic illusions she had attached to him would burn themselves out in time and through experience.

When the first stirrings of guilt edged their way into his thoughts, he told himself that every young woman had a first lover, and that he had merely been cast by fate and a few too many glasses of ale to assume that role in Melissa's life. There was no more to what they had shared than that, and he had forced himself to think no more of the incident.

But looking at her at the ball, dancing in the arms of another man, he knew that everything he'd told himself had been pure rubbish. He had lied to himself and to her from the first moment he had seen her in Cornwall. The damn girl meant something to him; past sexual desire, he couldn't say what, but the feeling was powerful enough to cause him to move toward her just as the music stopped.

With every step, he cursed himself for his loss of control, yet he was unable to stop.

He was actually grateful when one of the silly courtiers invited to the Duke's affair apprehended him halfway across the vast hall to speak of a trade operation he had in mind. *He was saved from himself.*

But as the man jabbered, Brandon heard nothing, his entire attention captured by Melissa Danfort. He had watched as Quentin left her. He had watched as a crowd of young male admirers immediately flew to her side like moths to a flame, encircling her, consuming her with their hot eyes.

He read their minds as surely as if he were in each of their heads: Melissa Danfort was beautiful and rich; each of them hoped to bed and wed her. One of them would.

No sooner did the music begin again, than Brandon claimed her—much, he noticed, to Quentin Danfort's obvious distress.

They were barely cordial to each other, yet he felt her tremble in his arms, and feelings he could not control, nor that he wanted to own, swept through him as they moved in time to the music.

He felt eyes on them, speculative, excited. A glance to one side showed him Quentin Danfort still watching them, his strange blue eyes overflowing with ill will, and joining him, the Countess Glenmillan Danfort, her own expression tight and nervous as she fixed her violet gaze on her stepdaughter.

And in a flash, he understood: their plan was for Quentin Danfort to wed Melissa. It was a sickening realization, all the more so because it was a plan of such certain success that it could as well be considered a fait accompli.

He forced himself to be cold. He forced himself to hurt her, letting her think he had come for Pavan and that there would be an assignation between them later that night. He allowed that fool Danfort to whisk her away... before he made the certain mistake of revealing his heart to her.

Damn him.

Damn her.

He wanted her. He wanted her for more than a single night of passion. He wanted her forever, just as every other man in the room wanted her. And that desire—for he could not bring himself to call it love, even then—was as doomed as his passion for Pavan de Noialles had been seven years ago.

Watching her as she moved away through the throng of lavishly plumed gossips, he knew that the girl he had met in Cornwall was no more, and a new woman, someone powerful and unfathomable, and perhaps even dangerous, had taken her place.

And there was no way he could ever have her....

He stood at the window until the light began to take over from the night, and before the city had come fully alive again he was dressed and in his offices.

But the day began no better than the night had ended for him. Ross McKay was upon him first thing, stewing over their prospects for survival. With the Danfort voyage canceled, they stood to lose everything they had worked for over the past seven years if, or rather, when, the Duke pulled their charters in revenge. Not only that, but Ross reminded him that they were in desperate need of new commissions to offset the loss of one of their ships, which had foundered off the coast of New England the month before.

"Your job is to advise, not command," said Brandon, standing at a table where he had navigational charts unfurled. "Your position is to keep accounts, not make policy," he snapped. "You overstep yourself, Ross. You forget whose company this is."

"Begging your pardon, Cap'n," Ross replied sarcastically, "but it seems that you've forgotten you've got a company."

"This company's my life. You needn't worry. I won't see it founder on the shoals of financial disaster."

"Damn me to hell!" bellowed Ross, "but it's me you're talking to, not some stranger. I know...." he said darkly.

Brandon raised his brows. "Well? What is it, man? What do you know?"

"It's a bloody woman who's caused this mess."

Brandon looked away. He did not want to get into this subject.

"It's the Danfort girl who's caused you to bow out of the India voyage."

"I won't be owned. I won't be commanded," Brandon said.

"And what the hell do you think? That she won't own you this way?" Ross shook his head. "She already does, man. She obviously owns your head, not to mention that she's tampered with your heart—or at least your privates. And in due time, she and her grandfather'll have your company, too. So what in hell do you have to gain with your bloody pride?"

"My self-respect," Brandon barked. He slammed down his fist, so that the table shook for several seconds afterward.

Ross's face reddened. "The company's overextended. You've taken too many chances too fast. We can't last unless a miracle walks in this door." And with that, Ross McKay left the room, slamming the oak door after him.

Brandon stared at the closed door. McKay had been right about everything.

After the ball there were a thousand invitations for Melissa to attend all manner of social events. They arrived, literally, by the hour, borne on little silver trays by the footmen Glenmillan employed, and whom she seemed to run ragged fetching and delivering messages. Nothing made Glenmillan happier than to receive these bids to attend socials, unless it might be any attention Melissa showed Quentin, who buzzed about her like a bee from morning to night.

For the most part, Melissa ignored him. Since realizing that Brandon was out of her life for good, she found little that claimed her interest. Even when Quentin brought her the occasional gift—another string of pearls, or the latest present, a pair of emerald and diamond earrings—she could barely manage a suitably polite response. And to his poetry, outpourings of tender and fervent rhymes proclaiming his devotion to her, she could do no more than avert her face as she murmured some polite disclaimer of her worthiness. How sadly ironic that only days before she had secretly thrilled to any romantic turn of phrase heard in passing—even when not meant for her. In her mind, she had reassigned the endearment to a sentiment Brandon might someday declare for her. Well, all that was lost now, all the dreams, all the foolish romanticism. There was only harsh reality to face. Brandon was gone from her life. He had never truly been a part of it, except in her own mind.

But whereas she had contrived various means to avoid Quentin's romantic overtures, she was not so fortunate in banishing her grandfather's influence over her life. Whenever she was summoned to his quarters, she appeared at once, out of respect and also because she sensed that in spite of his outer gruffness, he had a genuine fondness for her. It was a feeling she returned in small, quiet ways. Open affection put him off.

All their meetings were the same. A challenge of stubborn wills ensued, her grandfather setting the tone, which would on occasion take the form of subtle manipulation or at other times explode into a scene of blazing temperament. The topic of their conferences never varied. The subject was always Brandon, and it was always torture for her to endure. Each time his name was spoken, the sound registered as a whiplash to her heart.

On this latest occasion, the game of wits between them was finally brought to a head.

He awaited her arrival in his private closet. "Well?" the Duke asked from his favorite armchair. One of his prized leather-bound Greek volumes was in his hand—*Platonic Dialogues,* this time. He placed a marker in it and put it aside, turning his attention to her. "So, once again I inquire. Have you made your peace with de Forrest?"

Melissa looked him over carefully, silently voicing her own question. She wondered at his health. Today he had not dressed, but sat bundled in a blue velveteen robe. A burgundy-colored blanket was draped over his lap and legs. His only concession to formality was the white periwig.

The room was dark, but for the glow shed by a candelabra on an Italian chest behind him. It was impossible to tell that it was the beginning of June and that beyond the drawn curtains, birds sang in warm sunshine.

Melissa remained standing, as she always did unless invited by him to sit. She stood calmly before him, aware that his mood was somehow different. There was an urgency this time that resembled desperation more than the usual willfulness.

"I have not mended our troubles," she responded quietly, not wishing to escalate the tension that already existed between them. She was weary of these discussions; they hurt her, they hurt him. They were talks that would forever be without resolution.

The Duke of Danfort stared at her for a long moment. Once he narrowed his hazel eyes, but not at her; she sensed it was something else he was seeing.

He scowled at her through the dim light. "There's no time left for your emotional self-indulgence. I want you to get de Forrest back. The India voyage is necessary. We all need this voyage—he as much as you and I."

"No matter what is said or done, he won't go—"

"Of course he'll go! The man's rational when it comes to business. His only weakness is his sense of independence, which you've clumsily managed to injure. Once you make an appeal to his ego, he'll reconsider his decision to abandon our project and we can be underway with all our plans.''

But Melissa knew quite differently, and at various times she had attempted to convince her grandfather that his hopes were futile. Brandon de Forrest was lost . . . lost to both of them, because of her stupidity, just as her grandfather had accused.

Of course she could say nothing about her visit to Brandon's offices, a visit that had managed to finish off any possibility of a business relationship between them. It had been a desperate and foolish maneuver on her part; what good would it do to share her humiliation with her grandfather? Nothing would be changed in doing so, and if anything, she would earn his disrespect.

She held herself straight, determined not to flinch when the punishment she deserved was meted out. "I do not intend to deal with Brandon de Forrest again. Not now. Not ever. I swear to you, there is no power on this earth that will compel me to do so."

Rather than bark back in response, the Duke was uncustomarily silent. He considered her, looking into her face as if seeing something new there. "I see." He paused. "Well, then, you know that you will never see your mother."

She watched him watching her, waiting for her reaction, waiting to see which way she would jump. But he would be disappointed. She would not move as he had expected. If he had meant to wound her into compliance, he was mistaken. "Yes," Melissa replied, "I've considered that possibility."

"Probability."

"Probability," she corrected herself. "On the other hand . . . there are other ships sailing to India."

The Duke's hazel eyes flared, his lips twisting into a wry smile. "Ho! Are there now? And I suppose you will fund a voyage yourself? Or perhaps, with your somewhat exaggerated notion of your abilities, you'll swim the way." He turned his head, registering his disgust at her childish stupidity.

"I'll do whatever's necessary," Melissa said without bravado, unwilling to match his outburst with one of her own. What was the sense of this needless, hopeless sparring?

Her fiery disposition had always earned criticism from Goodie and Darben, and even she had to admit the sparks she sent out at a moment's provocation had caused her and others trouble. But the experiences of the last few weeks had made their impression. The series of small and great miseries, disappointments and revelations had made an impact on her personality. The fire within burned still, and intensely, but with more control now.

The Duke turned his back to her, his expression incredulous. "Do you actually dare to challenge me? You're nothing more than a stubborn, troublesome child. I've a mind to pack you back off to Cornwall, where you won't trouble me or anyone else."

"You can't," she said tiredly, half wishing it were possible to go back in time to the blissful peace and innocence of her former life. To that time before she had seen the handsome horseman galloping toward her, a splendid and fearsome spectacle against the glowing skyline.

"Can't I?" the Duke snapped, sitting straighter in his chair, so that the blanket over his knees slid slightly downward.

"I no longer pack as easily. Maybe you haven't noticed. I've grown far too large these last few weeks for the box you once put me in."

"Your impudence exceeds the reality of your position, madame. Don't push your luck." Their eyes locked, and she saw that he was not nearly as angry as his voice attempted to convey. Yes, she thought, warmth mixing with her perpetual melancholy, her grandfather loved her, as she loved him.

The Duke watched his granddaughter as she left his company, her head high and proud, her spirit as untamable as his had been at an earlier age. Behind her back he smiled, satisfied with what he saw in her. She was everything he had hoped Philip might have been, but wasn't, not really, although he had loved his son just the same. The girl had fire, and she was growing tougher, more realistic; she was adventurous and bold in her thinking, and certainly she was unyielding . . . all sterling qualities. She was exactly like him, the Duke decided. And she was precisely the woman for de Forrest.

The Duke closed his eyes, settling back into his armchair once again, and began to search for a plan. The situation was proving to be more of a challenge than he had counted on. Melissa was stubborn, too unyielding, and he was unable to second-guess her. Strange, but he knew de Forrest's mind better than the girl's.

If the Duke had known what his wayward granddaughter was about the following day, he would have worried more.

While others at the afternoon garden party tittered, Melissa was one of the few in attendance who listened raptly to the impassioned rhetoric being expounded by none other than the Duchess of Beltonwick, that very same lady who had been the mistress of Celia Allen.

In fact, for the first time since Melissa had accepted the fact that Brandon was out of her life forever, she felt a faint quiver of life flowing through her veins. The hint of purpose began to form in her mind. As she was never to marry—at least not for love—she would have to live for some other cause, and, like the Duchess, who railed at the carelessness of the government and heartlessness of the populace, Melissa's kind nature was easily stirred to champion the downtrodden who had no means to end their own misfortune.

After all, her own humble origins were not so far behind her. For all her newly acquired silks and jewels, she had not forgotten that she had been raised in Cornwall by simple and good people, nor would she ever forget the great courage of her friend Celia, a common servant, whose selfless bravery had saved her from rape, possibly from death. She knew firsthand the plight of the poor and of those others who could not fend for themselves.

When the Duchess called for supporters to follow her in a public display of condemnation for slaving operations, Melissa readily lent her full patronage. And probably because of Melissa's growing popularity, and as a lark, several other women also joined the ranks.

But three days later, the march through the wharves was not quite as heroic an endeavor as Melissa had envisioned.

Most of the onlookers gaped at the band of women, with children in tow, who passed out handwritten leaflets to whomever they met. The leaflets contained information on how to inform the Duchess of known or suspected slaving operators.

Some of the rabble who had come to gawk complained that if the Duchess and her well-dressed comrades were so concerned about the welfare of the common man, they might spend less time on their hair and less money on their jewels and fine clothes.

Rather than receiving accolades for their efforts, Melissa and the others found mud clods and rotting vegetables hurled at them, along with a barrage of crude invective.

Some in the crowd rushed boldly forward and began to grab at the jewelry and hats and wigs. In a tussle with a woman who grabbed at her necklace, Melissa found herself thrown face forward into a puddle of rainwater and street filth.

She rose sputtering and furious, the fire that had slept in her for the past two weeks suddenly bursting into a roaring inferno. She beat her attacker back, and, further standing her ground, took over for the Duchess, who was being tended by others for a cut suffered when a rock hit her head.

Undaunted by the discomfort of her wet, fouled garments, Melissa climbed atop a stack of precariously balanced pallets. Tomatoes still sailed through the air. An egg crashed at her feet. But in a voice ringing with passion, she cried out loudly on behalf of the poor, summoning in her mind the vision of Celia to sustain her conviction.

"If you care so much, my lady, why don't you risk your own skin?"

"Go get them yourself, you big mouth!"

"Or shut your trap!" heckled still another from the sidelines.

And rather than an insult, it was as if she'd been tossed a bouquet of roses. Warmth flooded through her, as if a river of love coursed into every vein, and though she looked into the jeering, disapproving and disbelieving faces of the surrounding crowd, she saw another scene in her mind's eye.

She saw herself on a ship riding the crest of a wave, white sails full and billowing above her, as she sped to liberate Celia.

From his carriage, stopped some distance away, Quentin Danfort saw a far less romantic scene. In fact, what he heard made him shiver with fear.

The damn girl was hell bent on destroying him! What would she think of next?

He had been happily on his way through the wharves to negotiate a new contract for a voyage to the Caribbean, where he was to deliver a cargo of twenty to thirty women as chattel to plantation owners. It was an excellent venture, full of prospects. The money he had assembled to fund the scheme was partially made from his last undertaking, that which had transported Melissa's friend—the Celia person—to India, and partially borrowed at flagrantly usurious terms from a goldsmith.

And now what did he find? He found Melissa...Melissa covered in filth like a guttersnipe; Melissa waving her arms about like an orator atop a mountain of wooden pallets and crates; Melissa haranguing a mob of drunken seamen, whores, fishwives and tattered children—along with the odd aristocrat whom he could see smirking from the sidelines, God help him!—about ending the inhumanity of slaving!

The little bitch was out to ruin him—socially and economically!

Well, he couldn't just sit there and brood about the on-going misfortune brought on by this upstart half-caste; he had to do something, had to act to save himself. With a long sigh and an enormous show of concern, he flung himself from his carriage and, with all the bravura of Lancelot spiriting away Guinevere, snatched a protesting Melissa from the mocking crowd, taking a lump of horse manure in his back for his trouble.

And the jade actually chastised him for interfering. She actually accused him of humiliating her before her friends and her audience. Audience! It was enough to make him choke.

It did make Glenmillan choke.

"Surely," she said, at first laughing when Quentin rushed into her room, fresh from delivering a still-protesting Melissa to her quarters to repair her appearance, "you're making up this delightful farce. Really, Quentin, you are such a tease, a regular wit sometimes."

Quentin's face, looking over her shoulder as she sat at her vanity, peering into her mirror, was anything but humorous. His expression was dark and serious. "This is no entertainment, Mother."

Glenmillan's face fell. "Oh. My God." She moaned, closing her eyes against the truth. The violet eyes batted open again. She stared at Quentin. "She *didn't.*"

"Oh, didn't she, though?" Quentin spun on his heels, stalking to the center of the room. He sighed deeply and, clasping his hands behind his back, stared up at the ceiling with its painted oval of a Grecian scene—a satyr frolicking amid ferns and Ionic columns with a bevy of seminude maidens. "And do you know what she told me? She said that she was going to devote her life to undoing wrongs. She would make charity her life's cause. Charity!" Quentin shook his head, his expression turning sour as he said the word. "She said she was going to begin at once, by going off to find that—that girl, Celia. She said that she would not rest until she had liberated that—that—servant."

"Impossible. We must stop her. If she's serious—"

"Oh, she's serious. She's always serious, no matter how outrageous her schemes are. And now she thinks she's Joan of Arc." He raised one brow and looked back at Glenmillan. "Need I remind you that dear Joan, for all her good intentions, did not come to a pretty end."

"Tragic, tragic…" Glenmillan murmured, thinking not of Joan but of what it meant to them if something should happen to Melissa before she was safely wed to Quentin.

Quentin knew precisely what she was thinking. "It would be the finish of us." And it would be an additional tragedy if the girl, through her confounded meddling, brought to public scrutiny his little business ventures. He seriously doubted the Duke would take kindly to his somewhat seamy enterprises in the sale of human bodies. No, slaving did not reflect well on the Danfort name, which was noted for financial cunning and ruthlessness of a far more refined nature. Well, thought Quentin, when you're rich, you can afford to dabble in such elevated financial machinations. When a man hardly knows where the funds for his next cockfight are coming from, he's prone to be somewhat more inventive in his monetary schemes.

After some discussion, it was finally decided they had no other choice but to enlist the aid of the Duke. Although the old man consistently seemed to delight in confounding any plan he and Glenmillan made, in this instance he would surely intervene in putting a stop to the girl's foolishness.

They were right.

The Duke listened, for once with complete attention, as Glenmillan breathlessly repeated the horror story of Melissa's intentions to rescue Celia. Sitting beside his mother on the sofa in the Duke's closet, Quentin, like a well-rehearsed actor, "tsk"ed and sighed and made small moaning sounds on cue.

"And so," concluded Glenmillan primly, folding her hands in her lap, "I trust you will intervene and stop the poor child from making a grievous error in pursuing this dangerous scheme."

"Indeed," the Duke said, looking thoughtful, "I can't thank you enough for bringing this matter to my attention."

He even smiled at them—benevolently.

Had it not been for the smile, both Quentin and Glenmillan might have felt easier as they left Danfort's apartments.

"He hasn't smiled at me in years," said Glenmillan as they passed down the corridor leading to Glenmillan's chambers.

"He hasn't ever smiled at me," muttered Quentin with a scowl.

"I know," said Glenmillan worriedly. "He's always had this strange, uncommon hatred for you."

"And now he suddenly smiles." Quentin furrowed his brow, trying to puzzle it out.

"Don't worry. It's nothing. We did him a service. He actually seems to dote on the jade."

"Don't we all," Quentin sighed.

In the eyes of Ross McKay, the Duke of Danfort seemed to fill the entire space of Brandon's office.

An old man now, the Duke still retained an imposing presence. Sitting stiffly in the chair opposite Brandon's worktable, his body, encased in its layers of velvet, silk and lace finery, appeared visibly shrunken in size, his pallor verging on ghostly. The eyes, however, remained clear. They had not lost their quickness, nor their hard light. For Ross, there could be no doubt that the Duke of Danfort was still a force to be reckoned with . . . and, also, that the long-dreaded moment of reckoning was upon them.

"The time for patience has passed, de Forrest," the Duke said, putting voice to Ross's fears. "I am no longer amused by our little pastime of cat and mouse. And I have grown infinitely weary of your self-indulgent conceits . . . these magnificent shows of prideful arrogance that celebrate your supposed autonomy from the constraints placed upon other . . . lesser men. Sadly, for your sake, you are deluded. All of us forfeit pieces of our soul in order to survive the realities of this planet. We all make our pacts with the devil—the only difference is for what and how much. If not, then we perish." Danfort spoke to the air before him, his inflection monotonous, heavy like a dirge, and Ross found the drone somehow even more chilling than if the Duke had been in a fiery rage.

Ross, as fascinated as he was horrified by the scene he was witnessing, looked to Brandon, who had moved to the window. He stood there with his back to the other two men.

No matter that they had been spoken to by the enemy, there was truth to the Duke's words, and Ross prayed that Brandon would accept the reality of the situation. If he did not bend to the Duke's will, then Brandon would find himself without a company to run. Subsequently, he would find himself a slave to not just one miserable old master, but to a thousand petty tyrants who would exact their wills on him if he hoped to survive economically.

Brandon spoke without turning. Perhaps, Ross thought, in Brandon's mind, to face the Duke would have symbolized deference. Stubborn to the end—and Ross truly feared it *was* the end—Brandon refused to yield.

"I will pay whatever price I must for my ideals, but not to any devil who holds the purse strings."

The Duke wasted no more time. He rose quietly from his seat and, reaching into a flat leather case embossed with the famous crest of the House of Danfort, he removed a sheath of papers and threw them upon the charts spread across Brandon's worktable. The pages fanned over the maps, covering carefully plotted routes of voyages that now would never be taken: the King's insignia was clearly visible upon the revocations of charters granted to the de Forrest Company.

Although Brandon did not move from his place, he flinched as the papers fell upon his table, much as if he had seen with an inner vision before Ross had what was physically present.

"Then you will pay now," said the Duke, moving through the silent gloom to the door. "And dearly."

Ross wasted no time in following the Duke from the room. His fury was so great at what Brandon had allowed to happen, that he was afraid to remain. At that moment he felt like killing the man he had grown to love like a brother, a man he had respected and admired beyond any other.

He halted halfway through the door and, turning back, said, "Fool! Damned, bloody fool! Holding yourself so rare and high above the lot of us low human louts, you with your lofty, pristine ideals of nobility. The honest truth, Captain . . . the honest truth?" Ross lashed out, his body trembling with rage, "You're far less than any of us! You're a dishonest, cowardly blackguard if ever there's been one! You lost it all for fear of what a woman could do to you! And that's the bleedin' truth. You lost your whole damn life all on account of that bloody Danfort wench. You think you've triumphed? Think again, Captain! It's she who's the winner here! I must say, my friend, a pitiful sight—your fine pride. I'd laugh myself, if the carnage wasn't so great."

At that, Brandon spun about on his heels, his body rigid with violence, ready to uncoil and make a deadly strike. The sight silenced Ross, who instinctively backed away. He'd gone too far; still he found himself too depleted emotionally to muster any regret. Anyway, what he had said was the truth.

"Laugh at me, will you, McKay?"

"Aye, sir, I'd be laughing, but it's my tears you most deserve. Anyway, the rest of London'll be splittin' their sides soon enough when it comes known you've lost everything for nothing."

Brandon's fist clenched and flexed, and Ross knew he was going to get a beating, but he didn't care. He welcomed it. Maybe the physical pain would dull the misery of his soul. He'd loved Brandon, he'd loved the de Forrest Company; both had become his whole life. And now it was all finished.

"Get out of here before I kill you."

"Aye, and you would, too. Only you'd be doin' me a favor, Cap'n."

They stared at each other, their eyes burning across the space that separated them. Then Ross left, not bothering to close the door.

A moment later, Brandon kicked it shut.

Reeling back around, he stalked to the table and lifted the papers lying across his charts, examining them one by one, reaffirming what he already knew in his heart.

Yes, it was so, what the Duke had said: he would pay the price dearly.

The old man had seen to it that the Crown had revoked his every license to sail as a merchant seaman. That was for the immediate present. For the future, he could project an auction of his ships when he was unable to support his enterprise; Danfort would foreclose on his loan, take what he was due by the terms of their original contract. And whatever he could not legally claim from it, he would probably buy a pence to the pound on the auction block.

Ross was right, damn him...and so, also, was the Duke. Damn them both.

Brandon dropped the pages, one by one, to the table, letting them float as they might until almost no part of the map was visible. The last paper was about to fall along with the others when Brandon's grip tightened on the page.

There was no stamp on it, no signature by the King, revoking his charters. Instead, it was an agreement. His eyes skimmed the page, reading hungrily. He could sign the paper and reclaim everything.

All he had to do was say that he would take Melissa Danfort to India and back. All he had to do was to fall on his knees before the accursed House of Danfort....

Chapter Twelve

"I had been playing brilliantly up until then..." Quentin explained for the third time within the past five minutes, his expression bewildered. "And then it...well, it all began to fall apart." The light opalescent eyes were watery from defeat and red-rimmed with the fatigue brought on by the previous night's debauchery. "I should have stopped when I was ahead. I should have *known.*"

Melissa—who had been drifting in and out of Quentin's version of a gaming loss at White's the previous night—was for once sympathetic to her stepbrother's plight. If she herself had been more prudent, had not made a mess of everything with her impetuousness, she would be going to India. She would be going to India with Brandon—

But she broke the thought before it led to another maddening progression of images from the past. She had to live now, in the present. But there was nothing to look forward to anymore.

Quentin droned on, and she closed her eyes, making at least a momentary escape from her surroundings.

In place of the cozy octagonal breakfast room, India rose magically in Melissa's mind, growing out of a thick, enchanted mist. With domed minarets and turrets, with strutting peacocks and waving, dancing cobras it stretched before her, lush and exotic. Such a fantastic land, waiting for her...its faint, gossamer impression looming in her heart. Dreaming about it was her only panacea in a life of soul-deadening monotony.

"Of course, I was cheated," Quentin complained to Glenmillan, with a side glance at Melissa.

As usual, he noted with consternation, she didn't appear to be listening. It always made him nervous when he found her deep in thought. Her ruminations boded more mischief—mischief with injurious effect to his scheme of grasping the ever illusive Danfort fortune.

"Anyway," he went on dourly, arching an eyebrow as he stretched his hand to examine the luster of his nails, "one cannot feel humiliated when cheated, can one? I mean, really, one can feel outraged, but not humiliated. Humiliation is for losers, and I did not lose. Technically I did not lose."

Glenmillan sat opposite him at the breakfast table, she, too, absorbed in her own concerns—namely her appearance, which along with her dwindling supply of funds was very much on her mind these days. Money had never ranged far from her thoughts. Even when she had first luxuriated in her inheritance from Philip, when it was new to her, overflowing and intact, she had fretted over one day scraping the bottom of the fortune's coffers.

That day was upon her now, as she sat in her morning gown of silver and mauve, a combination that threw a soft, rosy glow against her complexion and took years off her face. An illusion, of course, but a happy one.

It was not easy being continuously in Melissa's youthful presence. Physical comparisons were inevitable, and there was no getting around it, age, the universal and eternal malady, had finally befallen even her. She had always used her beauty for personal gain. Now what was she to do? She had only Melissa to rely upon.

With that thought, she bestowed a fleeting glance Melissa's way, as if to reassure herself that the projected remedy for all her woes was still in place. And, yes, there the girl sat, the mass of luxuriant golden hair arranged neatly, as Glenmillan had instructed Annie to do, atop her head in gentle curls that softly framed the delicate oval face. The slanted, almond-shaped green eyes were serene now, glassy with thought. Well, let the girl dream away, thought Glenmillan, as long as she never strays physically.

With a wave and a shrug, Quentin said, "Cheated, you see. Otherwise I would have made a spectacular showing last night." The lace cuffs peeking from the sleeves of his wine-colored jacket flounced like the wings of small, nervous birds on the verge of flight. "Actually, as it happened, I *was* making a spectacular showing until the rogue showed up, and—"

"Really, my dear," drawled Glenmillan, as she spread plum jelly on a shortbread biscuit, "I see no point in going over the tiresome details. After all, it's only money." She popped the biscuit in her mouth, stifling the urge to giggle hysterically. *Only money, indeed!*

Melissa, who was still thinking of India, chose that moment to glance up, and in doing so, discovered her two breakfast partners trading a collusive look that belied Glenmillan's statement about money.

For an instant Melissa was too stunned to look away. It was as if she had inadvertently blundered into a room she was never meant to enter. Then, quickly, she lowered her eyes, exiting the forbidden scene before being noticed.

But how extraordinary. Not once had it occurred to her that a shortage of money might have a place in the glittering lives of her newly acquired steprelatives.

Certainly Quentin spared no expense in the constant stream of gifts he lavished on her. Only the day before, Melissa recalled, he had presented her with a jeweled music box, its tinkling song a popular sentimental ballad of love. She had put the present away immediately. She did not want to think of love—she would put that part of her nature behind her, storing away her heart as she had Quentin's gift.

So, she thought, with more amusement than anything else, Quentin's desperate affection for her had a pecuniary foundation. And the hunger she always read in his eyes... well, that was certainly desire—but not for her.

Musing, Melissa bit into an apricot-filled biscuit and looked past Glenmillan's shoulder to the window, beyond which a flock of birds flew in playful circles against the blue sky. The fact was, she really did not mind about Quentin. Not at all. Contrary to being wounded, she felt oddly relieved. She was now released from the subtle obligation of returning his affections.

Still, what she had seen, what she now knew—or at least strongly suspected about Glenmillan and Quentin—was yet another pretty bubble burst. Nothing in her life was as it seemed . . . nothing.

For a while the pervasive gloom she had felt since her interchange with Brandon at the ball had lifted; now it descended again, weighing her down. From lovers to family, was the world beyond Cornwall made up entirely of deceit?

"Anyway, I was thinking," said Glenmillan, suddenly brightening her voice, "wouldn't it be wonderful for the three of us to take a tour this summer? Italy!" Her face glowed. She looked around the table, seeking confirmation from the other two. "Venice would be splendid, don't you agree, Quentin?"

Quentin sprang into fevered animation. "Venice is splendid, splendid in the summer . . . yes, we must plan a journey!"

Both he and Glenmillan awaited Melissa's reaction.

None came. The emerald green eyes were indrawn, her attention far from matters at hand.

Her thoughts had flown to India. . . .

She imagined scenes of a triumphant voyage, herself in charge of a band of mercenaries. She saw herself riding boldly with her soldiers, sweeping into the lair of the Indian potentate who was said to possess Celia and others.

If only this fantasy would take form in reality; it would be a personal triumph on many levels. She would leave Quentin with his greedy intentions; she would escape from Glenmillan's constant hovering, her continuous pressures to spend time with Quentin, and her prodding to appear at every social gathering thought up by every simpering gossip. That was not life; that was a life sentence of boredom.

Alternatively faraway India would give her life meaning. There was Celia to rescue, and she would meet her mother, her own mother!

And best of all, most crucially, distant, mysterious India would separate her from the tormenting thoughts of Brandon. There would be nothing in India to remind her of him as there was here, where his name popped up continuously and where there was always the dreaded chance of meeting him at a social affair.

India—so far removed in every way from England and memories of an impossible love—would be her salvation.

Well, she thought, she might as well wish for the moon as think about going to India.

Glenmillan's cheery, lilting voice cut through Melissa's downwardly spiraling mood, carrying her back to the breakfast room.

"I shall write to Prince Lodavico today. He'll want us to stay with him, just as before," said Glenmillan with her usual assurance.

"I'll need new outfits," Quentin considered aloud. "Vivid colors.... Opulence is the watchword for Italy."

"And I, as well," agreed Glenmillan breathlessly. "Of course, you'll have Venice on its knees, my dear," she said to Melissa. She paused, stopped by a new thought. "I can't recall, are you fluent in Italian as well as French?"

Melissa brought her mind back to matters at hand, barely aware of the ongoing conversation. "Latin," she replied, somewhat mystified by the question. "Not Italian."

Glenmillan's violet eyes cut into her, their expression rapacious even as her lips formed a gentle, forbearing smile.

"Well, then . . . the Italian will come easily."

"You will love Italy," Quentin said expansively. His strange, light blue eyes glittered like sunlight skipping across water. "The Duke's palace has been renovated by Palladio. It's always been my dream to have a summer home designed by him. Of course that would take a great deal of money." He eyed Melissa for a protracted beat, then, as if roused by the next thought, went on quickly. "Italy is so romantic," he exclaimed, widening his arms. "I promise you paradise there!" He closed his eyes, the ghost of a smile drawing up his mouth as he savored the future.

And before Melissa, the images of India dissolved into nothingness.

The final blow to her dreams of India came the following day during a rare family meal, where the Duke, Glenmillan, Melissa and Quentin sat together at one table.

"Yes. I'm pleased about this Venice trip," her grandfather suddenly announced, as he helped himself to a second serving of venison proffered on a silver platter by a butler. "Melissa should travel, and Italy will provide a sense of cultural perspective to her education."

Melissa sat in rigid, furious, impotent silence, hating all of them for the power they exercised over her life.

Glenmillan, on the other hand, became suddenly enlivened.

Encouraged by the Duke's good humor, she seized the moment and began to wax poetic about the Grand Canal, and even Quentin had the temerity to suggest they all be outfitted in new wardrobes in order to make a proper showing.

That proved a mistake. The Duke's acerbic reply to this ill-conceived suggestion took five minutes, followed by a thundering silence that lasted until the meal's end.

Melissa almost but not quite felt sorry for Quentin, whose greed seemingly outdistanced his good sense. Her ears were still ringing with her grandfather's last scathing remarks about her stepbrother's character when the greatest surprise of the evening, perhaps of the year and maybe in all of Quentin's and Glenmillan's lives occurred.

The Duke, being the first to rise from the table, suddenly halted and said with grave consideration, "But wait.

Perhaps I've been too hasty...too shortsighted in my evaluation of your suggestion, Quentin. You were correct. Tomorrow you three must begin to completely refurbish your wardrobes—everything, from head to toe. The trip to Italy must be done in the grandest of manners. Spare no expense, Glenmillan.''

Glenmillan and Quentin merely stared, for once with nothing to say, as if the wind had been knocked from their lungs.

And Melissa...Melissa knew there was no hope left for her at all.

India was now as lost to her as Brandon. She would have, instead of her heart's desire, many nice new gowns. And she would have Quentin. If Glenmillan was to have her way, most certainly she would have Quentin.

Late that night, as Melissa sat brooding in her bedroom, having given up her attempts to enjoy a translation of Homer's *Odyssey* recommended by her grandfather, there was an urgent rapping at her door.

She sighed, staring in the direction of the racket, but made no move to rise from her chair. It would be Quentin. Or Glenmillan. Again.

Ever since the meal, they were as if possessed. They had each appeared two or three times already that night, eager to discuss the next day's plans to ravish Oxford and Bond Streets of whatever goods were available in the way of fashionable items, before the merchants came calling in person at Danfort House. It was as if they were compelled to check on her every few minutes, lest she evaporate before they go on their orgy of spending.

Clearly, if Italy promised paradise, she was the vehicle that would carry them there.

Annie had already retired, and Melissa received her caller herself, opening the door with a martyr's forbearance.

But it was not Glenmillan; nor was it Quentin. Instead, the Duke stood before her. She found herself straining to believe her eyes—his presence was so completely improbable. He had never come to her quarters before; in fact, Melissa had never known him to call upon anyone, unless, of course, it was the King. And mysteriously, Annie stood behind him, her eyes round with worry.

"Well, well. Don't just stand there. Step aside, girl, let us pass," Danfort commanded brusquely. "There're matters to attend." He brushed by Melissa, continuing into the room. "Shut the door," he commanded to Annie, as Melissa stared in wonderment. "Hurry, hurry, I haven't got forever. And you two have far less—not even a night to waste with dillydallying."

Her grandfather had come dressed in an evening robe, yet certainly there was nothing retiring about him. To Melissa he looked as formal and fearsome as if he were in full Court costume. The garment's green background was richly embroidered with gold threads. Now and then a strand caught the candlelight and seemed to spark as he moved. She could smell the faint aroma of rose oil scenting his periwig. Still stunned by his untimely visit, she trailed mutely after him.

"You sail for India 'afore sunup," the Duke informed her bluntly, his back to her. He turned, and the hazel eyes fell briefly on Melissa's stricken face. His thin mouth twitched somewhere between a grimace and a smile.

Then, allowing her no time to comment, he removed a paper from a pocket and handed the list he had made to Annie. "I've accounted for everything you'll need for the voyage. Take exactly what I've instructed. No more, no less. All has been carefully planned."

Annie's face had paled. Clearly the notion of a voyage to India did not inflame her with enthusiasm. "But if your lordship pleases—"

"Pack, pack," he ordered. "That's what I please. Not a breath to waste on any buts!"

Two red spots appeared on Annie's ashen cheeks, but she dipped a frantic curtsy and gamely rushed off to do as she was bid.

Melissa was not so compliant. She spun around, the heavy folds of her dressing robe swinging gracefully with her movement. Her loose hair against the peach-colored material looked like a river of flowing honey.

"India? Before the sun's up! What madness is this?" Her heart had been seized by equal parts fear and hope. It could be that this was merely a dramatic ruse, another of his strategic ploys to manipulate her into a confrontation with Brandon.

But then again, what if the scheme was legitimate? Could such a thing possibly be? Was she truly to be off to India as she had so fervently dreamed?

Her grandfather's sharp eyes flashed at her. She could see him reading her thoughts, always a jump ahead of her, confound the man....

"My body shrivels, but rest assured my wits are quite intact—never fear for that." The Duke reached again into the robe's deep pocket. Retrieving a second paper, he extended it to Melissa. A light flamed briefly in the old man's eyes. She had a fleeting image of how he once must have looked, vigorous and handsome, as a young man. "You may consider this a victory."

She took the paper and, head bent, moved slowly toward the lighted candle on a nearby table, her eyes scanning the script. "No..." she murmured, and stopped short in her tracks. "No, this can't be." She lifted her face, confronting the Duke with a look of outrage. "Of what victory do you speak? Certainly, it can't be this! Do you think I'm such a fool? You can't possibly mean for me to imagine this could be real." She brandished the paper. "Brandon de Forrest would never agree to take me to India."

The Duke was calm. "Ah, but you can see for yourself. The proof. His signature is in your hand. His worthy seal affixed. Ah, yes...he has capitulated."

But Melissa was not convinced. Sighing wearily, she let her hand with the paper fall to her side. Her vision turned inward as she spoke. "Oh, again, again...this is some miserable trick you are playing." She looked now at the Duke, her words listless. "Aye, Grandfather, and a poor one, too. Not one of your better schemes. Because seal or no seal, I don't believe it for an instant," she added with narrowed green eyes.

With a sudden shrug and a defiant toss of her head she started toward her dressing table. The long golden skein of tresses flowed with the movement, catching and absorbing the nearby glow of candlelight. "I am weary," she said, "and so must you be. Tired of this whole India matter." As if it were a piece of lint, she dropped the purported contract amid a jumble of boxes and glass toiletries.

The Duke met her gaze in the vanity's mirror. "I promise you, not only does de Forrest know you are going, I can also assure you he is eager to make this voyage."

In the glass the green eyes flared back at the Duke. "Eager, is he? Ha! And I'll believe that when fish can fly."

"Such distrust. So unbecoming in one your age."

"Is it?" she said lightly, staring at herself. "A pity. But perhaps I've earned the right to my suspicious nature. In the time I've been in London, I've aged two hundred years. At least." She fumbled on the table for her brush.

"You could always go back to Cornwall. There you can rot from boredom, dying without a wrinkle of care on your brow."

"Perhaps Brandon *did* sign your paper," she said reconsidering. Her green eyes met the Duke's through the looking glass. "But if he did, then I'm sure it had nothing whatsoever to do with his own free will. So please, don't expect me to believe this other myth—that he looked gladly upon a voyage with me."

She gave her hair two violent sweeps with the brush, then spun around on her stool as Annie returned from the adjoining room, her arms filled with garments.

"Put them away, Annie," Melissa ordered. "There will be no voyage to India for us."

"Pay her no mind," the Duke contradicted firmly, with a discounting wave of his arm. "Continue to pack. You're to be on board the *Falcon* before the sun has fully risen."

Melissa stood, whirled on him. "And I tell you, we are not going to India!"

The Duke let her outburst die, then went on serenely. "Now you are being the fool."

Melissa sniffed indifferently.

"Oh, yes...a fool. Cutting your nose to spite your face. India was your dream."

"Aye, and it's still that—a dream. Nothing more. Because I will not be made a spectacle! I will not be used like a toy! I will not, for your monetary purposes, stand aboard a ship to be despised and scorned for months on end, by a man who reviles me!" *And who loves another woman,* she thought bitterly, clenching and unclenching her fists, as she remembered Pavan in his arms the night of the ball.

"On the contrary!" the Duke returned, matching her forceful tone. He lowered his voice, saying conspiratorially, "Don't you understand? It's plain. If anyone has groveled, then it is de Forrest. By signing this agreement he's virtually on his knees to you. All his pride...all his talk of independence... all his nobility.... He has signed it away. And to you."

Momentarily disarmed by the picture her grandfather's words painted in her mind, Melissa said nothing. *On his knees.* It was as if her grandfather had stolen the phrase from the depths of her heart. *On his knees....* Indeed?

It was this that she had dreamed about ever since the night in the tavern when Brandon had played with her, treating her deepest feelings as inconsequential. An annoyance, that's what she had always signified to him. *To have Brandon on his knees to her...she had always wanted that satisfaction.*

Of course, she would have preferred to have won him herself, by way of her charms. But what her grandfather had said *did* indeed have some merit to it: Brandon had bent his principles by signing the paper. That, at least, was something. From his present vantage point it would not be nearly so easy to sneer down at her. And in the meantime, she would have the opportunity of his company, during which time she could truly conquer him.

The Duke sensed an advantage and slipped his voice deftly between her thoughts. "And also there is that girl...that Celia. Does she not depend upon you? If not you, who else will come to her aid? Your friend the Duchess of Beltonwick is too old to make such a strenuous journey—besides which her husband would never permit it. You are the girl's only hope.''

"Very well," Melissa said. "I'll go. But not because of your interference. For my own sake, for the sake of Celia, I'll sail to India.''

"But of course," said the Duke, "a wise decision." And they both knew equally well the decision had been made by him. He collected his contract from the vanity table and turned to leave.

"Tell me," Melissa called after him, "how long have you known of these plans?''

"Ah, for a while...." he returned noncommittally.

"For a long while, I'll wager.''

"There were arrangements to be made. And had you known before, you would have conspired against me.''

"And the trip to Italy you promised Glenmillan and Quentin?''

"Ah, yes...that." He halted and swiveled half-around, a faint smile of delight playing on his face. "A wicked little amusement, I confess.''

And in spite of herself, Melissa also had to smile.

It would not be pleasant tomorrow to be around her stepmother and Quentin.

Brandon stood on the quarterdeck taking stock of his domain of wood and coiled hemp and iron and rolled canvas. Behind him a diffused lantern glow shed an amber pool of light behind his silhouette, carving his form out of the night.

He saw that the last of the iron was loaded, along with broadcloth and woolens to be traded in India; everything going was hauled aboard and stowed high and dry in the ship's hold.

He saw, also, that daylight would be upon them within the hour.

A shiver passed through him, and reflexively he tightened his arms across his chest. But it was not the cold that afflicted him; it was his mind.

Below, men who suffered no such complexities of spirit bustled about efficiently. They were experienced at their jobs, old salts to the very last of them, and eager to be borne atop forty-foot crests, to ride the trade winds to new fortune. If only he could share in their enthusiasm. Brandon gauged the tide; it was high—ideal for casting off into the moonlit channel that would take them into the open sea.

For the first time in his career as a seaman, he was not gripped by the thrill of adventure lying before him. Instead, as he stared beyond the roofs of warehouses into the sleeping city, he clung to the scents of brick and mortar, of plank and earth, of a million and one petty civilized indulgences that were a part of a world he had always found stifling, but now would have gladly suffered rather than take this journey.

On this voyage he would have a green-eyed hellcat on board, a constant reminder that he was as far from being a free man as any slave. It was one of the strange and cruel paradoxes of life: being always denied that which he most wanted, while those selfsame gifts seemingly poured like rain upon the heads of others. He had sought autonomy, and instead found enslavement to the Danforts.

An image formed of Melissa as she might be even that instant. He saw her lying in a silken nest of perfumed sheets, the face serene, the devil in her temporarily stilled by sleep. Imagining her so—the small emerald-eyed tigress at rest—a fleeting smile came to his face, more gentle than he would have liked if he had seen himself.

In the background, he heard Ross dealing with the ship's purser, delivering official papers to be presented to the officials at their port of entry in India.

A long, shrill whistle from the crow's nest wound through the night, enveloping the ship with a new sense of urgency. It was a signal to those still loading that departure was now imminent.

And out of the mist, as the high keening died, Melissa Danfort emerged suddenly, like an enchantress from the night.

At water's edge, she stood on the glistening moisture-coated cobbles, in the company of another woman, probably her chambermaid. Ross was quickly there to assist her up the gangplank. But she hesitated, her head rising suddenly, and the hood of her dark green cloak fell back, exposing the determined and lovely face Brandon had grown to know all too well since their meeting in Cornwall. He saw the heavy mass of golden hair framing the delicate features, and shivered slightly, remembering the feel of it trailing against his heated flesh during their lovemaking. She looked upward, her eyes searching until they came to rest where he stood.

A bolt of terror such as he had never felt during any pirate attack passed over him. It was as if her eyes bound him to a future he could not refuse; and the worst of it was, he could not even say truly if he wanted to refuse what she offered.

There had to be sixty feet separating them, yet at that moment they might have been touching, so potent was the look they exchanged: enemies and lovers…forever apart, forever together…torture and ecstasy, all of this combined.

Yes, a slave he was, his heart and mind bound to this misery.

Overhead an early gull circled noisily, like a gray wraith screaming, "Danger!"

But it was too late to back away from what had begun that afternoon in Cornwall. Now the green-eyed witch had begun her ascent up the wooden walk to his ship. *His ship?* No, it was now, curse her, curse her grandfather, *their* ship. And she knew it.

His bos'n also appeared just then, temporarily distracting him from his misgivings as he asked about storing Brandon's trunk in his cabin or carrying it below deck. Of wood and bronze construction, the trunk had seen the world with Brandon. On this voyage it held pistols and fine brandy and a formal outfit to be worn should he be required to sit in the company of the Mogul or other dignitaries. He also had packed various gifts of different value, including bribes to port officials, who would certainly require them. India was rife with corruption.

Below, the figures of the two women disappeared in a veil of fog blowing across the deck. A second later the fog cleared and the women were truly gone, led into their own cabin.

At the first hesitant light of day, the *Falcon* was gliding down the Thames toward the open sea, the sails unfurled and tinged with pink from the sky. Brandon stood at the quarter gallery railing.

Below him, he saw Melissa, the fair hair streaming behind her, caught by the wind, and fiery in the rosy light of daybreak. Her green cloak rose, billowing and spreading and rippling like the wings of some rare, magical bird. He thought he had never seen such a beautiful sight as that dawn...and that woman...and he hated her all the more for the desire he felt.

He was studying a map of Rajputana when the expected knock sounded against his cabin door. Tensing, Brandon straightened himself for the ordeal to follow.

"Yes, come," he ordered, and turned to Melissa as she entered his cabin on the heels of his steward, sent to escort her.

As before, the deep green wool cloak covered her body. He noted the dark splotches of sea spray against the fabric. The cloak's hood was down, and her pale hair framed the delicate oval of her face. It was clear that she had made some attempt to arrange the curls into a becoming style, but the wind had undone her efforts. Still, no matter that she had come apart, she looked magnificent to Brandon—like a wild gypsy—and he remembered how once he had thought her a silly innocent as she danced atop a table. Well, she had changed. Greatly.

"How good of you to come." He gave a bland delivery, contrary to the quickening of his pulse.

"Not at all, Captain," she returned with equal offhandedness. She cast him a quick side glance. "I presumed I had no choice." Although she remained stationary, swaying slightly with the movement of the ship, the green eyes scanned his quarters. Clever eyes they were, almond shaped and curving slightly up at the corners, with a sweep of thick dark lashes to lend added emphasis to the exotic impression she cast.

"On the contrary," Brandon returned. "You were invited to dine." He shot a glance at his steward. "Those were my instructions, clearly given."

She looked back at him, her expression softening somewhat, but wary just the same. "Yes, they were clearly received. Your man is not at fault. But, really, how strange. You see, I was under the impression you did not enjoy my company. I was naturally suspicious of your sudden change of heart."

She held his eyes for a moment, and he read in hers a taunt that he was now under obligation to her.

"Yes, well, you see, it's the captain's duty to invite his guests to a private dinner on the first night's sailing."

Melissa felt the heat rising to her face. "Ah, yes... I see... a tradition. How charming. So civilized." *I will have him on his knees,* she reminded herself.

"You may leave us," said Brandon to the steward, who departed quickly, sealing them in with their cold fury.

When they were alone, Melissa said evenly, "Monsieur de Forrest, truly, you needn't go through the senseless charade of patronizing me. As we both fully know, I'm hardly a guest on this ship. I've been led to understand that it is solely because of the Danfort influence that you are able to sail under the flag of England at all. This voyage is a necessity to you. I am a necessity to you, not a guest. We needn't pretend."

"The devil take you, woman...." Brandon said, the dark eyes growing cold. "This voyage is long and difficult enough. Must you add to its unpleasantness?"

"I want you to know one thing. This is a voyage I preferred not to make in your company."

"I preferred not to make it at all."

"But here we are," she said. "Anyway."

"But you did not have to come," he said, arching one brow. "You had nothing great to lose."

"But something very great to gain," she said sweetly, giving him a penetrating look. She put her fingers to her neck and, with a tug, unfastened the hook binding the cloak. The material parted and showed a dark, rich, wine-colored velvet gown. The bodice was low and tight, pushing up and forward the mounds of her breasts. At the sight of her beauty, Brandon swallowed deeply. She had seen his reaction, and smiled again. The cloak slid off her shoulders and with a toss she let it fall upon a nearby chair.

His eyes coursed down her body, and she knew with every fiber of her being that she looked beautiful, desirable, and that he wanted her. The power of her sexuality warmed her, and against her will she found herself responding to the trap meant solely for him. But when he looked back up at her, his eyes were insinuating and mocking, which was precisely what she had anticipated.

"There are some things that even the Danfort power can't command."

"Oh," she said, feigning shocked surprise, "but you do misunderstand me. It's India I hope to gain. India, with all its wealth... for the Danfort name." A spray of ocean water dashed against a window, startling Melissa. The boat listed, then righted itself.

Across the room, Brandon loomed tall and handsome, every bit as desirable in the flesh as he had been in her memory. Yet, in his dark eyes, she read nothing but scorn for her.

A slow, painful fire burned its way from her most private chamber—that place where she had stored every sweet dream, every hopeful longing for this man who so clearly despised the very sight of her—and erupted into a storm of desperate, self-righteous pride. *She would never bend to him, never apologize, never explain!*

"I prefer to dine alone," she said, and turned again to collect her cloak, which she threw about her with a flourish. Then she reached for the door's iron handle. But in vain. The ship rolled, caught in a series of high swells, and what was meant to have been a proud and determined exit became instead a jerky and unbalanced performance as she was pitched back into the cabin. Instantly, she collected herself—even as she felt a red flush of humiliation rising to her cheeks—and, getting her bearings, again set forth.

From behind her, she heard, "Madame, for the time being we are stuck with each other. Be also aware that this is my ship, my commission. Neither you nor your meddling, scheming demon of a grandfather have any say aboard this vessel while we are on the open seas. *My* wish—not yours—is law here."

Melissa turned back, her entire being quivering with indignation.

She could think of nothing to say. Instead, looking at him, seeing him not only with her eyes, but with her heart, she would have to tell him that his greatest crime was simply that he did not love her.

"Damn you, Brandon. Damn your smugness." The ship pitched, and she jerked to the side. If she hadn't managed to catch hold of a cabinet, she would have found herself sprawled on the planks, rolling around at his feet.

He laughed again, this time with less mockery and more warmth. "And I thought that you had changed! But perhaps it takes more than a gown to create such a transformation. You never know when to stop...you never know when you have reached your limit."

She shot him a look of hatred, not only because he was ridiculing her, but also because what he said had more than a little truth to it. But, oh...how his male beauty stung her. The shining black hair was drawn neatly behind his neck, with the strands barely touching his shoulders, broad and straight beneath the loose white shirt. She saw him like a glowing, brilliant distant star, unreachable no matter how many times she wished upon it.

The ship gave another sudden roll, and Melissa lurched forward into a table set for the meal they were to share. She caught the table's miniature railing and clasped it with both hands, waiting for the next shift to upset her.

"Ah, it appears you're eager to dine after all," he said dryly.

"I would rather eat poison than dine with you," she said, looking up with enough fire in her green eyes to ignite kindling, only to find herself disarmed beneath his smile. Their eyes held. Though she struggled to draw herself away, the dark magic of his gaze enfolded her, rendering her helpless against her desire.

"I hate you," she said softly, tears coming to her eyes.

"So you've said before," he said, but gently this time. "Much, much has happened since we met. And not any of it particularly fortunate for either of us. We have this voyage to get through, and then..." He stopped, drew in a breath, and said as much to himself as to her, "Melissa...you know that we can't be more than what we were—and not even that again. You know that," he said, speaking as if she had argued the point.

"Yes! Yes, I know that. You've made that plain enough, haven't you? But I didn't plan this voyage. I want you to know that. You must believe me. I never wanted to see you again after the ball." Biting her lip, she looked away so that he could not see her tears, nor realize the weakness she had for him even now, after everything he had done to humiliate and wound her.

"I'm sorry," he replied, this time without coldness or sarcasm. "What happened was not intended to cause you grief."

"Still, you knew what that night meant to me—what you meant to me."

"Perhaps...yes," he admitted, nodding slightly, and added somewhat sadly, "I knew, but—"

"But you didn't care...." Melissa whispered, even then remembering her hurt.

"I didn't want to care," he admitted, suddenly fearful that he might tell her exactly how he felt. She was incredibly beautiful, more desirable in her fury and sadness than she had ever been. For a fleeting moment he didn't care about the consequences that would follow his speaking the truth. To make love to her every night for the whole of the voyage was worth the sentence to hell such honesty would bring about in his life.

"You did not care for me, anyway." Melissa gave a weak laugh, torturing herself with the image of Brandon holding Pavan in his arms. She needed to remember, needed the strength of hatred to save her from humiliating herself by loving him.

"No, I didn't want to care for you," he responded in seriousness. "Melissa—" he began, knowing exactly what people meant when they spoke of the madness of love.

But she broke in before he had exposed himself. "I'm wondering, really... how could you bear to leave her for so long?" There was no reason to speak the name. They both understood it was Pavan. "Aren't you afraid that someone will claim her... again, while you sail the seas?"

At her cutting words, the feelings that collected in Brandon evaporated. They were replaced by an empty coldness that brought sanity to him as he recalled the years of humiliation and suffering he had endured for another beautiful woman.

Melissa wanted to look back at him, to see if she had hurt him with her barbed reference to the past. But she couldn't trust herself for fear that she might succumb to her own feelings of buried longing and despair. How wretched life was!

For what seemed an interminable time, Brandon was quiet. Then he said without inflection, "A meal's been prepared for us. I suggest we put aside our personal differences and sit down to eat it."

"I'm not hungry."

"Very well. It's up to you," he said without emotion.

When she had gathered the courage to face him, she saw that his eyes, although fixed on her, were a dark wall of disinterest. She could have borne anything—even hate or scorn—but not his infernal disinterest.

"I'll take all my meals in my cabin."

"As you wish," he said with a slight shrug.

She twisted the door open and began to step out. But just as quickly, Brandon pulled her back, swinging her in to him. For that instant they were close, close enough that their lips were almost touching. His breath held the scent of ale and was warm against her skin, reminding her of when they had made love in his office. She closed her eyes, her pulse racing faster than the wind speeding the *Falcon* over the green depths. Her lips parted; her heart pounded with such force she feared he would hear its thunder and know....

Oh, pride be damned! The future be damned! She loved him, would always and forever love him. He did not need to kneel to her....

But there was no kiss.

Instead she heard, "You aren't to walk about on your own," and his hold on her went limp. Slowly, as she opened her eyes—eyes that were glazed with fading desire and renewed regret over her weakness to resist her own nature—he drew completely away from her. "It's too dangerous," he said, and she realized that he was trembling, too.

Grabbing a coat, he threw it over his shoulders and ushered her into the howling night. Water drenched over them before they had made it across the deck and down into the corridor where her cabin, plus Annie's, were located. At her door he hesitated.

"You can have all your meals here, if you'd like. Don't walk about without an escort. There are no angels aboard this ship. Only men...." Her face was wet and her hair streamed over her cloak, with some of the strands plastered against her skin. He removed two strands trailing across her nose, holding on to the last lock longer than was necessary. "We're only men," he repeated and left her with a look that haunted her through the night.

Brandon took the watch that night and refused to be relieved. The ship rode high on the waves until dawn, when the sea turned tame and he retired to his cabin. His eyes were red and hollow from lack of sleep, but the devils in his soul had been vanquished by the elements. He slept soundly, and when he awoke in midafternoon, he did not remember that in his dreams he had made love to a woman with golden hair and green eyes, until he saw her standing on deck with her maid.

She stared up at him from below, looked at him knowingly, like a witch, and he wondered if it had truly been a dream.

In London, Glenmillan Danfort sat in the middle of her room, which she had spent the morning reducing to rubble. Her face was puffy from hours of tearful rage. The drapes had been clawed down. Every figurine and bowl and clock and mirror and perfume bottle had been smashed upon the floor. Tables had been upended and chairs hurled one upon the other until they splintered.

In another part of London, Quentin Danfort was in a raging drunk and hardly realized that he had lost one hundred pounds at cards. He was not so drunk, however, that he failed to hear a man, standing nearby, say to his companion, "I hear that Quentin Danfort's finished, quite done for...financially, socially, done for entirely. You won't find him on my guest list, I can assure you."

"Nor mine," drawled the other.

Quentin looked up, tears in his eyes, as the two men turned their backs, walking to another table where voices rang gaily as someone took a large win.

He noticed, peripherally, how nicely dressed the two men were, and it was perhaps this that saddened him the most, that brought reality crushing down upon his shoulders—for there would be no fine new threads for him to wear, no Italy, no anything, for there was no longer any Melissa.

Melissa had abandoned them.

Melissa had escaped.

Chapter Thirteen

For days turning to weeks, the *Falcon* rose and fell, crashing down deep green troughs and rocketing upward to ride mountainous swells. Then there were other times, moments of calm, when the vessel hoisted full sail and raced over a glassy, suddenly friendly sea.

The shifting colors, the mercurial moods of the sea—all of this brought to Melissa's mind the likeness of her own unstable nature, as, on course, the ship followed the cold current down the west coast of Africa, then for a time sailed with the warm trade winds.

In remote bays, where on shore the heat formed yellow clouds of dust into high funnels, Brandon would drop anchor to replenish their supplies, and whenever possible engage in trade of spices and fabrics and exotic woods and ivory, in return for his woolens and iron. During these stops Melissa, exiled aboard through her own pride and willfulness, would lean against the ship's railing, longing to go forth into the world as did Brandon, yet having to content herself to whatever her hungry eyes could take in from a distance.

Walvis Bay was their last port before rounding the Cape of Good Hope, originally named the Cape of Storms—and for good reason, Melissa had been warned. This was a perilous stretch of water, and more than a few ships had foundered and gone to the depths.

At Walvis she was, as always, commanded to stay aboard while the men took their liberty among the natives.

She was mad to go ashore, fevered with curiosity, overflowing with energy having no outlet. Still, no matter how great her desire for solid earth, her will was steel.

She had made a vow to herself, promising that she would never again stoop to begging Brandon for any favor. And since that first night, when she had refused to dine in his company, she had never wavered from her aloof stance.

Dullness and predictability proved to be the price for her stubbornness and pride.

Every meal was taken with Annie within the confines of their cramped quarters; all walks above deck were in the company of an escort chosen by Brandon for, she supposed, his lack of intellect.

The fact was, she was no better than a prisoner. How she longed to break free from her self-imposed constraints! She was desperate for adventure!

Such was her strained state as, unobserved and feeling forgotten, she looked landward from the *Falcon*'s railing, her green eyes fixed on Brandon's figure. If only she might join him. He moved among the local tribesmen in their loincloths or long robes, some men wearing coiled white cotton cloth turbans, atop their heads, as required by their religion.

But, unique as these sights were, they did not occupy her interest nearly so much as did Brandon's far more familiar figure. For, as long as he was in sight, her attention rarely strayed to other scenery.

It was always so. Brandon mesmerized her, rendered her all but witless in his presence. From the first fateful glance she'd had of him in Cornwall, as he came thundering over the hillside with his cape flying, it had been so for her. Long ago that was, and she an innocent then....

But even now the sight of him thrilled her, causing her mind to kindle thoughts that set her body afire with longing. So tall he was, and even more handsome now that he was in his favored element, with his skin sun-burnished from the days at sea. His black hair glistened blue-black as a raven's feathers, as in the equatorial heat he strode at ease within the noisy crush of local inhabitants.

In contrast to the natives' scant clothing, and although others in his crew had shed their usual outfits for makeshift sarongs and short breeches, Brandon remained a dignified and imposing figure in his traditional seaman's garb: the soft, white linen shirt open to the waist, the full sleeves catching a breeze, billowing the fabric like miniature sails. And beneath the clinging moist fabric of long pants, the powerful legs flexed, reminding Melissa of the passion they had known locked in each other's embrace.

She had no way of knowing that Brandon, walking on shore, was equally aware of the female form standing at the rail of the *Falcon*.

Beside him walked the Shahbandar, the fat and officious local head of customs, who spoke in a low voice of certain gratuities that were expected if Brandon hoped to conduct business in his port. It was a pressing issue, one that required full attention, but Brandon found it hard to concentrate.

His mind no longer belonged to him. It strayed continuously to the *Falcon*, to the woman who haunted his thoughts from daybreak to nightfall and even tormented him in his restless sleep.

It was a humiliating position, this unwanted possession of his faculties, and he had at first attempted to blame it on biology. After all, he had been without the physical pleasures afforded by female company for many weeks. The alluring body of a beautiful young woman was enticement enough for any man.

But no, he could not live with such facile self-deception. The pressure within—growing, it seemed, not with the days but with the very hours!—was not entirely physical.

That first night he had been stunned by his feelings for her. And it was with a cruel sense of relief that he allowed her to box herself into her present circumstances. Since then she had existed as a prisoner, hardly venturing from her cabin but for her escorted walks, and not once leaving the ship when they docked.

But revenge lost its appeal, and her discomfort rapidly became his own as he caught sight of her during her short strolls above deck. Proud as always, beautiful as ever, she floated over the planks with the forced air of the wounded determined not to show pain.

More than once he had come close to capitulating. He had been tempted to suggest they make the best of their situation and declare a truce. They would coexist politely, with distant but agreeable cordiality. But each time, at the crucial moment, he had been saved from this bit of idealistic foolishness by more sound judgment.

He doubted that he would be able to resist a physical encounter. Past experience had proved that he had little resistance to the beckoning force of her slanted green eyes. And then there was the body: a sailor's most exotic dream come true—but a sane man's downfall.

And he was a sane man. At least he was attempting to be so.

But he could feel her eyes following him as he moved through the jostling, curious crowd of locals come to meet his ship.

On two occasions he turned, caught her watching him and quickly looked away, feeling as foolish and out of control of his emotions as an enamored schoolboy.

It struck him then, with a sickening force, that he was frightened of her. In her inaccessibility, she had finally gained power over him. It was a dangerous power, and one he decided to obliterate that very day by taking advantage of the hospitality of the local ruler, who had organized an elaborate festivity for the white-skinned *feringhis*.

The heat, the wine—brought from his own ship—and the music conspired to aid in his cause, and by the time the moon was high that night, shining large and full on the glassy waters of the bay, Brandon had regained his sense of independence.

He was, in fact, so certain of himself that he turned away from the woman who had been selected by his host to please his carnal appetites and dared to board the ship and fearlessly face the green-eyed demon.

Melissa paced the deck.

Her forehead—in fact, her whole body—was slick with sweat. She told herself it was the heat, only the heat, but that was a lie. She had watched with misery as Brandon and the bulk of the crew, who had been granted freedom on shore, were lured inland to an entertainment she knew included wine, women and song. Dim shouts, male laughter and the strains of atonal music, heavily accentuated by the drive of drumbeats, stirred not only the thick night air, but also her blood.

He would have a woman this night.

Unable to stand the moon, so alive with the promise of passion, she went below to her cabin and shut the door.

But she did not escape the images that arose in her mind, maddeningly clear, as if what she dreamed had actual life.

She thought of killing him. She thought of throwing herself overboard and ending it all. She imagined him hearing of the tragedy. He would shrug, mark it down in a log book, continue sailing....

The man had infected her with madness!

The little room was so close. The heat bore down on her, coating her lungs. She ripped open the bodice of her gown and gasped for air. But it wasn't any use. The heat was as much within her as it was without.

She couldn't bear it any longer and returned to the deck, forgetful that she had broken the cardinal rule of not being there unescorted. For a moment she was nervous. But no one was around now to harm her, nor even see her and report her actions to Brandon. Whoever had been left on board had retreated to their quarters or to tend ship's business below.

Outside it seemed better, but only for a moment. Within seconds, the music again pierced her serenity, and all the images of Brandon locked in embrace with another woman set upon her again, driving her to the far side of the ship, where she leaned over the railing, gasping again for relief.

The moon lay like an enormous silver coin upon the water. For a time she stared at it, finding calm in its unmoving image, and finally she let her mind drift, like a piece of jetsam floating past the ship. Without any thought, she undid a lower button, and feeling a hint of breeze upon her skin, dared yet one more, until finally, in a burst of defiant abandonment, she released the strings of her bodice. With that, her physical comfort was much improved—and she felt liberated spiritually as well. This small rebellion was the most exciting thing she had done for weeks.

The music from shore still carried to her ears, but so did the gentler sound of water slapping rhythmically against the ship's hull. Between the two competing orchestrations she did not hear the footsteps behind her, until the voice accompanying them startled her, causing her to whirl around—forgetful entirely that the front of her gown was open. Too late she realized that the strings of her bodice had widened; had, in fact, become all but undone.

"Melissa!" He had spoken her name sharply, and intended to follow the single-word admonition with a lecture.

But all thought halted at the sight of her beauty.

It was as if he had been stunned senseless by an invisible attacker. He could only gape at the vision she created beneath the moonlight—skin like silver, hair tumbling from its upsweep, eyes wide and startled. And the body... breasts round and full, darkened tips thrust into hardening points....

He swallowed, trying to control his instincts. But the wine he had imbibed suddenly flowed through his veins like strings of fire.

Melissa stepped back, as if singed by his thoughts.

She made an attempt to shield her bosom, an attempt that only half succeeded. "I—I..." she began, but at a loss, she suddenly grasped her skirts and made a second attempt to bolt from his company.

But the wine and moonlight and music had taken their toll, obliterating all former thought of strength and prudence. Across the water, the beat of the drums matched the pulse of his groin, and everything—the night, the wine, the music, the woman—melded. Only this...this need, this desire...mattered, as he pulled her to him.

"No! No!" she objected, and made a motion to free herself.

But he countered it easily and brought his mouth hard against hers. She yielded, but only for an instant, after which she pushed hard against him and landed backward against the railing she had been looking over a moment earlier.

"Drunk!" she accused. "You're completely sotted!"

"Absolutely," he admitted, finding it amazingly easy to admit to human frailty. He should have thought of it before. "I'm flesh and blood, after all." He laughed again at the realization.

"You're drunk, is the long and short of it!"

"Drunk on your beauty," he countered expansively.

"On the wine, sir, on the wine."

"On the moon, madame." He laughed. The world seemed suddenly light and topsy-turvy, with everything, even reason, inverted. Above him the moon floated, and below, beyond the railing Melissa was poised against, it floated as well.

She again started forward. "You were quite right—I shouldn't be up here. It's not safe. There're bad characters about. Besides, you're making a spectacle of yourself."

"Spectacle, you say?" And he caught her, spinning her in to him. "This is a spectacle, my little cat...." He ran his gaze over her breasts, then glanced up, laughing as her nipples responded to the touch of his eyes. His head was spinning. It was partly the wine but it was her nearness as well. He was dizzy with the desire of weeks of wanting her. "Were you waiting for me, Melissa?" he asked, his voice soft, only partly jesting.

She recoiled from the suggestion, averting her eyes from him. "Oh, your conceit! If you really want to know, I had no idea that you'd be back. In fact, I was sure you'd be locked in the arms of some wild woman by now."

"I was," he said blandly, and saw her face change. The proud self-righteousness shattered and the eyes glistened with a hurt she couldn't disguise. "But I couldn't make love to her," he amended, this time with a heartfelt tenderness. And once the feeling began, it was as if a tide had suddenly begun to flow and there was no stopping the warmth, for he went on in a rush, "I thought of you and—"

"No!" Melissa put her hands against her ears, shutting her eyes, like a child wishing to banish a terror.

"Wanted you."

The green eyes were open again, and this time blazed with indignation. "You think I'm so stupid? So easily pliable?" She paused as if gathering courage, then went on, choosing her words with effort, then losing her bearings in pure emotion. "I'm not the girl from Cornwall any longer. Nor am I the pathetic fool who threw herself at your feet—and into your bed—in London. You said once that I had much to learn. Well, I've learned. I didn't mean for this to happen, this voyage. And I won't allow myself to be used, to be made a fool of by you again. You don't love me—you only want me!" Her tone had escalated into a breathless sob, half rage, half sorrowful, regretful accusation. "But you can't have me. Do you hear? You can never have me again!" she finished, now weeping.

In the moonlight the tears on her cheeks appeared to Brandon as lovely and precious as pearls. She was enchantment itself. She *had* grown up. God help him, but the girl was a woman now, and wine and prudence be damned, he had never in his life wanted any woman as much as he did this one.

With her hand across the open bodice of her dress, she darted away from him. This time he didn't attempt to stop her. Instead he watched silently as she moved over the deck. In another instant she had disappeared through the door leading down to her quarters, and he was alone.

A cloud passed over the moon. Brandon looked up. Dark shapes appeared against a lighter sky overhead. The air was suddenly heavier, the water rougher. Melissa had roused the gods.

Safe in her cabin, she shut and locked the door.

Leaning against it, she took deep breaths of air and shivered. How she had wanted him! Waves of desire spread through her body. They could have lain together. She closed her eyes. It was impossible not to touch herself, impossible not to pretend that it was Brandon's hands running over her breasts as his eyes had done.

She had refused him!

Oh, God...she thought, groaning softly, what a miserable triumph. What a price to pay for pride.

Only the moonlight, drifting past her small window, touched her that night as she lay unclothed on the small, narrow bed, crazed with need.

Brandon retreated to his quarters—that safe haven, that monkish retreat that had always been his refuge from trouble or confusion. This time peace did not come as, stripped to nothing, he lay atop his bed, stiff with need and burning with desire.

He wanted her, hated her, feared her, worshiped her.

Heaven help him, but he would not rest until she was his again....

Chapter Fourteen

At last they reached India. No, that was not quite accurate. It was the reverse, Melissa thought cynically: India, it seemed, was upon *them* . . . and with a vengeance.

She surveyed her situation from atop a swaying elephant covered in embroidered silk. The fabric itself seemed alive. Hundreds of tiny mirrors had been sewn into its pattern, each piece of glass reflecting the agonizing sunlight.

Whatever Melissa had expected of her mother's native land, she had not imagined the heat. Africa had seared, but nothing could compare to the stifling closeness of India's tropical climate.

From the time they set foot on land she complained to Annie, who mostly suffered Melissa's tirades in silence, too listless herself to provide many words of consolation.

"I've managed to cross oceans—treacherous seas, mind you—and survived intact. But here, on firm land, I will surely drown. I will swallow dust and perish!" And Melissa would cough and fan the air and beat at her clothes, only to send up a new wave of fine dirt, making conditions all the worse.

"Soon you'll be in your mother's care. All will be well," Annie ventured without conviction, her own face flushed scarlet.

"Ha! My mother will make the acquaintance of my cold corpse!"

The worst of the weather could have been avoided, but that the voyage around the Cape had not been easy. In fact, they could count themselves lucky to be alive. In the crossing, the *Falcon* had sustained serious damage to its masts and minor damage to the hull. Consequently, their progress was delayed by several weeks in order to make the necessary repairs. This brought them into premonsoon season. The later date also meant that their business in India would have to be concluded with all due haste, lest they be trapped by the rains and wind soon to be unleashed over the parched plains.

With each delay, the image of Celia's circumstance, held in Melissa's mind, became more dire.

But at least some things went on course.

The soldiers of the Nawab were at the port of Dwarka, where they had camped for weeks, waiting to meet the *Falcon* upon its arrival.

The contingent provided more than a welcoming party. Their mission was also to assure the foreigners' safe passage to the Nawab's inland fort near Ahmadabad. Violent unrest was upon the land, as Hindu insurgents attacked Muslim strongholds. Although both sides warred in God's name, their image of the Almighty was not the same, and bloodlust seemed to have taken dominance over both religions' doctrines of brotherhood. There was little chance that any unprotected caravan could make it through the countryside with heads intact.

Although Brandon said nothing to show his concern, Melissa noted that a tense watchfulness had replaced his typically stoic demeanor. Furthermore, during those few occasions when they did not take the usual pains to avoid each other's company, his manner toward her was uncommonly solicitous.

More than anything else, this show of consideration alarmed her. It was entirely out of character. There had to be some reason, and what other than a grave one?

"Is our situation that crucial, then?" she asked him, contriving a tone of cool and elegant disinterest when he came to her tent.

He appeared like that every night, an official visitor making his rounds through their camp, and every night—though she hated herself for it!—her heart would give its usual leap upon his arrival.

"You needn't concern yourself," he said, looking down to where she sat on a pallet of carpets and silken cushions.

The tent was box-shaped, made of a strong cotton weave in striped design. Its roof, which was steeply pitched and gathered at its center peak, allowed for a fully grown man to stand without stooping. Anyway, she could not imagine Brandon bending down to anyone, for any reason. There was even room enough for the carved chest of aromatic wood, filled with various gifts sent by her mother.

To her annoyance, Melissa noted that he had spoken almost gently—not abruptly nor dismissively as was his former habit.

This, too, was strange. Had the heat affected his mind?

She surveyed him more closely, on guard for what surely had to be some trickery. The tent was adequately lit with small flares set inside filigreed brass coverings. If his brain had curdled, physically at least he did not look ailing; to the contrary, he looked fit, his skin darkly alive with the sun's glow, his physique hardened by the months of activity at sea. No, she considered, there was nothing wan about the man standing before her. He appeared as proud and arrogant and commanding and fit as ever. *But there was something afoot, something he knew and was keeping from her, and which she intended to discover.*

"Oh, but I must take an interest," she insisted primly, and went on with a noble attitude. "Have you forgotten? My reason for making this miserable expedition is to rescue a friend in dire need. Celia Allen has no one in the entire world but me on whom to depend. Anyway," she accused, eyeing him with growing unease, "it's entirely obvious that you aren't yourself."

His face suddenly altered from strange agreeableness to cynical amusement. For an instant she was relieved. The old Brandon, her darkly handsome, beloved foe, stood before her, looking down his beautiful, straight, aristocratic nose at her. And, further, as always in the past, he seemed suddenly anxious to take leave of her company.

"And I see you're every bit the same," he returned dryly. Clearly there was no compliment in the observation.

There, she had been mistaken; there was no cause for alarm. She relaxed, as he gifted her with a final discounting look.

But at the tent's opening, he turned back and said abruptly, "If you'd prefer not to have the eunuchs attend you—that is, it could be disconcerting—I can speak to the Nawab's captain and have—"

Melissa's eyes widened. Dramatically, she threw up her hands, entreating unseen help from above. "What!"

"I can speak—"

"No, no," she said, shaking her head. "Not what…but *why?* Truly, sir, this concern for my welfare baffles me. Are you quite well in your mind?"

Brandon's face clouded. Did a flush come? She expected a wicked reply; instead, he appeared ruffled by her accusation, even took it seriously.

"The responsibility's unsought. Thrust into my hands…it's unavoidable that I—"

"Oh, yes, *that* I can understand…all of *that* I've heard before. But you've never been one to lavish such *kindly* concern in the performance of your miserable, unsought duty toward me. This—this sudden *respect* you're showing me, well—" she raised one brow quizzically "—it's unnatural. Only the aged or infirm, or someone destined to leave the earth at any moment would merit such consideration from you. Naturally one can only think the worst."

"My profoundest apologies," he said stiffly. "I'll take care to be less respectful in the future. You may sleep soundly, madame…without fear for your safety or for my mind's stability." He began to leave again.

"Ah, wait!"

Brandon turned slightly. His glance was mocking.

"Witty though you are, Monsieur de Forrest, you can't escape so easily," she said laughingly. But her voice turned serious. "I want the truth. I demand it, Brandon. That is," she said quickly, and more moderately, "I've a legitimate right to know. Tell me . . . and be frank, sparing not an ounce of whatever horrible knowledge you're keeping to yourself." With dignity, she drew herself up from the collection of pillows. "So, what do you hear from the Nawab's men?"

"Hear? Why, madame, all manner of gossip. Unfit for such innocent ears."

"Ah, you see," she said dryly, "you treat me too kindly."

"Very well. You're soon to be cut into small pieces by assassins lurking in the hills."

"So I expected. And I'm to be fed to the vultures."

Brandon's eyes glinted in the soft, flickering light. "No. Too cruel to the birds. They'd die within minutes. . . ."

She couldn't help but smile, and for a moment they were linked by the humor. Their gazing into each other's eyes lasted longer than either had intended, and the frozen moment filled with unspoken emotion, grew taut, became alive with dangerous potential. Brandon's face darkened perceptively, and Melissa's heart began to pound, then race. *Ah, to make love again. . . .*

But the moment broke as Brandon abruptly excused himself, and for a while Melissa remained too shaken by the power of her feelings to remember her inquiry. Later, she did not ask if they truly were in imminent danger. She could not trust herself to another personal encounter with him. That was certainly too dangerous.

The journey took six days, the slow-moving caravan consisting of ornately bedecked camels and horses and painted elephants, one of which Melissa rode atop, surrounded by pillows and a canopy and secluded behind silken veils. An army of men carrying crossbows and sabers, and many bearing muskets, rode before and behind, and guarded their flanks.

The curtains—meant to shield her from dust and male eyes—were, of course, in vain. She continuously popped her head out to peer at the surroundings and ask questions unfitting for a woman, generally causing the mouths of guards to purse and dark eyebrows to raise in consternation over fierce black eyes. For once Annie was too sick and terrified to suggest Melissa adjust her ways to society's expectations, and as for Brandon, he knew better than to waste his energy.

It was a tiresome journey, consisting of many stops to rest the animals, and others for the saying of prayers. The chants filled the air with a haunting singsong cadence five times every day, as the faithful prostrated themselves in the direction of Mecca.

If this were not enough, a few detours were also necessitated by reports of trouble ahead. Not only were the Hindu dissidents intent upon driving out all traces of Allah and installing Shiva as the reigning image of God, but there was threat even from the Muslim foes of the Nawab who sought to usurp his territories.

And daily, the heaviness continued to gather in the firmament, pressing down upon them all and affecting their moods, while dust from the many hot months without rain turned the air into a fine golden haze so that the whole world glowed with an eerie light.

At night camp was set up, and fires would burn continuously on the outskirts, illuminating the area as a protective measure against stealthy attack. Tension gripped every face, and even Melissa—generally immune to brooding on danger—found herself perpetually on edge.

On the fourth night she could bear the climate no more. In a fit of frustration over being confined behind veils and tent flaps and locked into the constraining garments of the civilized world, she shed her proper English costuming and appeared for dinner in a silken sari, a gift from her mother.

Brandon had been engaged in conversation with the captain of the Nawab's guards when Melissa appeared. As on all nights, a circle had been formed, the perimeter marked with thick oriental carpets and the area covered in embroidered silk cushions. It was here where the men of rank convened. In the center a fire burned, illuminating the faces of four musicians playing sitar, tambura, drums and flute.

Dinner was already underway, the officers being waited upon by servants bearing silver platters and bowls with jewels encrusted in the designs.

For an instant, upon Melissa's arrival, Brandon could do no more than stare. He forgot the serving spoon he held midair. He forgot the eunuch who hovered beside him, crouched with a heavy platter of rice and lamb.

But he was not alone in his stunned admiration. Every male in attendance felt the same, their expressions naked with carnal speculation.

It was a stunning transformation.

In truth, Brandon might not have recognized her, but for the green eyes and light-colored hair. Except for these familiar features, she appeared entirely altered, from Western to Eastern. It was not only in the dress. Even in her bearing, the assimilation of her Asian heritage was complete.

Was it the silk, wound loosely about her slender body? Was it something more intangible?

Where once there had been a spriteliness to her movements, there now existed a languid, sensual flow of form, with the pink and red and magenta silk drifting like a rainbow mist as she moved.

Staring, the captain whispered reverently, with the disbelief reserved for the supernatural, "May Allah be my witness... a living goddess...."

And it was true. Brandon could barely concentrate as he listened to his host's talk of politics and military strategy.

During the last weeks, it had been all but impossible to keep his emotions to himself; in fact, she had come close to guessing that there was something amiss when she had challenged his kindness to her that night in her tent.

A thousand times he had cursed himself, fearing he was falling in love with the girl.

Now, he nodded politely, his mind moving in and out of the conversation with the Nawab's captain.

His rational senses weakened with every glance he sent the girl's way. Dark magic was being done to him, and he was powerless in its grip.

He told himself it was India—not Melissa. India was reputed to play havoc with a Westerner's sensibilities... he would not be the first to fall spellbound. It was a temporary aberration.

The musicians played their flute and sitar and drums, driving the beat of the raga into a frenzy, while across the circular expanse Melissa coolly dined.

But clearly, she was no longer Melissa...

And she herself knew it.

It was as if, upon slipping into the sari, she had slipped out of her old self and into the body of an enchantress. There was nothing strange in claiming this new self; she felt, rather, that this was her true self, that only a half of her had existed until India, and now she had been re-united at long last with her missing part.

India. It was more than a mysterious, faraway land; it was another world entirely, a place turning reality inside out, making the impossible actual and heightening what had been only ordinary before.

As she sat atop a silken carpet surrounded by pillows, the dusty air seemed transformed into a heady bouquet of scrub trees and spices and exotic oils. Every sound became music to her ears. Even the elephants' trumpeting, and the restless pawing and snorting of horses in the darkness beyond the camp, achieved the beauty of a melodic chorus. The very air throbbed with secret and ancient wisdom.

This was who she was, who she had always been: she was India. India flowed in her veins like rich, dark, enchanted wine.

She saw Brandon watching her and for once did not look away. Nor did he. And in his eyes, she saw that he, too, understood that she was no longer the same.

He came to her that night.

A slight breeze arose. Beyond the tent in which Melissa lay, the rustling of some dry vegetation interrupted her sleep, so that she hung suspended between waking and dreaming, her mind belonging to neither world.

Again the air outside shifted, but this time, amid the distant, restless braying of beasts she heard the fall of steps. In the light from the moon she saw a silhouette pause against the material of her tent. The eunuch guard outside roused himself, standing at attention, and for a moment the two male forms melded together.

Melissa sat up, watchful.

The silhouette moved on, turned, passed again, stopped briefly, then began to fade again.

She felt a rush of fever, followed by a chill of fear. *It was him.* She hesitated, then moved to the tent's opening and parted the material.

At the unexpected sound the guard whirled, his hand on the hilt of his long, curved saber. His eyes were fierce, frightened, and she drew back with a cry as the steel blade flashed above her, ready to strike.

But the sound brought Brandon, too, reeling around. His hand went swiftly to his dagger, lodged in a sheath, and he might have hurled it at that instant had the guard not realized his mistake and lowered the blade.

In haste, the sentry bowed deferentially to Brandon, acknowledging the mistake, then bowed to Melissa, whom he had frightened.

Brandon's eyes were also on her, burning through the night with a torment she could feel. How well she understood his indecision.

"I will be safe," she said quietly to the guard, and he dissolved discreetly into the darkness, to watch from a distance.

And she waited, knowing Brandon would have to come.

"You're restless," she said softly when he stood before her, sculpted in moonlight.

Brandon's gaze strayed, drinking in the length of her. "It's a difficult night," he said. "The heat..."

In sleep her hair had become unbound, and it hung loose now, shimmering in waves over her shoulders. The night-dress provided by Saluina was of diaphanous white cotton. It was cool, so fragile as to be almost weightless against her skin. Now, as the breeze found it, the thin covering outlined her full breasts.

Brandon swallowed hard, his throat constricting, and looked back to her face.

"Yes, it's close tonight," she said. "Perhaps the monsoons will come sooner than—"

"Melissa..." he interrupted fiercely, not listening to her, then paused, as if suddenly at a loss. "I—I'm..." He tensed. "Not myself."

Some leaves skittered over the dry earth, sounding like laughter.

"The heat...?" she chided. *Of a different nature.* She could so easily take her revenge. "You're not used to wanting someone," she said quietly, with a gentle seriousness, and met his eyes.

He shifted his attention to the surrounding darkness. "I told myself that it's India."

"Maybe it is."

He looked back at her. "No. Things... things are different now." He searched her face. His eyes narrowed and she could see him struggle against his feelings, turning his thoughts around. "Damn..." he whispered, the word bitter. "Do you know how much I want to make love to you?"

Now it was her turn to be afraid, to look quickly away. "I told you—it will never happen again. It can't," she whispered, in spite of her own longing, and she slipped from him and from the dangerous moonlight into her tent.

But in the space of that second, Brandon also moved into the dark enclosure.

He gripped her wrist and drew her in to him. "Melissa," he said, "my God, I have never wanted any woman as much as—"

She shivered, the familiar pleasure beginning, and she felt her resolve waning. Struggling, she said, "Yes... but what you want from me, and what I want for myself are different things, Brandon.''

''We want precisely the same things. . . .'' He kissed the side of her neck. ''You cannot deny it. . . .''

Her pulse quickened. She could feel his heart, as quick as her own. ''No—not with my body. But I can with my mind.'' The firmness in her voice returned, and responding to it, he loosened his hold and she was able to step back. ''Once I was content just to lie with you, oh, yes. . . .'' She closed her eyes. ''You burned in my mind, like a terrible flame.'' Memories leaped before her and she grew silent. She recalled the web woven of desire and defeat. Looking at him again, she spoke with conviction. ''I've come to India to do something important. And I must do it. For Celia I must—and for my own self. As I said before, there are also the negotiations I intend to make on behalf of my grandfather.''

''On behalf of—my God, woman . . . *that again!*''

In spite of herself, she flinched under his mockery. How could he understand that half of everything she did was to gain his respect? But the other half was for her own sense of self-worth, and she could not betray herself now, not even for the love and desire she felt for him. ''Yes, I thought you'd forgotten that.''

''Perhaps because there's good reason.''

''The reason being I'm only a woman?''

''Not *only,* but because you are a woman,'' he said, and reached for her. But she evaded him, drifting into the shadows before he could prove her frailty.

Her voice came softly from the folds of darkness. ''I'll earn my place in the world. Just as you have. I'll not be commanded and used and tossed aside . . . not ever again. Leave me . . . leave me now. . . .''

''The world's not ready for your schemes of greatness, Melissa.'' His voice was closer.

She moved farther back. ''That matters nothing to me. Leave me. . . .''

''Very well. If you want.'' In the dark she heard him draw away.

And, though knowing better, her heart sank. "Brandon..."

He found her instantly, pulling her into his arms. His mouth opened against hers, and his thighs pressed hard against her body. She could feel his readiness and she wanted him as much.

His mouth moved against her breasts, and she cried out softly in an explosion of pleasure. Clutching him closer, she called his name, wanting more of him, forgetful of all her fine, noble intentions.

He was laughing now. "Ah, my Melissa...my beautiful, hot, passionate Melissa! This is what you are...this is what you were meant for...what we are meant for together...." He sent fevered kisses over her body and, lifting her in his arms, drew her across the few feet into the pillows making up her bed on the carpet. Lowering her, he fell atop her, and in a stroke he lifted her gown over her breasts, even as he fought to free himself from his own clothes.

"No!" Melissa cried in a panic. She wrenched her gown down, covering herself. "No! What am I doing? Not this...not this...." She was breathing rapidly, fighting against the passion that had almost claimed her. "I'm gone mad from this heat, from this moonlight. I'll not be your whore again—not ever. For that's *all* I was! And all you want now, as well."

"So...this was your revenge, was it?" His voice was strained, and she imagined a cold violence gathering beneath his words.

"Think what you must," she said. "But you know it's not so. I want to—"

"Oh, yes...that again. You have heroic deeds to accomplish. Great acts to perform. Armies to outwit. Empires to build." She heard him drawing away from her, the sound of his clothes being rearranged. "Be advised that people who climb mountains often fall, Melissa."

"I won't ask you to pick me up."

"Nor would I."

He left her.

Melissa watched from within the tent as the silhouette of the man she loved faded from view and his quick steps turned to silent night.

Her promise to herself was still intact.

The satisfaction seemed a poor consolation; pride was a cold bedfellow.

Chapter Fifteen

The sun was a great glowing red ball in the darkening sky as their caravan approached the fort of the warrior Nawab, Alviradi Khan.

But for the rumble of their small army over the dried plain, the rest of the world seemed silent and suspended. Not a leaf twisted on a branch; no bird sang or moved against the sky.

The calm before the storm.... thought Melissa, shivering slightly in spite of the heat.

Now her heart quickened as horns sounded their arrival from atop the fort's parapets, and she looked up to where the towering walls of the citadel bled into the crimson night.

So... here in this place, her life had begun. And what a meager, senseless life it had been—not hers at all. From her first breath she had been tossed about like a ball in the hands of others.

But soon that would change, she reminded herself, attempting to regain her confidence, which had been momentarily shaken as the shadow of the awesome fortress encompassed their caravan. She had returned full circle to her origin, and in doing so would at last become the mistress of her own fate.

As she thought it, an enormous gate opened on its hinges and a drawbridge lowered. Behind that a second iron gate began to move, looking to Melissa like the yawning maw of a voracious beast.

Brandon, who had been behind riding with the guard, suddenly galloped forward, raising a cloud of dust. But reaching Melissa, he reined in and kept a slower pace with her high, lumbering mount. For a while he said nothing, acting as if she were not there. She saw he had changed into a clean shirt and wore a leather jerkin; even his boots shone to a glistening finish. Melissa herself had taken pains to prepare herself for the arrival. From the chest of gifts sent by Saluina, she had chosen to drape herself in blue silk, embroidered with silver stars and moons. In the twilight its hue was a deeper indigo, the embroidered symbols flashing with her movements.

They had hardly spoken since she had rebuffed his advances, and then only perfunctorily. Now, looking up to her high perch, he said with a half smile that mocked their last serious conversation, "So, the gates of your long-awaited paradise are opening to you."

"I don't expect miracles," Melissa returned evenly, although she would gladly have welcomed any that came her way.

"You may find you'll need them." He gave a nod ahead.

She followed his glance toward the monstrous structure they were about to enter. Before its mass, it was impossible not to feel small, not only in size, but in spirit. "I only expect what I can accomplish myself," she said stoically.

"Well, then, your moment of truth awaits. At long last we'll see of what stuff you're made. Will it be empty words . . . or will you show the world actual deeds?" He raised an eyebrow, following his words with a cynical smile.

Melissa looked away. She fumbled for a reply, but nothing came. She was truly frightened. The building stretching before her was larger than any she had ever seen, with towers and minarets and walls within walls, and on the outskirts, clusters of village huts. Where the gates had parted beyond the drawbridge, she could see only a shadowy interior, and her thoughts flew to the dark cell she had once shared with Celia. How arrogant of the English to feel so superior. This was might far beyond any displayed in their small isle. Above, hundreds of men dressed in military garb dotted the defense posts, some already bearing lit torches against the settling of night.

Brandon was right. What might she—one small, inexperienced Englishwoman—expect to accomplish here, in this wild land with its heathen people and pagan customs?

And then she remembered: she herself bore that same savage blood in her veins.

Turning her face down to Brandon, she said with renewed courage, "You needn't worry on my account. When I leave here, I'll have accomplished everything I've set out to do. Don't you recall, this is my home," she added confidently, sweeping a hand toward the fort. "I've family within."

In the last of the day's light, his black eyes flashed. "Family or not, I'd advise you to take care, Melissa. Although I'm sure you won't," he added as a dry aside. "These Muslim rulers have little patience with the plans and demands of foreigners. They've even less regard for the schemes of women—including their own." He paused, as if considering saying more. This time he spoke to the air in front of him rather than face her directly. "Before, I said I wouldn't help you. I take that back. You have only to ask."

"That won't be necessary," she returned with a cold look. For a moment—only a moment—he had disarmed her with his generosity. But he had only meant to show his superiority, and she quickly recovered from her goodwill.

"Then good luck to you," Brandon said, catching her look and holding it an instant longer, as if he had more to add. Whatever it had been, he kept it to himself as he spurred his horse forward.

Melissa watched him gallop away, the black hair, tied in its leather strap, gleaming behind him like a velvet streamer. A thrill passed through her, as it always did when she could look upon his natural grace, his incredible male beauty, unobserved. He and the animal he rode moved almost as one, with a majestic dignity, easily taking the lead in the front ranks.

He was first to cross the drawbridge, with the Nawab's captain at his side.

Melissa made her entrance some moments later, crossing into her birthplace just as the sun made a final thrust against the sky, turning the scene bloodred, and sank rapidly behind the horizon.

The first sight of her mother was under official circumstances in the Hall of Public Audience. The Nawab sat amid a cloud of cushions on a high platform of carved marble. Below his dais and to the side, Saluina sat, veiled and still, in the company of eight others of the Nawab's principal wives, of which she was the most exalted.

Melissa had expected a formal presentation to her mother; she had expected pomp, and to be welcomed as the guest of honor.

She found herself mistaken.

Instead it was Brandon who was received as the honored guest.

In fact, she might have thought herself invisible, had the Nawab not asked Brandon if it were not so that "the girl" was heir to the Duke of Danfort's estate.

Only this reference to her grandfather drew any attention her way.

"She is," replied Brandon. "His sole heir, the future powerful head of the House of Danfort." His lips curled slightly.

The Nawab was a tall man, with high cheekbones and a straight nose, beneath which a long and drooping mustache flowed. He dressed simply, in white silk, and at his side was a curved blade, gleaming wickedly when he moved, its handle encrusted with precious gems. About his head was wound a turban of brilliant cerise, decorated with a single huge emerald, appearing to Melissa as a third eye. His other two eyes were black points of interest, dissecting Melissa's person.

But even then she was not directly acknowledged for herself, but merely surveyed like a possibly useful object.

After a long look, the Nawab turned back to Brandon and said, "You will tell me about your English weapons."

And she was forgotten, left to hide her humiliation and disappointment as best she could.

But her mother had seen and understood.

They met two long days later, when Saluina had been granted official permission by the Nawab to visit Melissa in her quarters.

"I could see that you were offended. But you must understand," Saluina said, "in India a woman is for pleasure, for beauty. She is a possession to a man. Perhaps it is not so in England."

Melissa smiled disparagingly. "Oh, yes...it's exactly so in England. I'd counted on it being different here. There's so much I had planned on accomplishing." And she explained to her mother about Celia and about needing to prove herself to her grandfather by securing a trade agreement with the Nawab.

"But these things are impossible," Saluina said in amazement. She shook her head, then said gently, "You must not think of such things again. They'll only bring you disappointment and grief."

Melissa widened her eyes, as if her mother had asked the truly impossible of her. "But it's impossible to put these things from my mind! I can't do anything *but* think of them."

Saluina laughed. "How much you look like your father. As I remember him. But of course, that was so long ago...."

"Do I?" Melissa asked, delighted.

"I will never forget him. I loved him with my whole being. There was never anyone else but him for me—in spite of..." She seemed to be apologizing, and her face colored.

"Oh...no, please...don't. I understand, truly. You had no choice." And to herself, she added, *Just as I've had so little choice in my own life's course.*

Saluina's eyes were moist as she looked at Melissa. "Can you? Can you understand how it is to love one man, only one man, to never forget him...even though there were times when I thought I would go mad from the memory of him?'' She searched Melissa's face and answered her own question. ''Ah...'' she said in a whisper. ''You've loved someone, too.''

Melissa looked away. Her eyes filled. She tried to will the tears away. But she did not have to be proud and secretive now—this was her mother. ''Yes,'' she admitted aloud, for the first time to another person. ''I love someone.''

''Then I pray that your love will prosper. But how could you leave him for so long a time?''

''I didn't,'' Melissa said, feeling a slight flush spread to her cheeks.

Saluina was thoughtful, then nodding, said, ''Ah, so...of course. The captain. I've seen the way you watch him.''

''Alas, the captain,'' Melissa said with a sigh.

''A very interesting man...very powerful....'' Saluina stopped. ''He's not like your father, though. Philip was soft. This man is hard, a difficult man for a woman.''

''This man is the only one in the world for me.''

''Then, for all his difficulties, you must have him....'' Saluina said softly. ''At least my daughter will know love.''

''Then you must help me,'' returned Melissa. ''I must accomplish everything I've told you, if I am to have him.''

Saluina's eyes glowed with indignation. ''He won't take you without—?''

''No,'' Melissa laughed. ''I won't take *him*. He must respect me, he must see me as an equal, or it will never work between us.''

''An equal? But you're a woman.''

''Exactly,'' said Melissa.

She would have much preferred to act aloof and disinterested when Brandon at last came to see her. But after several days of being cooped up in the women's quarters, Melissa was half crazed with anxiety that she would never see freedom again.

"So. How goes the world, Monsieur de Forrest?" she said bitterly, no sooner had he entered the garden where she had been brought to receive him. She felt humiliated. Two eunuch guards stood sentry at the gated entrance.

"That depends on how you would wish it to be."

"As you can see, I'm a prisoner here. More or less." She spoke low, letting her words be covered by the soft music of the fountain in a shallow, lotus-filled reflecting pool. "Prisoners' wishes are not considered at all. There's nothing I can do, merely pace back and forth," and she began to demonstrate. "Nothing I can accomplish, unless it is to listen to harem gossip all day. I tell you, it's maddening." She slid him a resentful glance. "Of course, this must amuse you greatly."

"On the contrary," he said with surprising kindness. "But I'm afraid I've brought more bad news."

Melissa stopped her agitated wandering and turned. She noted that a heavy gold chain lay draped about his neck, a large ruby pendant dangling as its focal point. He followed her interest. "A gift from our host."

"You seem to be as popular as I am unpopular," Melissa commented. She sighed and said resignedly, "So... you've brought bad tidings...."

She listened as Brandon told her that the Nawab had located Celia. She was being held as a concubine within another ruler's walled city.

"I'm sorry, but there's no chance of rescuing her," he said firmly in conclusion. Turning away, as if to avoid the scene he knew she'd create, he started toward the gate.

"But I must!" Melissa cried, rushing after him and placing herself in his path.

"It's impossible." He looked at her sternly. "It would require a full battle. Even if the Nawab was disposed to rescuing English serving maids—which he isn't—he'd have to wage an all-out war. That would weaken his position in his own territory, leaving him vulnerable to attack from his enemies. He's fought for four years. His resources are already strained to their limit."

Melissa felt her energy draining into the shimmering white marble beneath her feet. "Then you must go with your own men," she commanded, summoning a last burst of passion.

"This is not my affair. I only came to tell you," he said, and began to leave again.

"Brandon!" she called, and her voice rang out plaintively.

Reluctantly he turned. She saw from his eyes that he had steeled himself against her, but desperate, she went on anyway. "You said that I could ask you for help. Then, all right, you see—I'm humbling myself. I ask you. I beg. There, you can claim your victory. Only please... help me."

"Save your humility for another time. I've only fifty fighting men in my company. The rest were left aboard the *Falcon,* to guard it. It would be impossible odds against a thousand or more trained soldiers. My agreement was to consider the possibility of liberating the girl—it was not to commit suicide."

"All the tales I've heard of your heroics!"

"Then you've listened to too many stories," he replied wearily. "I'm no god. No magician. I'm not going to die, nor am I going to lead my men into a death trap, either." He moved aside and started past her, then turned again and said over his shoulder, "In spite of what you may think, I'm sorry... I'm sorry for all of this—that you had to come all this way to be disillusioned. I tried to tell you how things would be. At least you've become acquainted with your mother."

She moved listlessly to the edge of the pool and stared into the rippling water. The walls around them had been carved by a master craftsman into marble lacework, through which the sun's rays danced and spread against the garden's vegetation. In one of the far corners, beneath high leafy plants, a peacock strutted. Nevertheless, for all the garden's beauty, she was a prisoner.

"She will die in India," Melissa murmured. She spoke not only of Celia, but of herself. For instead of being reborn here, as she had dreamed, her soul would finally perish. She would return to England, to a bleak future. She would marry. Perhaps—too downtrodden to resist his advances and Glenmillan's pressures—she would even marry Quentin. What did it matter who she married? And eventually she would die. Maybe, if she were lucky, she would catch cold and die in two days like Philip.

"It's true she's a prisoner, but it's not a hard life... as a concubine," Brandon said. "Once in a while she's called upon for her... for her favors." He phrased it delicately. "But there are many women for that purpose, and she can easily be forgotten for months, even years."

"It's not *her* life—not the life she chose to live." Melissa stared into the pool and saw Celia's small, brave face as she remembered it in the cell they had shared. And then the water rippled and it was her own face she saw, with tears tracing down her cheeks and Brandon behind her suddenly. Their eyes met and held in the still reflection.

Her lips parted, and she felt the heat of desire begin to rise in her. It must have also been so for Brandon, for he stepped against her, and their bodies touched full-length. His desire rose instantly, fully. She had assumed he had lain with the women of the Nawab's court, but she had been mistaken. The force with which he turned her to him and his kiss of savage hunger were both evidence that he was as starved for pleasure as she.

Melissa felt the eyes of the eunuchs on them, but didn't care as she felt Brandon's fingers in her hair, pressing against the small of her back, his lips on the hollow of her neck. She did not want to stop him, she could not stop him.... His hand found her breasts, ran lightly over the fabric, then pressed, feeling for her nipples. She would have him here, now.... Nothing else mattered, only this....

Her mother had said that the eunuchs were to be thought of as ghosts, not of this world, and ignored; otherwise one would go mad, for they were everywhere as servants and guards, often as spies.

Brandon, however, did not share this viewpoint, and when one of them stirred, he looked up suddenly, his desire failing as he remembered they were not alone.

"Damn them," he whispered, breaking from her. "I'd forgotten...." His face was still flushed, his body tense with frustration. "This evening, then.... I'll arrange to have you brought to my quarters...." And he left, not needing to hear her answer.

He received it later that night, when his serving man returned with Melissa's words.

"She said, 'I am a prisoner but not a concubine....'"

Thrown back in his face: his words about Celia.

Brandon stared, at first in disbelief and then glowering, for he had not stopped thinking of her for a minute the entire day. He wanted her now, yes...more than ever...almost enough to go to her, to have her against her precious headstrong, stubborn will. Perhaps then he could be done with her, once and for all. No woman was worth the aggravation of this one!

"Bring me a woman," he said abruptly to the servant who waited silently.

But when the man returned several minutes later, with a young woman of exquisite beauty, Brandon said, "No...she's very beautiful, but no...."

If Melissa could resist her nature, so could he.

The following day he was in private audience with the Nawab when a disruption in an outer hall brought the Indian ruler to his feet with a shout. "By Allah's name, what is there!" Automatically the warrior's hand went to the hilt of his saber. Brandon was also up, his sword drawn and ready.

The doors opened and before them stood four guards, their lances drawn against the doorway. Melissa was standing just beyond.

The Nawab looked at Brandon, who looked at Melissa, who was staring with fury at him.

"What is the meaning of this?" Alviradi Khan said beneath his breath.

"Allah only knows...Englishwomen are difficult," Brandon said.

"I might ask the very same!" Melissa replied, shrugging free of one of the guards who reached to restrain her.

The Nawab gave a motion with his head, and the girl was allowed to pass.

Dressed in green and gold silk, Melissa moved toward them like the flashing waves of an angry sea. "Are you so surprised to find me about? Yes, of course you are. How would I dare? A lowly woman. But, as you can see, even a woman has wits. I've escaped! I will not be kept as a coddled prisoner here any longer!" she said. Her voice rang out in the hollow marble room. A faint echo followed, sounding somehow childish.

The Nawab's fingers grew white as he gripped his saber. "Take her! Get her back to the harem!" he ordered, and the guards sprang forward.

"Then you will lose more than the pleasure of my company. I have something you want," Melissa announced. "I have something you *need.*"

The guards hesitated. But the Nawab glowered and shook his head, his mind made up, and Melissa's arms were seized.

"Guns!" she said. "I can get you many guns!"

Instantly, the Nawab's face changed, his thin nose lifting slightly, as if scenting the air, and he made a slight staying motion with his hand. Melissa was released. To Brandon, he said, "If this woman were not my favorite wife's only child, I would have her head. Maybe even so, I will have her head." He smiled slyly. "But she is rich, is she not?"

"That, among other things," Brandon replied caustically as he watched her coming toward them.

Imperiously, Melissa took her place beside the men. She began at once, knowing that she had to make her point quickly before the grace of whatever gods had accompanied her this far on her wild mission deserted her.

Her proposition: she would supply the Nawab with guns, in return for a trade agreement favorable and exclusive to the Danfort name.

Although the Nawab listened attentively, when she had finished he merely shrugged and said, "I do not do business with women."

Melissa felt the blood drain from her face. She had been so certain of herself. "But you need guns."

"Indeed. And I can get them elsewhere—and without your ridiculous restrictions and compromises and demands of exclusivity." He looked pointedly at Brandon.

"So, you've had another offer. But perhaps I can do better," Melissa said, understanding that this was precisely what the Nawab had in mind or he would never have listened to her in the first place.

"Tell her," the Nawab said in a bored tone. Then he helped himself to a dish of dates.

Brandon quickly outlined his terms. They were fair, certainly better than her own.

"Perhaps I can offer you a better arrangement."

"Can you?" the Nawab challenged.

Two sets of eyes awaited her reply—two sets of faintly amused, decidedly patronizing eyes.

Even more determined to prove herself, she thought quickly, then stated terms and conditions that matched Brandon's and that gave the Nawab a slightly better advantage.

She saw Brandon's face change in surprise that she had done so well, then grow darker. At the same time a light of interest gathered in the Nawab's clever eyes. *She had done it!*

"Interesting," the Nawab said, reaching for another date, which he selected with agonizing care. He chewed slowly. Melissa and Brandon watched each other. "But, no..."

Melissa thought she had heard wrong, but then the Nawab said, "I do not deal in business with women. But perhaps—" the Nawab slid his eyes from Melissa to Brandon, then back again, "—you will deal together."

"I think not," said Brandon with mild amusement.

"Never," said Melissa coldly.

"Ah! I see... Very well," said the Nawab, and he shrugged. "We will let things stand as they are... unless, of course, a new arrangement can be made that would be more, uh, beneficial."

And then Melissa understood. The clever bastard, she thought, playing her against Brandon. Brandon's offer was certainly fair and equitable, but she was hungry for glory and the Nawab knew it... plus, he also must have suspected that with the Danfort money behind her, she could afford to give up much of the profit. But there was no satisfaction in that. She would still be thought a fool, not only by the Nawab but by Brandon and her grandfather.

In the meantime, both men could toy with her, as cats with a mouse. No one had anything to lose but her.

She excused herself and left the room with her dignity in shreds, with guards on either side of her and her grandiose plans shattered.

She shuttered her room against the heat, against the world itself, and lay on her bed as if in a coffin. At every turn she was stopped from accomplishing what she wanted; at every turn she was bested by Brandon or her grandfather. If she were lucky, she might die as she was, locked in this tomb where no one could see her shame. She wouldn't even have to rot in London as Quentin's wife.

The following day her mother's voice broke through her veil of misery. Saluina drew apart the shutters, and light beamed across the bed on which she lay like a corpse.

"Of course I have heard of your unfortunate meeting," she said matter-of-factly, and seeing Melissa's surprise, she went on to explain. "The eunuchs gossip more among themselves than any women."

"Then please close the shutters. I wish to die here in the dark, unseen."

"I've arranged to lift your spirits. I will take you on a wonderful outing to the country. Nature will serve you well. There are springs near here and some fascinating hidden caves in which the old Hindu gods are said to dwell.

If you believe in such things, you may go and ask them for their help. Certainly it couldn't hurt," she ended kindly, and her eyes were soft when she looked upon Melissa. "I know you love him and how much it hurts you to have failed.... But there is always another day."

"No," Melissa said. "My days are fast becoming used up."

"Today is one more day, and it is not yet done. Have hope, daughter. Come, I will tell you the wonderful stories of these caves. It's said they have great powers...."

Melissa was doubly miserable about leaving her sanctuary when she found that it was not a small picnic they were on, but a major campaign, headed by the Nawab himself, and with Brandon in attendance.

For the duration of the two-hour journey, Melissa kept behind the veils of her sedan chair, and at the oasis she remained mute, not taking part in the games, nor eating any of the feast that had been brought for the party of two hundred.

The more she watched the gaiety, the deeper Melissa's gloom became, for in contrast to the surrounding levity, she could only imagine Celia's misery. Although many had sought refuge in the cool springs, Melissa had remained on the sidelines, determined to suffer. But the heat was relentless, and her fury at being powerless climbed with the mounting temperature.

The laughter of the pompous and luxuriating Nawab cut across her nerves. Finally she could stand no more of the celebrations, and rising, she marched to where the men sat beneath a leafy bower.

A hush fell. Every eye was on her. Her hair was heavy, with fallen strands clinging to the back of her neck, even though she had wound it earlier into a tight knot. Dirt had blown on her face and arms and had mixed with her perspiration. She felt dizzy; the heat was making her faint and light-headed, but she moved with as much determined authority as she could muster. Even the light silk sari clung like a heavy weight against her body. But it didn't matter what she looked like; she could think of nothing but venting her outrage.

She saw Brandon tense, start to rise. But it was too late, she had already begun, and the ill-chosen words came out in a torrent of indignation.

"You have the time for laughter and games and food. You have the power... and yet you do nothing to free a human being who—"

"Leave us!" the Nawab bellowed. "Or I will have your tongue!"

Melissa flinched, suddenly aware of her terrible mistake. The Nawab was dark with rage, one that made her own shrewish indignation pale in comparison. She remembered that this man had once hated her father and had tried to kill not only him, but her, as well. Of course he would do nothing to help her. He tolerated her only because of Saluina. And clearly, there were limits to that toleration.

India had turned into a hell for her!

She ran blindly, with her heart pounding, past the games being played, past the guards surrounding the area and even past the animals tethered on the outskirts. In the distance, through her blur of tears, she saw the high mountainous ridge where the holy caves of the Hindu gods were said to have been carved. There she could be alone...there she could hide from the heat, from herself, from the memory of Brandon's eyes on her....

She rode swiftly, without a saddle, on a small but swift horse taken easily from one of the handlers. Her hair tumbled about her shoulders, tangling and whipping behind her on her wild escape.

The cliffs, when she reached them, were far more formidable than they had looked from the oasis. She had to abandon the horse. There was a steep mountain of crumbling rock to climb by foot before she reached the high, level clearing near where the caves were located.

With dirt streaking her face and arms and her sari torn in several places where she had snagged it, she at last stood atop the rock butte. The sun blasted against the stone. The world here was baked pale, and it was deathly still. There were no shrubs, no trees, no protection—only a series of dark yawning holes cut into the rock cliffs behind her, where the ancient Hindu gods slept. Her mother had said they were powerful dens of magic. She had laughed, and so had Melissa.

Below her in the valley came the distant sounds of the revelers, and she tensed again.

She turned away from the joy of others, seeking silence and relief from the heat. Her shadow trailed after her, lengthening, as if it was reluctant to follow her into the cool black cavern with its fanciful history of arcane secrets.

Chapter Sixteen

The cave was possessed of a deep stillness. It was a quiet so intense that, paradoxically, the pressure of it began to pound in her ears, much as if an unseen hand beat slowly and rhythmically on a drum. Her heart itself took up the meter, even as her eyes adjusted to the dim light flowing into the cave's opening, and gradually, as Melissa stepped forward, the room she had entered came into a twilight focus.

A sharp intake of breath was her first reaction to her now visible surroundings. Next, a part of her mind urged her to turn, to run—told her she had entered a place she did not belong.

But that other portion—that dangerous part of her mind made of curiosity—held her fast.

A place of magic, her mother had called it. They had both laughed.

Her eyes moved slowly, hypnotically over the ancient, muted colors staining the rock. There, drawn in detail on the walls, were the male and female Hindu deities Saluina had told her about. Shakti, the voluptuous female consort of the Indian god Shiva, was entwined in her beloved's carnal embrace. The eyes of both were heavy-lidded, their mouths parted in sublime delight. Ecstacy was imprinted on their faces, and so real was the artist's portrayal, that their very limbs seemed fluid, in motion, trembling with the blissful tension of their physical union.

The soundless pulse of the drum grew faster in Melissa's mind and her heart raced, matching the cadence. Around her the room grew hot, whereas only a moment before it had seemed cool. She felt a madness beginning to grip her. Even the space about her seemed to shrink, narrowing, and with a sense of panic she felt her will being ripped from her. The figures before her undulated. *Impossible.* Did she hear the walls sigh? Did someone whisper?

No... impossible... impossible.

She tried to look away, but could not. It was hard to breathe, difficult to think. Only her body was alive, pulsing, close to exploding with sexual need.

She tore her gaze from the wall, seeking relief from the figures that had prompted the torturous longing.

But still it was no use. At once she found her eyes jerked back again—as if a power greater than her own possessed her will. Body and soul were aflame with desire.

She would go mad in this place!

And the room darkened.

Now her blood ran cold. The drumming in her mind stopped.

"Melissa!" And again, "Melissa!" Her name echoed through the rock hall, and as she grew faint with fear, the mask of darkness lifted and the twilight world was reinstated.

"You should never have come here alone...." The voice echoed off the walls. "Are you mad?" *Mad. Mad.* "There are cobras that live in the caves and—"

And suddenly she was a part of the real world again.

Melissa whirled about, never so glad to suffer Brandon's rebukes as she was then. Her voice joined with his, covering the echo. "Cobras! Yes... yes, you're completely right!" she said in a rush. "I should never have come... never, never...." And she was no longer the composed woman of India, but once again the girl Melissa, of Cornwall, unsure, frightened to her very core as she rushed toward Brandon and threw her arms about his neck, sobbing. "I was so frightened...oh, Brandon, I was so—"

"There, there...you're fine, safe and well. There's nothing here to fear...." Brandon's voice was no longer harsh. His words against her ear were a soft, comforting caress.

The echo had stopped.

She could not stop shaking. *What had come over her in this place? What if it returned?* "We must run!" she said wildly and tried to draw away, but his fingers brushed over her hair, calming her, and he held her back. "There's something terrible here," she insisted.

"Too much sun, Melissa...that's all. It happens to people sometimes, a disorientation. And the climb—"

"No, something...something is in this place.... It can steal your mind, your soul," Melissa whispered furtively, nestling closer against his chest. She closed her eyes, afraid that she might see the deities and be claimed by them again. Now she could feel his heartbeat, and she remembered the drum, the silent drum, the feelings of savage lust and of deep longing, the sweet pain and knife-edged torment...every emotion magnified in her being.

"Only us...there's only us here and nothing more, Melissa."

He was humoring her.

"No," she said. "They're here. Brandon, they're more than paintings, they're alive...." And for the first time since he had put his arms about her, she dared to look back at the painted gods, frozen in their timeless embrace. Her heart caught and she felt the pulse of desire begin to flow through her limbs again, like the riptides of Cornwall that would pull a man out to sea, never to be heard from again.

And Brandon looked, too.

A single glance. She felt his body tighten. *Of course; he felt them, too.* The stories her mother had told her were true, not just myths. The gods were alive; they were magical, potent forces, not merely static images locked for eternity on stone. *In India it was possible; in India anything was possible.*

"Melissa," she heard him say, but now his voice was different, too. "We'd better go. We must get back. Your mother saw you run off. They're—all of us—we're to leave for the fort."

But he made no move to go, and his eyes remained fixed on the paintings.

And she understood. He'd been captured by the feeling.

She could feel his thoughts through the touch of his fingers, now gently taking hold of her arm, just as if he truly meant to pull her from the cave's spell.

But, of course, he did not. He could not.

Instead, she was being guided around, against him again, and his lips were upon hers, tasting, searching, growing more hungry. And she was meeting that need and taking what she also desired from him.

How could it happen? She had sworn never to let herself be taken so easily again.

She would curse herself later, but when she found herself beneath him, her body warm against his, she had no thought other than to satisfy the burning flame within her.

Their cries circled the cavern as again and then again they met in ecstatic union.

At last, still trembling, they drew apart, staring at each other as if neither could understand or explain the immensity of the passion they had shared.

Beyond, the lovers on the wall glowed in the half light, suddenly still. Their faces were serene, their power exhausted.

She had imagined it all. The heat, as Brandon had said, had made her mad....

"We must go, you said." Her words were sharp, her voice tight. *What had she done!* Melissa began to gather her garments in haste. She couldn't bear to look at Brandon, so shamed did she feel for having abandoned her promise to herself. Brandon moved to help her, but she froze when his hand touched her fingers. "No!" she said violently, jerking away from him. "It meant nothing ... this meant nothing at all. To either of us," she finished bitterly, remembering a time when she had mistakenly believed his passion for her signified love.

Brandon might have said something, but a gunshot rang from somewhere nearby, and he raced to the cave's opening. The man below must have seen him, and there was some shouting that Melissa could not make out before Brandon turned back. "Hurry," he said, as he grabbed his own clothes, dressing rapidly. "There's been an attack."

They rode back to the camp at breakneck speed, for the man sent by Saluina to find them had brought two extra horses for their return. At the site of the happy picnic, there had been a slaughter of men, women and beasts. The Nawab and Saluina had fled safely back to the fort, leaving a small band of soldiers to accompany Brandon and Melissa.

The tension at the fort was palpable when they arrived, and in the days that followed an atmosphere as thick with foreboding as the heavy skies overhead, claimed every corner of the palace. Even the eunuchs, generally oblivious to anything unconnected with household matters, radiated fear. The walls surrounding the fort were thick with armed men, and within the Nawab's chambers, whispers of revenge were on the tongues of men, just as tears were present on the cheeks of the women.

As for Melissa, confined to the harem and her own quarters, she could do nothing but think and pace and languish by the perfumed pools with all the other women. If she had thought restrictions against women in England severe, she had not considered the virtual imprisonment of her sex in India.

Idle time lay far too heavily on her shoulders. Now thoughts she would rather have put aside crowded into every free moment of her waking day and even invaded her dreams. Back and forth her mind swung, thinking of her sexual liaison with Brandon with shame and misgivings one moment, only to feel the fierce need for his body the next.

She was a fool!

Knowing all that she did—that she would never have him if she could not earn his singular respect—she had allowed herself to lay with him like *any* woman. In his eyes she could be no more than a milkmaid with hot blood, or one of the Court trollops whose bodies were passed as easily from man to man as candy in a dish.

When she wasn't mentally punishing herself for her weakness in the cave—that strange, strange cave—she was searching her mind for ways in which to repair this latest mess she had made. She did not know if he would truly believe it had been the heat, that she'd been disoriented, frightened by the cave's darkness, but it was the only excuse she could find. Anyway, it was partially true.

True or not, she would not be able to sleep, or to look at her reflection in a mirror, until she had explained herself, had polished her image in Brandon's eyes.

With this in mind she sent three short notes by way of the eunuchs, asking Brandon to call on her. No reply came. The silence cut deeply into her pride. *So, she had been right after all: lying with a man and hearing his sweet words uttered under passion's influence signified nothing and guaranteed his disrespect when the sun shone brightly.*

Nevertheless, through the busy tongues of the eunuchs, gossip of the outside world filtered through to the women's jasmine-scented quarters. Melissa determined that Brandon was engaged in talks with the Nawab, having to do with the fort's defense and measures of offense.

So, she thought, burning, *so. . . .* Brandon would better his own position, while she was kept a prisoner.

When her fourth note received no answer, she decided she would act.

"You'll only make things worse," Annie pleaded when she understood what Melissa meant to do.

"Impossible. My prospects are as miserable as they'll ever be. I've angered the Nawab and humiliated myself before Brandon. I have nothing to lose. And I have everything to gain. This time I will show them both."

Threatening one of the eunuchs that she would disclose some piece of petty thievery she had discovered, she found

him more than willing to aid her in her escape from the
harem. With his help, she found a secret unguarded entrance into the Nawab's private audience room. As she had
hoped, Brandon was there.

Both men scowled when she appeared. But this time
neither seemed particularly surprised.

The Nawab merely glowered as she approached. The silk
of her sari whispered about her legs as she moved over the
cool inlaid marble tiles. The fabric was colored fuchsia and
orange and gold and was so bright and rich it seemed to
radiate a glow about her person. Brandon's eyes were on
her, dark as wells, following her every move. His lips
curved into a sardonic smile. He expected her to ruin herself once again.

He will be wrong this time, she vowed. *This time, may
the devil take my soul for all eternity...I will walk away the
victor.*

"What plans have you constructed between your-
selves?" Melissa asked bluntly when she had reached
them.

"That is none of your concern," the Nawab said, looking up at her. But he did not object in as brusque a manner as he might have. He was an intelligent, canny man;
like an animal, he sensed power in an opponent.

"You forget, perhaps, that I am the representative of my
grandfather, and that in his hands and my own rests the
authority of the House of Danfort with the King of England. If we do not want you to purchase arms, we can
forbid their sale by your supplier. Not only that, but all
trade agreements that Monsieur de Forrest arranges can be
revoked. Now, you will please outline for me exactly what
you intend."

The Nawab was silent. Brandon's eyes narrowed. She
could feel both men bristle. She knew their thoughts: *the
upstart woman!* And she smiled, knowing that she had already won, and that they knew it.

"You may sit," the Nawab said offhandedly, although
Melissa could well imagine what the invitation cost him.

The Nawab's man-at-arms read off the conditional agreement the Muslim warrior and Brandon had agreed upon. When he had finished, Melissa nodded.

"Very good. Except for one thing."

And she told them that the Danforts would have a half interest in the enterprise for guaranteeing that all shipments would be filled and delivered.

Both men were clearly stunned. She left them that way, staring in disbelief—and, of course, impotent to refute her demands.

She was no longer a pawn.
The Queen had moved.
At long last . . .

Naturally, she did not have to send another note to Brandon. He came on his own . . . and in a rage.

They met in an antechamber to her inner rooms. He strode back and forth as she sat upon a low sofa near an open portico. Beyond the walkway behind her, the sky was a dazzling display of color, with black clouds silhouetted against the crimson and gold and purple evening canvas. The cry of peacocks mingled with the trumpeting of elephants in the distance. Close to her, the harsh sounds of Brandon's boots scraped against the room's silence.

"Bravo for your clever maneuver. Equal to your grandfather's miserable tactics, I might add." He shot her a cold look. "Tell me, what is it that you truly want in life, Melissa?"

"I would think that was clear enough. As I said, half the profits to be earned in this trade venture."

"No," said Brandon, facing her, "that's not it at all. There's much more that you seek in all of this."

"Respect, then. I don't like to be bullied."

"You imagine that. You put yourself in positions that a woman has no right—"

"No right!" Melissa stood, rage making her forget all the love she had for the man standing before her. "I'm only supposed to lift my skirts? Is that what you would have me do?"

"You're a woman, I'm a man. We have our own natures. And when we stick to them there's no problem.... There's only this trouble because you insist on—"

"Get out of my sight!" she said, turning away from him and walking to the balcony.

He came up close behind her. She didn't have to see him, for she could feel him as certainly as if he had touched her. It was always like that. Damn fate that she had to have met him! Damn the man.... She felt the heat grow within her and swore an oath she had overheard from some of the Cornish lads when she had gone to market. So long ago...

But Brandon was speaking to her. "Whatever you do in this world, Melissa, you pay a price. If you love, you pay a price for that...and if you wage war, there's also a price."

"And if you do nothing—" she shot a quick glance back over her shoulder "—then you pay another price. I am treated neither as a woman nor a man, but as some puppet to be maneuvered by you, by the Nawab, by my stepmother, by my grandfather. But no more," she said. "I will manage my life as I choose. And if there is a price to pay...so be it."

"So be it...." Brandon repeated.

He left silently.

And she cried that night, cried softly into her pillow, knowing that what she had said was true and what Brandon had said was also true.

Cursed life! So complex, when what she wanted—this man's love—was so easy, so beautiful, always so near. And always impossible to claim.

Melissa had never felt more solitary—or more determined—than she did when she faced Saluina in her room.

"I cannot help you," Saluina said, her face pale with worry. "This plan of yours is madness, Melissa. You cannot go to get this girl, this friend of yours. Not even my husband and his men would attempt such a thing. It is doomed before it is begun."

"Very well," Melissa said. "You cannot help me." *But you cannot stop me either.* She kept this to herself, saying only, "You were very brave to have loved my father... and perhaps not very wise. But you followed your heart anyway."

"Yes... yes, I had to," her mother whispered. Saluina's doe eyes were moist with feeling, even after so many years.

"Then you will understand that whatever I do, I too have no choice."

Their eyes met and held. "I love you, my daughter," Saluina said, seeming to understand more than she wanted to. She turned away quickly, moving in her soft silks to the door.

"Then promise me that you'll not stop me?" Melissa called from behind her.

Saluina turned. "Could I?" And she smiled a little, but sadly.

"No," Melissa said. "No one can stop me now. Not even I...."

The plans she had made were worthy of even her grandfather's intricacies of deceit. With the help of a network of eunuch spies, she had devised a plot to enter the fort of the Muslim ruler holding Celia as a concubine. She would gain admittance by disguising herself as a woman captured for prostitution. Within the confines of the enemy camp she would be aided by other eunuchs, in return for their safe passage to England.

Everything had been arranged to take place in ten days' time. But the plan fell through within three.

Brandon gave her the news. "We leave port in eight days. Six will be needed for crossing overland to the port, with two extra in case of unexpected delays."

Melissa felt herself growing faint. *Again she was to have her plans thwarted! What kind of a curse rode her back!* Averting her face, she said politely, without challenge, hoping to hide her desperation from him, "But can't we wait just a few more days...perhaps three more? I've had so little time with my mother."

"There's no alternative," he said stiffly. And when she turned, did she only imagine he looked at her queerly, as if he read behind her eyes? "The ship's being readied. I will leave tomorrow, and you the day after under heavy guard. We've tarried long enough, and if we don't go at once we'll be caught by the monsoons. The Nawab must have his carbines if he's to survive—and I'm sure you're interested in protecting your investment in India," he added with a sarcastic smile.

But even so, she could only think, *How handsome he is,* until her thoughts turned to the seriousness of his words.

She had no time to waste. Her plan would need to be implemented immediately... the next day at the very latest. Her mind began to swim with plans....

"Brandon!" she cried suddenly, as she realized he was halfway to the door. "Brandon...."

He turned, reacting to the panic in her voice. His eyes were dark with his own thoughts, and she wondered if he even saw her now as she moved toward him.

When they stood close to each other, she said, "If we...if anything were to happen...." She saw that he grew impatient. He had much more to do now than listen to her prattle. But he did not know...he did not understand that she might never see him again. Certainly he would not know that what she did was not only for Celia, it was also for herself, so that she could gain her own respect and thereby be his equal. If she were to die on her mission, then she would lose her life for the love of him. *And all of this he did not know—could not know, in case he would stop her.*

"You will be under heavy guard, Melissa—and if you don't do anything foolish for a change, like leap from your chair or cause a stampede among the elephants, then I'll see you on board." He turned again, but she gripped his arm, holding him with her an instant longer.

"Brandon—whatever problems I've caused...whatever harsh words—"

"They're forgotten, Melissa." The black eyes were dark and flat, echoing the unemotional quality of his words. "They do not signify. Our relationship is as you've made it now... that of colleagues in business." He removed her hand from his arm. "Now I must go, there's much to—"

"Brandon! I've always loved you," she blurted.

Brandon stared at her. "No..." he said. "You're a Danfort through and through, a Danfort like your grandfather. I see that now. Once I believed differently. That was my brief mistake to allow myself to—" But he broke off.

"To love me, too?" Her words rushed out in a flood of hope.

"Perhaps I had a moment of such weakness... or came close to believing that there was that possibility.... But the time is passed now," he finished. "I see all too well what you may not even know about yourself. You're for the game, for the hunt, Melissa. You rush in where angels fear to tread... but only for the challenge and the sport of doing so."

"Then we are no different," she whispered, aching to touch his face, to kiss his lips just once before they parted—perhaps forever.

"Perhaps," he agreed with false amiability, and then grew cold as he said, "but with a difference. I don't muck up all that I involve myself in. And you, my dear, make a shambles of all your wild schemes. Pack your things and make ready," he ordered, showing her his back as he dismissed her from his mind and opened the door.

"Oh, Brandon..." she said to the empty room, not with sadness but with fury that life could be so cruel and unfair "... we may never meet again, and you will never know... that I loved you so. You did not want to know. You did not want me to love you."

And it was true. Brandon, walking from Melissa's chamber, felt sick with the weakness her presence always brought to him. Try as he might to forget her, the merest sight of her stirred something within him that he could not deny... and yet found it impossible to accept. How could he want one woman so much that he would toss at night, the need and the desire for her consuming him, and yet despise that part of her that was so much like himself that she might have been his female twin soul?

Well, he told himself, he would be well rid of the girl, once they were in England.

The official parting ceremony for Brandon and his men was held the following morning. Although there was pomp, there was no joyousness; there was only tension as the men rode away.

Melissa attended, her heart torn as Brandon passed her and the other women of the harem. Astride his horse he looked down briefly, delivering a last, dark look.

But she had no time to grieve.

Obscuring herself behind veils, she substituted an Indian woman in her place and, amid the commotion, slipped off in the opposite direction from Brandon's well-armed caravan with her band of eunuchs—poorly armed but clever and filled with the determination of the downtrodden to succeed against their persecutors.

It was Saluina who made the discovery of the missing eunuchs, and then of Melissa's escape with them, and with the threat of beating one of the remaining servants until his hide fell off, she was able to uncover Melissa's plot.

Not two hours later Brandon was accosted by Saluina's messenger. "My God!" Brandon closed his eyes upon hearing the story the rider brought. "She'll die this time...."

"Will you go then?" the messenger asked, his eyes pleading with Brandon. Clearly the man had a personal stake in the successful outcome of his journey. "I must tell my mistress that you will go to stop her."

"And how can I do that? I cannot stop her now—I never could stop her at all," Brandon said between clenched teeth. "She'll at last pay the price."

"But—"

"Enough!" And Brandon started forward, galloping far ahead of the band he led.

"But she will surely die!" the voice wailed behind him. Brandon did not turn.

Chapter Seventeen

Night had fallen, covering the landscape with a thick, brooding hush.

Melissa looked up to the heavens from where she was huddled near an outcropping of rocks and dry, scraggly shrubbery that had once been hearty and green by the now parched riverbed. Soon, she knew, the cracked earth would hold a rushing torrent. Even as she thought it there was a low, distant rumble, evidence that the monsoons gathered. But tonight the moon hung like a threshing sickle paused to strike, a pale arc of silver in the star-filled blackness above.

Her small band of desperate accomplices had ridden hard all day, and the horses needed to rest before they advanced to the fort. When they left again they would need all their strength and speed for their escape over the plains. *If,* Melissa thought, *there would even be an escape.*

In the distance she could make out a fortress, every bit as large as Alviradi Khan's. The ruler within was said to be cruel and clever and perpetually fearful—therefore he would be well guarded against surprise attacks.

Some distance away her makeshift army of half men stared silently toward the structure that was to prove their ultimate salvation or else bring their end. She knew their minds, their misgivings and their hopes. There was no turning back for them; they had chosen to defy the Nawab in the desperate quest for their freedom. He would show them no mercy if they came crawling back, penitents.

Yes, Melissa thought, within a few hours all their fates would be sealed. Until then they would rest.

And pray.

Although she had said her silent good-byes—should she fail—to Goodie and Darben, to Celia and to her grandfather and mother...it was Brandon's face that claimed most of her thoughts, and Brandon's memory that caused the tears to course down her cheeks.

So lost was she in her sorrowful misgivings that she did not hear the steps behind her until the instant she was wrenched up from the ground and shoved roughly against the boulder that had been her place of refuge.

A man's body pressed against hers, one hand gripping her waist. She struggled and would have shouted for help, but his hand, dusty and rough, clamped over her mouth. They were too close for Melissa to make out his features. His shape was no more than a dark blur in her frantic vision. *They had been discovered; all was lost before it had even begun!*

But the voice was not foreign; it was English, and hoarse from recent exertion as the assailant whispered against her ear. "Make no sound. I've just killed two men who would have slit your throats. I don't know if others are nearby. You fools...you'll all die if you dare ride on that place."

And then, releasing his grip slightly and taking his hand from her mouth, he stepped back, and in the dim light from above, she saw Brandon's drawn expression as he looked down at her. Her heart turned once at seeing him, in joy, in longing, as it always did no matter what the circumstances of their meeting. But she put aside her love, thinking instead of the words he had just spoken. *He was there to stop her.*

"Then I'll die," she said quietly, but with urgent passion, "because I must go to Celia. I *must*. You above all people have to understand that."

Quiet for a moment, he neither agreed nor disagreed, but then said wearily as his eyes searched her face, "I understand only that you are the biggest trouble that has ever come into my life. No storm, no tyrant, no shipload of the most evil-hearted pirates has ever been more of a misery. Do you know the odds against your success in this idiotic venture you've undertaken?''

''Yes, I do know, and charming me with your sweet words won't change my mind,'' she said caustically. ''Nor will you frighten me off.''

''Don't I know that.'' Brandon turned his head slightly, and for the first time she saw that he had ridden with a group of his own armed men, who waited beyond the outcrop of boulders she had chosen as her hiding place. ''So instead of you, I'm going.''

They glared at each other in silence, gauging the other's thoughts.

''No,'' she said.

''It's what you wanted of me. Now be happy.''

''But the odds,'' she mocked, ''the terrible odds... Surely you must be as mad as I am!'' She found herself more angry than relieved that he had come at last to her aid. Insane as her scheme might be, she had prepared herself for its undertaking and now felt cheated.

''That's most likely true. Regardless, my men and I will continue onward.'' He glanced to the fortress, looming black and ominous in the distance. ''You're to return with—'' he shook his head in disparagement ''—with your army, such as it is, and set out immediately to join the caravan to the port.''

She meant to object, but the orders were issued and she had no chance to dispute them. In a whirlwind of hushed commands and activity, Melissa found herself bodily thrust atop her horse. Then she was being led by one of Brandon's men in the opposite direction from the fort holding Celia.

She stared behind her, helpless as always to direct her life.

And Brandon... he was a dark shape against the open plain, doing what she had intended, riding with thirty men toward what she suddenly realized would be their certain doom.

She saw the future with such clarity! Her heart contracted, the horror of what she knew to be the future freezing her soul. *Never would they meet again!*

And as she thought it, Brandon made a sudden sweeping turn. As if he, too, knew there was no hope of returning, he raced back at a desperate speed, clinging low to his mount's back.

Taking her bridle in his hands, he pulled her close against his own horse and said almost angrily, "There may not be another time for this—"

"No...!" she cried softly, wanting to silence his words, for fear that speaking them would make the terrible vision an actuality.

"I don't care for heartfelt speeches—"

"Oh, please, then save your words...no, don't speak!" She pressed a finger to his lips. "You *will* come back...you must," said Melissa desperately.

But he removed the silencing finger and said, "From the beginning, Melissa...I loved you. Perhaps I didn't know it—I didn't want to know." A fleeting smile, ironic and sad, flickered over his face. "When I watched you dance...perhaps it happened then. At the inn. But you were only a child, or so it seemed. Ah, you're an impossible woman, the worst I've ever encountered. But I thought you should know... We may never meet again...."

His dark eyes burned into her. He closed them tightly, took in a breath, then abruptly jerked his reins and pulled away.

She reached out blindly for his arm. "No, Brandon...we *will* meet again!" she cried, tortured by his words. "Oh...don't go, don't go...."

His horse danced, agitated, ready to be off. "Ah, but I must," he said, flinging her own words back at her. "Where is there any other choice?" In the distance his men waited, their horses also restless to move on. "You were right to have wanted to help this friend of yours. Some things are not wise, but they can't be otherwise."

And she knew he spoke not only of Celia, but of himself, for coming this night to her aid, even for the folly of loving her.

"You must come back to me," she said softly. "If not, who will I have to feud with?"

He approached again, and leaning over, he wrapped his fingers in her hair and drew her face close, kissing her hard. Then he broke away, leaving her to watch desolately after him.

The attack was made in the still of night. The band of thirty trained fighting men met staggering odds. Beside Brandon's soldiers stood Melissa's company of rebellious eunuchs. Enslaved themselves, they fought now with fire in their eyes to defend another victim of cruelty. But they would have fallen, all of them to a man, were it not for the brotherhood of other eunuchs within the enemy camp, who joined them in the sabotage.

Among them—brandishing a sword taken from a slain foe—was a woman with green eyes gleaming and golden hair streaming wildly over her shoulders.

The man at her side periodically cursed his attackers and her as well as he sliced his Scottish dirk with the speed of lightning. "Damn you, woman! Didn't I tell you—"

But the rest of his sentence was drowned out by the woman's cry of victory as she downed an opponent with her sword.

An hour before the ship was set to sail—by prior instructions, with or without its captain—a small band on horseback arrived at the pier. They were exhausted and covered with dust, some with dried blood on their clothes, others nursing open wounds.

In spite of everything, all wore smiles.

Silently Brandon assisted Melissa in dismounting, and for once she allowed him to help.

"Once on board that ship you are free forever," Melissa said to the girl who had come up beside her. "Come,

Celia…'' She took her hand, and they walked together up the plank.

Behind them, the surviving eunuchs cheered, then made ready to board the same vessel.

Seven months later, the *Falcon* arrived in London.

Melissa thought at first that it was the dizzying environment of London, with its clattering coaches and its cries of street merchants—so different from India's serenity— that caused the queasiness to persist. Walls, walls, they were everywhere, seeming to crush against her spirits as she drove through the city with Glenmillan and Quentin pressed on either side of her in the carriage.

For two weeks, since she had returned on the *Falcon,* she had been feted at various social functions, a celebrity for her heroic deed of rescuing Celia.

And also for two weeks, since she had landed on English soil, she had not seen Brandon—though she had sent him at least four notes.

She could not understand that he did not come to her, that he did not at least reply, and perhaps out of dread more than pride, she could not bring herself to cross the city to confront him in person. Rather, she waited…day in, day out.

The night before their arrival in London, Brandon had held her close to him in his cabin, as he had during all the nights of their voyage home. Pressed against each other throughout those nights, Melissa had felt secure in his love, and there had been no need to speak of a future together once they were back in England. It was established in her mind that they would wed, that they would spend their lives together.

But now all her confidence in their love seemed like sand drifting grain by grain through the hourglass her heart had become, as days passed one after the next with no word from him. Had he reconsidered? Had India drained him of resolve and London again altered his senses?

But if she was sad, Glenmillan and Quentin exhibited overwhelming joy in her return.

"You can't imagine how we missed you," Glenmillan would coo several times a day as she rushed Melissa about, replenishing her wardrobe with the latest fashions.

As for Quentin, he seemed somehow aged. The careless, spontaneous elan that had formerly characterized his personality had been replaced by a tense, hungry eagerness to accommodate. The light blue eyes haunted her at every turn, seeming both emotionally distant and yet invasive of her thoughts.

"You do not feel well?" asked Quentin one morning when he came to call on her shortly after she had arisen. She sat in her dressing gown, staring out the window at the new leaves being born on bare, spindly branches. *Would Brandon come to her this day? Or did she hope in vain?*

"I am fine," Melissa murmured, even though the smell of the scones and tea made her want to retch.

"You haven't touched anything," he said, eyeing her intently.

She sighed listlessly and lifted a scone, then let it drop back to the plate. "I'm not hungry."

"You're pale, as well," Quentin commented. "Perhaps..." he said cautiously "...perhaps you've brought back something from India...."

Their eyes met. It was as clear as if he'd spoken the words: she was with child.

"A passing flu," she answered, panic rising within her.

"Of course," Quentin replied, but his eyes had hardened.

"It's as we thought," said Quentin to Glenmillan a few minutes later in her bedroom suite.

"How can you be sure?" said Glenmillan, her face growing pale beneath the powder she applied at her dressing table mirror.

"Because I have these," Quentin said, and he withdrew from a velvet pouch four letters. Languorously he tossed them on Glenmillan's dressing table and moved back to watch her as she read the contents. "They were intercepted by one of my loyal household friends," he said, recalling with some pain what he had had to pay the footman to get access to the letters and buy absolute silence regarding the treachery.

"My God..." Glenmillan gasped. "So it's true. She's pregnant." She swung around on her stool and looked up at Quentin, her violet eyes holding horror. In her forehead a muscle twitched spasmodically. "She writes as if they are firmly committed to each other. Then surely he'll marry her." Her expression hardened. "So it's come to pass at last. We are finished, Quentin."

"No. Not necessarily." And from the same velvet purse he took five other letters. "These were delivered here."

Glenmillan examined one after the next, reading as quickly as she could. "Good God, I never thought I'd live to see the day... Brandon de Forrest, mortal, after all."

"Disgusting, isn't it? The man's so in love he's all but spouting poetry. Nevertheless, it doesn't matter what he writes. As you've read, he's left London to tend to the business of securing weapons for that Indian potentate. And our little golden goose, who's bearing his egg, will receive none of his messages."

Glenmillan's eyes took on a gleam. "And none of her messages will reach him." Her face clouded. "But what's to stop him from coming to her?"

"Ah, yes... that," Quentin said, and he waved his handkerchief. "I've taken the liberty of having a lady friend with prettily fashioned penmanship write a rather chilly reply to our hot lover."

Glenmillan raised her eyebrow, a smile quirking the corners of her rouged lips. "Oh, Quentin, really? Why, you rogue."

"Indeed, Mother. Our Melissa has had second thoughts, you see.... The affair was one of those foreign things—the exotic locale, the moonlight at sea.... But, alas, with her senses now returned, she realizes that she must marry someone of lineage. You know de Forrest's pride, his previous situation with Pavan. He'll be done with her."

"And hearing nothing from the scoundrel, our little goose will become more distraught. And we, son, will not be finished after all, because—"

"Because I will be pleased to rescue her from this most embarrassing—not to mention heartbreaking—of situations."

"It will be the wedding of the century."

"At the very least."

Melissa sat opposite her grandfather in his study. He looked shrunken. Even his wig appeared too large. When she returned from India, he had greeted her himself at the entrance to Danfort House, and the tears of joy he'd shed were copious and unself-conscious. In many ways he was a man changed from the one she had left almost two years before. He was openly proud of her for rescuing Celia and impressed by the agreement she had reached to supply weaponry to the Nawab.

He was not as pleased by her reticence to speak of Brandon.

"There's nothing to tell," she said dully, the sickness in her stomach a constant reminder of Brandon. "There was India . . . the voyage back . . . and that is all. I've not heard from him once since I've returned."

The Duke reached for a paper and his quill. "Most strange."

"Strange? And why is that? Hasn't he always led an independent life?" she snapped, her nerves strained to the point of breaking. She did not know if she accused or defended him.

"I'll write to him and—"

"No!" she said fiercely, half rising from her seat. The sickness welled up, and she sank back, weak and frightened. "I've already written to him several times and received no answer."

"Perhaps the man is ill."

"If he were, someone would have let me know—his man, Ross McKay would have been sent to me. Or some note would have come. No," she said heavily, "Monsieur de Forrest is not ill." *But I am,* she thought. *I am sick of heart, and my body ails me as well.* "If anything, he is busy preparing for the shipment of arms to the Nawab." *But a man in love is never too busy to call on the woman who holds his heart—and now carries his child within her body.*

Melissa rose and went to the window. Beyond the small diamond panes were the Duke's gardens. Everywhere she looked she saw signs of nature's rebirth into a hopeful new season. But there was no joy in any of it for her.

She spoke without having the courage to face her grandfather. "I'm afraid I've inherited my parents' predilection for complex love affairs. I'm bearing Brandon de Forrest's child. I know I've disgraced myself."

The room became quiet, overflowed with silence.

And then at last the Duke spoke. "Of course it is a disgrace. And you must marry at once."

Oddly, in spite of his choice of words, to Melissa he sounded strangely happy rather than condemning. "Marry?" With a harsh laugh, she turned. "And, pray, how shall that be arranged? The man is not willing. I've written four times to him, telling him I'm carrying his child. He has chosen not to reply. That should be answer enough that there's to be no happy wedding."

"I'll go to him myself. He will not sail under any flag so long as he lives, if he—"

Melissa clenched her fists, her nails digging into her flesh. "Oh, you won't . . . you will not!"

"The child must have a name!"

"If you dare to coerce Brandon in any way . . . if you so much as even think to meddle in this affair . . . I swear to you, I shall run from here and never return so long as I live. Swear to me! Swear that you—for once!—will not plot to arrange things as you would have them!"

The Duke's face had gone entirely white. He sank back into his chair, looking small, like a child, as he said hollowly, "Have it as you wish then. . . ."

"Don't worry. The child shall have a father, shall be respectable, shall not disgrace our family name. But what shame there is, is due to my stupidity, not to any immorality. I loved him! And this humiliation will be born in silence by me. *This* I swear to you,'' she finished.

In her room, she sat quietly for some time, gathering her resolve, arranging her thoughts, before setting pen to paper. Even so, the letter she wrote took several tries before she felt that all had been clearly stated. She sealed it with wax and with a silent prayer that within the day she would have Brandon at her side—or at the very least a note of positive response from him. Surely, unless the man were made of ice and stone, he could not refuse her entreaty—unless, of course, he did not love her at all.

This was her last plea; her last hope.

She rang for the footman, whom she ordered to leave immediately. He was to give the letter to no one but Monsieur de Forrest himself, or if that were not possible, to Ross McKay.

Not five minutes later, Quentin Danfort sat in his room with his feet soaking in warm perfumed water while he read the words his future bride had written to her lover. He noted the blotches where tears had stained an occasional word.

Crumpling the page, he held it tightly in his fist as he tried to envision his next move.

No, there would be no next move. He would wait a bit longer, wait until Melissa was desperate.

Melissa stayed alone in her room for three days. She ate only for the baby's sake. No servants, save for Annie who brought her food, were admitted, and she refused to see Quentin, Glenmillan and her grandfather. Even Celia was denied entry when she came from the Duchess's to visit.

The woman who looked back at her in the looking glass was no one Melissa knew. Her eyes were dull and hollowed with dark rings. Her hair draped in a tangled web over thin shoulders covered in a nightdress she had not bothered to change.

On the third day she called for Annie to assist her in making herself presentable. She moved listlessly about the task, and when she was clothed in a somber gray dress, she sent for Quentin.

He sauntered into her presence two hours later, back from a visit to his tailor.

"I understand you wanted to see me?" He picked a bit of lint from his sleeve.

"Not particularly," returned Melissa, past the point of pretense anymore. She was sure he knew she was pregnant. "I do, however, want to marry you."

"Ah, do you?" he said, glancing up only briefly before he began to survey himself for other errant pieces of fuzz.

"I thought you might be pleased," she said sarcastically. "You've hounded me about marriage often enough."

"Yes, well ... that's true, isn't it?" He looked up at her again. "Very well, then. We shall do the expedient thing—since I presume this proposal has much to do with expediency. So, my love, when shall the happy occasion take place?"

"I am not your love. Nor are you mine," said Melissa coldly, without taking her eyes from his face. "Listen to me.... This marriage is, as you very well know, a business arrangement to you. So neither of us will suffer any great emotional pangs when I tell you clearly what you already know—I'm pregnant with another man's child. This child will be raised as yours. But you and I will have no physical relationship between us. Not ever. I have loved one man completely and fully. As I am not to have him as my partner in life, I will put my heart into exile. So...is all of this clearly understood and agreed upon?"

A faint smile preceded Quentin's nod. "Perfectly understood."

"And agreeable?"

"Tell me, madame, if I should say no, what other choice do you really have? You won't rid yourself of the child, because you love its father—of that, at least, I'm sure. And to go to someone else in such a rush would cast a great deal of doubt upon the legitimacy of the child, which in turn would stain the pristine name of Danfort and leave open the opportunity for any future heirs you would have with anyone else to claim inheritance. You're a beautiful woman. I doubt sincerely that you could wrest from any man such a guarantee of physical abstinence. Oh, certainly, you would find someone to swear to your demands. But though promises might flow copiously, so also would port, and one night you'd find your locked door kicked in and your stipulations lying in shreds along with your nightdress."

Melissa paled, for the first time fully realizing how much she had underestimated Quentin's ability to calculate, not to mention the cold precision with which he did so.

"And what choice would you have to turn me down now?" she said hotly. "Who will support your lavish ways?"

"Quite right," agreed Quentin. "So, then, you see, we both need each other."

"I despise you."

"That may be," he replied with a cold laugh, "but I can promise you it doesn't necessarily have to be as unpleasant an allegiance as you may think. For one thing, when we marry, I will by law have possession of your estate... and of you, as well, my dear Melissa." He moved from her and began to wander through the room, speaking thoughtfully, as if he dictated a letter to a secretary. "As you might have surmised, I have little interest in commerce—other than to make certain I have funds to support my pleasures. But you, apparently, thrive on such enterprise. So I'll keep out of your hair, and you can keep out of mine." He turned to her, smiling ingratiatingly. "There, you see, the arrangement you propose is not so black as you may have originally thought."

With a quick step he made his way to a table bearing a set of crystal glasses and poured them each a sherry from a half-filled decanter. Then he returned with a spritely bounce to where Melissa was seated stonelike on the small divan.

"To a successful partnership..." he said, handing her her glass. With gusto, Quentin downed his own.

Silently Melissa tasted the wine. It was bitter in her mouth and burned her throat like fire as she swallowed.

Although he did not realize it, Brandon still held the letter in his hand, gripping the paper so tightly that the tips of his fingers were white. He felt as if he had been punched hard in the gut. Gradually he became aware of Ross McKay speaking to him....

"I'm sorry. The news is not good, I take it. It came yesterday, while you were gone."

"Who brought it?" Brandon snapped, with a look that made Ross flinch.

"A footman under employ of the Danforts...." Ross took in a deep breath. "Perhaps the Duke has been meddling again and Melissa knows nothing of—"

"It's her hand," Brandon said, and still holding the letter, he moved to the window. Below him the seaport bustled with activity, much as if it were any day, any ordinary day.

"She might have been forced."

Brandon laughed sharply. "Melissa? Forced?" But he was quiet for a moment, desperate enough to consider even the most outrageous of possibilities. But it was no use. "What of the other letters I sent to her? Four of them while I was away. You brought them yourself, so we know they arrived. And there was not one response. Until this."

"There must be an explanation," murmured Ross. "It makes no sense that she would suddenly change her feelings."

"Why? She's a woman," said Brandon.

"Aye. Still, she's not one to be ruled by her head, is she? From all you've told me, that one is blown hither and yon by passion. It would not have grown cold overnight. Why don't you go to her?" Ross urged. "Find out for yourself."

"Find out what? It's all in here, isn't it?" Brandon said angrily, brandishing the letter. "It's her hand, her signature, the Danfort seal, brought by the Danfort messenger. No, Ross. There's nothing more to be done or said. Only that it seems I was a fool... again,'' he added quietly.

"I'll go myself to her—"

Brandon reeled about. "No, man! It's over. We'll make our plans to ship the weapons to India, as agreed. If Danfort means to stop us, then we will deal with that eventuality when it occurs. In the meantime, the past is past." His voice broke and he turned quickly to the window. "Leave me."

What irony! In his whole life, he had cared only for two women: the first when he was young and unschooled in the ways of the world and in the ways of women in particular; and the second in maturity, and only after he had resisted love for so many long years. And yet—damn him, damn them!—human love was sacrificed to the love of gold.

He would not have thought it of her. Of Pavan, yes... but not of Melissa. Even now, though he knew it as the truth, though he bore that truth in his hands—holding the paper as if in doing so he still kept something of her in his life—what she had written did not ring true with what he knew of her character.

But then, he considered further, could any man ever know a woman's mind and heart?

Pride and past experience took him from the window to the desk, where he set the last vestiges of his love for Melissa Danfort aflame.

He watched the paper curl and blacken in the pewter dish. His heart withered at the sight, then hardened as he turned and left his office to tend to the business of amassing his own share of gold.

Chapter Eighteen

Though it was late afternoon, the Duke of Danfort sat at his desk in the library, dressed carelessly in a gray and gold morning coat. He had much on his mind, all of it grave. Before him were the letters of credit he had signed, which would cover most of the extravagances Glenmillan had arranged for the wedding of her miserable cur to his granddaughter.

How bitter, defeat. No wonder he had all his life scrupulously avoided its bad taste.

Miserably, his weak hazel eyes traveled the length of the large room, with its bookshelves and its portraits of former Danforts, noble ancestors who had for generations risen valiantly—and shrewdly—over all manner of adversity.

With a sense of shame, the Duke returned his gaze to the list of guests and the itemized accounts Glenmillan had served him with two days ago, instructing him—*she* instructing *him*—to make haste in releasing the funds to cover the festivities.

And, of course, he had no choice, as Glenmillan well knew. Melissa was pregnant; urgency was a necessity if he was to protect the Danfort name and lineage.

For the first and only time in his life, he found himself powerless to effect his will against that of others. Had it not been so sad a situation, there might have been some humor to it—that he, the master manipulator, whose wealth and influence rivaled even that of the Crown's, was stripped of his power by a young woman.

But, alas, it *was* a sad case: reckless passion, not careful plotting, had achieved the final victory. And now Quentin Danfort, that miserable, conniving, spendthrift fop, would reap the benefit of his life's efforts. There was nothing—not a thing—he could do about it, lest he lose Melissa herself, as she had threatened, and the child she carried, who would someday bear the Danfort crest.

If he did not love the girl... yes, then he would have been able to stand his ground, to have bullied, to have forced her to his will. But it was no use: her pain was his own. And he found himself lying awake at night with worry, heartsick that she suffered alone in her own bedchamber and that there was nothing that he could do to save her heart from its agony.

Curse de Forrest!

But uttering oaths was all he could do, for wronged as Melissa was, she refused to let loose even one arrow of revenge de Forrest's way.

An impotent old man, that's what I've become, thought the Duke.

Lending credence to the claim, the door at the far end of the library swung open, and Glenmillan Danfort stood majestically in the doorway.

She paused for a moment as she surveyed the long room with proprietary violet eyes, resting them at last on the Duke. She had draped herself in yards of deep scarlet satin—something new, the Duke wagered, and expensive. He wondered how much it had cost him. Her hair was dark as midnight against the flawless pale skin. Even he had to admit she was a stunning creature, wickedly beautiful.

She acknowledged him with a nod, shoved the door closed, and in a gust of flowing, bloodred yardage, marched imperiously toward the desk.

She barely curtsied, but said in a rush, "I trust all is in order?" as her eyes pounced hungrily on the stack of documents protected by the Duke's right hand.

"That depends upon one's point of view. I've seen fit to omit certain of your requests—" he began.

"*Requirements*, sir!" snapped Glenmillan. "Hardly requests."

"Madame, take care," the Duke replied with an icy calm. "Your son is not married yet. Your arrogant presumptuousness is premature. And may prove to be very much to your detriment."

The violet eyes flared, then narrowed with resentment. "Old man, your days of torturing me and toying with my son are over. Even you know it."

The Duke's blood boiled, but he smiled enigmatically, saying nothing. Keeping his eyes on his adversary, he watched Glenmillan's expression of triumph fade slightly as doubt invaded her recent certainty.

But her eyes grew cold and hard again, and she said with assurance, "Your threats are meaningless. Quentin will marry Melissa. Not heaven nor hell can stop this marriage. Not," she said spitefully, "even you."

"Have you ever known me to lose, madame?" Holding his smile, the Duke passed the papers to her.

She looked down for a moment, hesitating, as if fearing a trap...then snatched them from his hand and pressed them against her breast. There, she was safe! Now all the city would be at her feet! She had financial license to throw London's largest, most lavish wedding in more years than anyone could remember. And once Quentin was wed to the girl, he would take control of the Danfort estate and she, Glenmillan Danfort, would be invulnerable to all the forces that would see her grovel for position. The Duke's threats were empty as air. She had won at long last.

"Soon, m'lord, very soon the final score to this match between us will be posted." She parodied a respectful curtsy, then in her dress of flaming silk tore from his presence, slamming the door shut on his ill will.

The Duke noted that she had not pestered him for the extra funds he had denied her.

Well, it was a small victory, but welcome just the same, and he thanked God for it, wondering as he did if there might actually be a God after all. If so, it could do no harm to make amends now, on the chance that his prayers be answered....

Closing his eyes, he drove away years of disbelief and clasped his hands devoutly before him, concentrating his thoughts. "Lord, grant me this last victory...this last, sweet revenge on that miserable jade...." And then, thinking it wise, he added with grudging humility, "Please."

Now and then the two young women, Celia and Annie, stole surreptitious looks at each other as they went silently and dutifully about their tasks in Melissa's room.

With dreary apathy Melissa surveyed the names of guests invited to the various post-wedding functions, marking any changes she required. Now and then she would sigh, not realizing she did so, and Celia would look up to see her staring into space, the green eyes, usually so brilliant with life, vacant of the joy one would expect of a bride-to-be.

Celia had a hundred questions and at least that many opinions about the wedding about to take place, but experience had taught her to keep silent about what was not her business. Mutely she continued to examine the wedding ensemble for loose threads. A thousand small, gleaming pearls had been hastily stitched into place by seamstresses working round the clock in an effort to meet the Countess Glenmillan Danfort's schedule. In their weariness they may have become careless. It would not do, Celia felt, to have Melissa unraveling before the whole of fashionable London society.

She had come willingly and gladly to the House of Danfort, excited to have been lent by the Duchess of Beltonwick to serve as Melissa's handmaid. She was to assist Annie in getting Melissa ready for the ceremony and for the string of balls and social gatherings that would follow the nuptials for the next two weeks. She had come with her own heart full of joy, expecting that Melissa would feel the same. Instead, she found Melissa lost in a haze of gloom.

She was further bewildered to find that the groom was not Brandon de Forrest.

"I'm sorry," Celia said at last in frustration, when Annie had left the room, "it may not be my place, but I don't understand. You were deeply in love with a man, and he with you—and yet now, suddenly, you are to marry someone else. You are not so fickle," she said kindly. She moved to where Melissa sat in a somber blue dress at her small desk and stroked her long golden hair. "How could this have happened? I see no joy in your eyes."

"Oh, Celia . . . Celia, I am pregnant! I am miserable beyond imagining! Better that I was dead than having to face the life ahead of me! How can I bear it?" The admission came in a burst of pent-up sorrow, and Melissa dropped the quill to the paper as if it were another burden she could no longer manage. Her shoulders trembled and she shut her eyes, fighting her tears. The merest thought of Brandon made her want to end her life, and if she hadn't been carrying a part of him in her womb, she might have thrown herself into the Thames and let the black waters take her, so deep was her pain.

Celia gasped slightly. "Then it is Monsieur de Forrest's child! And this marriage is doubly wrong!"

Melissa turned remorseful green eyes to her friend. "His child, yes. But he didn't want me, he didn't want the burden of a child. Oh, I was a fool, Celia—just as you were. Just as a hundred thousand women and more have been since the beginning of time," she said, sorrow and anger mixing in her voice. "Now please . . . let's not talk of this anymore. It serves no purpose."

It did not seem right. For the rest of the day, the phrase repeated in Celia's mind like a litany as she moved about the house, running errands, accomplishing small chores for Annie and Melissa.

During the voyage home, she had seen the way Brandon de Forrest looked at Melissa, and there was never a man more in love. How could he have abandoned the woman he loved? What was more, a woman who carried his child? No, *it did not seem right.*

Celia was thinking precisely this as she passed down the hall, carrying a basket loaded high with gifts recently arrived for the wedding couple. They were to be deposited with the steward, who would arrange the many treasures for public viewing by the guests. Scarcely able to see above the packages, she moved gingerly.

And it was then that she heard him.

She thought at first that her ears were playing tricks or that her mind had gone suddenly feeble.

But, no, even as her heart froze, a woman called his name: "Quentin!" And Celia heard that same laugh, the same arrogant tone of her former persecutor: "Mother, not now.... I've a game at White's and the will to win it."

"But I have Melissa's ring!"

"Very good, I'm sure it's in excellent taste and horribly costly."

The woman laughed. "Be sure of both!"

"I'll examine it later."

He passed within inches of Celia, not bothering to pay her—a mere servant—the slightest heed. His cologne was sweet, powerful...and chillingly reminiscent. She kept her head down, her face averted, lest he see her. And lest she see *him,* and suddenly scream or faint. *The man was as good as a murderer.*

It was *he* who had been responsible for her abduction! It was *he* who'd kept her in captivity to be sold as a slave— and Melissa as well, had she not been rescued by...

Quentin!

The name suddenly came back to her. So the man who had rescued Melissa and the man Melissa was to marry...and their two voices...were one and the same!

She was certain of it. She would never forget that voice, that cruel, careless laugh.

Melissa could not marry this man, this monster. No, no...Celia's head swam with terrible images.

Something must be done!

But what? And how? Would Melissa believe her? Would the Duke? She was a servant, uneducated, her opinions automatically suspect. Her story would be taken as preposterous. There could be dire consequences if she risked speaking out and was not believed. If Quentin knew that he was discovered, and that she might have some means of giving evidence against him, might not all their lives be in danger?

At the dark thought, the heavy weight of packages slipped from her fingers and crashed to the floor. Celia stared before her, lost in a bleak future, unaware that priceless crystal and silver and gold and lace lay scattered at her feet.

This wedding could not take place! If she had to kill this monster Quentin with her own hands, she would not let him marry Melissa.

But she looked down at her trembling fingers, small and rough and calloused from work, and knew a serving maid was no match for the power and cleverness of her adversary.

The door to Brandon's office burst open.

Brandon started, the pair of compasses he operated veering off the paper. Aggravated, he looked up. He had been deeply engrossed in a new set of navigational charts; besides that, everything set him off these days.

She was a blur at first, a streak of auburn hair and brown cloak entering his vision and a high voice mingling urgently with the shouts of Ross McKay, who barreled after her.

"I tried to stop the wench!" McKay bellowed, his face flushed and his chest heaving. "Like a greased pig she is!"

Brandon scowled, but he left his table and stepped to where the winded girl stood, her eyes wide and her face stricken with panic. He made a gesture, stopping Ross from lunging at her. "It's all right, I know my guest...."

Celia wasted no time in preliminaries. "You must help her, Monsieur de Forrest! You mustn't let that man marry her. He's a monster, a slaver, the same as a murderer!" Celia threw herself to her knees before him. "Oh, please, I beg you ... no matter that you don't want her, that you do not want the child she carries. You loved her once, I know you did. How could it be entirely gone? You must feel some bit of love and kindness for—''

''What?'' Brandon broke in sharply. ''What the devil are you saying!''

''You must do something to—''

Brandon grabbed her by the shoulders, raising her up to eye level. There was a coiled violence to his stance, and behind Celia, Ross McKay stood stock-still trying to gauge all that was happening.

''No, tell me about the child.... What child? What are you talking about?'' Brandon demanded.

And in a torrent of words and rushing emotions, Celia related everything she knew.

''Good God....'' Ross breathed.

Brandon glared. ''What game is this? I was away. I wrote several times to her. Not once did she answer. And then when I returned there was a letter telling me good-bye—a letter in her own hand.'' Brandon spoke angrily, as if reliving the experiences that had caused him so much grief. ''A child...I had no idea of the child,'' Brandon said, his thoughts turning inward. A strange look passed over his face, and Celia shivered in fear. Perhaps all this meant to him was that now he would be free of the responsibility of a bastard child.

''I can't believe she sent that letter...I can't. I know she loves you—''

''And yet she marries another man,'' Brandon said sarcastically.

''Tomorrow....'' Celia said, sick at heart.

''As I understand. Well, of course, it would have to be soon. The House of Danfort would not want a scandal. I'll be there,'' Brandon said coldly, and Celia realized he had forgotten her and was speaking to himself. ''I would not miss this happy occasion for all the world....''

It seemed to Melissa that her heart and not the clock on her mantle ticked off the time of freedom remaining to her. In less than an hour she would be married to Quentin.

Each time the door to her room opened, her breath caught, hoping for the impossible.

Let it be him! she would pray, dreaming of a miracle.

But it was only Annie or Celia, and four times Glenmillan, who watched her like a hungry wolf watches a lamb.

Her grandfather had come once himself, and though he had seemed miserable enough over the past few days, he now seemed reconciled to the marriage she had arranged with Quentin.

"I will never understand you," she said, feeling betrayed by his docile acceptance of her fate. "I thought you hated Quentin."

"Yes, well . . ." He paused. "I've taken to praying."

"You? Have you gone mad?" she asked bitterly.

The Duke smiled sweetly, which only added evidence to her suspicions. "Have faith!" he said, and he kissed her lightly on the forehead before excusing himself to greet those guests who even now arrived below in the great ballroom. Melissa had refused a church wedding; it would have been a travesty.

There was nothing sacred in her heart as minutes later the Duke guided her down the aisle lined by all the gaping notables of London. The air was thick with the scent of hundreds of flowers festooning the room, combining with those of many perfumed handkerchiefs being fluttered by disappointed dandies envying the groom his match. A group of musicians played the sickeningly sentimental refrains Glenmillan had chosen.

Melissa gritted her teeth, wanting to scream. *She had a child to think of now . . . Brandon's child; for his sake she would not disgrace herself.*

Delighted sighs and whispers accompanied Melissa's progress in the shimmering white froth of lace and silk and pearls. A black dress would have been more appropriate to the occasion, Melissa thought, nearing the raised dais where Quentin stood.

He smiled at her. He was resplendent in white velvet and satin, embroidered with the same pearl motif as her dress and train and headdress.

She would stab him to death if he ever entered her bed.

To the side, she saw Glenmillan, dressed in white and pale violet. Although she wore the expected smile of a mother whose son was about to marry into extreme wealth, her smile seemed to Melissa to be drawn and tense. The violet eyes, likewise, darted restlessly from the dais to the guests and back again, as if she would hurry the proceedings if she possibly could.

But they began soon enough.

The clergyman was pompous and dramatic, reciting the service with the flair of an actor playing Shakespeare's most weighty role.

Melissa felt oddly detached, as if she were not there but rather looking at herself from above. She saw her grandfather standing benignly at her side, no show of fight left in him, resigned to turning over his life's work to the two people he despised most in the world. The last two years passed before Melissa's mind as if in a dream. She recalled the day in Cornwall when she had first seen Brandon, her ill-met attempts to seduce him, the lovemaking they later shared. And India, with her triumphant rescue of Celia and her coup in besting the Nawab... all of this she remembered, along with the hopes and dreams she had envisioned of a life with Brandon when she returned to England.

All of it was history now.

The clergyman droned on.

Quentin was slipping a ring on her finger. *It was all a bad dream, a strange, horrible dream.* She looked at him, his eyes joining hers for an instant, their opalescent blue orbs shining like the large stone he slid on her finger. Its weight was ponderous. The marriage would be as heavy a burden.

And now it was her turn.

She hesitated, knowing that her entire life hung in the balance of the next moment, when with the ring on Quentin's finger, the final words binding her to a man she loathed would be spoken. And never could they be withdrawn, till death did them part....

She thought of the child within her, abandoned by his father just as she had been. She thought of her life in Cornwall, where she'd been loved by honest, good people. The open countryside was without the complexity and sham of London society. What if...?

Light-headed with the possibility she envisioned, she felt a sudden pressure on her hand and realized Quentin was squeezing her fingers, urging her to carry on with her part of the ceremony. The ring was like a burning coal searing her palm. The rest of her was cold, so cold.

Her eyes met his again.

The room had fallen silent.

She could hear her heart beating.

She could hear the breathing of the clergyman, waiting....

Panic...her face was growing warm...within her body was Brandon's child...this marriage of convenience was a sacrilege beside such love as she had known....

"Melissa!" Quentin hissed at her beneath his breath. "Put the ring..."

The whole world seemed to wait.

"Melissa!" she heard again, and startled, she opened her hand, the ring falling to the ground. Her heart gave a sudden start, a leap of defiant joy! She was free! She would never marry Quentin. She would never marry anyone!

"Melissa!" Her name was being called again.

But it was not Quentin who spoke it this time, for Quentin had turned from her and was staring, his shocked face a frozen mask of fear and hatred.

Glenmillan's voice rang out in a shriek, "What is the meaning of this outrage? Get him out! Get out, you devil! Get out!" She began to rush down the aisle, as if to drive away the intruder.

But Brandon de Forrest continued on his way. He strode without pause or comment toward Melissa, his progress fearless and determined as around him the gaping, buzzing, tittering spectators drew slightly aside. With a shove, he sent Glenmillan reeling and sputtering into the mass of bodies crowding forward to witness the drama.

But there was another show for them, as behind Brandon another voice rang out, "In the name of King George...."

And into the room marched a contingent of the King's men, bearing arms and the official standard of the Crown.

"Quentin Danfort is hereby under warrant for heinous and numerous crimes committed against the citizenry of London, under sworn protection of the Crown. Abduction, slavery, trafficking in prostitution, usury..." The voice droned on as the King's men marched forward down the aisle and wrenched Quentin from the dais.

"What outrage is this!" he shouted, pointing an accusing finger at the Duke.

The Duke laughed and shot a look to where Glenmillan stood, pale and still. Their eyes met, and for a moment it seemed that the Countess Glenmillan wavered, swaying in her purple and white gown as if she would faint.

But she did not.

Instead, she brought herself fully erect and went clamoring after Quentin and the guards, demanding explanations and shrieking threats of revenge.

All in all, it was a far better show than anyone there had expected, and even they, so used to all manner of outrageousness, were shocked into momentary silence.

Before they could regain their tongues, the Duke stepped forward, and with a glance at Brandon and Melissa, announced, "The arrangements for this wedding have cost me far too much to be abandoned now. I suggest the wedding continue, with, perhaps, a slight change...."

"If the lady is for once cooperative," added Brandon.

From the sidelines, Celia suddenly appeared, a smile on her face and tears in her eyes, to hand Brandon the ring he had entrusted her with. "Thank you for believing me," she whispered, as she placed it in his hand. "And you also, sir, for using your influence to see justice done," she said to the Duke.

"You!" Melissa said, widening her eyes at her grandfather. "Meddling again, sir?" But she laughed.

"And to typical good effect," he countered. "Now, shall we proceed?"

"Shall we?" said Melissa, looking into Brandon's eyes.

"I'm concerned only about one thing," he said, frowning. "There is a portion of this ceremony—to love, honor and obey...."

"Ah," Melissa said, nodding. "A difficult passage, that one. But I love challenges. Don't you, my love?"

"It's you I love, Melissa...."

"Till death do us part," said Melissa, her eyes filling with tender tears of joy.

"And far beyond that," said Brandon.

*   *   *   *   *

**THIS JULY, HARLEQUIN OFFERS YOU
THE PERFECT SUMMER READ!**

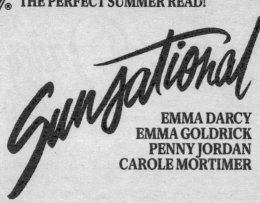

Sunsational

**EMMA DARCY
EMMA GOLDRICK
PENNY JORDAN
CAROLE MORTIMER**

From top authors of Harlequin Presents comes
HARLEQUIN SUNSATIONAL, a four-stories-in-one
book with 768 pages of romantic reading.

Written by such prolific Harlequin authors as Emma Darcy,
Emma Goldrick, Penny Jordan and Carole Mortimer,
HARLEQUIN SUNSATIONAL is the perfect summer
companion to take along to the beach, cottage, on your
dream destination or just for reading at home in the warm
sunshine!

Don't miss this unique reading opportunity.

Available wherever Harlequin books are sold.

Back by Popular Demand

Janet Dailey
Americana

A romantic tour of America through fifty favorite Harlequin Presents, each set in a different state researched by Janet and her husband, Bill. A journey of a lifetime in one cherished collection.

In July, don't miss the exciting states featured in:

Title #11 — HAWAII
Kona Winds

#12 — IDAHO
The Travelling Kind

Available wherever Harlequin books are sold.